The Son

ALSO BY PHILIPP MEYER

American Rust

The Son

Philipp Meyer

HARPER LUXE

An Imprint of HarperCollinsPublishers

THE SON. Copyright © 2013 by Philipp Meyer. All rights reserved. Printed in the United States of America. No part of this book may be used or reproduced in any manner whatsoever without written permission except in the case of brief quotations embodied in critical articles and reviews. For information address HarperCollins Publishers, 10 East 53rd Street, New York, NY 10022.

HarperCollins books may be purchased for educational, business, or sales promotional use. For information, please e-mail the Special Markets Department at SPsales@harpercollins.com.

FIRST HARPERLUXE EDITION

HarperLuxe™ is a trademark of HarperCollins Publishers

Library of Congress Cataloging-in-Publication Data is available upon request.

ISBN: 978-0-06-225402-3

13 14   ID/RRD   10 9 8 7 6 5 4 3 2 1

For my family

The Son

The Son

Acknowledgments

Thanks to my publisher, Dan Halpern, a fellow artist who gets it. Also Suzanne Baboneau. My agents, Eric Simonoff and Peter Straus. Libby Edelson and Lee Boudreaux.

I am grateful to the following organizations for their generous support: the Dobie Paisano Fellowship Program, Guggenheim Foundation, Ucross Foundation, Lannan Foundation, and the Noah and Alexis Foundation.

While any and all errors are the fault of the author, the following people were invaluable for their knowledge: Don Graham, Michael Adams, Tracy Yett, Jim Magnuson, Tyson Midkiff, Tom and Karen Reynolds (and Debbie Dewees), Raymond Plank, Roger Plank, Patricia Dean Boswell McCall, Mary Ralph Lowe,

Richard Butler, Kinley Coyan, "Diego" McGreevy and Lee Shipman, Wes Phillips, Sarah and Hugh Fitzsimons, Tink Pinkard, Bill Marple, Heather and Martin Kohout, Tom and Marsha Caven, Andy Wilkinson, everyone at the James A. Michener Center for Writers, André Bernard, for his sympathetic ear, Ralph Grossman, Kyle Defoor, Alexandra Seifert, Jay Seifert, Whitney Seifert, and Melinda Seifert. Additionally, I am grateful to Jimmy Arterberry of the Comanche Nation Historic Preservation Office, Juanita Pahdopony and Gene Pekah of Comanche Nation College, Willie Pekah, Harry Mithlo, and the Comanche Language and Cultural Preservation Committee, though this in no way implies their endorsement of this material. It is estimated that the Comanche people suffered a 98 percent population loss during the middle period of the nineteenth century.

RIP Dan McCall.

In the second century of the Christian era, the Empire of Rome comprehended the fairest part of the earth, and the most civilised portion of mankind . . .

. . . its genius was humbled in the dust; and armies of unknown Barbarians, issuing from the frozen regions of the North, had established their victorious reign over the fairest provinces of Europe and Africa.

. . . the vicissitudes of fortune, which spares neither man nor the proudest of his works . . . buries empires and cities in a common grave.

—EDWARD GIBBON

THE MCCULLOUGHS

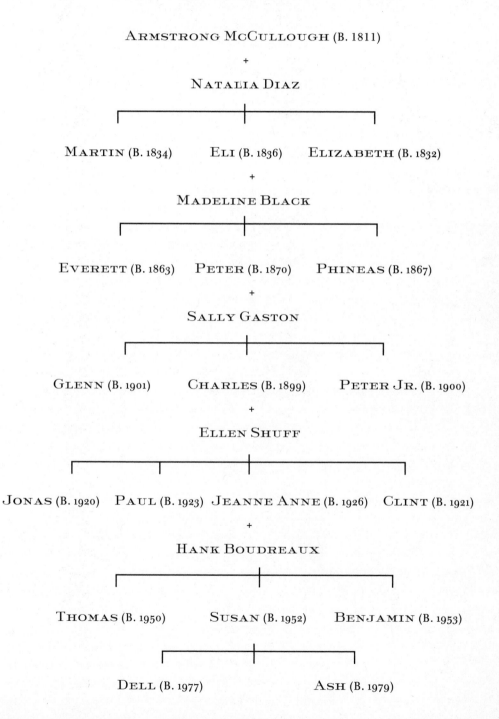

ARMSTRONG MCCULLOUGH (B. 1811)

+

NATALIA DIAZ

MARTIN (B. 1834)　　ELI (B. 1836)　　ELIZABETH (B. 1832)

+

MADELINE BLACK

EVERETT (B. 1863)　　PETER (B. 1870)　　PHINEAS (B. 1867)

+

SALLY GASTON

GLENN (B. 1901)　　CHARLES (B. 1899)　　PETER JR. (B. 1900)

+

ELLEN SHUFF

JONAS (B. 1920)　　PAUL (B. 1923)　　JEANNE ANNE (B. 1926)　　CLINT (B. 1921)

+

HANK BOUDREAUX

THOMAS (B. 1950)　　SUSAN (B. 1952)　　BENJAMIN (B. 1953)

DELL (B. 1977)　　ASH (B. 1979)

The Son

Chapter One
Colonel Eli McCullough

Taken from a 1936 WPA Recording

It was prophesied I would live to see one hundred and having achieved that age I see no reason to doubt it. I am not dying a Christian though my scalp is intact and if there is an eternal hunting ground, that is where I am headed. That or the river Styx. My opinion at this moment is my life has been far too short: the good I could do if given another year on my feet. Instead I am strapped to this bed, fouling myself like an infant.

Should the Creator see fit to give me strength I will make my way to the waters that run through the pasture. The Nueces River at its eastern bend. I have always preferred the Devil's. In my dreams I have reached it three times and it is known that Alexander the Great, on his last night of mortal life, crawled from his palace and tried to slip into the Euphrates, knowing that if his body disappeared, his people would assume he had ascended to heaven as a god. His wife stopped him at the water's edge. She dragged him home to die mortal. And people ask why I did not remarry.

Should my son appear, I would prefer not to suffer his smile of victory. Seed of my destruction. I know what he did and I suspect he has long graced the banks of the river Jordan, as Quanah Parker, last chief of the Comanches, gave the boy scant chance to reach fifty. In return for this information I gave to Quanah and his warriors a young bull buffalo, a prime animal to be slain the old way with lances, on my pastures that had once been their hunting grounds. One of Quanah's companions was a venerable Arapahoe chief and as we sat partaking of the bull's warm liver in the ancient manner, dipped in the animal's own bile, he gave me a silver band he had personally removed from the finger of George Armstrong Custer. The ring is marked "7th Cav." It bears a deep scar from a lance, and, having no suitable heir, I will take it to the river with me.

Most will be familiar with the date of my birth. The Declaration of Independence that bore the Republic of Texas out of Mexican tyranny was ratified March 2, 1836, in a humble shack at the edge of the Brazos. Half the signatories were malarial; the other half had come to Texas to escape a hangman's noose. I was the first male child of this new republic.

The Spanish had been in Texas hundreds of years but nothing had come of it. Since Columbus they had been conquering all the natives that stood in their way and while I have never met an Aztec, they must have been a pack of mincing choirboys. The Lipan Apaches stopped the old conquistadores in their tracks. Then came the Comanche. The earth had seen nothing like them since the Mongols; they drove the Apaches into the sea, destroyed the Spanish Army, turned Mexico into a slave market. I once saw Comanches herding villagers along the Pecos, hundreds at a time, no different from the way you'd drive cattle.

Having been trounced by the aboriginals, the Mexican government devised a desperate plan to settle Texas. Any man, of any nation, willing to move west of the Sabine River would receive four thousand acres of free land. The fine print was written in blood. The Comanche philosophy toward outsiders was nearly papal in its thoroughness: torture and kill the men, rape and kill the women, take the children for slaves or adoption. Few from the ancient countries of Europe took the Mexicans up on their offer. In fact, no one came at all. Except the Americans. They flooded in.

They had women and children to spare and to him that overcometh, I giveth to eat of the tree of life.

In 1832 my father arrived in Matagorda, common in those days if you viewed the risk of death by firing squad or a scalping by the Comanches as God's way of telling you there were great rewards to be had. By then the Mexican government, nervous about the growing Anglo horde within its borders, had banned American immigration into Texas.

And still it was better than the Old States, where unless you were son of a plantation owner, there was nothing to be had but the gleanings. Let the records show that the better classes, the Austins and Houstons, were all content to remain citizens of Mexico so long as they could keep their land. Their descendants have waged wars of propaganda to clear their names and have them declared Founders of Texas. In truth it was only the men like my father, who had nothing, who pushed Texas into war.

Like every able-bodied Scotsman, he did his part in the rout at San Jacinto and after the war worked as a blacksmith, gunsmith, and surveyor. He was tall and easy to talk to. He had a straight back and hard hands and people felt safe around him, which proved, for most of them, to be an illusion.

My father was not religious and I attribute my heathen ways to him. Still, he was the sort of man who felt the breath of the pale rider close on his neck. He did not believe in time to waste. We first lived at Bastrop, raising corn, sorghum, and hogs, clearing land until the new settlers came in, those who waited until the Indian dangers had passed, then arrived with their lawyers to challenge the deeds and titles of those who had civilized the country and vanquished the red man. These first Texans had purchased their holdings with the original human currency and most could neither read nor write. By the age of ten I had dug four graves. The faintest sound of galloping hooves would wake the entire family, and by the time the news arrived—some neighbor cut up like a Thanksgiving shoat—my father had checked his loads and then he and the messenger would disappear into the night. The brave die young: that is the Comanche saying, but it was true of the first Anglos as well.

During the ten years Texas stood alone as a nation, the government was desperate for settlers, especially those with money. And through some invisible telegraph the message went back to the Old States—this area is safe now. In 1844 the first stranger arrived at our gate: a barbershop shingle, store-bought clothes, a lady-broke sorrel. He asked for grain as his horse would founder on grass. A horse that could not eat grass—I had never heard of such a thing.

Two months later, the Smithwicks' title was challenged and then the Hornsbys and MacLeods were bought out at a pittance. By then there were more lawyers in Texas, per capita, than any other place on the continent and within a few years all the original settlers had lost their land and been driven west again, back into Indian country. The gentler classes who had stolen the land were already plotting a war to protect their blacks; the South would be cursed but Texas, a child of the West, would emerge unscathed.

In the meantime a campaign was launched against my mother, a Castilian of the old line, dark skinned but finely featured, it was claimed by the new settlers that she was octoroon. The plantation gentleman took pride in his eye for such things.

By 1846 we had moved past the line of settlement, to my father's headright on the Pedernales. It was Comanche hunting grounds. The trees had never heard an ax, and the land and all the animals who lived upon it were fat and slick. Grass up to the chest, the soil deep and black in the bottoms, and even the steepest hillsides overrun with wildflowers. It was not the dry rocky place it is today.

Wild Spanish cattle were easily acquired with a rope—within a year we had a hundred head. Hogs and mustang horses were also for the taking. There were deer, turkey, bear, squirrel, the occasional buffalo, turtles and fish from the river, ducks, plums and mustang grapes, bee trees and persimmons—the country was rich with life the way it is rotten with people today. The only problem was keeping your scalp attached.

Chapter Two
Jeanne Anne McCullough

March 3, 2012

There were murmurs and quiet voices, not enough light. She was in a large room that she first mistook for a church or courthouse and though she was awake, she couldn't feel anything. It was like floating in a warm bath. There were dim chandeliers, logs smoking in a fireplace, Jacobean chairs and tables and busts of old Greeks. There was a rug that had been a gift from the Shah. She wondered who would find her.

It was a big white house in the Spanish style; nineteen bedrooms, a library, a great room and ballroom. She and her brothers had all been born here but now it was nothing more than a weekend house, a place for family reunions. The maids wouldn't be back until morning. Her mind was perfectly awake but the rest of her seemed to have been left unplugged and she was fairly certain that someone else was responsible for her condition. She was eighty-six years old, but even if she liked telling others that she couldn't wait to cross over to the Land of Mañana, it was not exactly true.

The most important thing is a man who does what I tell him. She had said that to a reporter from *Time* magazine and they'd put her on the cover, forty-one and still sultry, standing on her Cadillac in front of a field of pumpjacks. She was a small, slender woman, though people forgot this soon after meeting her. Her voice carried and her eyes were gray like an old pistol or blue norther; she was striking, though not exactly beautiful. Which the Yankee photographer must have noticed. He had her open her blouse another notch and did her hair like she'd stepped out of an open car. It was not the height of her power—that had come decades later—but it was an important moment. They had begun to take her seriously. Now the man who'd taken the photograph was dead. *No one is going to find you,* she thought.

Of course it was going to happen this way; even as a child she'd been mostly alone. Her family had owned the town. People made no sense to her. Men, with whom she had everything in common, did not want her around. Women, with whom she had nothing in common, smiled too much, laughed too loud, and mostly reminded her of small dogs, their lives lost in interior decorating and other peoples' outfits. There had never been a place for a person like her.

She was young, eight or ten, sitting on the porch. It was a cool day in spring and the green hills went on as far as she could see, McCullough land, as far as she could see. But something was wrong: there was her Cadillac, parked in the grass, and the old stables, which her brother had not yet burned, were already gone. *I am going to wake up now,* she thought. But then the Colonel—her great-grandfather—was speaking. Her father was there as well. She'd once had a grandfather, Peter McCullough, but he had disappeared and no one had anything good to say about him and she knew she would not have liked him either.

"I was thinking you might make a showing at the church this Sunday," her father said.

The Colonel thought those things were best left to the Negroes and Mexicans. He was a hundred years old and did not mind telling people they were wrong. His arms were like gunsticks and his face was splotchy as an old rawhide and they said the next time he fell, it would be right into his own grave.

"The thing about preachers," he was saying, "is if they ain't sparkin' your daughters, or eatin' all the fried chicken and pie in your icebox, they're cheatin' your sons on horses."

Her father was twice the size of the Colonel, but, as the Colonel was always pointing out, he had a strong back and a weak mind. Her brother Clint had bought a horse and saddle off that pastor and there had been a setfast under the blanket nearly the size of a griddle cake.

Her father made her go to church anyway, waking up early to make the trip to Carrizo, where they had a Sunday school. She was hungry and could barely keep her eyes open. When she asked the teacher what would happen to the Colonel, who was sitting home that very minute, likely drinking a julep, the teacher said he was going to hell, where he would be tortured by Satan himself. *In that case, I am going with him,* Jeannie said. She was a disgraceful little scamp. She would have been whipped if she were Mexican.

On the ride home, she could not understand why her father sided with the teacher, who had a beak like an eagle and smelled like something inside her had died. The woman was ugly as a tar bucket. *During the war,* her father was saying, *I promised God that if I survived, I would go to church every Sunday. But just before you were born, I stopped going because I was* busy. *And do you know what happened?* She did—she had always known. But he reminded her anyway: *Your mother died.*

Jonas, her oldest brother, said something about not scaring her. Her father told Jonas to be quiet and Clint pinched her arm and whispered, *When you go to hell, the first thing they do is shove a pitchfork up your ass.*

She opened her eyes. Clint had been dead sixty years. Nothing in the dim room had moved. *The papers,* she thought. She had saved them from the fire once and had not gotten around to destroying them. Now they would be found.

Chapter Three
Diaries of Peter McCullough

AUGUST 10, 1915

My birthday. Today, without the help of any whiskey, I have reached the conclusion: I am no one. Looking back on my forty-five years I see nothing worthwhile—what I had mistaken for a soul appears more like a black abyss—I have allowed others to shape me as they pleased. To ask the Colonel I am the worst son he has ever had—he has always preferred Phineas and even poor Everett.

This journal will be the only true record of this family. In Austin they are planning a celebration for the Colonel's eightieth birthday, and what will be honestly said about a man who is lionized in capitols, I don't know. Meanwhile, our bloody summer continues. The telephone lines to Brownsville cannot be kept open—every time they are repaired, the insurgents blow them up. The King Ranch was attacked by forty *sediciosos* last night, there was a three-hour gun battle at Los Tulitos, and the president of the Cameron Law and Order League was shot to death, though whether the latter is a gain or loss, I can't say.

As for the Mexicans, to see the number of them shot in bar ditches or hung from trees, you would think them as ill a scourge as the panther or wolf. The *San Antonio Express* no longer mentions their deaths—it would take up too much paper—and so the Tejano die unrecorded and are buried, if at all, in shallow graves, or roped and dragged off where they will not bother anyone.

After Longino and Esteban Morales were killed last month (by whom we don't know, though I suspect Niles Gilbert) the Colonel devised a note for all our vaqueros: *This man is a good Mexican. Please leave him alone. When I am done with him I will kill him myself.* Our men display these notes like badges of honor; they worship the Colonel (along with everyone else), *nuestro patrón.*

Unfortunately for the Tejanos, the area cattlemen continue to lose stock. In the west pastures last week Sullivan and I found a section where the wire was cut and by nightfall we'd found only 263 cows and calves, versus the 478 counted during the spring roundup.

A twenty-thousand-dollar loss and all evidence, circumstantially at least, pointing to our neighbors, the Garcias. I myself would rather lose the kingdom than lay blood libel against the wrong person. But that is a rare sentiment.

I have always thought I ought to have been born in the Old States, where, though their soil is even more blood soaked than ours, they no longer need their guns. But of course it is against my disposition. Even Austin I find overwhelming, as if each of its sixty thousand inhabitants were shouting at me at once. I have always found it difficult to clear my head—images and sounds linger with me for years—and so here I remain, in the one place that is truly mine, whether it wants me or not.

As we examined the cut fences, Sullivan pointed out, quite unnecessarily, that the tracks led right into the Garcia lands, which border the river, which, as it has been so dry, can be crossed nearly anywhere.

"I do not mind old Pedro," he said, "but his sons-in-law are as vile a pack of niggers as I have ever seen."

"You've been spending too much time with the Colonel," I told him.

"He does *sabe* his Mexicans."

"I have found just the opposite."

"In that case, boss, I am hoping you will learn me the various honest explanations for a cut fence leading to Pedro Garcia's pastures while we are short two hundred head. Time was we would cross and take them back but that is a bit above our bend these days."

"Old Pedro can't watch every inch of his land any more than we can watch every inch of ours."

"You're a big man," he said, "and I don't see why you act like such a small one."

After that he had no further comment. He considers it a personal affront that a Mexican might own so much land in our day and age. Of course the vaqueros do not help: because of his weight and high voice they call him Don Castrado behind his back.

As for Pedro Garcia, trouble seems to follow him like a lonely dog. Two of his sons-in-law are being pursued by the Mexican authorities for cattle theft, a notable accomplishment given that country's views on such matters. I attempted to visit him last week, only to be turned back by José and Chico. *Don Pedro no feel good,* they told me, and pretended not to understand my Spanish. I have known Pedro my entire life, knew he would accept me as a visitor, but of course I turned my horse around and said nothing.

Pedro has been shorthanded so long that the brush is overrunning his land, and for the past two years he has only managed to brand half his calves. Each year he makes less money, each year he cannot hire as many men, and thus each year his income decreases yet again.

Still he has retained his good nature. I have always preferred his household to our own. We both enjoyed the old days, when it was a gentler land, with white caliche roads and adobe villages, not a thornbush to be seen and the grass up to your stirrups. Now the brush is relentless and the old stone villages are abandoned. The only houses built are crooked wood-frame monstrosities that grow like mushrooms but begin rotting just as quickly.

In many ways Pedro has been a truer father to me than the Colonel; if he has ever had a harsh word for me, I have not heard it. He had always hoped I might take an interest in one of his daughters, and for a time I was quite infatuated with María, the eldest, but I could sense the Colonel was strongly against it, and, like a coward, I allowed the feeling to pass. María went to Mexico City to pursue her studies; her sisters married Mexicans, all of whom have their eyes on Pedro's land.

My greatest fear is that Sullivan is right and that Pedro's sons-in-law are involved with the theft of our stock; they may not understand what the consequences will be; they may not understand that Don Pedro cannot protect them.

August 11, 1915

Sally and Dr. Pilkington are driving Glenn, our youngest, to San Antonio. He was shot tonight when we came across some riders in the dark. The wound is high in the shoulder and is certainly not life threatening and had it not been for the Colonel I would have gone to San Antonio with my son.

The Colonel has decided that the shooters were our neighbors. When I protested that it was too dark for any of us to have seen the guilty parties, it was implied that I was a traitor.

"If you'd learned anything I taught you," he said. "That was Chico and José on those horses."

"Well, you must have eyes like a catamount to be able to see in the dark past a furlong."

"As you well know," he told me, "my vision has always carried farther than that of other men."

About a quarter of the town (the white quarter) is downstairs. Along with the Rangers, all of our vaqueros, and the Midkiff vaqueros as well. In a few minutes we will ride on the Garcias.

Chapter Four
Eli McCullough

S pring 1849, the last full moon. We'd been two years on our Pedernales acreocracy, not far from Fredericksburg, when our neighbor had two horses stolen in broad daylight. Syphilis Poe, as my father called him, had come down from the Appalachian Mountains, imagining Texas a lazy man's paradise where the firewood split itself, the persimmons fell into your lap, and your pipe was always stuffed with jim-sonweed. He was the commonest type on the frontier, though there were plenty like my father—intent on getting rich if they could stay alive long enough—and there were the Germans.

Before the Germans came, it was thought impossible to make butter in a southern climate. It was also thought impossible to grow wheat. A slave economy does that

to the human mind, but the Germans, who had not
been told otherwise, arrived and began churning first-
rate butter and raising heavy crops of the noble cereal,
which they sold to their dumbfounded neighbors at a
high profit.

Your German had no allergy to work, which was
conspicuous when you looked at his possessions. If,
upon passing some field, you noticed the soil was level
and the rows straight, the land belonged to a German.
If the field was full of rocks, if the rows appeared to
have been laid by a blind Indian, if it was December
and the cotton had not been picked, you knew the land
was owned by one of the local whites, who had drifted
over from Tennessee and hoped that the bounties of
Dame Nature would, by some witchery, yield him up
a slave.

But I am ahead of myself. The problem facing my
father that morning was the theft of two scrawny
horses and a conspicuous trail of unshod pony tracks
leading into the hills. Common sense suggested the
perpetrators might still be about—no self-respecting
horse thief would have been satisfied with Poe's
mangy swaybacked mares—but the law of the frontier
demanded pursuit, and so my father and the other men
rode off, leaving my brother and me with a rifle apiece
and two silver-mounted pistols taken off a general at

San Jacinto. This was considered plenty to defend a sturdy house, as the army had come to the frontier and the big Indian raids of the early '40s were thought to be over.

The men rode out just before noon, and my brother and I, both between hay and grass but feeling full grown, were not worried. We had no fear of the aborigine; there were dozens of Tonkawas and other strays living nearby, waiting for the government to open a reservation. They might rob lost Yankees, but they knew better than to molest the locals: we all wanted an Indian pelt and would have collected one at the slightest excuse.

By the time I was twelve, I had killed the biggest panther ever seen in Blanco County. I could trail a deer across hard ground and my sense of direction was as good as our father's. Even my brother, though he had a weakness for books and poetry, could outshoot any man from the Old States.

As for my brother, I was embarrassed for him. I would point out tracks he could not see, telling him which way the buck's head had been turned and whether its belly had been full or empty and what had made it nervous. I saw farther, ran faster, heard things he thought I imagined.

But my brother did not mind. He thought himself superior for reasons I could not fathom. Whereas I hated every fresh wagon track, every sign of a new settler, my brother had always known that he would head east. He talked incessantly about the superiority of cities and it would not be long until he got his wish—our crops were heavy, our herds increasing—our parents would be able to hire a man to replace him.

Thanks to the Germans in Fredericksburg, where more books were stockpiled than in the rest of Texas combined, people like my brother were considered normal. He understood German because our neighbors spoke it, French because it was superior, and Spanish because you could not live in Texas without it. He had finished *The Sorrows of Young Werther* in the original language and claimed to be working on his own superior version, though he would not let anyone read it.

Outside of Goethe and Byron, my sister was the object of most of my brother's thoughts. She was a beautiful girl who played the piano nearly as well as my brother read and wrote, and it was widely considered a shame that they were related. For my part, I had a bit of a hatchet face. The Germans thought I looked French.

As for my brother and sister, if there was anything improper I never knew it, though when she spoke to him her words were made of cotton, or a sweet that dissolves on your tongue, whereas I was addressed as a cur dog. My brother was always writing plays for her to act in, the two of them playing a doomed couple while I was cast as the Indian or badman who caused their ruination. My father pretended interest while shooting me knowing looks. So far as he was concerned, my brother was only acceptable because I'd turned out so close to perfect. But my mother was proud. She had high hopes for my siblings.

The cabin was two rooms linked by a covered dog-trot. It sat on a bluff where a spring came out of the rock and flowed over a ledge to the Pedernales. The woods were thick as first creation and my father said if we ever got to where the trees didn't rub the house, we would move. Of course my mother felt different.

We fenced and gated a yard and stock pen, built a smokehouse, a corncrib, and a stable where my father did blacksmithing. We had a wood floor and glass windows with shutters and a German-built stove that would burn all night on just a few sticks. The furniture had the look of store-bought; it was whitewashed and turned by the Mormons at Burnet.

In the main room my mother and father kept a canopy bed to themselves and my sister had a cot; my brother and I shared a bed in the unheated room on the other side of the dogtrot, though I often slept outside in a rawhide I'd slung thirty feet or so in the air, in the branches of an old oak. My brother often lit a candle to read (a luxury my mother indulged), which disturbed my sleep.

The centerpiece of the main room was a Spanish square piano, my mother's sole inheritance. It was a rarity, and the Germans came over on Sundays to sing and visit and be subjected to my brother's plays. My mother was formulating plans to move into Fredericksburg, which would allow my brother and sister to resume their schooling. Me she considered a lost cause and had she not witnessed my issuance she would have denied responsibility in my creation. As soon as I was old enough I planned to join a Ranging company and ride against the Indians, Mexicans, or whomever else I could.

Thinking back, it is plain my mother knew what would happen. The human mind was open in those days, we felt every disturbance and ripple; even those like my brother were in tune with the natural laws. Man today lives in a coffin of flesh. Hearing and seeing nothing. The Land and Law are perverted. The Good Book says I will gather you to Jerusalem to the furnace of my wrath. It says thou art the land that is not cleansed. I concur. We need a great fire that will sweep from ocean to ocean and I offer my oath that I will soak myself in kerosene if promised the fire would be allowed to burn.

But I digress. That afternoon I was making myself useful, as children did in those days, carving an ox yoke out of dogwood. My sister came out of the house and said, "Eli, go out to the springhouse and bring Mother all the butter and grape preserves."

At first I did not reply, for in no way did I find her superior, and as for her supposed charms, they had long since worn off. Though I will admit I was often murderous jealous of my brother, the way they sat together smiling about private matters. I was not exactly on her good side, either, having recently stolen the horse of her preferred suitor, an Alsatian named Hiebert. Despite the fact that I had returned the horse better than I found it, having taught it the pleasures of a good rider, Hiebert had not returned to call on her.

"Eli!" She had a voice like a hog caller. I decided I was sorry for whatever unfortunate wretch got roped to her.

"We're near out of butter," I shouted back. "And Daddy will be mad if he comes home and finds it gone." I went back to my whittling. It was nice in the shade with nothing but the green hills and a forty-mile view. Right below me the river made a series of little waterfalls.

In addition to the yoke, I had a new handle to make for my felling ax. It was a bo'dark sapling I had found in my travels. The handle would be springier than what my father liked, with a doe foot on the end for slippage.

"Get up," said my sister. She was standing over me. "Get the butter, Eli. I mean it."

I looked up at her standing there in her best blue homespun and made note of a fresh boil that she was attempting to hide with paint. When I finally brought the butter and preserves, my mother had stoked the stove and opened all the windows to keep the house cool.

"Eli," my mother said, "go down and catch us a few fish, will you? And maybe a pheasant if you see one."

"What about the Indians?" I said.

"Well, if you catch one, don't bring him back. There's no sense kissing the Devil till you've met him."

"Where's Saint Martin?"

"He's out fetching blackberries."

I picked my way down the limestone bluff to the river, taking my fishing pole, war bag, and my father's Jaegerbuchse. The Jaegerbuchse fired a one-ounce ball, had double-set triggers, and was one of the best

rifles on the frontier, but my father found it cumber-
some to reload from horseback. My brother had first
claim on it, but he found its kick too ferocious for his
poetical constitution. It got meat on both ends but I did
not mind that. It would drive its ball through even the
oldermost of the tribe of Ephraim, or, if you preferred,
bark a squirrel at nearly any distance. I was happy to
carry it.

The Pedernales was narrow and cut deep into the
rock, and there was not much water most times, maybe
a hundred yards across and a few feet deep. Along the
banks were old cypresses and sycamores, and the river
itself was full of swimming holes and waterfalls and
shaded pools brimming with eels. Like most Texas
rivers it was useless to boatmen, though I considered
this an advantage, as it kept the boatmen out.

I dug some grubs from the bank, collected a few
oak galls for floats, and found a shady pool under a
cypress. Just above me on the hill was an enormous
mulberry, so heavy with fruit that even the ringtails
had not been able to eat it all. I took off my shirt and
picked as many as I could, intending to bring them to
my mother.

I began to fish, though it was hard relaxing because
I couldn't see the house, it being high above me on the
bluff. The Indians liked to travel in the riverbeds and

my father had taken the only repeating firearms. But that was not bad in its way because it made me watch everything, the water glassing over the stone, skunk tracks in the mud, a heron in a far pool. There was a bobcat ghosting through the willows, thinking no one saw him.

Farther up the bank was a stand of pecans where a cat squirrel was taking bites of green nuts and dropping them to the ground to rot. I wondered why they did that: a squirrel will waste half the nuts on a tree before they are ripe. I thought about teaching him a lesson. Squirrel liver is top bait; if the Creator was a fisherman it is all he would use. But it was hard to reckon a one-ounce ball against a bushytail. I wished I'd brought my brother's .36 Kentucky. I began to graze on the mulberries and soon they were all gone. Mother preferred blackberries anyway. She viewed mulberries the same as sassafras tea, low class.

After another hour of fishing I saw a flock of turkeys on the opposite bank and shot one of the poults. It was seventy yards but the head came clean off. I was allowed to aim at the head, my brother was not—the poult flapped its wings crazily, trying to fly while the blood fountained up. A shot for the record books.

I braced my fishing pole under a rock, swabbed the barrel clean, measured out a careful charge, seated a ball and capped the nipple. Then I waded across the river to retrieve my prize.

Near where the poult lay in a fan of blood there was a purple spear point sticking out of the sand. It was four inches long and I sat examining it for a long time; it had two flutes at the base that modern man has yet to figure how to replicate. The local flint was all cream to brown, which told me something else about that spear point: it had traveled a long way.

When I got back to my fishing pole it was floating downriver and I saw a big catfish had stuck itself on my bait, another one-in-a-million chance. I set the hook, thinking I'd lose the fish, but it pulled out of the water with no trouble. I decided to think about it. While I was sitting there I saw something in the sky and when I looked through my fist I realized it was Venus, that I was seeing it during the daytime. A bad sign if there ever was one. I took the turkey and catfish and my mulberry-stained shirt and hightailed it back to the house.

"That was quick," said my mother. "Only one fish?"

I held up the turkey.

"We were worried when we heard the shot," said my sister.

"I don't think it's good being so far from the house."

"The Indians won't bother you," my mother said. "The army is everywhere."

"I'm worried about you and Lizzie, not me," I said.

"Oh, Eli," said my mother. "My little hero." She appeared not to notice my ruined shirt and she smelled of the brandy that we saved for important guests. My sister smelled of brandy as well. It had gone to her head and she pinched my cheek sweetly. I was annoyed at her. I considered reminding her that Miles Wallace had been kidnapped not a month earlier. But unlike the Wallace boy, who had been taken by the Comanches only to be scalped a few miles later, I was not a wall-eyed cripple. I knew I would probably enjoy being kidnapped, as all they did was ride and shoot.

After double-checking our supply of patch and ball I went outside and climbed the tree into my rawhide hammock, where I could see out over the riverbed, the road, and the surrounding country. I hung the Jaegerbuchse from a nail. I had been meaning to shoot something while swinging in the hammock—that would be proper living—but had not yet been successful. Through the dogwoods near the spring I could see my brother gathering blackberries. The wind was calm and it was pleasant lying there with the smell of my mother's cooking. My brother had his rifle with him but wandered far from it, a sloppy habit. My father was strict about those things—if a gun is worth carrying it is worth keeping within arm's reach.

But that afternoon my brother was in luck, as we saw no Indians. Near sundown I spotted something moving in the rocks above the flood line, sneaking in and out of the cedar, which turned out to be a wolf. It was so far away it might have been a coyote, but wolves run with their tails straight and proud while coyotes tuck them under like scolded dogs. The tail was straight on this one and he was a pale gray, nearly white. The branches were in my way so I climbed down out of the tree, snuck to the edge of the bluff, and got into a good brace with the sights high over the wolf's back. He had stopped with his nose in the air, picking up the smell of our dinner. I set the first trigger, which made the second trigger only a twelve-ounce pull, then squeezed off the shot. The wolf jumped straight up and fell over dead. My father had us patch our bullets with greased buckskin, and our balls carried farther and straighter than if we'd used cotton patches, like most everyone else on the frontier.

"Eli, was that you shooting?" It was my sister.

"It was just a wolf," I shouted back. I thought about going down to get the skin—a white wolf, I had never seen one of those before—but decided against it, as it was getting dark.

Because of all the food being made, we did not sit down for supper until late. Seven or eight tallow candles were lit around the house, another luxury. My mother and sister had been cooking all day and they brought out dish after dish. We all knew it was to punish my father for leaving us alone, for being guilted into a wild-goose chase, but no one said anything.

My brother and I drank cool buttermilk, my mother and sister drank a bottle of white wine we had gotten from the Germans. My father had been saving the wine for a special occasion. Supper began with wheat bread and butter and the last of the cherry preserves, then ham, sweet potatoes, roast turkey, fish stuffed with wild garlic and fried in tallow, steaks rubbed with salt and chili pepper and cooked directly on the coals, the last of the spring morels, also cooked in butter, and a warm salad of pigweed and Indian spinach, cooked in more butter and with garlic. I had never eaten so much butter in my life. For dessert we had two pies: blackberry and plum, fruit my brother had picked that day. There was nothing left in the larder but hardtack and salt pork. If he wants to run with Syphilis Poe, my mother said, then he can eat like Syphilis Poe.

I felt guilty but that did not stop me from eating my share. My mother did not feel guilty at all. She wished for more wine. Everyone was falling asleep.

I carried the ham bone out to the springhouse, then sat watching the stars. I had my own names for them—the buck, the rattler, the running man—but my brother convinced me to use Ptolemy's, which did not make any sense. Draco looks like a snake, not a dragon. Ursa Major looks like a man running; there is not a bear anywhere in it. But my brother could not abide anything so tainted with common sense and thus my effort to name the heavens was aborted.

I put the horses in the stable, barred the door from the inside, and climbed out through the gap in the eaves. It would take any Indians a while to get at them. The horses seemed calm, which was a good sign, as they could smell Indians better than the dogs.

By the time I got back inside, my mother and sister had retired to my parents' canopy bed and my brother was lying in my sister's cot. Usually my brother and I slept in the room across the dogtrot, but I let him be. After gathering my rifle, war bag, and boots to the foot of the bed, I spit into the last candle and climbed under the covers with my brother.

Around midnight I heard our dogs rucking up a chorus. I had not been sleeping well anyway so I got up to check the porthole, worried my mother or sister would see what was sticking up under my nightshirt.

Which I forgot about. There were a dozen men near our fence and more in the shadows near the road and still more in our side yard. I heard a dog yelp and then our smallest, a fyce named Perdida, went running off into the brush. She was hunched like a gut-shot deer.

"Everyone get the hell up," I said. "Get up, Momma. Get everyone up."

The moon was high and it might as well have been daylight. The Indians led our three horses out of the yard and down the hill. I wondered how they'd figured their way into the stable. Our bulldog was following a tall brave around like they were best friends.

"Move over," said my brother.

He and my mother and sister had gotten out of bed and were both standing behind me.

"There's a lot of Indians."

"It's probably Rooster Joe and the other Tonks," said my brother.

I let him push me out of the way, then went to the fire and poked it so we would have light. Since statehood we'd had good Indian years; most of the U.S. Army had been stationed in Texas to watch the frontier. I wondered where they were. I knew I should load all the guns, then remembered I had already done it. A rhyme came into my head, *buffalo grip, barlow blade, best damn knife that was ever made.* I knew what would happen—the Indians would knock on the door, we would not let them in, and they would try to break in until they got bored. Then they would set fire to the house and shoot us as we came out.

"Martin?" said my mother.

"He's right. There are at least two dozen."

"Then it's whites," said my sister. "It's some gang of horse thieves."

"No, it's definitely Indians."

I got my rifle and sat down in a corner facing the door. It was shadows and dim red light. I wondered if I would go to hell. My brother was pacing and my mother and sister had sat down on their bed. My mother was brushing my sister's hair saying, *Shush now, Lizzie, everything will be fine.* In the dimness their eyes were empty sockets like the buzzards had already found them. I looked the other way.

"Your rifle has a nipple on it," I told my brother, "and so do the pistols."

He shook his head.

"If we put up a fight, they might just be happy with the horses."

I could tell he didn't agree but he went to the corner and took up his squirrel gun, feeling the nipple for a percussion cap.

"I already capped it," I repeated.

"Maybe they'll think we're not home," said my sister. She looked to my brother but he said, "They can see we have a fire going, Lizzie."

We could hear the Indians clanging things around in my father's metal shop, talking in low voices. My mother got up and put a chair in front of the door and stood on it. There was another gun port up high and she removed the board and put her face to it: "I only see seven."

"There are at least thirty," I told her.

"Daddy will be following them," said my sister. "He'll know they're here."

"Maybe when he sees the flames," said my brother.

"They're coming."

"Get down from there, Mammy."

"Not so loud," said my sister.

Someone kicked the door and my mother nearly fell off her perch. *Salir, salir.* There was pounding. Spanish was the language most of the wild tribes spoke, if they spoke anything but Indian. I thought the door might stop a few shots at best and I motioned again for my mother to get down.

Tenemos hambre. Nos dan los alimentos.

"That is ridiculous," said my brother. "Who would believe that?"

There was a long quiet time and then Mother looked at us and said, in her schoolteacher voice: "Eli and

Martin, please put your guns on the floor." She began to remove the bar from the door and I realized that everything they ever said about women was true—they had no common sense and you could not trust them.

"Do not open that door, Momma.

"Grab her," I told Martin. But he didn't move. I saw the bar lift and propped the rifle on my knee. The moonlight was coming through the cracks like a white fire but my mother didn't notice; she set the bar aside like she was welcoming an old friend, like she'd been expecting this from the day we were born.

It was said in the newspapers that mothers on the frontier saved their last bullets for their own children, so they would not be taken by the heathens, but you did not hear of anyone doing it. In fact it was the opposite. We all knew I was of prime age—the Indians would want me alive. My brother and sister might have been slightly old, but my sister was pretty and my brother looked younger than he really was. Meanwhile my mother was almost forty. She knew exactly what they would do to her.

The door flung open and two men tackled her. A third man stood behind them in the doorway, squinting into the darkness of the house.

When my shot hit, he windmilled an arm and fell backward. The other Indians sprinted out and I yelled for my brother to shut the door but he didn't move. I ran over to shut it myself but the dead Indian was lying across the sill. I was grabbing for his feet, intending to pull him in and clear the doorway, when he kicked me under the jaw.

When I came to there were trees waving in the moonlight and one loud noise after another. Indians were standing on either side of the doorway, leaning to shoot into the room, then ducking back around the corner. My sister said, *Martin, I think they've shot me*. My brother was just sitting there. I thought he'd taken a ball. The Indians took a break for the powder smoke to thin so I jerked the rifle from his hand, checked that the hammer was cocked, and was swinging it toward the Indians when my mother stopped me.

Then I was on my stomach; at first I thought the house had fallen, but it was a man. I grabbed at his neck but my head kept chunking against the floor. Then I was outside under the trees.

I tried to stand but was kicked and tried again and was kicked again. Now a man's feet, now the ground next to them. Now a pair of legs, covered in buckskin. I bit his foot and was kicked a third time and then my hair was being pulled like it would come out at the roots. I waited for the cutting.

When I opened my eyes there was a big red face; he smelled like onions and a dirty outhouse and he showed me with the knife that I would behave or he would cut my head off. Then he lashed my hands with a piggin string.

When he walked away, he did not look like any Indian I'd ever seen. The aborigines living among the whites were thin, light bodied, and hard wintered. This one was tall and stocky, with a square head and fat nose; he looked more like a Negro than a lathy starving Indian and he walked with his chest out, as if taking everything we owned was his natural right.

There were fifteen or twenty horses outside the gate and as many Indians against our fence, laughing and making jokes. There was no sign of my mother or brother or sister. The Indians were stripped to the waist and covered with paint and designs like they'd escaped from a traveling show; one had painted his face like a skull, another had the same design on his chest.

Some of the Indians were rummaging the house and others rummaging the stables or outbuildings but most were leaning on the fence watching their friends work. All the white men I'd ever seen after a fight were nervous for hours, pacing and talking so fast you couldn't understand them, but the Indians were bored and yawning like they'd just come back from an evening constitutional, except for the man I'd shot, who was sitting against the house. There was blood on his chest and his mouth was frothing. Maybe he'd jumped sideways when the cap popped—they said the aboriginals had reflexes like deer. His friends saw me staring and one came over and said *taibo nʊ wʊkupatʊ?i,* then knocked me in the head.

I had a long dream where I was brought before a man to judge me for my sins. It was Saint Peter, only in the form of the teacher of our school in Bastrop, who had disliked me over all the other students, and I knew I was going to hell.

Then most of the Indians were standing looking at something on the ground. There was a white leg crooked in the air and a man's bare ass and buckskin leggings on top. I realized it was my mother and by the way the man was moving and the bells on his legs were jingling I knew what he was doing to her. After a while he stood up and retied his breechcloth. Another jumped right into place. I had just gotten to my feet when my ears started ringing and the ground came up and I thought I was dead for certain.

A while later I heard noises again. I could see the second group of Indians a little farther down the fence but now I could hear my sister's voice whimpering. The Indians were doing the same to her as my mother.

Finally I realized I was in bed. I was having a dream. It was nice until I woke up all the way and heard war whoops and saw I was still in the yard. My mother was naked and crawling away from the Indians; she had reached the porch and was trying to make it to the door. Inside the house, someone was pounding on the piano and there was something waving out from my mother's back that I realized was an arrow.

The Indians must have decided they did not want her in the house because they began shooting more arrows into her. She kept crawling. Finally one of them walked up to her, put his foot between her shoulders and pressed her to the ground. He gathered up her long hair as if he was fixing to wash it, then pulled it tight with one hand and drew his butcher knife. My mother had not made a sound since I woke up, even with the arrows sticking out of her, but she began to scream then, and I saw another Indian walking up to her with my father's broadax.

I had been puddling and moaning but that is when I dried up for good. I did not look at my mother and I might have heard a sound or I might not have. I tried to find Martin and Lizzie. Where Lizzie had been I made out a small white patch and then another and I realized it was her and that she was lying where they had left her. Later, when they led us out, I saw a body with its breasts cut off and its bowels draped around. I knew it was my sister but she no longer looked like herself.

I was dragged over to the fence next to my brother. He was crying and going quiet and crying again. Meanwhile nothing was coming out of me. I gathered myself up to look over at my mother; she was on her belly with the arrows sticking out of her. The Indians were going in and out of the house. My brother was sitting there looking at things. I began to choke and air my paunch and when I was done he said: "I thought you were dead. I was watching you for a long time."

It felt like a wedge had been stuck between my eyes.

"I was thinking Daddy might come home, but now I think we'll be miles away before anyone knows what happened."

A young Indian saw us talking and threatened us with his knife to shut up, but after he walked off Martin said: "Lizzie was hit in the stomach."

I knew what he was getting at and I thought about how he'd sat there while our mother unbarred the door, sat there when I tried to get the Indian out of the doorway, sat with a loaded rifle while Indians were shooting into the house. But my head hurt too much to say any of it. I saw spots again.

"Did you see what they did to her and Momma?"

"A little," I said.

The Comanches went in and out of the house, taking what they wanted and throwing the rest into a pile in the yard. Someone was attacking our piano with an ax. I was hoping the Indians would kill us or that I would pass out again. My brother was staring at my sister. The Indians were carrying out stacks of books that I thought were meant for the fire but instead they put them into their bolsas. Later they would use the pages to stuff their shields, which were two layers of buffalo neckhide. When stuffed with paper the shields would stop almost any bullet.

The mattresses were dragged out and cut open and the wind caught the feathers and spread them over the yard like snow. My mother was in the way. The feathers were falling over her. The ants had found us but we barely noticed; my brother kept staring at my sister.

"You shouldn't look at her anymore."

"I want to," he said.

When I woke up it was hot. The pile of everything the Indians didn't want, mostly smashed furniture, had been lit. An agarito was cutting into me. The fire got bigger and I could see into the shadows where our dogs were lying dead and I wondered if the Indians meant to throw us into the fire. They were known for strapping people to wagon wheels and lighting them. Then I was looking down on myself as you would a lead soldier. Interested in what I might do but not really caring.

"I can already shimmy my hands," I told my brother.

"For what?" he said.

"We should stay ready."

He was quiet. We watched the fire.

"Are you thirsty?"

"Of course I'm thirsty," he said.

The fire was getting bigger and the moss in the branches above us was flaring and smoke was coming off the bark. The embers of our own burned things were singeing our faces and hair; I watched the sparks climb up. When I looked over at my brother he was covered in ash like a person who had been dead a long time and I thought of how my mother and sister had looked when they sat together on the bed.

The Indians brought all my father's tools to be examined by firelight and I decided to remember everything they were taking: horseshoes, hammers, nails, barrel hoops, the bucksaw, the broadax and felling ax, the barking iron, an adze and froe; all the bits, bridles, saddles and stirrups, other tack; my brother's Kentucky rifle. My Jaegerbuchse they decided was too heavy and smashed against the side of the house. They took our knives, files, picks and awls, bits for drilling, lead bullets, bullet molds, powder kegs, percussion caps, a horsehair rope hanging in the dogtrot. Our three milch cows heard the commotion and wandered up to the house for a feed. The Indians shot them with arrows. They were in high spirits. Burning logs were pulled from the fire and carried inside the house; people were tying their bundles, checking their cinches, making ready to leave. Smoke was coming from the doors and windows and then someone untied my hands and stood me up.

Our clothes were thrown into the fire along with everything else and we were walked naked out of our gate, across the road, and into our field. A big remuda had been driven up, Cayuse ponies mixed with larger American horses. The Indians were ignoring us and talking among themselves, *ums* and *ughs*, grunts, no language at all, though they had words that sounded Spanish, and one word, *taibo*, they said to us often, *taibo* this and *taibo* that. We were barefoot and it was dark and I tried not to kick a prickly pear or be tromped on by the horses stamping and pacing. I felt better that at least something was happening, then I reminded myself that made no sense.

We were lifted up and our legs tied to the animals' bare backs with our hands tied in front of us. It could have been worse as sometimes they just tied you over the horse like a sack of flour. My pony was skittering; he didn't like the way I smelled.

The other horses were stamping and snorting and the Indians were calling back and forth across our field and my brother began to cry and I was mad at him for crying in front of the Indians. Then I began to blubber as well. We trotted out through our lower pasture, three months of grubbing stumps; we passed a stand of walnut I had picked for board trees. I thought about the men who had pushed us out of Bastrop, calling my mother a nigger and suing for our title. Once I had killed all the Indians I would go back and kill all the new settlers; I would burn the town to the bedrock. I wondered where my father was and I hoped he would come and then I felt guilty for hoping that.

Then we were going at a lope with the bluestem whipping our legs. We stretched into a column and I watched as the Indians disappeared into the woods ahead and then my horse passed into the darkness as well.

We crossed Grape Creek at the only spot you didn't have to jump, took a path through the bogs I had not known was there, came out at a gallop at the base of Cedar Mountain. Our cattle were white spots on the hillside. We were making ground in a long flat bottom with the hills all around, into the trees and out again, darkness to moonlight and back to darkness, the Indians trusting the horses to see, driving every animal in the forest in front of us. I looked for my brother. Behind me the riders were suddening out of the trees as if they'd been called out of the blackness itself.

Despite the dark and the uneven ground my horse hadn't slipped and had plenty of wind. We were coming to the base of Packsaddle Mountain. It was the last piece of land I knew well. I could turn the horse into the woods, but I doubted I would make it and my brother had no chance alone. Farther up the white hillside, I caught sight of the mustang pack I had intended to rope and break. They stood watching as we passed.

Two hours later we changed horses. My legs and backside were already raw and I'd been whipped by branches across the face and chest and arms. My brother was cut even worse; his entire body was caked with blood and dirt. We remounted and took up the same hard tempo. Later we came on a river that had to be the Llano. It didn't seem possible we'd made it that far.

"Is this what I think?" said my brother.

I nodded.

We waited for the horses to cross in the dark.

"We are fucked," he said. "This is a whole day's ride."

Sometime later we hit another river, probably the Colorado, after which we stopped to change horses again. I could smell that my brother had shat himself. When they stood me on the ground I squatted with my hands tied in front of me and the water dripping off and the horses pacing all around. My legs were cramped and I could barely hold a squat. Someone kicked me but I did not want to be riding in my own mess so I finished shitting and they stood me up by the hair. I doubted there was any skin left anywhere below my waist. I was put on another pony. The Comanches didn't trust the horses raised by whites.

Sometime after first light we stopped to change horses a third time, but instead of remounting we stood around at the edge of a river. We were in a deep canyon, I guessed it was still the Colorado but not even the army ever went this far up. The sun hadn't risen but it was bright enough to see color, and the Indians were standing around waiting for something. They were drinking from the river or leaning and stretching their backs, packing and repacking their saddlebags. It was the first time I'd seen them in the light.

They carried bows and quivers and lances, short-barreled muskets and war axes and butcher knives, their faces were painted with arrows and blooming suns and their skin was completely smooth, their eyebrows and beards all plucked. They all wore their hair as a Dutch girl might, two long braids on either side, but these Indians had woven in bits of copper and silver and colored beads.

"I can tell what you're thinking," said my brother.

"They look like a pack of mollies," I said, though I didn't really believe it.

"They look more like actors on a stage." Then he added: "Don't get us in any more trouble."

Then a stocky brave walked over and pushed us apart with his lance. There was a dried bloody handprint on his back and a long dark smear down the front of his leggings. What I had thought were pieces of calfskin on his waist turned out to be scalps. I looked up the river.

Ahead of us was a high overlook and behind us the Indians were rotating the horses in and out of the grass along the banks. There was a discussion and then most of the Comanches made their way on foot toward the overlook. One of them was leading a horse and tied to the horse was the body of the man I'd shot. I hadn't known he'd died and I got a cold feeling. My brother waded out into the river. The two Indians guarding us drew their bows but when I opened my eyes my brother was still in one piece, standing splashing himself—he was covered in his own waste. The Indians watched him, shriveled and pale and shivering, his chest caved from reading too many books.

When he was clean he came back and sat next to me.

"I hope it was worth getting shot just to wipe your ass," I said.

He patted my leg. "I want you to know what happened last night."

I didn't want to know any more than I already did but I couldn't tell him that so I stayed quiet.

"Momma wasn't going to make it but I don't think they meant to kill Lizzie. When they saw she was wounded they took off her shirt and looked over her gunshot pretty carefully; they even rigged up a sort of torch so this old Indian could give his opinion. They must have decided it was bad because they all went and talked for a while and then they came back and pulled off the rest of her clothes and raped her." He looked upriver where the Indians were climbing up the canyon. "Lizzie Lizzie Lizzie."

"She's in a better place."

He shrugged. "She's in no place."

"There is still Daddy," I said.

He snorted. "When Daddy finds out he will likely ride straight for that woman he keeps in Austin."

"That is low. Even for you."

"People don't go around saying a thing unless it's true, Eli. That's another thing you ought to know."

The guards looked back. I wanted them to stop our talking but now they didn't care.

"Momma knew she could save you," he said. He shrugged. "Lizzie and I . . . I dunno. But you're a different story."

I pretended not to understand him and looked around. The canyon walls went up a few hundred feet and there was bear grass and agarito spilling out of the cracks. A gnarled old cedar stuck out of the face; it looked like a stovepipe and there was an eagle's nest in it. Upriver were big cypresses with knock-kneed roots. Five hundred years was nothing for them.

When the sun hit the upper walls of the canyon a wailing and chanting went up. There was a shot and the burial party began to file back down to the river and when they reached us they knocked us down and kicked us until my brother shat himself again.

"I can't help it," he said.

"Don't worry."

"I'm worried," he said.

Several of the Indians thought we ought to be marched to the burial site and killed along with the dead man's horse but the one who was in charge of the war party, the one who'd dragged me out of the house, was against it. *Nabituku tekwaniwapi Toshaway*, they would say. My brother was already starting to pick up bits of Comanche; Toshaway was the chief's name. There were charges and offers and counteroffers, but Toshaway would not give in. He caught me watching him but gave no more account than if I were a dog.

My brother got a philosophical look and I got nervous.

"You know," he said, "the whole time, I was hoping that when the sun came up they would see us and realize they had made some terrible mistake, that we were people just like them, or at least just people, but now I am hoping the opposite."

I didn't say anything.

"What I am getting at is that the very kinship I had hoped might save us might be the reason they kill us. Because of course we are completely powerless over our fates, but in the end they are as well and maybe that is why they will kill us. To erase, at least temporarily, their own reflections."

"Stop it," I said. "Stop talking."

"They don't care," he said. "They don't care about a word we say."

I knew he was right but just then the debate ended and the Indians who had been for killing us came over and began to stomp and kick us.

When they finished my brother lay in a puddle of water among the stones, his head at an angle, looking up at the sky. There was blood running into my throat and I threw up into the river. The rocks were floating all around me. I decided as long as they killed us together it would be fine. I caught a wolf watching me from a high ledge but when I blinked he was gone. I thought about the white one I'd shot and how it was bad luck, then I thought about my mother and sister and wondered if the animals had found them. I got to blubbering and was cuffed in the head.

Martin looked like he'd lost twenty pounds; his knees and elbows and chin were bleeding and there was dirt and sand stuck everywhere. The Indians were changing their saddles onto fresh horses. I was hungry and before they could put me on another horse I sucked water from the river until my stomach was full.

"You should drink," I told him.

He shook his head. He lay there with his hands cupping his privates. The Indians jerked us up.

"Next time," I said.

"I was thinking how nice it was that I didn't have to get up again. Then I realized they hadn't killed me. Now I'm annoyed."

"It wouldn't be any better."

He shrugged.

We continued to ride at a good pace and if the Indians were tired they didn't show it and if they were hungry they didn't show it, either. They were alert but not nervous. Every now and then I'd get a glimpse of the entire remuda trailing behind us in the canyon. My brother would not stop talking.

"You know I was watching Mother and Lizzie," he said. "I had always thought about where the soul might be, near to the heart or maybe along the bones, I'd always figured you'd have to cut for it. But there was a lot of cutting and I didn't see anything come out. I'm certain I would have seen it."

I ignored him.

A while later he said: "Can you imagine any white man, even a thousand white men, riding this easy in Indian country?"

"No."

"It's funny because everyone calls them heathens and red devils, but now that we've seen them, I think it's the opposite. They act like the gods were supposed to act. Though I guess I mean heroes or demigods because as you have certainly helped demonstrate, though not without a certain cost, these Indians are indeed mortal."

"Please stop."

"It does make you wonder about the Negro problem, doesn't it?"

At midday we climbed out of the canyon. We were on a rolling grassland thick with asters and primrose, ironweed and red poppy. Some bobwhites scuttled into the brush. The prairie went on forever; there were herds of antelope and deer and a few stray buffalo in the distance. The Indians checked their pace to look around and then we were off.

There was nothing to protect us from the sun and by afternoon I could smell my own burning skin and was going in and out of sleep. We continued through the high grass, over limestone breaks, briefly into the shade along streams—though never stopping to drink—and then back into the sun.

Then the Comanches all reined up and after some chatter my brother and I were led back to a stream we'd just crossed. We were pulled roughly off the horses and tied to each other back to back and put in the shade. A teenager was left to guard us.

"Rangers?"

"This one doesn't look too nervous," said my brother.

We were facing opposite directions and it was strange not seeing his face.

"Maybe it's Daddy and the others."

"I think they would be behind us," he said.

After a while I decided he was right. I called the young Indian over. There were grapes hanging all along the stream.

He shook his head. *Itsa aitʊ.* Then he added *itsa keta kwasʊpʊ* and when he still wasn't satisfied I understood, he said in Spanish, *no en sazón.*

"He's saying they're not ripe."

"I know that."

I wanted them anyway and I was so hungry I didn't care. The Indian cut a section of vine and dropped it into my lap. Then he rinsed his hands in the stream. The grapes were so bitter I nearly aired my paunch. I thought they would help my fever. My lips were itching.

"They're good," I said.

"For tanning hides, maybe."

"You should eat."

"You are not making any sense," he told me.

I ate more of the grapes. It felt like I'd swallowed boiling water.

I said, "Scoot over to that stream and lean over it," and we did. My brother let his head rest in the water, as sunburned as I was, but I could tell he wasn't drinking. Something about this made me want to puddle up but I kept drinking instead. The young Indian stood on a rock and watched. We sat up again. It seemed like my fever was going down and I could stretch my legs.

"What's your name," I said to our guard. *"Cómo te llamas?"*

He didn't answer for a long time. Then he said: "Nuukaru." He looked around nervously and then walked off as if he'd given away some secret and when I saw him again he was upstream, lying on his belly, sucking up water. It was the first time I'd seen any of the Indians eat or drink much of anything, except for a few swallows. When he stood up he arranged his braids and checked his paint.

"I wonder if they're cockchafers," my brother said.

"Somehow I doubt it."

"You know the Spartans were."

"Who are the Spartans?" I said.

He was about to say something else when there was a rattling of shots far off. There was a scattered return volley and finally the slow knocking of a single repeating pistol. Then it got quiet and I knew it was just the

Indians using their bows. I wondered whose bad luck it had been.

Another young Indian came bounding down the rocks and then we were tied back on the horses and led out of the streambed. My fever had gone down and I didn't mind the sun. After crossing a stony plateau we descended to a prairie that seemed to be mostly larkspur and wine-cup. A red dirt wagon road went up the middle and it was a pleasant sight with the blue sky and a few bright clouds and wildflowers everywhere.

The Indians were milling around a pair of ox-drawn freight wagons. A third wagon was far ahead in the grass, turned on its side, a mule team standing dumbly in front of it. Someone was screaming.

"I don't want to see this," said Martin.

There was something white at the edge of the road; a small tow-headed boy in a boiled shirt. An arrow shaft had stuck through his eye and a big red-headed woodpecker was tapping a branch over his head.

Farther up the road blood was dripping from the wagons as if someone had splashed a bucket. There were four or five Texans sprawled in the red dirt and another curled up like a baby in the back of the wagon. Off in the grass and larkspur the Indians were doing something to the last teamster and he was shrieking in a high voice and they were imitating him.

With the exception of the two dealing with the remaining teamster, no one was wasting any time. The mule team was cut loose but they didn't move; they stood with their heads down as if they had done something wrong. A spotted pony was dead in the ditch, his neck covered with blood, the owner trying to free his saddle. Another Indian pony, a handsome strawberry roan, was standing blowing pink froth out of a hole in its chest. His owner removed his saddle, blanket, and bridle and set them carefully in the road. Then, while hugging and kissing the roan's neck, he shot it behind the ear.

Everything was pulled from the wagons, including two more bodies we hadn't noticed. It was hot and the red dust was settling over the flowers. The dead men's pockets were searched, those who hadn't been scalped were scalped; the last teamster had gone quiet. One of the Indians had a poultice applied, a pear pad split and tied with cloth; most of the hide shields had fresh lead streaks and a tall brave with Karankawa blood was cleaning his lance with grass. Others were going through the cargo, mostly flour sacks, which were cut and dumped in the road. A keg of whiskey was tomahawked and smaller kegs of gunpowder were strapped to horses along with several small crates, which from their weight must have been lead. Knives and blankets were taken, plugs of tobacco, bullet molds, a pair of axes and a handsaw, some calico fabric, a few repeating pistols. The locks and mainsprings on the rest of the guns were checked and the ones still good were taken. There was a brief debate over a scalp. Two plum pies were discovered and divvied up with the bloody knives.

The younger Comanches were combing the grass for stray arrows, the mules were put into the horse pack, a few quick circles were made to be sure nothing and no one had been missed, a piece of interesting fabric recovered, then all the guns were recharged and the quivers repacked, straps and hitches tightened, mouths rinsed. The oxen bellowed their final protest as someone cut their throats; by then the rest of the blood in the road had turned black and the bodies covered over with dust. They looked like they'd always been there.

The Indians split into three groups and left a wide set of tracks leading toward civilization, opposite the direction we were actually headed. Everyone was in a good mood. One of the braves rode up and slapped a fresh scalp on my head, the stringy gray hair hanging down. A man's bloody hat was crushed down on top of it, which the Indians found hilarious. We continued northwest, the grass tall with scattered thick motts of oak and the mesquites with their flickering leaves and the yuccas in bloom with their white flowers.

After a few hours the brave decided he didn't want to soil his trophy any further and took it off my head, tying it to his belt and throwing the dead man's hat into the bushes. The scalp and hat had been keeping the sun off and I asked for the hat back but we rode on. By then the other groups had rejoined us.

At the next change of horses, the Indians passed around some jerky they'd taken off the teamsters. My brother and I were offered a few bites. It was still hot but the Indians didn't care about drinking water, and when one of them offered me tobacco I was so thirsty I couldn't take it. My brother was not offered tobacco. He stood with his legs in a straddle and looked miserable.

When the sun finally went down my mouth was so dry I thought I would choke. I reminded myself to pick up a pebble to suck but then I was thinking about the spring near our house, of sitting and letting the water rush over as I looked out past the river. I began to feel better.

It was dark and at some point we stopped at a muddy hole and the horses were held back while the Indians tore up grass and piled it on the mud and took about two swallows each. My brother and I stuck our whole faces in and drank our fill. It tasted like frogs and smelled like animals had been wallowing but we didn't care.

After he'd swallowed enough my brother started to cry, and then the Indians were kicking him in the belly and giving him the knife at the throat. *Wʉyupaʔnitʉ,* quiet down. *Nihpʉʔaitʉ,* stop talking.

They were planning something. They changed their mounts but we were kept back with the horse herd.

"I think we've come a hundred miles. We must be right below the San Saba."

"Do you think they'll let me drink again?"

"Sure," I said.

He put his face back in the muddy water. I tried again but now I couldn't stand the smell. My brother drank and drank. It hurt even just to sit in the dirt now. I wondered how long it would take to heal; weeks maybe. We huddled together as best as possible. There was a bad odor and I realized my brother had shat himself.

"I can't stop."

"It's all right."

"There's no point," he said.

"All we have to do is keep going," I told him. "It is not that much when you think about it."

"And then what? What happens when we get where they're taking us?"

I was quiet.

"I don't want to find out," he said.

"There was John Tanner," I said, "Charles Johnston, you yourself have read those books."

"I am not the type to live on bark and gooseberries."

"You'll be a legend," I said. "I'll visit you in Boston and tell your friend Emerson that you're a real man and not just some cockchafing poet."

He didn't say anything.

"You could try a little harder," I told him. "You're risking our hair every time you piss them off."

"I'm doing the best I can."

"That is not true at all."

"Well, I'm glad you know."

He started to cry again. Then he was snoring. I was mad because he was just being lazy. We were not being fed any less, or driven any harder, than the Indians were driving themselves; we'd both had a lot more water than they had and who knew how long they'd been going like this? There was a logic but my brother couldn't see it. If a man has done it, so can you: that is what our father used to tell us.

Then we were slapped awake. It was still dark and they tied us to the horses and there was a bright light in the distance that I knew was a burning homestead. I hadn't thought there were whites this far out, but the land was rich and I could see why they had risked it.

A few braves came up and I could tell they were pleased with the youngsters for getting us mounted.

In the darkness we saw another dozen or so horses driven into the remuda. There were two new captives; by their crying we knew they were women and by their language we knew they were German, or Dutch as we called them back then.

By sunrise we'd gone another fifty miles, changing horses twice. The Germans didn't stop crying the entire night. When it was light enough we climbed a mesa, winding around the far side before coming up to watch our backtrail. The land had opened up; there were mesas, buttes, distant views.

The Germans were as naked as we were. One was seventeen or eighteen and the other a little older, and while they were both covered in blood and filth it was obvious they were at the peak of their female charms. The more I looked at them, the more I began to hate them and I hoped the Indians would degrade them some more and I would be able to watch.

My brother said, "I hate those Dutch women and I hope the Indians give them a good fucking."

"Me too."

"You seem to be holding up, though."

"Because I don't keep falling off my horse." We had stopped twice that night so they could lash my brother on tighter.

"I've been trying to catch a hoof in the head, but I haven't been so lucky."

"I'm sure Momma would be happy to hear that."

"You'll make a good little Indian, Eli. I'm sorry I won't be there to see it."

I didn't say anything.

"You know the reason I didn't shoot is because I didn't want them to hurt Mother or Lizzie."

"You froze up."

"They would have killed Mother anyway, that's obvious, but they would have taken Lizzie with us. It was only because she'd been shot that . . ."

"Shut up," I said.

"You didn't have to see what they did to her."

I was looking at him. He looked the same as always with his squinty eyes and thin lips but he seemed like someone I'd known a long time ago.

A little later he told me he was sorry.

The Indians passed around a few pieces of jerked meat from the teamsters. One of the Germans asked me where I thought we were going. I pretended not to understand her. She knew better than to talk to Martin.

The next day the views got longer. We were in a canyon ten miles wide, the walls going up a thousand feet above us, all red rock. There were cottonwoods and hackberries but not many other trees and we passed a magenta spear point in the sand, twin to the one I'd seen below our house. There were stone creatures in every rock and stream bank: a nautilus big as a wagon wheel, the horns and bones of animals larger than anything still alive on the earth.

Toshaway told me in Spanish that by fall the canyon would be full of buffalo. He was appreciating the scene. There were long tufts of black hair streaming from the cedar and mesquite; the buffalo had been using this place a long time.

The Indians showed no sign of tiring or of wanting a proper feed, but the pace had slowed. My mouth was watering; any number of fish could have been speared as we passed: the water was full of yellow cats, eels, buffalo fish, and gar. I lost count of the whitetail and antelope. A cinnamon grizzly, the largest I'd ever seen, was sunning himself on a ledge. Springs flowing down cliff faces, pools underneath.

That night we made our first real camp and I fell asleep in the rocks holding my brother. Someone put a buffalo robe over us and when I looked up, Toshaway was squatting next to me. His smell was becoming familiar. "Tomorrow we'll make a fire," he said.

The next morning we rode past sandstone mesas with figures scratched into the rock: shamans, men in combat, lances and shields and tipis.

"You know they're going to separate us," Martin said.

I looked at him.

"These guys are from two different bands."

"How would you even know?" I said.

"The one who owns you is Kotsoteka," he said. "The one who owns me is Yamparika."

"The one who owns me is Toshaway."

"That's his name. He's from the Kotsoteka band. The one who owns me is Urwat. They've been saying that Urwat has a long way to go, but the guy who owns you is not that far from home."

"They don't own us," I said.

"You're right. Why they might have that impression is completely beyond me."

We continued to ride.

"What about the Penatekas?"

"The Penatekas are sick right now, or something else bad is happening to them. I can't tell except that none of these are Penatekas."

Despite Toshaway's promise, we made another cold camp that night. In the morning we climbed out of the big canyon and onto the plains. There was no timber, no trail, no lines of brush to mark a stream, it was nothing but grass and sky and my stomach felt wobbly just looking at it. I knew where we were: the Llano Estacado. A blank space on the map.

After riding an hour nothing had changed and I was dizzy again. We might have gone ten inches or ten miles and by the end of the day I thought something had come loose in my head. My brother fell asleep and rolled all the way under his horse and the Indians stopped, beat him, and tied him back on.

We made camp at a stream cut so deep into the plain you could not see it until you were on top of it. It was our first fire and because there were no trees to reflect the light, it could not be seen from any distance. A pair of antelopes were thrown on, skin and all, and Toshaway brought us a pile of steaming half-cooked venison. My brother didn't have the energy to eat. I chewed the meat into small pieces and fed it to him.

Then I climbed out of the streambed to have a look. The stars came down to the earth on all sides and the Comanches had pickets looking for other campfires. They ignored me. I went back to our pallet.

A catamount screamed at us for nearly an hour, and wolf calls were echoing from one side of the plain to the other. My brother began to cry out in his sleep; I started to shake him, then stopped. There wasn't any dream he could be having that would be as bad as waking up.

The next morning they didn't bother to tie us. There was nowhere to go.

My brother, despite having eaten real food and slept six hours, was not any better. Meanwhile the Indians were laughing and cutting capers, riding their horses backward or standing up, calling back and forth with jokes. I fell asleep and woke up in the grass. We stopped and I was tied on again, slapped a few times but not beaten. Toshaway came over and gave me a long drink of water, then chewed up some tobacco and rubbed the juice into my eyes. Still I spent the rest of the day not knowing if I was asleep or awake. I had the feeling that somewhere ahead of us was the edge of the earth and if we reached it we would never stop falling.

That afternoon a small herd of buffalo were spotted and run down and after a discussion my brother and I were taken off our horses and led to one of the calves. It was cut open and its innards pulled out. Toshaway cut into the stomach and offered me a handful of curdled milk but I did not want any part of it. Another Indian forced my brother's head into the stomach but he shut his eyes and mouth. I was given the same treatment. I tried to swallow the milk but instead I aired my paunch.

This was done two or three times, with my brother not swallowing at all, me trying and throwing up, until the Indians gave up trying and scooped out all the curdled milk for themselves. When the stomach was empty the liver was cut out. My brother refused to touch it and I saw the way they looked at him so I forced myself to keep it down. The blood turned in my gizzard. I had always thought blood tasted like metal but that is only if you drink a small amount. What it actually tastes like is musk and salt. I reached for more liver and the Indians were happy to see it and I continued to eat until they slapped me away and ate the rest of the liver themselves, squeezing the gallbladder over it as a sauce.

When the organs were gone the calf was skinned out and a piece of meat held up to the sun in an offering and then the rest distributed to everyone, about five pounds apiece. The Indians finished their allotment within a few minutes and I was worried they would take mine so I ate quickly as well.

It was the first time I'd had a full belly in nearly a week and I felt tired and peaceful but my brother just sat there, sunburned and filthy and covered in his own vomit.

"You need to eat."

He was smiling. "You know, I never thought a place like this could exist. I'll bet our tracks will be gone with the first wind."

"They're going to kill you if you don't eat."

"They're going to kill me anyway, Eli."

"Eat," I said. "Daddy ate raw meat all the time."

"I'm quite aware that as a Ranger, Daddy did every-thing. But I am not him. Sorry," he said. He touched my leg. "I started a new poem about Lizzie. Would you like to hear it?"

"All right."

" 'Your virgin blood, spilled by savages, you are whole again in heaven.' Which of course is shit. But it's the best I can do under the circumstances."

The Indians were looking at us. Toshaway brought another chunk of buffalo and indicated I ought to give it to my brother. My brother pushed it away.

"I was sure I would go to Harvard," he said. "And then Rome. I have actually been there in my mind, you know, because when I read, I actually see things; I physically see them in front of me. Did you know that?" He seemed to cheer up. "Even these people can't ruin this place for me." He shook his head. "I've written about ten letters to Emerson but I haven't sent them. I think he would take them seriously, though."

Any letters he'd written had been burned in the fire but I didn't mention this. I told him he needed to eat.

"They're not going to turn me into some fucking filthy Indian, Eli. I'd rather be dead."

I must have gotten a look because then he said, "It wasn't your fault. I go back and forth between thinking we shouldn't have been living out there in the first place, and then I think what else could a man like Daddy do? He had no choice, really. It was fate."

"I'm going to make you a pile of food."

He ignored me. He was staring at something on the ground and then he reached over and pulled up one of the blanketflowers—we were sitting in a big patch. He held it up for all the Indians to see.

"Note the Indian blanket," he said, "or Indian sunburst."

They ignored him.

He continued in a louder voice. "It is worth noting that small, stunted, or useless plants—such as Mexican plum, Mexican walnut, or Mexican apple—are named after the Mexicans, who will doubtless endure among us for centuries, while colorful or beautiful plants are often named after Indians, as they will soon be vanquished from the earth." He looked around at them. "It's a great compliment to your race. Though if your vanquishing had come a bit earlier, I wouldn't have complained."

No one was paying attention.

"It's the fate of a man like myself to be misunderstood. That's Goethe, in case you were wondering."

Toshaway tried a few more times to give him meat, but my brother wouldn't touch it. Within half an hour there was nothing left but bone and hide. The hides were rolled up and put on the back of someone's horse and the Indians began to mount.

Then my brother was looking at someone behind me. "Don't try to help."

Toshaway pinned me to the grass. He and another Indian sat on me and tied my wrists and ankles as quick as my father might have tied a calf. I was dragged a good distance. When I looked over, Martin hadn't moved. He was sitting there taking things in; I could barely see his face above the flowers. Three Indians had mounted their horses, including Urwat, my brother's owner. They were riding in circles around him, whooping and hollering. He stood and they slapped him with the flats of their lances, giving him an opening and encouraging him to run, but he stayed where he was, up to his knees in the red-and-yellow flowers, looking small against the sky behind him.

Finally Urwat got tired and, instead of using the flat of his lance, lowered the point and ran it through my brother's back. My brother stayed on his feet. Toshaway and the other Indians were holding me. Urwat charged again and my brother was knocked down into the flowers.

Then Toshaway got my head down. I knew I ought to be getting up but Toshaway wouldn't let me, I knew I should get up but I didn't want to. *That is fine*, I thought, *but now I'll get up*. I strained against Toshaway but he wouldn't let go.

My brother was standing again. How many times he'd been knocked down and gotten back up I didn't know. Urwat had discarded his lance and now rode toward him with his ax but my brother didn't flinch and after he fell the last time the Indians rushed forward and made a circle.

Toshaway later explained that my brother, who had acted like such a coward the entire time, was obviously not a coward at all, but a *kʊʔtseena,* a coyote or trickster, a mystical creature who had been sent to test them. It was very bad medicine to kill him—the coyote was so important that Comanches were not allowed to even scratch one. My brother could not be scalped. Urwat was cursed.

There was a good deal of milling and confusion and three of the Indian kids held me while the adults talked. I was telling myself I would kill Urwat. I looked around for a friendly eye, but the German women wouldn't look at me.

The shoulder bones of the dead buffalo were cut loose and several of the braves began to dig. When there was a passable grave my brother was wrapped in calico taken from the freight wagon and lowered into the hole. Urwat left his tomahawk, someone else gave a knife; there was buffalo meat left as well. There was discussion about killing a horse, but it was voted down.

Then we rode off. I watched the grave disappear from sight, as if the blanketflower had already grown over, as if the place would not stand for any record of human life, or death; it would continue as my brother had said it would, our tracks disappearing in the first wind.

Chapter Five
J.A. McCullough

If she were a better person she would not leave her family a dime; a few million, maybe, something to pay for college or if they got sick. She had grown up knowing that if a drought went on another year, or the ticks got worse, or the flies, if any single thing went wrong, the family would not eat. Of course they had oil by then, it was an illusion. But her father had acted as if it were true, and she had believed it, and so it was.

When she was a child, her father often gave her orphaned calves to look after, and, every so often, she would fold the grown ones in with the steers when they were shipped off to Fort Worth. She made enough money off her dogies to make investments in stocks, and that, she told people, is what taught her the value of a dollar. *More like the value of a thousand dollars,* some reporter once said. He was not entirely masculine. He was from the North.

The Colonel, though he drank whiskey the entire ten years she'd known him, never slept past sunrise. When she was eight, and he ninety-eight, he had led her slowly across a dry pasture, following a track across the caliche she could not see, around clusters of prickly pear and yellow-flowered huisache, following a track she was certain her great-grandfather was imagining, until finally they arrived at a particular clump of soapbrush and he had reached into it and pulled out a baby rabbit. Its heart was pounding and she cradled it against the skin under her shirt.

"Are there more?" She could not have been more excited. She wanted all of them.

"We'll leave the rest with their dam," he said. His face was brown, cracked and furrowed like a dry riverbed, and his eyes were always running. His hands smelled of cottonwood buds, the sap that was like sugar and cinnamon and some flower she couldn't name; he was always stopping among the cottonwoods to rub the bud sap onto his fingers, a habit she adopted as well. Even at the end of her life she would stop at an old tree and scrape the orange sap onto a thumbnail, that she might smell it the rest of the day, and think of her great-grandfather. Balm of Gilead, someone once told her, that's what the sap was called, though it didn't need a name.

She had taken the kit home and given it milk but the next day the dogs got it. She knew she could go back to the brush for more, but the dogs would get them all eventually, so she decided to leave the remaining rabbits where they were, a decision she knew to be very grown-up and merciful. And yet she could not stop thinking about the kit's fur against her belly, a nearly liquid softness, her great-grandfather's hand on her shoulder, leaning on her for support.

She was a small, thin girl with light hair and a snub nose and skin that went brown in the sun, though she imagined that when she grew up, she would have dark hair and pale skin and a long straight nose like her mother. Her father snorted at this. *Your mother didn't look like that at all,* he said. *She was a towhead, like you.* But that was not how Jeannie thought of her. Her mother died young, giving birth to her at twenty-six. There were only a handful of pictures, none of them close up, or good, though there were plenty of pictures of her father's horses. But in the pictures of her mother, her hair *did* look dark and long, and her nose *was* straight, and after thinking on it, she decided that her father was simply wrong, that he had no eye for she-stuff, unless it were cattle or horses. She knew that if she had ever seen her mother alive she would have noticed a thousand things that her father had not.

What her father noticed was if an old cow had been left in the brush during roundup, or if another cow was open a second year, or if a new man, who claimed to be a top hand, missed his throws, or didn't charge into the brush with proper enthusiasm. Her father noticed if a *ladino* bull, living wild as an old buck, was mixing with his heifers, and what the Mexicans said about rain, and how much work his sons did, and whether she, Jeannie, was getting in the way. Despite her grandmother's discouragement, Jeannie rode out every morning with her brothers, so long as it was not a school day. During roundup she rode drag, though she knew she was simply extra; her father did not figure her into the head count, and at the branding fire, while her brothers did their best to rope, learned throwing from the *tumbadores* or branding from the *marcadores*, she was only allowed to carry the bucket of lime paste to dab on the fresh brands. Sometimes she would help make the calf fries, scooping them from an overflowing bucket to roast on a bed of coals specially raked out for that purpose. They were sweet and so tender they nearly burst in your mouth, and she would eat them by the handful, ignoring her brothers' snide comments, which she only half understood, about her enthusiasm for that particular delicacy.

Calf fries were one thing—if she even stood near the *tumbadors*, her father would be on her immediately. She had taught herself anyway. By the time she was twelve, she could flank and mug as well as her brothers, she could forefoot anything that moved, but it didn't matter. Her father didn't want her working among the men and her grandmother found it embarrassing. The Colonel, had he been alive, would have supported her; he had always seen in her what no one else did, her unshakable sense of her own perfectibility, her certainty that if she set her mind to something, she would master it. When the Colonel told her, as he often did, that one day she would do something important, she barely took any notice. It was as if he'd pointed out the grass was green, or her eyes large as a deer's, or that she was a pretty girl, if a bit small, that men and women alike enjoyed her presence.

So while the cattle drives struck her as boredom incarnate, a slow trudge behind an endless dusty line of steers, her rope flicking at their feet, walking at the slowest of walks toward the holding pens at the rail station—despite all that—she went on every drive she could. Despite the heat and thirst of the branding fire—best done in August, when it was too hot even for blowflies—she went out anyway, throwing calves when her father wasn't paying attention, her hands covered in their slobber, running the iron if the *marcador* let her, light pressure if the metal was hot, heavy pressure as the iron cooled; she did not allow herself to make mistakes. The vaqueros found her amusing. They knew what she was doing and while they would never have let their own daughters come to a branding fire, they were happy to let her take their place so they could rest in the shade and escape the heat. As long as she didn't make mistakes. And so she didn't.

There had been a time when this was not unusual. A time when the wealthy were exemplars. When you held yourself to a higher standard, when you lived as an example to others. When you did not parade your inheritance in front of a camera; when you did not accept the spotlight unless you'd *done* something. But that obligation had been lost. The rich were as anxious for attention as any scullery maid.

Perhaps she was no different. She'd hired a historian to compile a history of the ranch, a history of the family, but in ten years he'd done nothing but notate every letter, receipt, and slip of paper the Colonel had ever touched, scanning them into his little computer, going to Austin to look at microfiche. He was, she saw, incapable of writing the book he'd promised. *You can make any story of this you want,* he told her. *Well, pick the best one,* she said. *That would be lying,* he replied.

He was a pudgy, infuriating little man and she could not remember why she'd ever thought the process should be so mysterious. She'd opened her checkbook and the fund-raisers had picked up the scent, a check here, a mention there, another check, another mention; the Colonel's name had spread like roots from a mesquite. The next year he'd be appearing in the new state history books, the ones all the liberals had fought against.

If you did not work, you did not eat. If you did not wake up in the dark, be it ten degrees or a hundred, if you did not spend all day in the dust and thorns, you would not survive, the family would not survive, you had received God's blessings and been profligate.

Later, when she was old enough to look at the books, she realized the family had been safe all along. But it was too late. She could not sit still without thinking of the coyotes watching her calves, windmills that needed their gearboxes greased or sucker rods checked, fences flattened by weather or animals or careless humans. Later, when she stopped worrying about cattle, it was oil. Which wells were producing more or less than she'd hoped (less, she thought, it was always less), what new fields might be in play and what old plays the majors were giving up on. Which drillers might be hired, who was out of credit, what could be bought on the cheap. All wells went dry—the moment you stopped looking for new ones was the moment your fortunes began to decline.

Why am I on this floor, she thought. She looked around her. There was a haze in the room. She wondered if there was a problem with the flue. And the throbbing in her head; it was not the pain of a stroke. There had been someone in the room with her, she was sure of it.

The thing that had gone wrong in her children . . . she had always assumed some weakness from Hank's side, though it might also have been the city, the schools they attended, the friends they had made, their liberal teachers. There were things children did in the city, but work was not one of them, and spending weekends riding with the vaqueros was just another form of entertainment, like dressage or skiing. Making it worse, in order to get to the ranch and back in time for school on Monday, it was necessary to fly there. Her children were not stupid. They knew that real vaqueros did not take private planes to work.

Meanwhile they had no constitution. Working them during the summer was out of the question. July and August were the hottest of hot months, hot as the plains of Africa, a branding fire you could never escape. Clothes soaked through in minutes, a filthy paste over every inch of skin, and while she'd grown up thinking this was normal, unpleasant but normal, her children could not stand it even for an hour. Susan had passed out and fallen off her horse.

J.A. was embarrassed by this, though no one else was. She had begun to doubt herself. It was only later, when the children were grown, that she knew she had been right, that once people grew used to free money, to laboring only when the mood struck them, they began to think there was something low about work. They became desperate to excuse their own laziness. They came to believe that their family property was something inherent to life itself, like water or air or clean sheets.

You ought to give all this money away right now, she thought. But it was too late. She had ruined her daughter; perhaps her son as well. She thought about this and felt sick . . . the money was not the only thing; she knew what she had done to her children. She could not figure out if leaving them more money was penance or some strange form of additional punishment. *You are a bad Christian,* she thought.

When her father died she had immediately stopped going to church. If prayer could not even keep your family alive, she did not see what good it was. But after she and Hank moved to Houston, she had started going again. You were marked if you didn't. She did not really think about whether she believed, though in the past decade, her faith had come back, and they said that was all that mattered. Being old, you had no real choice—salvation or eternal nothingness—and it was no wonder who you saw in church, it was not young people with hangovers and their entire lives ahead of them.

She remembered a sermon in which the minister named some of the interesting people you would meet in heaven: Martin Luther King Jr. (for the blacks), Mahatma Gandhi, Ronald Reagan. Except the minister would not have mentioned Gandhi. John Wayne, maybe. You wondered: all the interesting people in heaven, everyone would want to talk to them. It didn't take much thinking to realize that there would have to be a separate heaven for famous people, just like on earth, a place they would not be bothered, a private community. She wondered if she would go there. But in heaven there was no such thing as money, so perhaps people would stop caring about her. Trump, Walton, Gates, herself; they would be no more interesting than the garbagemen.

Of course it would be nice to be reunited with Hank, with her boys Tom and Ben, her brothers as well, but what about Ted, who had been her lover for twenty years after Hank? Someone would be jealous. And Thomas—that small detail—would he be there?

If you listened to what they said about heaven, it was a massive city with twelve gates. No eating, bowel movements, or sex; you lay around in a trance listening to harp music. Like a hospice you could never leave. She would sleep with every nice-looking man she met. Which of course meant she would be sent to hell.

Do not let me die, she thought. She opened her eyes. She was still on the floor of her living room, lying on the burgundy rug. The fire was still burning. Was the light growing? She couldn't tell. She willed her head to move, then her legs, but there was nothing.

Chapter Six
Diaries of Peter McCullough

The newspapers are already running their version, straight from the mouth of the Colonel. The following will stand as the only true record:

Yesterday our segundo Ramirez was riding in one of the west pastures when he saw men driving whiteface cattle toward the river. As the Garcias still run mostly unimproved stock, it was obvious to whom the cattle belonged.

It was just after sundown when we caught them at the water. Most of the stock had already been crossed and the range was extreme, nearly three hundred yards, but everyone—Glenn, Charles, myself, the Colonel, Ramirez, our caporal Rafael Garza, and a handful of our other vaqueros—began shooting

anyway, hoping to scare the thieves into abandon-
ing the herd. Unfortunately they were old hands and
instead of leaving the cattle, a few of them dismounted
to shoot back while the others continued to drive the
beefs into the *brasada* on the Mexican side. Glenn was
hit in the shoulder, a Hail Mary shot from across the
water.

Back at the house two Rangers were waiting along
with Dr. Pilkington, whom Sally had called when she
heard the shooting. The bullet had missed the artery
but Glenn would need surgery and Pilkington thought
it best to take him to the hospital in San Antonio. While
he and Sally patched up Glenn, I spoke to the Ranger
sergeant, a hard-faced little blond boy who looks like
he escaped from a penitentiary. He is perhaps twenty
but the other Ranger is conspicuously afraid of him.
Beware the small man in Texas; he must be ten times
meaner to survive in this land of giants.

A gang of Mexicans does not just shoot a white
teenager without retaliation and I had wanted as many
lawmen around as possible, but one look and I knew
these Rangers were not going to help things. Still it was
better than Niles Gilbert and his friends from the Law
and Order League.

"How many more of you are coming?" I asked the
sergeant.

"None. You are lucky we are even here. We are supposed to be in Hidalgo County." He went to spit on the rug but then stopped himself.

Of course the King Ranch has an entire company permanently stationed, but it was not worth mentioning.

We loaded Glenn into the back of Pilkington's car. Sally climbed in after him. Glenn looked pitiful and I wanted to ride with him but I knew I was the only voice of reason within twenty miles; if I left I did not want to imagine the scene I might return to.

Sally leaned out of the window and whispered: "You need to go kill every one of those bastards."

I did not say anything. Around here, talk like that turns quickly to action.

"You're the Colonel's son, Pete. Tonight you need to act like it."

"I think it was José and Chico," Glenn called out. "The way they sat their horses."

"It was pretty dark, buddy. And we were all pretty worked up."

"Well, I'm sure of it, Daddy."

Another kind of man would not be doubting his own son as he lay pale in the back of a car. But of course it was not him I was doubting at all; it was my father.

"All right," I told him. "You're a brave man."

They drove off. I doubted that Glenn really thought that he'd seen José and Chico until he'd heard the Colonel say it. My father can put ideas into other men's heads without them realizing.

The mood was to ride on the Garcias immediately, before they had time to barricade their casa mayor. All the vaqueros had gathered and were waiting outside, smoking cigarettes or chewing tobacco, ready to spill blood for their patrón.

A dozen or so white men had arrived as well: Sheriff Graham from Carrizo, two deputies, another Ranger, the new game warden. Additionally: Niles Gilbert, his two sons, and two members of the Law and Order League visiting from El Paso. Gilbert brought a case of Krag rifles and several thousand rounds of ammunition from his store, as he'd heard that others were coming as well.

"Coming for what?" I said.

"To help you all run them copper-bellies out."

"The copper-bellies in question are across the river," I said.

He gave me a look. I nearly pointed out that I have four years of college to his four years of grammar school. But he is one who believes that power is best

used for the humiliation of other men. I might as well
have explained myself to a donkey.

I have always possessed a near-perfect recall, of
which both Charles and my father are quite aware, but
neither supported me when I pointed this out to the
others. It had been less than three hours, but the facts
were already changing—men who had appeared as
apparitions, their white shirts barely visible in the dusk,
were now seen clearly. I reminded everyone that it had
been too dark to identify any man—so dark, in fact, that
the flashes from our guns left us blind—but it no longer
mattered. In the light of memory, it was bright enough
to see faces, and the faces belonged to the Garcias.

I suggested we might wait for more Rangers or the
army—I was anxious to delay until daylight, when men
become harder to lynch—but Charles, who spoke for
most in the room, said firstly we could not let them get
away with shooting Glenn, and secondly that the army
would not be coming at all, as General Funston had
made clear that he would only interfere if his soldiers
were directly fired upon. He would not put his men
to chasing common cattle thieves. Unless of course the
cattle are King Ranch Brahmas.

At this I got even more depressed. The soldiers are
the only government agents in South Texas who have
no marked tendency to shoot Mexicans. As for the

Rangers, they are both the best and the worst. The sergeant pointed out that there were only thirty-nine of them in the entire state of Texas; the fact we had three in the same room (a third had arrived from Carrizo) was a miracle.

A miracle for whom, I thought. The room had the atmosphere of a cattle association, old friends politely discussing grazing rights and which politicians we ought to be supporting and how we were going to keep our stock competitive in the northern markets. The Colonel chimed in from the peanut gallery and laid out a long argument in support of Charles, in what I have now begun to consider their usual unholy alliance. He claimed that Glenn's wounding was his responsibility, as he'd had a chance fifty years ago to push the Garcias off this land forever, and had not taken it, and damned if he was going to let the same thing happen twice in a single lifetime.

I pointed out that due to various events on our land our family tree had already shed quite a few leaves. My father pretended to ignore me.

"I have lost my mother here and a son and a brother," I said. "And now another son is on his way to the hospital. I would prefer to wait until daylight."

All agreed that our family had suffered great tragedies, but the best thing was to take Pedro as soon as

possible. This was the community's problem now—
not just ours—no telling who the Garcias' next victim
might be.

I laid out another argument, namely that Pedro
Garcia was as proud as any other man, and if pressed
by a mob, he would certainly not give up his *yerno*, or
any other member of his family, but if asked by the law,
in the light of day, it would be a different story.

"We *are* the law," said the Ranger sergeant.

The others agreed. Not one of them would have considered surrendering to an armed mob in the middle of
the night, but they did not see why the Garcias ought
not to. I considered mentioning this but instead I said:
"With due respect it might be better to wait until the
sun comes up. Pedro will give up the guilty parties if
they have anything to do with his family."

Not only was this suggestion dismissed, but now
there was rumbling that I might retreat to the kitchen
and sit it out with the other women. We would hold a
little longer for reinforcements, which were certainly
coming, as by now the word was out all over the four
counties.

A shoat was killed and set roasting; a loin of beef set
out with tortillas and beans, the good linen, the fireplace lit and coffee served. Men lounged in the great

room, talking or flipping through old issues of *Confederate Veteran*, boots up, rifles askew in the palatial dark room with its drawings of Florentine ruins, its busts and statues, idly thumbing the engraving on the chairs and tables, resisting the urge to whittle with their pocketknives, everything around them bought wholesale from a dead Philadelphian, the contents of the entire house including the Tiffany windows bought and shipped, the house built to contain them. Not a single man asked about the marbles; they stopped to admire the picture of *Lee and His Generals*, a dime-store print they have in their own homes, then moved on for another serving of beef or coffee.

Around three A.M., fifteen more men arrived; an hour later another dozen drove up in two Ford trucks. Until then I'd been hopeful the plan would be scotched, as we had less than forty men, versus the Garcias' twenty or so, and them holding a virtual fortress. Now we had over sixty, all with repeating rifles, a few with Remington and Winchester automatics. The Colonel could not contain his satisfaction.

"One of your grandsons has been shot," I told him, "and the other is about to go to war. What you might be happy about I cannot fathom."

He gave me a look that said, for the thousandth time, how sorry he was that I had abandoned my studies to return to the ranch. I reminded myself that he is from another era. He cannot help it. Of course there is the third grandson I did not mention, my namesake, buried now next to my mother and brother.

I went upstairs to my office, lay in the dark among my books—the only comforting thing I have. An exile in my own house, my own family, maybe in my own country. Outside the coyotes were yipping in the distance; on the gallery the vaqueros were talking in quiet Spanish. Someone told a joke. If they were nervous or had second thoughts about attacking their own countrymen, I could not hear it. I knew things would get worse.

I must have fallen asleep because I heard someone shouting my name. At first I thought it was my mother calling me down for supper; we were back in the old house in Austin with its green fields and woods and streams running all night. My mother and her soft hands, the scent of roses lingering everywhere she walked. I thought about those things and allowed myself to forget where I was, and for a few moments I was certain I was young again, that we had not yet moved out to this monstrous country where all our misfortunes began. How the Colonel can love the place that has claimed so many members of our family, and may yet claim a few more, I don't know.

It was nearly five in the morning when we rode out.
Nearly seventy men. Everyone had been up all night
but was as somber and awake as if we were riding to
Yorktown or Concord. The Colonel wore the buckskin
vest that is famous in town, everyone believing that it
is made from Apache scalps. Even the Rangers were
deferring to him, as if they were in the presence of a
general, rather than an old man who was not even a
real colonel, but a brevet colonel, and had fought for
the cause of human slavery.

The vaqueros formed a flying squad around him;
the Colonel has no great respect for the Mexicans and
yet they are all willing to die for him. I, on the other
hand, consider myself their ally—no patrón has ever
been more generous—and they despise me.

An hour before sunrise we hobbled the horses and
made our way on foot toward the Garcias' house,
which overlooks the surrounding country with its
watchtower and high stone walls and parapets. A hundred years ago it was a bastion of civilization in a desert, a stronghold against a wilderness of Indians, but
now, in the minds of the men marching toward it, it
had come to be something else: the guardian of an old,
less civilized order, standing against progress and all
that was good on the earth.

I slipped off into the brush. I noticed the Colonel squatting nearby. He looked at me and grinned and I couldn't tell if he was smiling because he was looking forward to the gunplay or because he was proud of me for coming out for the old family ritual.

As for our neighbors from town, they all considered themselves great heroes but not a single one had lived here during the old days; they had kept their distance until it was safe. I wondered how I had ended up on the same side as men like that. For that reason alone I thought I ought to be making my stand with the Garcias.

Shortly thereafter I came across Charles. He was very nervous and I asked him to come home with me, to wash his hands of whatever was about to happen, but it was out of the question. He thought he was about to take part in an important ritual; he was about to become a man. I had always worried he might be bitten by a snake or kicked by a horse or gored or trampled, but he had survived all those things and somehow I had still failed him. Here he was, sweating despite the cool night, gripping his rifle, ready to make war on men who had attended his christening.

The Garcia casa mayor overlooked what was left of their old village, a few small buildings and an old *visitas,* all built of adobe or caliche blocks, several acres of *corrales de leña.* A stone wall surrounded the yard—a leftover from the days when you fenced cows out, rather than in—and that was where we made our line, the house surrounded on three sides, at a distance of fifty or sixty yards. The somber mood had not changed. This was no mere lynching; it was an overturning of the ancient order, the remaking of things for a new world.

Then Pedro was standing there. His thick gray hair was combed neatly back; he was wearing a clean white shirt and his pants were tucked into clean boots. He looked surprised as he searched the crowd, noting his many neighbors, men whose families he knew, whose wives and children he knew. With the stiff shuffle of a man mounting the scaffold, he walked out onto the gallery, to the edge of the stairs. He began to speak but had to clear his throat.

"My sons-in-law are not here. I don't know where they are but I would like to see them hanged the same as the rest of you. Unfortunately they are not here."

He gave an embarrassed shrug. If there is a worse sight than a proud man brought to terror, I have not seen it.

"Perhaps some of you might come inside and we can discuss how to find them."

I set down my rifle and stepped over the wall and walked until I was standing in the middle of Pedro's yard, between our men and his. Everyone on our side looked nervous, but they quickly got angry, as they saw I intended to rob them of their fun.

"I am going to talk to Pedro," I told them. "If the sergeant and his men would care to come inside with me, we can figure this all out."

I looked at the sergeant. He shook his head. Maybe he worried it was a trap; maybe he worried it *wasn't* a trap—it was hard to tell.

"Most of you know that Glenn is my son," I continued. "And the cattle lost were mine as well. This is no one's fight but my own. And I do not want it."

Everyone stopped looking at me. Glenn and our cattle no longer had anything to do with this. They settled on their knees and haunches, as if, without a single word exchanged, they had all decided that I did not exist, the way a flock of birds changes direction without any individual appearing to lead. There was a shot somewhere to my right, and then, all at once, a rolling volley from our line. I heard and felt the bullets crack past my head and I fell to the grass.

Pedro fell as well. He lay on the porch clutching his stomach but two men rushed out and pulled him inside as the bullets splintered the doorframe around them.

Over the top of the low rock wall I could see all our neighbors, their heads and gun barrels showing, the smoke puffing out and the shiny brass casings levering through the air, the spray of dust and stone as bullets slapped into the wall. I couldn't move without being shot by one side or the other so I lay there with the grass underneath me and the bullets over top. I felt strangely safe, then wondered if I'd already been shot; there was a feeling of drifting, as if I were in a river, or in the air, looking down from a great height, it was all pointless, we might as well have never crawled from the swamps, we were no more able to understand our own ignorance than a fish, staring up from a pool, can fathom its own.

The bullets continued to snap overhead. I was looking at Bill Hollis when a pale cloud appeared and his eyes went wide as if he'd had some realization. His rifle clattered over the wall and he lay down his head as if taking a nap. I had a vision of him playing the fiddle in our parlor while his brother sang.

Meanwhile the house was being shot to pieces. The heavy oak door, three hundred years old and brought from a family estate in Spain, was nothing but splinters. The parapets were disintegrating, the top of the stone tower as well. The caliche *sillares* were remnants from another era, suitable for stopping arrow and ball but not jacketed bullets, there was a thick cloud of dust rising from the house, the dust of its own bones.

Finally there was no return fire. Sometime during the fight the sun had risen and the beams of light were shining through the old gunports. Every door and window hung from splinters; except for the fresh dust the house might have been abandoned a century ago. I began to inch toward the wall.

"Reload," someone shouted. "Everyone reload."

I reached the wall and crawled over it. The young Ranger sergeant was talking to the men gathered: " . . . I go through the door, you follow me, get out of the doorway as soon as you can but don't move faster than you can shoot. The Mexicans will be in the corners. Do not pass a corner, do not turn your back to a corner, unless you or someone else is shooting into it."

He raised his head so everyone could see him.

"When I stand up," he called out, "I want you to empty your guns at the building. But as soon you see me clear this wall, you stop firing. You hear?"

I did not trust that anyone had heard. Between the ringing ears and the spectacle of destruction before us, everyone was in his own world. But somehow most agreed and those who did not had the instructions shouted into their ears.

When the sergeant stood up, there was a long volley that did not stop until finally he waved his hands and shouted for a long time and then he and a dozen other men, including Charles, rushed for the gallery. I called for Charles to come back, but he didn't hear me, or pretended not to, and then I noticed that fat old Niles Gilbert had not gone, nor had either of his two sons.

The front door was so shattered they just walked right through it. The shooting began again, the tempo increasing as each man entered the house until it was nearly continuous. We couldn't see any of what was happening inside, dark shapes passing behind the doors or windows, a few bullets leaking out and kicking up dirt in the yard. Then it got quiet and then there was a sudden *pop pop pop*. Then it got quiet and then there were more orphaned shots. After that I couldn't bear to look. In the distance I could see the Nueces and the green river flats all around, the sun continuing to rise, catching in the pall of dust, the air around the casa mayor turning a brilliant orange as if some miracle were about to occur, a descent of angels, or perhaps the opposite, a kind of eruption, the ascent of some ancient fire that would wipe us all from the earth.

I looked for some sense in it. It was the best piece of land for miles—high, well-watered ground—we had not been the first to fight here. If we were to scratch the earth we would find the bones of crushed legs, ribs gashed from spears.

Then someone was waving his hat. It was Charles. His shirt was in tatters and his arm was bleeding. He shouted for us to put down our guns, but no one moved so I stood and stepped over the wall again, waving my arms and walking up and down the line so the others would lower their rifles.

I attempted to tend to Charles's arm but he pushed me away. It appeared to be birdshot.

"Let me look at it," I said.

"It doesn't even hurt yet." Then, as if I had some disease, he would not allow me any closer.

Inside the house, it looked as if workmen had been called to perform a demolition. Or vandals let into a museum. Antique furniture shot to pieces, upholstery shredded and the stuffing spilled as if the house had been invaded by a swarm of birds, ancient dark paintings of matriarchs and patriarchs, a Byzantine portrait of Christ, antique quilts, sketches, weapons, crosses, all punctured or smashed or knocked onto the floor. An illuminated Bible, the pride of Pedro's family, fallen from its place in the *altarcito* and splayed open in the plaster.

In the living room I counted five dead men and one dead woman, shot so many times that every drop of blood had leaked from their bodies and mixed with the splinters and dust and gutted upholstery. One looked old enough to be Pedro but when I turned him over it was Cesár, a vaquero, a man who had helped us on roundups since I was a boy. In kneeling to turn him my pants soaked through and when I stood up the fabric stuck darkly to my legs.

Underneath one of the sofas something caught my eye: a young girl in a blue dress. Next to her a boy of six or eight, dead as well. By then a barricade had gone up between my eyes and mind; I saw them with scientific interest; here was the blood, there were the holes. Smaller details: standing pools of bright crimson, handprints and bootprints and long smears where the wounded had been dragged, bloody spray over the walls indicating some final moment, some story which would never be told. A young man with the white of his spine, another stretched out as if drunk; his brains had been spooned out onto his shirt. I saw others looking with the same cool interest; when blood does not belong to your kin it might as well be wine or water.

In the kitchen, six dead; three of Pedro's vaqueros—Romaldo, Gregorio, and Martín—along with Pedro's middle daughter, Carmen. Two men staring at each other over the crumpled bodies of Pedro's twin granddaughters, the same white dresses and pigtails. The room smelled like an abattoir; blood and the musky smell of opened bellies, waste from the bodies, but there was something sweet as well—roses—which I suspected my mind had invented from a swamp of confused sensations.

I went to Pedro's office. It was surprisingly untouched and I felt tired; I sat down in the chair opposite his desk as I had done many times. I resolved I would let the others make the necessary discoveries. Though of course that would be worse. There was no absolution. I got up and followed the scent of rosewater toward one of the bedrooms, where the door was perforated with two large holes from a shotgun, plaster dust grinding under my feet.

At the far end of the room, in the middle of his canopy bed, Pedro lay on his back as if taking a nap. The scent of rosewater was so strong I nearly retched. A small price. When I got closer I saw his face, the pillow and bedclothes stained. Something—a pair of teeth—had been knocked from his mouth. A few white feathers had settled on his face.

There had been a fight here—the back wall was pocked by bullets, the dressers and wardrobes splintered, jewelry scattered. I thought I heard Pedro speaking, but it was just a trick of my ringing ears. Near the foot of the bed lay Aná, Pedro's youngest daughter, her church dress soaked to the waist, her back and neck arched as if she had gathered her energy to shout something. There was an old Colt Army.

Lourdes Garcia was on the other side of the bed, still gripping a Spanish fowling piece.

Just then the game warden came into the room, surveyed the damage, and told me not to touch the bodies.

"If you do not get the hell out of here," I told him, "you will be looking for another job tomorrow."

I straightened Aná's skirts and placed her and Lourdes in the bed with Pedro. It was a pointless gesture. They would soon be carried outside. I left the room.

In one of the closets in another bedroom we found a woman in her thirties. She was alive. *¿Estás herida?* I guessed it was María, the unmarried daughter, but her face was so filthy and bloody and her eyes so wild I couldn't be sure. She looked at me. She submitted as I ran my fingers over her scalp and through her hair to check for wounds, then opened her shirt quickly to check front and back for the same, then closed it again, then lifted her skirts to check her hip and waist area. She was not injured. She sat dumbly as I straightened her clothes.

I led her outside and turned her over to Ike Reynolds and his sons, whom I know to be respectable. A minute later they rode off. What family she has left I don't know; the Garcias have been in this country far longer than any of the white families. They were once proper hidalgos, having been granted this land by the king of Spain himself. Pedro never spoke of any family in Mexico; he did not think of himself as Mexican.

Outside the sun was all the way up. Charles and one of the Rangers had both been hit by birdshot, but the pellets had not gone deep. I thought of the shotgun lying next to Lourdes. I wondered if Charles had killed her, or if he had killed Pedro, or maybe Aná.

Niles Gilbert's friend from El Paso, who had been so anxious to "naturalize" some Mexicans, had been shot through the mouth. A brief sense of satisfaction rose within me, then slipped away; he would go down a martyr. The small blond Ranger sergeant had been hit in the hand and forearm and the stock of his carbine split by a bullet.

Wounded or not, the twelve living assaulters sat dumbly on the porch, some lying on their backs, others dangling their legs over the edge, staring at the roof or into the sky. Sullivan was lifting their shirts to check them for injuries, shouting instructions into their ears. I wondered again if Charles had been the one to shoot Pedro and Lourdes, but pushed away the question a second time.

Meanwhile, the men at the wall had begun to come forward. Bill Hollis had been laid out in the shade. His brother Dutch was sitting next to him. Four others were carried over. I could tell that one was a vaquero of ours, though I did not have the heart to get up and see who it was.

A few hours later the photographer showed up. The Rangers posed with the bodies of the male Garcias, the faces shot off most of the dead men, a detail that would be lost in the printing. They would look blurred, overdirty, as the faces of all dead men do.

No one commented on the absence of Pedro's sons-in-law. It was just as he had told us—they were not in the house. The bodies of the women and children were placed in the shade, away from their men, perhaps out of some old-fashioned impulse, perhaps so they would not show in the pictures.

Watching the photographer take pictures of townspeople posing with the Garcias—a loose queue had formed—I began to feel even more tired. I knew what anyone looking at the pictures would think, or rather not think, of the Garcias, whose remains were so matted with dust and dried blood that they were barely distinguishable from the caliche. The audience would notice only the living men, who had done a brave thing, while the dead would not even register as men. They were props—like a panther or dead buck—they had lived their entire lives in order to die for just this moment.

People from town continued to arrive, women and children now. Our vaqueros disappeared, taking the body of their fallen comrade, while the vigilantes and their wives went through the cupboards. The furniture inside the casa mayor was all quite valuable; most had come from the old country: old Spanish weapons and armor, a good deal of silver. The Garcias had once been quite wealthy and I knew when I returned I would find the house completely plundered.

As for myself, I have always known I will leave nothing behind me in this place, no sign I ever passed, but for the Garcias it was different, because they had hoped, and believed, that they would.

Chapter Seven
Eli McCullough

Two days after my brother died I was still in a fever. The Indians kept me tied to my horse. I was still in a fever and we were still on the Llano, and on the morning of the third day I saw something shining in the distance, which I took to be a city, and as we got closer I saw it was floating in the air, a shining city on a hill, and I knew my mother had been right, that the heat or my fever or some hilarious Indian had killed me and I would soon be joining the rest of my family. I knew I ought to be happy but I felt sadder than I'd ever been.

When we got closer I saw it wasn't a city at all. It was a box canyon and it was still floating miles above us, as if a range of mountains had been carved out of the earth; there was a long shining river and drifting herds of deer and my mother had not been right at all. I was being taken by the Indians to their happy hunting ground, where I would remain their prisoner even in death.

I had a dauncy spell but no one heard me over the wind. Soon after, we reached the thing itself. It was a proper canyon cut into the earth but some mirage in the sky was reflecting it. It was even larger than the mirage made it look—a dozen miles across and a thousand feet deep, with fins and towers and hoodoos like observation posts, mesas and minor buttes, springs flowing brightly in the red rock. There were cottonwoods and hackberries, and the valley floor was thick with grass and wildflowers.

We took an hour dropping into it, then made an early camp next to a clear stream. There was a skull with an enormous tusk all turned to stone and sticking out of the bank. I wondered what my brother would have made of it. The Indians were relaxed. For my own protection I was kept tied to a tree, though the Germans were allowed to wander and by her yellow hair I could see one sitting on a far butte. The Indians were not worried; there were wolf and grizzly and panther tracks everywhere and it was no place to be playing a lone hand.

A few deer were killed and a yearling buffalo. Wild potatoes and turnips and sweet onions were dug up, braided, and roasted in the fire. The animals were carefully skinned, the meat filleted from the bones, coals raked out and the big roasts placed on them. The bones were put in the fire and when everything was ready they were cracked and the marrow spread on the potatoes. There were handfuls of chokecherries for dessert and a lemonade made from sumac. Everyone was full as a tick but finally the hump of the buffalo was dug out of the coals; it was dripping with fat and came apart in our fingers. It was the best I'd eaten since I'd left home and at the thought of that I got dauncy again and Nuukaru came over and slapped me.

By sundown the walls of the canyon looked to be on fire and the clouds coming off the prairie were glowing like smoke in the light, as if this place were His forge and the Creator himself were still fashioning the earth.

"Urwat leaves tomorrow," Toshaway said. When the others turned in I was tied down for sleep as I'd been since my brother died—my arms and legs roped to separate stakes in the ground. Toshaway put his buffalo robe over me. The stars were too bright to sleep, the Dipper, Pegasus, the serpent and dragon, Hercules; I watched them turn while meteors left smoking trails that stretched across the canyon.

A few of the Indians had their way with the Germans. This time I tried not to listen.

The next morning the spoils of the raid—weapons, tools, equipment, horses, anything valuable including the German girls and me—were set out and divided. The older girl went with Urwat's group; the younger girl and I with Toshaway's. The younger girl was crying as Urwat's group rode away with her cousin, and there was a patch of long dark hair, my mother's, tied to the saddle of a horse in Urwat's band. Nuukaru came over and slapped me. I knew he was doing me a favor.

After climbing back onto the Llano we didn't see water all day. A few hours before sundown we camped at a small playa lake sunk beneath the level of the grass. It was invisible from more than a hundred yards distance and how the Indians had navigated to it, I had no idea, as the plain was so flat and empty you could see the curve of the earth.

Toshaway and Nuukaru led the blond girl and me to the far end of the lake and after we washed ourselves we lay on our bellies while they lanced all the boils and blisters from riding and cleaned our other wounds as well. Our legs and backsides were rinsed with a bark tea and covered with a poultice made from pear pad innards and coneflower root. Despite the sunburn and saddle sores on her legs and rear end, now that she was cleaned up, the German girl was quite beautiful. I looked at her and hoped we might connubiate but she ignored me. I guessed she'd been a haughty one like my sister. Then I couldn't look at her.

Mostly they treated her like an expensive horse, taking care with her feed and water but hitting or throwing sticks if she did anything that got their ire up. I was given plenty of lather myself but never without an explanation; Toshaway and Nuukaru spoke to me constantly, pointing things out, and I was picking up the language already: *paa,* water; *tuhuya,* horse; *tehcaró,* eat. *Tunetsuka*—keep going.

A few days later we came to a big river that I guessed was the Canadian. The country improved. By then, neither I nor the girl were tied up at all. We'd been riding at an easy pace, eating and drinking and nursing our wounds, and even the horses were putting on flesh.

Two buffalo calves were killed and for a change the liver was put on the coals along with all the heavy bones, the warm marrow spread on the liver like butter. Toshaway kept passing me more meat and there was more curdled calves' milk, which got sweeter each time I tried it.

The next morning I woke up thinking about my father and how even with a group of willing men he never would have been able to catch us. Even a young

Indian like Nʉʉkaru would have lost them. The Comanches left conflicting trails at every patch of soft ground, changed direction at every stretch of rock or hardpan, took note of the natural line of travel across a landscape and rode a different way. A detour that cost them a few minutes would confuse a pursuer for hours. I had never felt so alone in my life.

I got up to find the Indians. I could hear voices at the river and found all the warriors bathing themselves, scrubbing off the dirt and old war paint. Some were sitting naked in the sun, looking into tiny hand mirrors or small pieces of cracked glass, and, with steel tweezers they must have gotten from the whites, they were plucking all the hair from their faces. When that was done they took small pouches of vermilion and other dyes from their possibles, which they ground with spit to form a paste, then put on their paint, color by color. Each man parted his hair down the middle and rewove his braids and dyed the part red or yellow. *Puha nabisarʉ,* said Toshaway. He was working on his braids as well. Everyone was feeling grandacious, as if getting dressed for a night of beauing.

I was put to scrubbing down the horses with grass. Each warrior repainted his pony with stripes and handprints. Two of the younger Indians rode away over the hills and didn't return.

The captured scalps were washed and brushed and attached to the tops of lances. I knew my mother's was gone and I couldn't see my sister's, either. I decided it had been Urwat's men who'd killed her.

The girl and I were tied to the horses for the first time in days. To our left the southern bank of the Canadian was a sheer cliff and to the north it was shallow breaks and hills and buttes. We followed a small stream up into the trees and came on a procession of Indians, hundreds of them, all in their best bib and tucker, painted leggings and buckskin dresses, copper bracelets and earrings sparkling and jouncing. The younger boys were naked and they came shouting and dodging among the horses. We kept going and reached the main body; it was like the parade they had when my father returned from the war. Women were calling to men and neighbors calling to neighbors and a somber old grandmother was carrying a pole with scalps attached. Some of the braves tied their scalps to the pole. The children avoided me but the adults all pinched or slapped me as I rode past.

Then we reached the village. The tipis went on out of sight, swirling designs of warriors and horses, soldiers stuck with arrows, soldiers without heads, mountains and rising suns. The air smelled like green hides

and drying flesh; there were racks standing everywhere with the flayed meat hanging in the sun like old
clothes.

A group of angry-looking Indians pushed through
the others. The women were wailing and keening
and the men were thumping their lances in the dirt.
They beat my legs and tried to pull me off my horse.
Toshaway let this go on until one of the old women
came at me with a knife. No one paid any attention to
the German girl.

There was a long negotiation over my future, with
the group of wailing women believing it should be settled with a knife or something worse. Toshaway was
defending his property. I was sure it was the family of
the man I'd shot, though Toshaway was the only person
who could have known I was the culprit.

Nɯɯkaru later explained that the dead man's family
was expecting spoils from the raid, but what they got
instead was news that their man had taken a ball in the
chest. They asked for a white scalp only to hear that
my mother's and sister's scalps had gone north with the
Yap-Eaters, that my brother had not been scalped as
he had died too bravely, and that I was innocent (a lie)
and more important I was Toshaway's property and he
would not allow them to give me a haircut. They asked
after the three scalps on his belt, but those had been

taken from soldiers during such legendary combat that he could not be expected to part with them. He could offer them two rifles. An insult. A horse, then. Five horses would be an insult. In that case he could offer them nothing. They knew the risks and they would be well taken care of by the tribe. Fine. They would take a horse.

Meanwhile, as it was a big haul of guns, ponies, and other supplies, the village was preparing a party. Of the seventy-odd horses captured, Toshaway gave most away to the men who had gone on the raid, one to the family of the dead man, and a few to some poor families who had come to him directly. You could not refuse to give a gift if someone asked for it. He was left with two new horses and me. Stingier war chiefs might keep the entire haul for themselves, but Toshaway's status was greatly improved.

After Toshaway settled with the dead man's family, he and I and Nuukaru rode to all the tipis. I stayed tied to the horse. At each place an old squaw would come over and pinch my leg to bruise it. There was frantic talking and laughing. After several hours I was hot and bored, stiff from being tied up; I could tell there were stories being told about me. Finally we arrived in Toshaway's neighborhood. Everyone was standing waiting. There was a good-looking teenage boy and girl, who I gathered were Toshaway's children, a woman in her late twenties, his wife, and a woman in her late thirties, his other wife.

When everyone finished catching up, three old men came over and untied me and told me to follow them. We were off just like that, between the tipis, around cookfires and staked-out hides, racks of drying meat, tools and weapons scattered everywhere. An old squaw came out of nowhere and slapped me between my legs. I was already sick from nervousness and the rotting meat and the flies swarming. Then a young brave came out of nowhere and hit me in the jaw. I turtled up as he kicked but then he stopped and had a talk with the old men. He had blue eyes and I knew he was white and after a few minutes he walked away as if nothing had happened.

The three old men found a place to sit near someone's tipi. It was late in the afternoon and nice in the sun, the land was open and rolling, the forest was behind us, there were horse herds grazing in the distance, several thousand animals at least. I sat listening to the creek. I'd dozed off when two of them pinned my arms back and rolled me over. The oldermost squatted at my head, I could smell his reeking breechcloth; I was sure I would air my paunch, which bothered me more than the idea of dying, and then Nuukaru came over and I relaxed.

The oldermost was doing something in the fire. When he came back he knelt next to me with a hot awl that he stuck through my ears a few times. Nuukaru was sitting on top of me so I had no air to protest. They threaded strings of greased buckskin through the holes in my ears and let me up.

Then I was given some sumac lemonade and some meat was skewered on sticks that were poked into the ground over the fire. As we sat waiting, a young fat squaw came up and hugged me, slapped me, pushed me into the grass, and climbed on top of me, wrestling the way you might with a dog. I let her drag me around and sit on me and stick my face into a mud puddle that smelled like feet. She held my nose so I'd have to open my mouth to breathe in the mud. After a while she got bored. I went back to the fire. Someone passed me a gourd of water to wash up. Someone else was heating up a kind of sauce in a small metal pan, honey and lard, stirring it with the rib bone from a deer. Everything was smelling finer than cream gravy, but just when we began to eat, Toshaway's son came over and said something. The old men clucked and shook their heads. I saw the family of the dead man making their way toward us and I knew they'd decided to dig up the hatchet.

Nuukaru clapped me on the back for support, then everyone followed as I was led by the neck to an open area in the middle of the village. A big post had been driven into the ground. I was tied to it. From looking at the people gathered it was clear Judge Lynch was holding court and then three teenage Indians were pacing around me, pointing pistols at my head.

Their sap was up and I expected them to shoot but they were waiting for more people. Finally most of the village was there; children running in and out of the crowd, putting pieces of wood and brush around my legs until there was a pile to my waist.

The young Indians cocked their pistols and pressed them to my temple, into my mouth. My guts went loose. An old squaw came over with a skinning knife and I nearly released my innards, thinking I was about to be unshucked whole, but all she did was give me a few bleeders. Then I had to let some air out, which everyone found hilarious because they knew I was scared. *Pakatsi tsa kuya?atʉ. Pakatsi tsa tʉ?ʉyatʉ!*

Nʉʉkaru was standing at the front of the crowd, watching things; he was the same awkward age as my brother, tall and gangly, he would not be much help. The old woman walked away and one of the boys aimed his pistol and pulled the trigger. It pocked my face and singed my eyebrows but he hadn't loaded a ball. The other two did the same. Then a kid ran up with a torch and feigned at lighting the pile of brush. I nodded at where I thought he ought to start the fire. I encouraged him and finally he lit the brush. The hair between my thighs began to sizzle and I was about to give up when Toshaway walked over and kicked away the burning sticks.

Toshaway made a speech to the villagers, the gist of which was I hadn't minded the idea of being burned or shot to death. The Indians highly approved of that outlook and a few of them slapped me on the back as I returned to Toshaway's tipi. His wives poured tea over my cuts and burns and cleaned my face and dressed me in a new breechcloth. But before all that I went and squatted in the brush till I'd got the evil out of me.

The party began at suppertime. Later Nʉʉkaru told me this wouldn't normally have been done because a man had been lost on the raid, but in this case no one liked the family and it was hoped they would move on.

There was venison, elk, and buffalo, quail and prairie dog, bones roasted so the marrow could be spread on meat or mixed with mesquite beans and honey for dessert. There were potatoes and onions, corn bread and squash they'd gotten from the New Mexicans. The Comanches traded with the New Mexicans for nearly everything, and also the people at Bent's Fort on the Arkansas River. For corn, squash, and pumpkins, white and brown sugar, tortillas and hard breads, guns, powder, bar lead, and bullet molds. Ornaments for horses, percussion caps and steel knives, hatchets, axes and blankets, ribbons, linens and shrouds, gartering and gun screws, lance- and arrowheads, barrel hoops, bridles, steel wire, copper wire, gold wire, bells of all sizes, saddlebags, iron stirrups, iron pots, brass pots, mirrors and scissors, indigo and vermilion, glass beads and wampum, tobacco and tinder boxes, tweezers, combs, and dried fruit. The Comanches were the wealthiest of all the Indian tribes and spent half of what they made on baubles and cheap jewelry, though they did not, as some have written, care much for the white man's clothing, for top hats or stockings or wedding veils.

After everyone had eaten his fill the oldermost of the tribe began the dance and a warrior was called out and handed a long slender pole with scalps attached. The warrior told a story of bravery and called another warrior, who took the scalp pole and told a story and called up someone else. To tell a lie would bring a curse on the entire tribe and finally a brave was called who didn't have any story better than the ones already told, and instead of talking he took up the scalp pole and began to dance. The people followed him in a big milling circle. I was standing watching. I had been scrubbed

clean and painted and was wearing my breechcloth.
The three old men had plucked out my eyebrows and
the few scraggling hairs off my chin and upper lip. The
drums beat and the Indians stepped in time; I was put
into the circle and the scalp pole was handed to me and
I was pushed to the front. After a few minutes I tried
to hand it to the man behind me but he shoved me
forward. The drums went faster, the air was red from
the setting sun, I saw the wives of the man I'd killed
and the next time I saw them they hadn't moved and
I knew the scalp pole was protecting me. They would
not touch me as long as I held it. Several hours later the
moon was up and I could barely stay awake, my feet
hurt from stamping and my shoulders burned, but the
Indians kept me at the front; there was grunting and
whooping, the calls of bear and buffalo, panthers, deer,
and elk.

When I woke up everything was black. I was under a
robe. A small disk of dark sky over my head, a dying
fire off to one side, the sound of someone breathing.
It was peaceful. I was in a tipi on a soft bed of skins;
I'd been washed again and rubbed with oil and my
wounds dressed; I was clean and warm and rolled in
a soft blanket. There was something about the person
breathing, I got to feeling dauncy and it was like the

Bible-thumpers say when you're dunked: you think the world is one way and then you come up and find you've been wrong about everything.

I got up from my pallet and went outside. There were stars and as far as I could see there were tipis glowing from their nightfires, around the bonfire people were still awake, talking softly. Women leaning on their men, children asleep against their parents. From some of the tipis there was snoring and in others there was giggling and in others there were women moaning, which went on for a long time and I got excited and then I thought of times I had heard my mother and father doing that, not to mention the few times I had imagined doing it to my sister, which of course I was ashamed of, more now than I'd been before.

I heard someone rustle in their sleep, either Nuukaru or Toshaway's son Escuté. I decided I would find Urwat and the rest of the Yap-Eaters and I would take from them a collection of scalps so long it would trail behind my horse ten miles.

As for Toshaway and his family, he had saved me and he had tried to save my brother. He might have saved my mother and sister if he had known better. But the Indians had their rules same as we had ours. My father and I had once shot at a pair of runaway slaves collecting pecans from under our trees. My gun snapped and misfired and my father's shot went yards high. I couldn't understand as the niggers were barely at eighty paces and my father the best rifle shot in the county. Then they were dark streaks running through the forest. I said we ought to get Rufe Perry and his nigger dogs but my father said it was likely to rain and we had rows yet to hoe. I asked where the slaves were headed and he said Mexico, most likely, or to live out with the Indians, who would take in Negroes and other types as long as they lived according to their laws. I said how can they take in niggers to live among them? He said plenty of people do. I could not think of anything except I was sorry my gun had snapped and he told me one day I would be thankful for small mercies.

I could hear Nʉʉkaru and Escuté breathing deeply. I listened as long as I could before I fell asleep myself.

Chapter Eight
J.A. McCullough

She was young again, riding an old wooden roller coaster, but something was going wrong—the cars were running faster and faster until finally at the very top, the whole train of them leaped from the tracks. She was flying and then she was not, she was watching the ground, everything was taking a long time, *This is very serious,* she thought, and then all the cars came down on top of her.

Then she was in the desert. The biggest frac job of her life, the engineer directing tankers like the conductor of a symphony; the lines were charged, twelve thousand PSI, and then a coupler broke. A solid iron pipe whipped like a snake. Her eyes were stinging, she was looking right into the sun, there was a Life Flight on the way, but it wouldn't do any good. *Yes,* she thought. *That is what happened.*

She opened her eyes again. Except there had been a man, she was certain of it. She wondered if he'd gone for help. She watched the logs and embers in the fireplace. The burgundy rug spread beneath her, its birds and flowers and curlicues, the busts of old Romans. She was dreaming.

She wondered how people would remember her. She had not made enough to spread her wealth around like Carnegie, to erase any sins that had attached to her name, she had failed, she had not reached the golden bough. The liberals would cheer her death. They would light marijuana cigarettes and drive to their sushi restaurants and eat fresh food that had traveled eight thousand miles. They would spend all of supper complaining about people like her, and when they got home their houses would be cold and they'd press a button on a wall to get warm. The whole time complaining about big oil.

People thought Henry Ford had ushered in the automobile age. False. Cart before the horse. It was Spindletop that had begun the automobile age and Howard Hughes, with his miraculous drill bit, who had completed it. Modern life was born at the Lucas gusher, when people suddenly realized how much oil there might be on earth. Before that, gasoline was nothing more than a cheap solvent—used to clean gears and bicycle chains—and all the oil that made

John Rockefeller a millionaire was burned in lamps, a replacement for whale oil. It was Spindletop and the Hughes bit that had opened the way for the car, the truck, and the airplane, which all depended on cheap oil the way a church depended on God.

She had done right. Made something out of nothing. The human life span had doubled, you did not get to the hospital without oil, the medicines you took could not be made, the food you ate did not reach the store, the tractor did not leave the farmer's barn. She took something useless under the ground and brought it to the surface, into the light, where it meant something. It was creation. Her entire life.

Once, she had not been unique in this. The industrialists built the country, the oilmen made it run. Now it was just the oilmen. The industrialists, or whatever they called themselves these days, led lives based on destruction, closing down factories and moving them abroad. She did not expect to be loved but there were bastards and there were bastards; those men had taken apart the country brick by brick and if there was anything she hated more than unions, it was people who couldn't work.

Other memories came back in a rush. Visiting the houses of the Mexican hands with her father, the women out of another century, pregnant and carrying water buckets from distant wells, irons over a wood fire, bluing to steaming washpots, wringing the boiling clothes. Canning fruits and vegetables in the worst of the summer heat—hotter in the jacals than it was outside. The men in the shade, braiding lariats from horsehair. *Why don't they buy their ropes from the store?* she asked, but her father didn't answer.

Walking through the pasture hours before sunup, crouching low to find the horses against the dark sky. All around her, the hands roping their mounts. Blowing of horses, clicking of cinches, voices soothing in Spanish. Some of the ponies gave in to the rope, others bucked and kicked, not wanting to spend the day running in the sun and thorns. Many of them were nothing but scar tissue from wither to hoof; the brush took all the hair off.

A never-ending creak of windmills, kneeling with the Colonel to study the wet ground at the stock tanks, the night's fresh tracks. Cattle, deer, foxes, javelina, rabbits, paisano, hares, mice, raccoons, snakes, turkey, bobcats. The appearance of a panther track brought her father and brothers, an old Mexican with his dogs. At some point, she did not remember when, the Colonel began to put his hand over every panther track he saw, obliterating it completely. *Don't tell anyone.* The adult world ran on secrets. The derision of her father and brothers when she said she wanted to see a wolf or bear. They are better in zoos, said her father. They are better gone forever.

And what had she learned? She had lost half her family before their time. The land was hard on its sons, harder yet on the sons of other lands. Her grandmother had once proposed a bounty for each pair of Mexican ears—*treat them the same as coyotes.* She thought of her brothers killed by the Germans, her uncle Glenn blown to bits in a trench.

She had tried to retire twelve years ago. She had been a child kneeling by the stock tank and then her own children were middle-aged; she had not been perfect, she wanted to patch things, she wanted to know her grandchildren. There had been a window. But oil had been low, cheaper than water, they said, and the bids she got for her leases were a fraction of what they should have been. She knew it was her last chance to make things right with the family. But to sell at such a bottom—the thought made her physically ill.

Then the Arabs hit New York. She began hiring drillers. Her children had their own lives, they did not need her, oil began to climb. To see a well come in where there had just been desert, to see flow after a good frac job, from a hole everyone had given up on— that was what she lived for. Something out of nothing. Act of creation. There would always be time for family.

Chapter Nine
Diaries of Peter McCullough

AUGUST 13, 1915

Memory is a curse. When I close my eyes I see Pedro's shot-off face and the weeping hole in Lourdes's cheek, a clear fluid issuing forth like a tear. Aná's blood-soaked dress. When I sleep I am back in their room. Pedro is sitting up in bed, pointing at me, speaking in some ancient language, and as I get closer I realize the sound is not coming from his mouth, but from the hole in his temple. Upon waking I lie still a long time and hope for my heart to stop beating, as if death might absolve me from my place in this.

What happened at the Garcias' was only the beginning. In town, there are at least a hundred armed men that no one knows, carrying rifles and shotguns as if it were half a century ago, as if there were no town at all.

Amado Batista was murdered sometime in the night, his store looted, an attempt made to burn the building though the fire did not catch.

The Garcias are described in all the papers as Mexican radicals; in truth they were the most conservative landowners in Webb and Dimmit Counties. The picture of their bodies is reprinted in every corner of the state and in Mexico, where, despite the fact that old landowners are not quite in favor, they will doubtless go down as martyrs.

Glenn remains in San Antonio, recovering at the hospital. Neither he nor Sally reacted to the news of the Garcias' annihilation. I wonder if I am going crazy or if I do not love my family enough, or if it is the opposite, if I love them too much. If I am the only sane person I know.

Meanwhile, the rooming houses are full of the worst sorts the Rio Grande Valley has to offer and the Rangers are having trouble keeping order. I suggested to Sergeant Campbell (Was he the one to shoot Pedro and Lourdes? Was it my own son?) that he send for the rest of his company, but they are occupied up and down the border, guarding other ranches.

Campbell, despite his mean looks, is troubled that half the dead were women and children. I refuse to talk to him about it. People like him think you can apologize things away, that you can confess over and over until you are free to repeat your crime.

Our house was busy all day with well-wishers; at one point I drove into town to escape them, whereupon I came on two trucks with a dozen men each, well armed and hoping to make battle with Mexican insurgents. I told them everyone was dead. They looked disappointed but after some discussion they decided to go into town anyway: no point giving up hope just yet.

Returned to find Judge Poole eating our beef and drinking our whiskey and taking statements from all present. I gave him my story—*just the facts*—he corrected me several times—*not your interpretation.* Finally he asked me to step outside, away from the others.

"This is just a formality, Pete. Don't let anyone think I'll side with a wetback over a white man."

Nearly pointed out that *we* are the wetbacks, having swum our horses across the Nueces a century after the Garcias first settled here. But of course I said nothing. He clapped me on the back—his butcher's hands—and went in to eat more free beef.

People continued to arrive at the house, bringing cakes, roasts, and regrets that they had not been able to reach us in time to help—how brave we were to assault the Mexicans with such a small force. By that they mean seventy-three against ten. Fifteen if you count the women. Nineteen if you count the children.

AUGUST 14, 1915

Sally asked why I had not yet come to see Glenn at the hospital. I explained my reasons:

Three houses were burned last night and eight townspeople killed, all Mexican except Llewellyn Pierce, who had a Mexican wife.

Sergeant Campbell shot at least three looters, though two escaped into the brush. The dead man is from Eagle Pass. The three were in the process of setting fire to the home of Custodio and Adriana Morales. The Moraleses were already dead. I thought of Custodio and how he loved our fine horses; he always charged too little to repair the tack and other goods I brought him. I had been meaning to invite him over to ride for twenty years now.

Campbell confided that one of his men refused to shoot at white looters. Also a sheriff's deputy was found dead, but no one knew any details.

Campbell has cabled again for the rest of his company but was told that they were busy with bigger problems farther south.

"We need to do something about these Mexicans," he told me. "They're not going to be safe here."

He had not seemed very concerned about the safety of the Garcias. I did not say this but he must have read my face.

"Our job is to enforce the peace against anyone who disturbs it," he said. "I don't care what color they are."

Several Tejano families—the Alberto Gonzaleses, the Claudio Lopezes, the Janeros, Sapinosos, and the Urracas—left town this afternoon with all their belongings.

Campbell thinks tonight will be worse than last. His men are outnumbered fifty to one. "They've been talking about buying us machine guns," he said. "They should have done it already." Then he asked: "What do you think about this Sheriff Graham?"

"I think he will be sad if he misses out on all this looting."

"That's what I thought."

It was quiet. We sat there on the porch looking out over the country.

"What is it like to have all this?" he said.

"I don't know, really."

He nodded as if he'd expected this answer.

"Would you like some supper to bring with you for later?" I said.

He didn't reply. We looked toward the town but you cannot see it from the porch.

"Your old man is something, I'll say that."

"He's something all right."

"My daddy is dead," he said.

Something made me wonder if he were responsible for this condition. Still, I liked him. He could not have been over five foot five in boots and every man in town was afraid of him.

"What are you planning to do about tonight?"

"Shoot a lot of people, I guess."

"That does not sound like much of a plan."

"Well, that's what we got."

"Have you done much work like this?"

"I shot two guys in Beaumont. But this is like turkey season compared to that."

It was quiet.

"How do you do it?"

"You use your sights," he said.

AUGUST 15, 1915

The light of several fires visible from my window last night; gunfire sporadic but constant.

By morning another dozen Mexican families were gone; they appear to have left under their own power. Fourteen more dead, six of them white. On the phone, Campbell admitted that he was the one who shot the deputy the other evening. The deputy was wearing his badge and looting a house.

Charles and I drove into town and came on a Tejano man hanging from a live oak.

"That's Fulgencio Ypina," Charles said.

We stopped and Charles climbed the tree and cut him down. We lifted and deposited him as gently as possible in the back of the truck. Fulgencio had cleared brush for us for years. His body was already beginning to swell.

"Who is going to bury these people?" said Charles.

"I don't know."

"Is the army coming?"

"I don't know that, either."

"We should call Uncle Phineas."

"He is on a fishing trip."

"Well, you need to do something."

"Like what?"

"I don't know. But you need to."

The streets were empty. There were handwritten signs posted everywhere:

ANYONE FOUND ON THESE STREETS AFTER DARK (INCLUDING WHITES) WILL BE SHOT. ORDER OF THE TEXAS RANGERS.

When we found Sergeant Campbell, he had been shot again, this time through the upper part of his calf.

He was sitting in a chair in the back of the feed store with his boots off and his pants down.

"At least people seem to aim for your extremities," I joked. The leg did not look bad—the bullet had missed the bone and the artery.

Campbell was watching the doctor. "You get hit in the hands because your hands are in front of your chest when you aim a gun. And I got hit in the leg because when I shot the guy last night, he discharged his weapon when he fell over." He looked at me as if our ages were reversed.

"You can tell every Mexican family in town that they can come to my ranch," I said.

"That will make things easier on me." He did not seem to consider it a big favor. He continued to watch Guillermo Chavez, who at twenty-five is the town veterinarian, having taken over from his father. Chavez unbandaged his hand and arm.

"Who did these dressings?"

"I did. Are you a real doctor?"

"Mostly with animals."

"Licensed?"

"Look at me and take a guess."

Campbell shook his head: "This is a goatfuck."

"I am happy you are here," said Guillermo. "Which is something I never thought I would say to a *Rinche*."

Campbell ignored the insult. "What's gonna happen if those bones knit like that?"

"You'll have trouble with your hand." He shrugged. "But the forearm is the real trouble, because there is a lot of bruising and that will need to be cut out."

"Or I lose the arm?" His voice cracked and for an instant I saw Campbell for what he was, a scared twenty-year-old; but the mask quickly returned.

"Just keep packing this powder into it. When it begins to ooze and get sticky, add more. Always keep dry powder in the wound."

"That looks like yellow sugar."

"Sugar and sulfa."

"Table sugar."

"It's a reliable remedy. The sugar alone would be enough."

"This is fuckin' stupid."

"Use it or not, I don't care. Your colleagues in Starr County murdered my cousin, your colleagues in Brownsville murdered my uncle and his son, and here I am, fixing you up."

"There's rotten ones in every barrel," said Campbell.

"Tell that to Alfredo Cerda or Gregorio Cortez or Pedro Garcia. Or their wives and children, who are also dead. Your colleagues arrive and stir things up and the army comes and settles them down. But this is obvious. It is not even a matter for serious discussion."

Campbell was flexing his fingers to see if he could still grip his gun. "Do you have morphine?" he said to Guillermo. To me he said: "We can't pay you for the use of the ranch."

"When is the army getting here?"

"Never," he said.

"Well . . . One riot, one Ranger."

"Sure. Unless you're the one Ranger."

Sally was furious that I'd invited all the Mexicans in the town to our house and immediately demanded I put Consuela on the phone. I could hear her ordering Consuela to have the other maids hide the silver and take up the expensive rugs. Consuela handed the phone back.

"What is wrong with you, Peter?"

"These people are going to die if they don't come here."

She didn't say anything.

"Glenn is going to be fine," I told her.

"You can't say that," she said. "You can't say that when you're not even here with him."

I hoped the Mexicans would make the move quietly, but by dark, half the Tejano residents of the town, nearly a hundred people, had walked, driven, or ridden up to the ranch, carrying, pushing, or pulling their valuables in donkey carts or handcarts or on their backs.

Midkiff and Reynolds, without being prompted, both sent men to help protect the Mexicans. *They are protecting our ranch*, the Colonel corrected me, *don't be an idiot.*

Campbell came to check in in person, deputized the eight men (though he had no legal power to do so), and returned to town, limping badly, his right arm in a sling. Somewhere he acquired a .351 Winchester, which can be operated with one hand. I did not ask how he got it. We have chained and locked the gates to the ranch and Charles and the vaqueros have dug themselves in by the road.

Chapter Ten
Eli/Tiehteti

1849

The Kotsoteka Comanche lived mostly along the Canadian River, where the Llano ended and the dry plains turned into grassy canyonlands. Historically they'd ranged down to the outskirts of Austin; Toshaway knew my family's headright better than I did. The Texans had signed a treaty saying that there would be no more settlements west of town, but in the end they were a certain breed, and when an agreement became troublesome, they did not mind breaking it.

"One day a few houses appeared," said Toshaway. "Someone had been cutting the trees. Of course we did not mind, in the same way you would not mind if someone came into your family home, disposed of your belongings, and moved in their own family. But perhaps, I don't know. Perhaps white people are different.

Perhaps a Texan, if someone stole his house, he would say: 'Oh, I have made a mistake, I have built this house, but I guess you like it also so you may have it, along with all this good land that feeds my family. I am but a *kahúu*, little mouse. Please allow me to tell you where my ancestors lie, so you may dig them up and plunder their graves.' Do you think that is what he would say, Tiehteti-taibo?"

That was my name. I shook my head.

"That's right," said Toshaway. "He would kill the men who had stolen his house. He would tell them, '*Itsa nʉ kahni*. Now I will cut out your heart.'"

We were lying in a grove of cottonwoods, looking out over the valley of the Canadian. The grass was thick around us, grama and bluestem, more than could ever be eaten. The sun was going down and the crickets were sawing away and the birds were making a slaughter. On our side of the river the cane was glowing like it would spark at any minute but across the water, toward the south and the white settlements, the cliffs had already gone dusky. I was thinking of all the times I'd been mad at my brother for keeping a candle lit and I'd gone to sleep by myself outside.

Toshaway was still talking: "Of course we are not stupid, the land did not always belong to the Comanche, many years ago it was Tonkawa land, but we liked it, so we killed the Tonkawa and took it from them . . . and now they are *tawohho* and try to kill us whenever they see us. But the whites do not think this way—they prefer to forget that everything they want already belongs to someone else. They think, *Oh, I am white, this must be mine.* And they really believe it, Tiehteti. I have never seen a white person who did not look surprised when you killed them." He shrugged. "Me, when I steal something, I expect the person will try to kill me, and I know the song I will sing when I die."

I nodded.

"Am I crazy to think this?"

"*No sé nada.*"

He shook his head. "I am not even slightly crazy. The white people are crazy. They all want to be rich, same as we do, but they do not admit to themselves that you only get rich by taking things from other people. They think that if you do not see the people you are stealing from, or if you do not know them, or if they do not look like you, it is not really stealing."

A bear came down to the water and flights of teal and wigeon were settling in the far pools. Toshaway continued to braid his lariat.

"*Moowi,*" he said.

"*Moowi,*" I repeated.

"I have watched you many times, Tiehteti. Your father has seen me twice, but allowed himself to believe he had seen nothing. I have watched your mother feed the disgraced starving Indians who come to her door, I have watched you lying on your belly studying deer tracks, and I have watched when you killed the big *tʊmakupa* that night." He sighed. "But the Yap-Eaters smelled the smoke from your evening meal, and when I lied and told them I knew the family that lived there, that you were very poor, *nabukuwaatʊ,* they insisted that for a poor family, you seemed to be eating very well, and then Urwat decided to check for himself."

I looked out past the hills and saw my mother on the porch and my sister in the grass and my brother in a shallow pit. I wondered if my brother and sister had done something and that was what brought the Indians on us. Then I wondered if my sister had been winking in and out the way I was. My mother would not have let herself. But my sister . . . She would have let herself wink out, I decided. She had not been awake for most of it.

Then I was thinking about my father. I pushed him out of my mind. There was nothing but shame between us.

"*Moowi,*" I said to Toshaway.

"*Moowi,*" he said.

———

Toshaway had no idea how old he was, though he looked around forty. Like the other Comanche purebloods he had a big forehead, a fat nose, and a heavy square melon. He looked like a field hand, and on the ground he was slow as an old cowboy, but put him on a horse and the natural laws did not apply. The Comanches all rode like this, though they did not all look like Toshaway: they were darker or lighter, they were lathy as Karankawas and fat as bankers, they had faces like hatchets or Spanish kings, it was a democratic-looking mix. They all had a few captives somewhere in the bloodline—from other Indian tribes or the Spanish, or more recently, the Anglos and Germans.

Unless I wanted a hiding, I was up before the stars set, walking through the wet grass, filling the water jugs in the cold stream and getting the fire going. The rest of the day I did whatever the women didn't feel like doing. Pounding corn for Toshaway's wife, cleaning and flaying game the men brought in, getting more water or firewood. Most Comanches used a flint and steel, same as the whites, but they made me learn the hand drill, which was a yucca stalk you spun between your palms while leaning it into a cedar board. You spun and leaned with all your strength until a coal formed or your hands began to bleed. The coal was the size of a pinhead. Usually it broke up before you could get it into the bundle of cattail down or punk or whatever you'd collected for tinder.

Meanwhile, when they weren't hunting, Escuté and Nʉʉkaru spent their days sleeping, smoking, or gambling, and if I tried to talk to them when others could see, I would be ignored or beaten, though it was nothing compared to the beatings the women gave me.

When everything else was done I was set to making *ta?siwoo ʉhʉ*—buffalo robes—which was like printing money on a slow press. Each robe took a week. It would then be traded for a handful of glass beads and end up in the coat of a soldier who was out fighting other Indians or perhaps on a sofa in Boston or New York, where, having wiped out their own aboriginals, they held a great affinity for anything Native.

But all that was women's work. If Toshaway called me over everything else stopped. Sometimes to catch and saddle his horse, sometimes to light his pipe or paint him for his evenings out. When he got back from a raid or trip I would spend a few hours picking lice, lancing his boils, cooking his dinner, plucking any beard hairs that had come in, and then his paint. He spent more time getting himself up than my sister ever had, going through slews of makeup and spending hours raking his hair with a porcupine brush, greasing and rebraiding it with slivers of copper and fur until it looked just like when he'd started.

Depending on what was in season, I was also put to gathering. Fruit from the *wokwéesi* (prickly pear), *tʉahpi* (wild plum), and *tunaséka* (persimmon), beans from the *wohiʔhuu* (mesquite), *kʉʉka* (wild onion), *paapasi* (wild potato), or *mutsi natsamukwe* (mustang grapes). I was not allowed to carry a knife or gun or bow, just a digging stick, and there were wolf and bear and panther tracks everywhere.

No white person, even an Irishman, would have spent an hour digging a handful of runty potatoes, but I knew I had gotten off easy. I had not taken the big jump. I still got the feeling of a full stomach, a hot fire against a cold night, the sound of other people sleeping close. I knew what it would look like with the grass waving over me; the road to heaven would be slick with my own blood.

It would be nice to expound upon the kinship I discovered between myself and the black Africans my countrymen kept in bondage, but, unfortunately, I made no such discovery. I thought only of my own troubles. I was an empty bucket that needing filling with whatever food or favors the Indians would allow, crippling my way through each day, hoping for extra food or praise or a few easy minutes to myself.

As for escaping, there were eight hundred miles of dry wilderness between the ranchería and civilization. The first time I was caught by the other children. The second time I was caught by Toshaway, who turned me over to his wives. They and their mothers beat me hollow, cut up the soles of my feet, and had a long discussion about blinding me in one eye, and I knew the next time I bucked would be the end of me.

To prepare a hide, you stretched out the skin in the grass, hair side down, staking the corners. Then you knelt on the bloody surface, pushing and scraping off the fat and sinew with a piece of blunt bone or metal. If the tool was too sharp or you weren't careful you would push through to the other side, ruining the hide, for which you would be beaten.

Between scrapings I spread a layer of wood ash so the lye would soften the fat; while that was happening I was sent for more water or wood, or I would skin, bone, and flay out a deer one of the men or boys had dragged in. The only thing I didn't do was repair or make clothing, though the women would have taught me if they could have—they were always months behind what the men needed: a new pair of moccasins or leggings (one hide), a bearskin robe (two hides), a wolf robe (four hides). The hides had to be cut so the shape of the animal matched the shape of the wearer, and, as it took all day to finish even a single deer or wolf hide, mistakes could not be made.

In addition to making all the tools the band needed—axes, awls, needles, digging sticks, scrapers, knives and utensils—the women also made all the thread, rope, and twine. The band went through miles of it—for tipis and clothing, for saddles and bridles and hobbles, for every tool or weapon they made—everything in their lives was held together by string, which had to be twisted inch by inch. The leaves of a yucca or agave would be soaked or pounded, or the fibers separated from grasses or cedar bark. Once the fibers were loose they were braided. Animal sinews were also saved—tendons from a deer's ankles were chewed until they split. The sinews along the spine were longer and very easy to work with, but these were in short supply and saved to make weapons, and the women were not allowed to use them.

If you were in a tight spot, cordage could be made from rawhide, but there were better uses for it and it stretched when wet. A hide would be laid flat and a spiral cut into it an inch or two wide, starting from the outside and cutting inward until the entire hide was one long strand. A single lariat required six different strands, though mostly the men made their own lariats, unless a woman was seen sitting with nothing to do.

The Comanches had no patience for the ignorance of their white captives when they themselves had been raised knowing that whether it took a minute or an hour to build a fire or make a weapon or track a man or animal might, at some point, be the difference between living and dying. When there was nothing to do, no one could match them in laziness; otherwise they were careful as goldsmiths. When they looked at a forest they saw each individual plant and knew its name and the seasons they could eat or use it as medicine; they saw the tracks of every living thing that had passed through. Any of them might have been dropped naked upon the earth and within a few days would be living comfortably.

By comparison we were dumb as steers. They could not understand why they had not defeated us. Toshaway always said that white women laid crops of eggs like ducks, which hatched every night, so it didn't matter how many you killed.

As for me, I dreamed about scraping hides and woke up with the feel of the scraper in my hands. Once a hide was scraped and dried, we took a rawhide bowl and mashed in whatever brains were around, tallow, soap water from yucca (which I had dug up, cut up, carried back to the camp, then pounded and boiled), and maybe some old liver. Bear tallow was used most of the time, and this was the main reason bears were killed. My father and the other frontiersmen considered bear meat and honey the king's supper, but the Indians would only eat bear if there was no hoofed creature to be found.

As for the hides, if the hair was left on, you tanned one side; if the hair was off, you tanned both sides. Then it was the worst part of the process—two days of kneading and twisting to get the hide broken. The final step with buckskin was to smoke it to make it waterproof, though not if it was for trade.

One day in August, Nʉʉkaru caught up to me as I was fetching water. I was happy to see him as he'd been gone most of the summer, and even though we shared a tipi, we hardly got the chance to augur, because the women kept me working from can't see to can't see.

He'd come back from his last raid with a scalp, so even though he still looked like a boy, with bony arms and legs, the women now wanted his approval and the men invited him to their gambling. The Comanches had no ceremony for ending boyhood—no vision quests or hooks through the nipples—when you felt like it you started going on raids, watching the horses until gradually you were allowed into the fight.

"It's women's work," he said, by way of greeting me.

I was carrying water up the hill. After I delivered it, I would go dig for potatoes in the mud. "They make me do it," I said.

"So tell them you won't."

"Toshaway will beat me."

"Definitely not."

"Then his wives and mother and the neighbor woman will."

"So what?"

We kept walking.

"What do I say to them?"

"Just stop doing it," he said. "The rest is just details."

We continued to climb the hill. The afternoon was cool and the women had not been asking so much of me. I saw no reason to stir the kettle. Nuukaru must have sensed this, because he turned and punched me suddenly in the groin. I went to my knees.

"For your own good you will give me your full attention now."

I nodded. It occurred to me that in the old days I would have wanted to kill him; now I just hoped he wouldn't hit me again.

"Everyone in the world wants to be *Nɇmɇnɇɇ* and here it is being given to you, but you are not taking it. When the Indians starve on their reservations, for instance the Chickasaw, Cherokee, Wichita, Shawnee, Seminole, Quapaw, Delaware"—he paused—"even the Apaches and Osages and plenty of Mexicans, they all want to join our band. They leave their reservations, they risk *ooibehkarɇ,* half of them die just trying to find us. And why do you think that is?"

"I don't know."

"Because we are free. They speak Comanche before they get here, Tiehteti. They speak their own language and they also speak Comanche. Do you know why?"

I looked after my water jug.

"Because Comanches don't act like women."

"I have to get the water," I said.

"Whatever you want. But soon it'll be too late and no one will think of you as anything but a *na?raiboo.*"

The next morning Toshaway's wives and mother and the neighbor woman were straightening up camp. The men were sitting around the fire, smoking or eating breakfast.

"Get me some water, Tiehteti-taibo." That was my full name. It meant Pathetic Little White Man. It was not bad as Comanche names went, and I went for the water carrier without thinking about it. Then I felt Nʉʉkaru's eyes on me.

"Go on," said Toshaway's daughter. She gave Nʉʉkaru a look; she must have known what was happening. The work that wore me out had equally worn out her mother and grandmother, and if I quit, it would fall to them again.

"I'm not getting any more water," I said. "*Okwéetuku nʉ miarʉ.*"

The neighbor woman, who had a voice like a burro and outweighed me by six or eight stone, picked up a hatchet in one hand and grabbed for my wrist with the other. I lit a shuck between the tipis, dodging around pots and equipment. The men were hooting and finally she threw the hatchet at my head, which, in my best stroke of luck in months, hit handle first. My bell was ringing but she stopped chasing me. She was trying to catch her breath. I slowed to a walk.

"I will kill you, Tiehteti."

"*Nasiinʉ,*" I told her. Piss on yourself.

The men looked in the other direction and began to talk in loud voices about a hunting trip they were planning.

"I'm going to the river," I repeated. "But I am not getting any more water."

"In that case fetch some wood," called Toshaway's mother. "You don't have to get water anymore."

"No," I said. "I'm done with those things."

I followed the stream down to the Canadian and sat in the sun. There were elk on the opposite side and Indians a couple of furlongs downstream. I fell asleep awhile and woke up feeling narrow at the equator—I'd left camp before eating breakfast—but I had no knife and all I was wearing was a breechcloth. There were plenty of old mesquite beans, but I wanted meat, so I went into the cane and spent half an hour catching a turtle. Fish were taboo but turtles weren't. I had nothing to kill him with so I carried him around until I found a good piece of rainbow flint, then stepped on his shell till his head stuck out and cut through his neck with my flint. I sucked down a bit of the blood and it was fishy but not too bad so I drank some more of it and then turned the turtle upside down and sucked him dry.

Then I thought my mother wouldn't be happy if she saw me drinking turtle blood like a wild Indian. I figured I'd been with the Comanches six months, but I'd had no time to think, just work and sleep, and I wondered if my mind had been rubbed clean. When I thought of my mother I saw a pretty woman's face, but part of me was not sure it was really her. I forgot about the turtle and sat down. I watched the other Indians downriver. They had a new captive with them, a red Mexican. I waved and they waved back. That made me feel better.

Meanwhile the turtle was still leaking blood. I wondered if Nʉʉkaru was right or if he had played me for a gump. If the women were allowed to cut me up again—the only fun they ever got to have—it would be better to carry water.

I saw another turtle sunning himself and decided to catch him, then saw two more. After I cut their heads off I had nothing to make a fire. That was fine; I found some dead cedar and shaved off the bark. I found another flint to dig the notch for a fireboard and a short straight stick for the drill. My hands were hard and I got a coal in a few minutes and the tinder caught easily.

When Toshaway's father rode up I was dozing in the grass with my belly full of turtle. He looked at the empty shells.

"You leave any for me, fat boy?"

"I didn't know you were coming."

He sat there on his horse, looking out over the river and thinking about things. "Get on behind me," he finally said. "You don't have to worry about the women anymore."

The next morning I slept the latest I had in months, waking up to the sound of Nʉʉkaru and Escuté chattering.

"The white one becomes a man," said Nʉʉkaru as I emerged from the tipi. I could not believe how long I'd slept.

"Actually," said Escuté, "he has become a boy." They offered me some meat they'd been roasting, and some sumac lemonade, a couple of small potatoes. We sat and smoked.

"What are we doing today?"

"*We* are doing nothing," said Escuté. "*You* are going out with the other children."

I looked at them but they were not joking. Being retarded in all things they found important, the men had decided that I was best matched with the eight- and nine-year-olds.

By the age of ten, shooting a rough bow he made himself, a Comanche child could kill anything smaller than a buffalo. At the Council House Fight in San Antonio, when the great chiefs came in for peace talks and the whites massacred them, an eight-year-old Comanche boy, hearing the news that his people were betrayed, picked up his toy bow and shot the nearest white man through the heart. He was trying to retrieve his arrow when the mob of whites killed him.

The children I was sent to play with were smaller than they would have been if they had grown up among the Anglos, but they'd spent every minute of their short lives riding, shooting, and hunting. They could sit a horse that would have thrown any white man, they could hit each other with blunt arrows at a dead run. There had never been any church or lessons; in fact, nothing had ever been asked of them, except to do what came naturally, which was to be out hunting and tracking, playing at making war. By the time their short hairs came in they would be going on raids to watch the horses, until the practice for making war and the making of war itself had become the same thing.

They were also encouraged to steal, though only if the owner of the item were present, and only if the item were returned. Toshaway's butcher knife was taken from his sheath as he ate lunch, his pistol was stolen from under his robe. The whites knew that an Indian could steal your horse while you were sleeping, even if you'd tied the reins around your wrist, and for a Comanche to say "that man is the best horse thief in our tribe" was nearly the highest compliment that could be paid, a way of saying that a person could walk into the heart of an enemy camp without being seen and, horses being common currency among both whites and Indians, was likely to become rich. The Comanches were just as happy to steal all the horses of a group of Rangers or settlers as they were to actually kill them, knowing that the buffalo wolves, mountain lions, or sparse water would eventually do them in.

After a few weeks of instruction I was considered ready to go hunting with the bow, and so three other boys and I went down to the canebrakes near the river and sat waiting a long time. There was nothing moving and one of the boys took a section of reed and put it in his mouth, which, when he blew through it, made a sound like a fawn in distress. Within a few moments we heard stamping, then nothing, and then more stamping. Then I saw a doe walking slowly through the tall grass and blowdown. She pricked her ears and looked straight at me and I knew I couldn't draw the bow without her seeing me. Not to mention arrows wouldn't cut through the frontal bones, only the ribs.

The ten-year-old made a noise with his mouth that seemed to come from the other side of the thicket. The doe turned her head, but her body was still facing us.

"Now would be a good time to shoot," he whispered.

"But the chest . . ."

"Shoot her in the neck."

"Remember to aim low so she ducks into it."

I drew the bow and began to feel better about everything—the deer still hadn't moved—but at the sound of the string she crouched and took a leap. By a miracle the arrow went into her, but it only cut muscle. Then she was running at full speed with her flag up.

The youngest one shook his head. "*Yee*," he said, "*Tiehteti tsa? awinu.*"

"What do you think?" I said.

"*Aitu*," said the oldest. "Very poor. We will be tracking her all day."

The others sighed.

We snuck down to the river and looked for turtles to catch, made a few snares, and when the boys decided the doe had calmed down and likely begun to stiffen from her wound, we followed her through featureless tall grass to where she was bedded a half mile away, using four spots of blood and a scuffed patch of moss on a log. She took off running but was hit with three more arrows. We sat awhile longer and when we found her again she was dead.

I said: "That seemed like cheating, using the call to bring her in."

"So next time get closer and use a lance."

"Or a knife."

"Or go after a bear."

"I was only saying about the fawn call."

The oldest one waved his hand impatiently. "We were told to bring a deer back, Tiehteti, and they'd be mad if we didn't get one. And next time you might try to break the neck so we don't have to track the deer all day."

"It would also be fine to hit one of the big arteries."

"You're rolling your fingers," said the eight-year-old. He drew an imaginary bow. "You have to pop them away from the string."

"Like we showed you," said the oldest.

I didn't say anything.

"If you roll your string, you will never shoot straight."

"Toshaway will tell you I'm a good shot with a gun."

"So go find us a sapling, Mr. Good Shot."

The boys made their own bows and arrows, but the people who made the real weapons were the old men, retired warriors who had become too blind or too slow to go on raids, or maybe their wind had given out, or maybe, unbelievably to us, they had grown tired of killing and wanted to spend their last years making items of an artistic nature.

Osage was preferred for the bows—though ash, mulberry, or hickory could substitute—and dogwood for the arrows. We carried the big *ohapuupi* seeds with us, planting them anywhere they might grow, and as this had been done by the various tribes for hundreds or maybe thousands of years, bois d'arc trees were found all along the plains. Equally important was the *parua,* or dogwood. When we found a grove of them we would prune back the trunks almost to the ground. The next spring each trunk would send out dozens of thin new shoots, which grew very straight and were easy to make into good arrows. The location of these arrow groves was kept track of, and they were harvested carefully, making sure that the trees would survive.

A regular bow—better than any factory could make today—was worth one horse. The upper and lower limbs had to release with even pressure while pulling a specific weight at a specific distance from the grip. A fancy or unusually good bow was worth two or three horses. They were all about a yard in length (short compared to the eastern tribes', as, unlike them, we fought from horseback) and backed with the spine sinews from a deer or buffalo. If times were bad, the bowyers would turn out bows very quickly; if times were good—if our warriors were not being killed and their equipment not being lost on raids—the bowyers would take their time and their bows would be the stuff of legend.

Arrows were no different. It could take half a day to make one just right: straight, the proper length and stiffness, the feathers all in alignment—though in a single minute of fighting you might need two dozen. The shafts were felt and squeezed and held up to the light and straightened in the teeth. A crooked arrow was no different from a bent rifle barrel. The Comanches expected their bows to reach fifty yards when they were shooting quickly, hundreds of yards if they were taking their time. On a calm day I saw Toshaway kill an antelope at a full furlong, the first shot going over the animal's back (though falling so quietly it was not noticed) the second falling just short, also in silence, and the third finally telling between the ribs.

The strings were commonly sinew, which when dry shot arrows the fastest but could not be depended on when wet. Some preferred horsehair, which shot slower but was reliable in all conditions, and still others preferred bear gut.

The best feathers for fletching were turkey feathers, but owl or buzzard feathers were also fine. Hawk or eagle feathers were never used as they were damaged by blood. The best shafts were grooved along their length. We used two grooves and the Lipan used four. This prevented the arrow from stanching the wound it had just cut, but it also kept the shaft from warping.

The blades of hunting arrows were fixed vertically, as the ribs of game animals are vertical to the earth. The blades of war arrows were fixed parallel to the earth, the same as human ribs. Hunting points were made without barbs and tied tightly to the shaft so they could be pulled from an animal and reused. War arrows had barbs and the blades were tied loosely, so that if the arrow was pulled, the head would remain lodged in the enemy's body. If you were shot with a war arrow, it had to be pushed through the other side to be removed. By then all the white people knew that, though they did not know that we used different arrows for hunting.

All the plains tribes used arrows with three feathers, though some of the eastern bands used only two, which we looked down on, as they were not accurate. Of course the eastern Indians did not care much, as they lived on a weekly meat allowance from the white man and were drunk most of the time anyway, wishing they had died with their ancestors.

Occasionally, throughout the fall and winter, I would see the German girl who'd been taken captive with me. Most families had at least one slave or captive, often a young Mexican boy or girl, as Mexico was where they did most of their raiding and horse stealing—the Comanches' toll on that country was on another scale, entire villages wiped out in a single night—Texans had nothing to complain about.

Of course there were numerous white captives as well, from settlements near Dallas, Austin, and San Antonio; there was a boy who had been snatched in far East Texas; there were captives from other tribes. But as I was considered to have a great future, I avoided talking to them.

The only one I broke this rule for was the German girl, whose name was *Suhiʔohapitʋ*, Yellow Hair Between the Legs, but who was mostly referred to as Yellow Hair. Whatever she had been to her family, to the Comanches she was invisible, a nonperson. She spent all her time scraping skins, hauling wood and water, digging *tutupipʋ*, everything I had done my first six months. But for her, there would be no end.

In spring, I ran into her in one of the pastures, looking after the horses. She looked well fed, though her muscles were ropy for a white woman and she didn't have much fat. She appeared to have grown water shy. I could smell her from a good distance and her back was dotted with *mohtoʔa* as if she had not bathed in months.

"It's you," she said in English. "The chosen one."

I could tell she was sulking.

"I see they're treating you well."

It threw me off to hear English. I told her—in Comanche—that she might consider washing herself. Which was not fair, but I was mad at her for saying I ought to be read out as some kind of deserter.

"Why should I?" she said. "I hoped it would make them stop touching me, but it hasn't."

"They aren't supposed to do that anymore. They could get in big trouble."

"Well, they are."

"Well, they're not supposed to."

"That's very useful of you to say."

"Is it like before?"

"It's one or two in particular," she said. "Though why that makes a difference I don't know."

"How are the horses?" I said. "That one with the sore foot, I could get some wet rawhide."

"Do you think about what we are?" she said. "Me, if I speak to them, they pretend not to hear me. They've given me a new name, because of this." She pointed between her legs. "That's all I am."

I didn't say anything.

"The only thing that makes me happy is the thought that if I die I'll cost them money, because they'll get fewer hides finished." She looked at me. "And you, Tiehteti"—she used my Indian name—"can you see yourself?"

"Sure," I said.

"You're too young. They were smart when they got you."

This annoyed me as well. "You know I can help you if you just ask," I said, though I was not sure what I meant by that.

"Then kill me. Or take me out of here. I don't care which one."

She went back to scraping her hide. I looked around for Ekanaki, the red-eared pinto Toshaway had given me. The sun was getting low and it was cold and there was horseshit everywhere.

"I need to fetch my pony," I said.

"That's what I thought."

I would have been happy to never speak another word to her in my life.

"Tiehteti," she called after me, "if I know it's you I won't fight back." She pointed to the side of her neck, where you'd put a knife in. "I promise. I just can't bring myself to do it."

Chapter Eleven
J.A. McCullough

The house had been dead a long time; she was the last of its children. She willed herself to get up. The chandeliers hung quietly above her, indifferent to her suffering. *Get up,* she thought. But nothing happened.

During her childhood it been a gay, chattering place, not a moment of silence or privacy; the idea that she might one day be lying alone, the house silent as a graveyard . . . When she came home from school there was always someone talking in the great room or on the gallery or she would wander around and there would be the Colonel, a cluster of his friends talking and drinking or shooting clay pigeons. There were serious-looking young men who came to take notes, ancient plainsmen living out their last days in rented rooms, and there were others who, like the Colonel, were millionaires.

There were reporters and politicians and Indians who came in great bunches, six or eight to a car. The Colonel was different around the Indians; he did not hold court as he did among the whites but rather sat and nodded and listened. She did not like to see it. The Indians did not dress the way they should have—they might as well have been grangers or Mexicans—and they smelled strongly and did not pay her any attention. She would find them stalking around the house and her father thought they stole. But the Colonel did not seem to mind, and the Indians got along fine with the waddies; many mornings she came into the great room to discover a dozen old men asleep among their former enemies, spilled beer and whiskey, a beef quarter half-eaten in the fireplace.

It was the Colonel's house, there was no mistaking it, though he mostly slept in a jacal down the hill. Her father complained about the noise and grandstanding and endless strangers and houseguests, about the food bills and the size of the domestic staff. The Colonel did not care for him, either; he found her father's interest in cattle quite taxing. "We have not made a dime off the dumb brutes in twenty years" or "That man can't take a shit without asking the county agent."

The Colonel was in favor of oil, in favor of Jonas going to Princeton, and as for Clint and Paul, they would make damn fine hands. But you, he would say, tapping her on the shoulder, you are going to do something. She had not known how fragile that all was. Now, looking across the dim room from her place on the floor, she saw the house as it would soon be: a haven for bats and owls, for mice and coyotes, the deer leaving footprints in the dust. The roof would give way and brush would begin to grow inside the house until there was nothing left but stone walls in a desert.

Aside from the Colonel, her grandmother was the only one who paid her any mind. On hot days they would sit in the library while her grandmother sorted, for the thousandth time, the contents of various boxes, pictures and tintypes, here was her first husband, who had died before they had children, here were her two sisters, dead of typhoid, here was Uncle Glenn in his army uniform. There were more pictures of Glendale—who had been shot by the Mexicans but had died fighting the Huns—than there were of Jeannie's mother. If her grandmother knew a single thing about the woman who'd brought Jeannie into this world, she didn't share it. *Here is your great-grandfather Cornellius, the most famous lawyer in*

Dallas, your great-great-grandfather Silas Burns, who owned the biggest plantation in Texas before the Yankees ran the niggers off. Jeannie did not know much about niggers, except for the few she'd seen working on the trains. They said East Texas was full of them. But she did know something about the old men in the tintypes, their ridiculous collars and mustaches, coats buttoned to their necks, looking like they had sat on a splinter. She did not care what her grandmother said; she was not related to them and never would be.

Invitations to parties, calling cards, gaudy pins. Cheap jewelry only a child would wear. The engagement ring from her first husband, who had died before she met Peter McCullough. Jeannie's grandfather. The Great Disgrace.

Her grandmother occasionally took her riding; a hand would prepare her horse and sidesaddle, the only one in Dimmit County. She was a fair horsewoman, even on the awkward device. She scolded Jeannie for going bareback and for climbing fences. *You will do things to yourself you will be sorry about later.* What those things were, she wouldn't say, and sometimes, if Jeannie fell asleep during the stories of her grandmother's dull girlhood, she would awake to a firm pinch.

Her grandmother and the other grown-ups did not mind being boring; they often went on until Jeannie wished *she* were the dead one, instead of the person in the story, who was always more clever, or handsome, with more style and grace and wit than anyone Jeannie had ever met. If the Colonel had any boring stories, he must have forgotten them. He never said the same thing twice. Here was where to find a hawk's nest or a pair of bucks who had died with their antlers locked, here was a leaf fossil or old bone or piece of purple flint. They kept a box of things they had found together, the skulls of little mice, squirrels, raccoons, and other animals.

When there were no visitors the Colonel would sit on the gallery making arrowheads or whittling cedar. Once, after whittling a piece into shavings, he told her: "If I wasn't so old we'd get into the airplane business. We could build 'em here and sell 'em to the government and they would fly 'em at that field near Sanderson."

He had tried to teach her to make arrowheads, but it had not taken. She had gashed her palm on a piece of sharp flint, at first surprised that a simple rock could cut her so deeply, then fascinated by the free flow of her own blood, then nauseated. The Colonel had come out of his trance and they had hobbled into the kitchen, where he bandaged her up and brought her back to the porch.

"I guess you're off drinks duty," he said, and winked. He went to the cart and made her a julep without the whiskey, and, against her father's rules, let her sip straight from the cold silver shaker, the two of them conspiring against all that was right and good. She sat happily, forgetting the pain in her hand.

"It's a foolish activity," he said, taking up the arrowhead she'd begun. "Though if you make a knife, you can do anything. One day I will take all the arrowheads I've made and scatter them around the ranch and then maybe in a thousand years, some historian will find them and make up stories that aren't true." Then he looked up. "There is a thrush in that granjeno."

She looked out over the pasture, but she didn't see anything. The sun was bright but it was early in the year; the grass was still green and the live oaks beginning their springtime shed.

"They have told me there is a German named Hertz," he said, "who has given his name to, among other things, the way flint breaks when you strike it. It is always the same way." He held up a chip. "Though of course Hertz did not discover this. In fact the man who did discover it has been dead two million years. Which is how long people have been knocking rocks together to make tools." He took another flake. "Remember that," he said. "None of it's worth a shit until you put your name on it."

Chapter Twelve
Diaries of Peter McCullough

AUGUST 16, 1915

The shooting could be heard as soon as it got dark. Near midnight about fifty men came to the gate, carrying torches, shouting for us to turn over the Mexicans.

They hesitated there in the road—fifty men or not, it is no small thing to trespass on McCullough land—but after a long period of milling around, one of them put his foot on the bar and began to climb over. At which point we opened fire over their heads. Charles put his automatic Remington to good use, unleashing all fifteen rounds as the crowd broke and fled down the road. We spent a good deal of time afterward stomping out the fires that started when they dropped their torches.

Later Niles Gilbert and two others from the Law and Order League drove up and pleaded with me to kick the Mexicans out, lest the town be burned.

Charles shouted: "So go shoot the assholes who are burning your town. It ain't like you don't have enough guns."

"How many men do you have, Peter?"

"I've got enough. And I've armed all the Mexicans as well." Which was not true.

"This isn't going to turn out well for you," he said.

Consuela and Sullivan had been cooking all night so there was plenty of beef and cabrito. By morning half the families had asked permission to stay at the ranch until the town was safe. The other half loaded up with food and water and began to walk or ride across our pastures, toward the river and Mexico. They are going into a war zone but apparently it is preferable to this.

Naturally they all believe the Colonel is responsible for their salvation—who else could it be but Don Eli? This rankles greatly but I did not bother to correct them. How they will ever get democracy I don't know—they are very comfortable with the idea that powerful men rule their lives. Or perhaps they are simply more honest about it than we allow ourselves to be.

My father was well behaved, entertaining all the children on the gallery with his Indian stories, showing them how to start a fire with two sticks, giving archery demonstrations as well (he can still draw his old Indian bow, which I can barely pull back myself). He was happy and at ease and laughed a lot—I do not remember seeing him like this since before my mother died. Perhaps he was meant to be a schoolteacher. As we watched the refugees walking and riding toward the river, their belongings piled on mules and carts, he said: "That'll be the last time we see any of 'em moving south, I'd imagine."

And yet they love him. They go back to their jacals at night, which are hot in the summer and cold in the winter, while he goes back to our house, a sprawling white monstrosity, a thousand years' salary for them, or a thousand thousand. Meanwhile their children are stillborn and they bury them near the corrals. *Who are you to say they ain't happy?* That is what a white man will tell you, looking you straight in the eye as he says it.

After the largest group of Mexicans left, a group of us went door-to-door in town and gave everyone we didn't recognize five minutes to be on their way. Campbell put up new signs: ANYONE CARRYING A FIREARM WILL BE SHOT AND/OR ARRESTED.

By six o'clock the streets were deserted. Fourteen houses have been burned. Sergeant Campbell is leaving tomorrow to get medical attention for his wounds. Apparently he has gotten quite a hiding for not going south to protect the big ranches: two hundred sections is considered middling. But, thanks to Guillermo's sugar remedy, his arm does not appear to be getting any worse.

To help me relax I read the newspapers for the first time in a week. A storm hit Galveston yesterday, killing three hundred. A great victory as the last one killed ten thousand, ending Galveston's reign as our state's queen city.

Sally called at five A.M. Glenn's fever appears to have broken.

AUGUST 18, 1915

Today at the meeting of all the remaining townspeople, I suggested that the train station be named after Bill Hollis (killed at the Garcias'), a motion seconded and carried. Feel extremely poorly for Marjorie Hollis. While Glenn was repeatedly mentioned by name in all the newspaper articles as having been wounded, and Charles singled out for leading the charge on the Garcia compound (each time mentioning he is the grandson of the famous Indian fighter Eli McCullough)—Bill Hollis was only mentioned once, in the local paper.

Afterward I wondered why I did not suggest the station be named after one of the many dead Mexicans.

AUGUST 20, 1915

Storm giving us a good soaking. Everyone in high spirits. Except me. Can't sleep—faces of the Garcias have returned—spent most of the morning in a nervous daze, searching for things to do, as if I did not find something to occupy my mind . . . I avoid looking into the shadows, as I know what I'll find there.

Visited with the Reynolds family, inquired about the surviving girl, who we all now know was María Garcia. Apparently she locked herself in their spare bedroom and then disappeared during the night, stealing an old pair of boots, as she had no shoes.

Ike motioned for me to follow him out to the gallery, where the others couldn't hear us.

"Pete, don't take this the wrong way, but if I were that girl, I might believe I was the only living witness to a murder." He held up his hands. "Not that I'm saying she is, but from her point of view . . ."

"I was against it from the start."

"I know that." He scuffed his boot. "Sometimes I wish there was another way to live here."

Chapter Thirteen
Eli/Tiehteti

1850

By the time I'd been with them a year, I was treated the same as any other Comanche, though they kept a bright eye on me, like some derelict uncle who'd taken the pledge. Dame Nature had made my eyes and hair naturally dark and in winter I kept my skin brown by lying out in the sun on a robe. Most nights I slept as gentle as a dead calf and had no thoughts of going off with the whites. There was nothing back there but shame and if my father had come looking for me, I hadn't heard about it.

Escuté and Nuukaru still ignored me so I spent my time with the younger boys; we'd graduated to breaking the band's horses and soon we would go to hold the remuda during the raids. A steady trickle of unbroken ponies came off the plains: whenever a herd was spotted, the fastest braves would ride out and rope them and the animals whose necks didn't break would be brought back to camp. Then their nostrils were held shut until they sagged to the ground. They were tied that way and left for us to handle.

There is something in the white man that loves a sorrel but the Indians had no use for them; there were only five horses we cared about: red paints, black paints, Appaloosas, red medicine hats, and black medicine hats. The medicine hats had dark bands around their heads and dark ears and a blaze in the shape of a medieval shield on their chests. There was one type— the *pia tso?nika* or war bonnet—that had black eye patches as well and from a distance looked like a skull or death's head. Centuries of hard living had made them as frothy as panthers; they had as much in common with a domestic horse as a wolf has with a lapdog and they would stave in your ribs if you gave them half a chance. We loved them.

I slept when I wanted and ate when I wanted and did nothing all day that I didn't feel like doing. The white in me expected any minute that I would be ordered to do chores or some other form of slave labor but it never happened. We rode and hunted and wrestled and made arrows. We slayed every living thing we laid eyes on—

prairie chickens and prairie dogs, plovers and pheasants, blacktail deer and antelope; we launched arrows at panther and elk and bears of every size, dumping our kills in camp for the women to clean, then walking off with our chests out like men. Along the river we dug up the bones from giant bison and enormous shells turned to stone and almost too heavy to lift; we found crayfish and shards of pottery and carried it all to the tops of cliffs and smashed it on the rocks below. We arrowed bobcats at night while they stalked ducks in the cane and the weather was warming and the flowers coming out, the yucca had shot their stalks and big white flowers hung ten feet in the air; there were patches of bluebonnet or blanketflower or greenthread that went on for miles, now it was green, now it was blue, now it was red and orange as far as the eye would carry. The snow was gone and fat high clouds hung everywhere, and the sun blinked on and off as they moved across the wind, heading south toward Mexico, where they would burn away forever.

It was considered a sure thing that a few of us would be asked to go raiding. I was the oldest, the only one whose short hair had come in, but I was also deficient; I shot fine from the ground but the other kids could hit pheasants and rabbits from a gallop. Still, when Toshaway came out to the pasture one morning carrying his pistol and a new buffalo-hide shield, it was me he picked out of the crowd. The others made comments but I ignored them.

We walked a good distance and set the shield against a runty cottonwood and he handed me the gun.

"Go ahead."

"Just like that?"

"Sure."

I shot and the shield fell over. It was smeared with lead but not dented. He grinned and set it up again and I shot it until the gun was empty.

"Okay," he said. "A shield will stop a ball. But if a ball ever hits a stationary shield, you are an idiot." He put the straps over his arm and moved it in quick circles. "Always it's moving. Of course the feathers hide you, but more important is that a stationary shield will only stop a pistol ball. A rifle ball will go through it, the same as if you jump from a high tree and land on flat ground, you will break your legs, but if you land on a steep hill, you will be fine. A moving shield will stop a rifle ball. *Nahkʉsuaberʉ?*"

I nodded.

"Good," he said. "Now we come to the fun part."

We walked a few more minutes to the middle of an old pasture at the edge of camp. Whatever was going to happen, everyone would see it. A dozen or so braves were sitting in the sun playing *tʊkii* but when they saw me they got up and retrieved some equipment. Each man was carrying his bow and a basket of arrows.

"Okay," said Toshaway. "This will be very easy. You will remain standing here and these men will shoot you. I would prefer if you used the shield as much as possible."

"Where are you going?"

"I don't want to be shot!" He grinned and patted me on the head.

The braves formed a skirmish line a hundred yards away and when everything was arranged Toshaway shouted at me and waved an arrow. "*Ke matʊʊ mutsipʊ!* They are blunt!" The warriors found this humorous. "They have no spikes!" he repeated.

People were trickling out from their tipis to watch and I wondered if Toshaway had actually checked each arrow, as by certain lights it would be a very funny joke if there were a few spikes mixed in with the blunt ones. I was only worth a horse or two and plenty of people in the village still had no use for me.

"*Tiehteti tsa maka?mukitʊ-tʊ!*"

I nodded.

"Keep the shield moving!"

I made myself small. Arrows take a few seconds to go a hundred yards, which seems like forever unless they're coming toward you. Most thumped off the shield; one or two missed entirely; others hit me in the thigh and shin and then again in the same shin.

This was thought hilarious and several of the warriors began to imitate me, hopping around on one foot and calling out *anáa anáa anáa* until Toshaway made them go back to their places.

"You have to move!" he shouted. "It is too small to hide you!"

The hilarious Indians opened fire and my legs took another pounding. One arrow grazed my forehead where I had looked over the shield.

"You don't have to block the ones that will miss you," someone shouted. I was in a crouch, trying to make myself as small as possible; it was the funniest thing the Indians had ever seen and it went on until they were out of ammunition.

I started to limp back to the village, but there was an uproar from the audience so instead the braves and I switched sides so they could collect their arrows.

"It is for your own benefit," someone yelled, but now the sun was in my face. I squinted at one particular arrow that seemed to not be moving at all.

Sometime later I woke up. Toshaway was standing over me, murmuring like a pulpiteer.

"What?" I said.

"Are you awake now?"

"Haa." I felt my breechcloth. It was dry.

"Good. Now if you can listen for a moment I will tell you something my father once told me. The difference between a brave man and a coward is very simple. It is a problem of love. A coward loves only himself . . ."

I got very dizzy and I could feel the cold ground. I wondered if my skull was cracked. You could shoot a blunt arrow through a deer if it was close enough.

" . . . a coward cares only for his own body," Toshaway said, "and he loves it above all other things. The brave man loves other men first and himself last. *Nahkʉsuaberʉ?*"

I nodded.

"This"—he tapped me—"must mean nothing to you." Then he tapped me again, on my face, my chest, my belly, my hands and feet. "All of this means nothing."

"Haa," I said.

"Good. You're a brave little Indian. But everyone is bored. Get up and let them shoot you."

A short while later I was down again. The warriors went back to the shade and gambled while Toshaway gave me cool water and wrapped my head with a blanket scrap. Only my eyes were exposed. This caused more hilarious laughter but it worked like a helmet and

I stopped being afraid. By the end of the day they had cut the distance in half and the shooters were working hard to get their hits. After a week they couldn't hit me at all.

As a graduation ceremony I held the shield while a big fat buck named Pizon, who made no secret that he thought I ought to be a *na?raiboo* rather than a member of the tribe, aimed at me with Toshaway's pistol. All the slack went out of my rope but I blocked each shot and kept the shield moving the whole time. Pizon gave me a look that said he would have liked if I had gotten my lamp blown out, but I got to keep the shield. Being a sacred item, it was kept in a protective case far from camp. If a menstruating woman ever touched it, it would have to be destroyed.

The hunting that spring was the worst anyone could remember. Toshaway had grown up with herds of buffalo blackening the prairie for weeks, but none of the younger Indians had seen anything like it. There had been a drought in parts of the plains, but mostly it was because of the eastern tribes, whose numbers were growing by the month in the Territories. They all took liberties in our hunting grounds and we spent as much time killing them as we did the whites. It was considered a good way to break in the youth without having to ride too far.

When the yucca were done blooming Toshaway and I and a few dozen others rode out to patrol for buffalo or trespassing Indians. After a few days we came on a small herd moving west, toward New Mexico and the drier part of the plains, which meant something was disturbing them. The scouts rode east while the rest of us killed buffalo and then it came back that a group of Tonks had been seen. Some of the fort Indians were treated with caution, but the Tonkawa had a great taste for firewater and it was not considered much to kill one. A decade later they would be wiped out completely.

Nʉʉkaru, who had been coaching me on the skinning, put his knife into his sheath and was into his saddle in three long steps. I had misplaced my bow and by the time I got mounted the entire party was riding to haul hell out of its shuck.

The prairie is not as flat as it looks, it is more like the swells of an ocean, there are peaks and troughs, and, being in less of a hurry to kill a Tonk, it wasn't long till I lost sight of the others. It was a nice day, the grass going down and standing up in waves, in all directions, the sky very clear and blue with a few clouds lingering. The sun was nice on my back. The idea of running down a Tonk could not have seemed less appealing. I was not allowed to carry a firearm and even with both feet on the ground I was only average with the bow; unless the target was standing still, directly in front of me, shooting from a moving horse was impossible.

The horse knew something was wrong and he kept trying to catch the others. He had a good smooth lope so I held him there. I made a note of the sun and it occurred to me that I might just turn southeast, toward the Llano breaks; I could hunt easily enough with the bow and it was maybe a two-week ride to the frontier if I wasn't caught. There were patches of small red flowers, *puha natsu*. I thought about the English name but I didn't know it. I thought about my father. Then I gave the horse his head and we were running.

A few minutes later I could hear shots and hollering and then there were riders and horses. Toshaway and Pizon and a few others were standing around a man on the ground. He was lying in a patch of blanketflower with several arrows sticking out of him. He had lost enough blood to paint a house and it was bright in the greenery around him.

"Tiehteti-taibo, very nice of you to come."

The Comanches were breathing easy and their sweat was dry and their horses were off grazing. Except for Nuukaru, who was holding his lance in case the Tonk got his sap back, not one of them had a weapon in hand. They might have been judging the quality of a deer or elk they'd brought down. As for the Tonkawa, he was chanting and wheezing, his torso smeared and his chin dripping with blood as if he had been feeding on human bodies.

Toshaway and Pizon had a word and then Pizon took an old single-shot pistol from his sash and handed it over butt-first. It was a .69 caliber, a cannon as handguns went.

"Go ahead, Tiehteti."

Pizon added: "If it were him, he would be slicing off your breast and eating it in front of you."

The man looked up and recognized me, then stared out over the prairie. His chanting got more insistent and there was no point lingering so I squeezed the trigger. The gun snapped into my wrist and the man leaned farther against the rock. His music stopped and his legs began to twitch like a dog in sleep.

He was a good-looking brave with long beautiful hair and Pizon took the entire scalp beneath the ears. The ball must have loosened something because when Pizon ripped off his hair, the man's head fell open as if it were hinged at the bottom, his face going forward and the back of his head going the other direction. No one had ever seen a pistol ball do that. It was good medicine.

The others got distracted but I continued to stare, the man's face looking down at his own chest, all his secrets open to the wind.

"You're acting very strange, Tiehteti-taibo."

"*Haa*," I said. "*Tsaa manusukaru.*"

Nuukaru and I were sent to retrieve the dead man's weapons and anything else he had dropped and there was something about him lying there with the blanketflowers all around stained with blood and I rode after Nuukaru as quickly as I could. After an hour we found the Tonk's rifle. It was a fire-new Springfield musket and Nuukaru couldn't believe it—the Tonks were poor and their equipment was usually poor as well. "This thing must have come from the whites," he said. "And his horse also."

I didn't care. I was bored looking for the man's valuables—I doubted he owned much and didn't intend on spending the rest of the day looking for a filthy war bag. I wondered if I was the only one who knew how many rifles and horses the whites had.

The rest of the group was out of sight; it was waist-high grass in every direction, then sky. My horse was eating flowers; bluebonnets were hanging from his mouth. I wondered if they would let me keep the Tonk's scalp.

One of the Tonks had gotten away, but as he was afoot in unfamiliar territory, and being a reservation Indian probably only a few notches above a white man, he was almost certain to die eventually, so we didn't bother chasing him. Not to mention that with the confusion of the fight over, he would easily spot us before we spotted him, making it likely he would be able to shoot at least one of us. Unlike the whites, whose noble leaders were willing to sacrifice any number of followers to kill a single Indian, the Comanches did not believe in trading any of their own for the enemy. It was another unfortunate character trait, as far as fighting the Anglos was concerned.

So instead of following the lone Tonk, we prepared for a celebration, taking their scalps and horses and brand-new rifles, whose newness, though no one said it, was another sign of a storm coming. Nuukaru found the Tonk's war bag, which contained dozens of paper cartridges, another luxury from the whites.

"Look at this shit," he said.

No one paid any attention. We made our way back to the buffalo we'd killed, having a big feast of the liver and bile and then building a fire of mesquite and buffalo chips and roasting the meat and marrow. The Tonk's scalp belonged to Pizon. My shooting him was just a formality.

The next morning the wind had shifted and there was a faint rotten smell. I could barely pick it up and of course things were always dying on the prairie, but the other Comanches thought it noteworthy, and after we packed the buffalo's meat back into their skins and tied the bundles onto the spare horses, we began to ride. A few hours later we came to a small canyon, the grass tall and a creek running down the middle, and as we rode into it the smell became worse, and then the horses refused to go farther.

There was no sound except the wind and the running of the stream and the flapping of tent skins. There were several hundred tipis, with thousands of black vultures tottering among them, as if they had decided to give up their wild ways and become civilized.

I leaned over and retched and someone behind me did the same. It was decided that I would go in alone and make an inspection while the others stayed back.

"Are you joking?" I said.

"There are no living people in this drainage except us," said Toshaway. He gave me a cloth to tie over my mouth and nose.

"Then give me your pistol."

"You won't need it."

"Let me have it anyway."

He shrugged and handed over the revolver, then leaned to help me tie the cloth over my face. "Remember to lift it if you have to vomit. Otherwise you will be very sorry."

A few of the buzzards flew off, others stepped aside to let me through, and the flies took off and landed in great black waves. The ground was covered with human bodies, whether hundreds or thousands I couldn't tell; they were all pulled apart and rotted, partially eaten, blackened and contorted and uncountable. My horse stepped gingerly at first, but soon saw it was hopeless and began to tread directly on what was left of the people.

There were heads and sections of spine, feet and hands, rib cages, the muscle black and the bones very white, lumps of fat stuck to rocks, arms and legs wedged in the branches of cottonwoods where they had been dragged by cougars or bobcats. There were rifles and bows and knives scattered and starting to rust. There were so many dead that not even the wolves and coyotes and bears had been able to eat them. The sun had blackened everything but I could see that none of the people had been scalped. I could not think of who had done this to them.

Most of the horses had been driven off by the wolves, or eaten, but a few dozen of the most loyal or helpless grazed the periphery; there was a big dun mare still saddled, though the saddle had rolled all the way under her belly and she could barely walk. I nickered and rode up next to her and she stood resigned to whatever I might do. I cut the cinch and at the sound of the saddle hitting the ground the mare stepped away, then shook herself and broke into a trot. She had an army brand on her hip, though she had been wearing an Indian saddle, and I wondered about the things she had seen.

One of the tipis had been sealed shut, rocks and brush piled around it, and without dismounting from my horse I took hold of the flaps and cut the ropes. Inside there were two dead vultures and dozens of small bodies, carefully placed in rows and stacked on top of one another. Whoever had put them there was too weak to bury them, or maybe they had been dying too quickly; it was either smallpox or cholera or some other disease and I turned my horse and kicked him and went back to where the others were waiting for me.

"They still had their hair?"

"Yes," I said.

"How many?"

"Hundreds. Maybe thousands."

"I think around one thousand. Did you touch anything?"

"Not really. A tipi that was in the sun."

He squinted and looked around. It was a pleasant little canyon. "I guess there are worse places to die."

"Who were they?"

"I think that is Kicking Dog's band. Tenewa Comanche. They are outside their territory so something was not going well when they put their camp there, they were running from something. *Tasía*, probably." He dotted his face with a finger. "The gift of the great white father."

I rode my horse into the middle of the stream and scrubbed his feet and legs with sand, then did the same to my own body. I slept by myself that night, a good distance from the others. A few days later, before we reached camp, I went to the river to scrub myself again and asked Nuukaru to bring me a bowl of yucca soap and place it on the ground. I cleaned the horse again as well.

When I reached the village they were preparing a big celebration and scalp dance. One of the medicine men took me into a tipi and made me strip. He swallowed breaths of cedar and sage smoke, blew them onto me, then rubbed my body with leaves. I told him I had already used soap, but he figured the smoke was better.

—————

A few weeks later a group of Comancheros came through the camp and said they had seen more Indians killing buffalo. Toshaway told me we were going on another scouting trip. I acted enthusiastic.

"Give me one of the Tonk rifles," I said.

He must have thought something would happen because he handed it over without comment, along with a dozen of the paper cartridges.

At night we had fires but only in gullies and far away from any trees so there was nothing to show the light. Finally the scouts came back and reported a party of Indians cutting up buffalo: they appeared to be Delawares, who, though the Comanches would never admit it, were the best hunters of all the eastern tribes, good trackers and men to be taken seriously.

We decided to make a cold camp and sleep before we laid into them. The Delawares made a cold camp as well, though they did not know they'd been seen, and I thought of them out there in the dark, they'd once been the kings of the east as we were the kings of the west, but now they'd killed twenty buffalo and couldn't even have a fire to celebrate.

The light was flat and gray and a slick mist was rising from the grass. There were horses going in all directions and everyone shouting and I was staring at one man who had taken four or five arrows but stood calmly tamping a charge into his musket. Someone came from behind and pinned him with a lance. It was Nuukaru. There was something about the man squirming on the ground but Nuukaru didn't seem to mind.

The rest of the Delawares were quickly unroostered, but one managed to make a clear swing. I had stayed on the outskirts and he went right past me; he might as well have been standing still, though he didn't react to the shot and with the smoke I wasn't sure I'd hit him.

I watched him ride off. I knew what I had to do. There was no time to reload the rifle, and even with all the fighting I knew Toshaway and Pizon were probably watching me. While I was thinking this, the two of them finished killing the man they had started to kill, saw the escaping Delaware, and took off after him.

I fell in behind. I had never whipped a horse so hard but the four of us were strung out in a long line across the prairie with the Delaware at the head. He was riding a legendary animal, putting ground on us with each step, he was nearly a half mile ahead, but there was nowhere to hide, no canyons, no forest, just open prairie, and we began to close. Then Toshaway's pony stumbled and collided with Pizon's and I went around them.

As for the Delaware, I could see a shiny slick down his back where my ball had gone in and I whipped the horse even harder, though I had no plan for what I would do if I caught him.

Then he was on the ground. There was a gulch he'd tried to jump and the horse had thrown him. He was lying in the tall grass.

I was on him before I knew it and I nocked an arrow but it went several feet wide. I tried to nock another but my hands were shaking and the horse was skittering so I slid off onto the ground.

The Delaware hadn't moved. I felt better about everything, I was looking down at my string, trying to get the arrow set, and I looked up to see him spin and draw and shoot in the same movement.

There was an arrow sticking out of me. It seemed like I ought to sit down. Then I was looking at myself; then I decided there was nothing wrong. I grabbed the arrow and pulled it out.

Later I realized that the Delaware was so weak he hadn't been able to fully draw his bow. My quiver strap had stopped his arrow—but right then I picked up my own bow, which I had dropped, aimed carefully, and shot the Delaware in the stomach. The arrow went to the feathers.

He was looking around for his quiver. It had gotten separated in the fall. I shot another arrow, then a third, which went between his ribs. He was tugging at the one where it was stuck into the ground and I knew he would send it back to me. I shot the rest of the arrows I was holding and he gave up, though he was not quite dead. I knew I should go and thump him but I didn't want to get any closer, I was ashamed of his breathing and gurgling, of my bad shooting, of being afraid of a man who was nearly dead, and then someone kicked me in the backside.

It was Toshaway and Pizon. I hadn't heard them come up.

"*Kuʔe tsasimapu.*" Toshaway nodded at the Delaware.

"Do it quickly," said Pizon. "Before he dies."

The Delaware was lying on his side and I rolled him onto his belly. I put my foot on his back and grabbed his hair and he raised his arm to stop me, but I cut all the way around. He was slapping at my hand the whole time.

"Snap it off," called Pizon. "One big motion."

The scalp came off like a cracking branch and the Delaware lost his fight. I walked a few yards and looked at it: it could have been anything, a piece of buffalo or calf hide. The sun was coming up and my leg began to hurt: I'd cut myself on my own arrow spikes where they'd come through the Delaware's back. He gave a last moaning rattle, and, looking at him there on the ground, stuck through from every direction with my spikes and the grass matted with his blood, it was like a haze clearing from my mind, like I'd been dunked again, like I'd been chosen by God Himself. I ran over to Toshaway and Pizon and grabbed them.

"Fucking white boy," said Pizon. But he was smiling as well. He turned to Toshaway. "I guess I owe you a horse."

There was a big dance when we got back, eight scalps had been collected, but before it began, Pizon told the story of how I'd gone after the Delaware alone, like a proper Comanche, with nothing but my bow, and he said we know what a great talent Tiehteti is with his bow. There was general laughter, which annoyed me. But this is serious, he continued, this was not some filthy *Numu Tuuka,* but a warrior, and Tiehteti's only weapon was one he cannot yet use from his horse. And to be shot in the heart, only to have the arrow refuse to go in? What does that say about Tiehteti?

For the rest of the night the medicine man who'd cleansed me of smallpox told everyone that he had given me his bear medicine, as only that could have stopped the arrow, but no one believed him. I knew the Delaware was almost dead when I reached him, that he had taken a ball in the lungs and been thrown from his horse onto the rocks, that if I had caught him five or ten minutes earlier he would have driven his arrow to my spine. That even in his final condition, if the buffalo-hide strap of my quiver hadn't been hanging just so, the spike would have reached my heart. But by the end of the night those details meant nothing, and this was the point of the scalp dance, we were eternal, the Chosen People, and our names would ring on in the night, long after we'd vanished from the earth.

Sometime before morning I opened my eyes. I was lying in the yard of our old house and there was an Indian standing over me. I was watching the arrows go in but decided not to believe what I was seeing; I remembered I'd hit my head and was probably confused. The Comanche was young and there was something familiar about him and after a time I began to recognize his face.

When morning came I could still feel the hollow where the arrows had gone. The sun had risen and was shining directly through the open door of the tipi and Nuukaru and Escuté were outside smoking. I went and sat with them. The three boys who had taken me hunting, all of whom were still better hunters, riders, and bowmen than I was, came over and said hello, but didn't sit—I was now their superior—and then Nuukaru waved them away. "You're done with those kids," he said.

Escuté called his mother to bring us something to eat and then there were sugarberry cakes, which were hackberries and tallow mashed together and cooked over a fire. Nuukaru and I thanked her. Escuté just took the food and ate. He must have seen the way I looked at him because he said: "We could get killed every time we leave camp. They all know this. Half of us will be dead by the time we reach forty winters."

A short time later Fat Wolf, Toshaway's eldest son, came by with his wife.

"So this is the famous white boy?"

Escuté said, "You're a man now, Tiehteti, and I'm sure Fat Wolf appreciates the respect but you don't have to stare at the dirt."

Fat Wolf leaned over and gripped my chin, then his hand softened. "Don't listen to my asshole brother. I always put him in a bad mood." He pointed over his shoulder. "This is Hates Work. Obviously you've noticed her before, but as you are a man now, you may talk to her, and take note of her unfortunately soft hands."

Hates Work, who was standing a ways back from her husband, smiled and waved, but didn't say anything. She was by far the most beautiful Indian I'd ever seen, in her early twenties with clear skin and shining hair and a good figure; it was widely thought a tragedy that she would soon be ruined by children. Her father had asked fifty horses as a bride-price, which was outrageous according to Nʉʉkaru, but Toshaway, because he spoiled his sons terribly, as anyone spending time with Escuté might notice, had given the fifty horses and the marriage had been approved.

Fat Wolf himself was as tall as his father, but while his face was young, he already had the thin arms and heavy paunch of a much older man. He looked as Toshaway might if Toshaway had stopped hunting and raiding. I nodded at Hates Work and tried not to show too much interest.

Fat Wolf had lifted my poultice and was touching me gently, the open skin and bone, the cut still weeping. "Motherfucker," he said. "I have never seen a wound like that on a living man." He looked me up and down. "My father talked about you, but he likes everyone and we thought he was going soft. Now we see he was right. It's no small thing." He took me by the shoulders; he was a very touchy Indian. "You ever need anything, you come to me. And don't hang around my brother too much, he's a bitter little fuck." Then he walked away with his pretty wife.

"What a fat fuck," said his brother, when the pair were out of earshot.

"Escuté has been hoping that Fat Wolf will send her his way, but Fat Wolf is not interested in sharing yet."

"I get plenty of *tai?i* on my own. I don't need a hand-out from the fat one." He looked at Nuukaru: "You, on the other hand . . ."

"I get plenty."

"From old women, maybe."

"Like your mother."

"I wouldn't put it past you," said Escuté.

It was quiet. I'd invented a number of stories about the various girls I'd been with, but Nuukaru and Escuté knew better than to ask.

After lunch I went to the stream to clean my trophy. I scraped the inner skin to remove all the meat and fat, rinsing it in the water, rubbing it with a coarse stone and rinsing it again, teasing off the silverskin with my fingers, repeating until the inner scalp was white and full and soft. Then I took a wooden basin, filled it with water and yucca soap, and carefully washed the hair, separating the strands, trying not to pull too hard, as if the Delaware might still feel what I was doing, teasing out each burr and grass seed, the dandruff and dried blood. I rewove his braids, replacing all the beads, which were turquoise and red glass, in the same places he had put them. I made a paste of brain and tallow and rubbed it into the inner skin, allowing it to dry and then rubbing in more of the paste. I stretched it on a willow hoop to dry, then carried it back to the tipi to hang in the shade.

That night we stayed up late talking. I'd hung the scalp above my pallet and I watched it turn all night in the warm air from the fire. The embers went dark and we all drifted off and there was a rustling at the tipi flap and the sound of someone trying to come inside and I heard the other two wake up as well. By her hair I could tell the visitor was a woman, but otherwise it was too dark.

"If you are here for Escuté, I am over here."

"And Nuukaru is straight ahead of you, on the other side of the fire."

"You are both dreaming," said the woman. "Forget I am here."

"The wife of Fat Wolf. You are joking me."

"Where is Tiehteti?"

"He is right here," said Escuté. "You are talking to him right now."

"Is he in here or not?"

"I don't know. Tiehteti, are you here? Probably not. I saw him heading out to the pasture; Fucks a Mare was going to show him something."

Hates Work said: "You are a serious asshole, Escuté."

"But funny?"

"Sometimes."

"Nuukaru, I have bad news. For the one-thousandth time, a woman has come to the tipi and she has no interest in you."

"Fuck off," said Nuukaru.

"As for Tiehteti," he pronounced, "it is time for him to become a man. It is a process that requires physical contact, and so at some point, unless you would simply prefer to watch a master at work, you will have to tell this woman, who is among the most beautiful of all Comanches, though also the laziest, where you are located in the tipi."

"I'm over here," I said quietly.

"Nuukaru, you skinny pervert, don't think you can lie there and masturbate; get up and give Tiehteti his privacy."

"*Noyoma nakuhkupa.*"

"I would prefer not to," said Escuté. "For I am wise, and a great leader, and one day I'll be your chief."

He and Nuukaru took their blankets and left.

"Tiehteti? Say something so I can find you."

"Follow the wall to the right," I said.

I felt her touch my pallet. It was too dark to see her, or to even know who she was except by her voice, but I could hear the rustling as she took off her dress. Then she slipped under the robe. Her skin was smooth against me. She began to kiss my neck and drift her fingers along my stomach, I tried to touch her, but she put my hand back and continued to rub my belly, then my thighs, it seemed I ought to be doing something, I tried to reach between her legs, touched hair, but she stopped that hand as well. I began to feel docious. Nothing was expected of me; she was a grown woman and she had the reins.

She was of this same opinion. She ran her fingernails up and down, across my chest and down my legs, while slowly kissing my neck. This went on much longer than I thought it properly ought to, but finally she climbed on top of me and then I was inside.

There was a noise. Escuté poked his head into the tipi.

"How long, wife of Fat Wolf? One minute? Or, let me guess, he is already *pʉa*."

"Out," she said. "Go masturbate yourself with Nʉʉkaru."

She kissed me on the nose. She was leaning over me, being very still. I wanted to start moving but she held me in place.

"How does that feel, brother-in-law?"

I made some noise.

She moved her hips. "Should I do this?"

"Yes."

"Hmmm. Maybe not."

I didn't say anything.

"I think we will just stay like this," she said.

I cleared my throat.

"It feels good to me also," she said.

This seemed like an unbelievable coincidence. At some point she began to move slowly. She was leaning forward and our foreheads were touching and she was holding my hands. Her breath was sweet. "Hates Work is not my real name," she said. "My name is Single Bird."

By the time Nʉʉkaru and Escuté came back, I had slept with Single Bird five times. I expected Escuté to have something to say but he didn't; he and Nʉʉkaru whispered something to each other and then Nʉʉkaru went to his pallet but Escuté, instead of going to bed, slipped over to us very quietly. He felt Single Bird's hair, and then he gently felt my face, and then he patted me on the chest and said something in Comanche I did not understand, and Single Bird murmured something in her sleep, and Escuté leaned forward and kissed her hair and patted me again and then kissed me on the forehead. Then he went back to his pallet.

I was awake. I woke up Single Bird and we did it again.

In the morning, when the faintest of gray light was coming through the smoke flap, I felt her get up. I pulled her back.

"No," she whispered. "It's already late."

"Tell me why they call you Hates Work."

"Because I only do the work of ten men. Instead of fifty." She leaned over and kissed me. "Don't look at me in public. This will probably never happen again. This is the first time my husband has sent me to anyone, and I don't know what kind of mood he's going to be in when I get back."

A few hours later, Nuukaru and Escuté and I were sitting around the fire, eating dried elk and watching the bustle of the camp. Something was wrong with Escuté; normally he did his hair carefully into an a fan on the top of his head but that morning he had not even painted himself.

"Is Fat Wolf going to be angry at me?" I said.

"He's going to cut your dick off. I hope it was worth it."

"Don't listen to him," said Nuukaru. "Everyone wants to sleep with Hates Work and you're the only one who has, except the guy who paid fifty horses for her."

"My father paid fifty horses, not my fat brother. If it was my father getting her I wouldn't care."

"Escuté is especially pissed, as you can tell."

"Why shouldn't I be? Where are my fifty fucking horses if I wanted to marry? Meanwhile, Hates Work gets sent to Tiehteti."

"Who do you want to marry?" I said.

"No one. That's the point. Who the fuck can I marry now that the fat one has taken the best-looking girl anyone has ever heard of?"

"Her sister is not bad," said Nʉʉkaru.

"I am fucked, is the point. He is a fat coward but I still end up looking like the bad one. Eight of the horses that went to her bride-price were horses I gave to my father. When was the last time my brother even went on a raid?"

"You should stop," said Nʉʉkaru.

"I don't care who hears me."

"You will later."

We sat for a while. I couldn't see what Escuté had to worry about. He had six scalps and while he was shorter and slimmer than his father and brother, he was nicely built and had an easy way of moving and all the young Indians, men and women alike, looked up to him. Then I thought maybe he was right: Hates Work was his only real equal in the band.

"There is a very beautiful captive owned by Lazy Feet, the blond one? The German?"

"Yellow Hair," I said.

"Yes, her. She is the equal of Hates Work."

"I'm not marrying a fucking captive. No offense, Tiehteti."

"We're all from captives at some point," said Nʉʉkaru.

"Yes, but still I am not doing it."

"You weren't angry last night," I said.

"No, I wasn't. I'm not angry at you, Tiehteti; I'm glad you got a taste, you deserved it. It's just my father, because the fat one is the oldest, he can do no wrong, and fifty fucking horses, he didn't even try to negotiate."

"We all know you'll be a chief," said Nʉʉkaru. "Everyone knows that. Your brother won't be. He's just a man with a rich father."

"Yes, and if I get killed on a raid before I get to be a chief? While my father supports the fat one and buys him a few more wives?"

"Then I'll make sure you don't get scalped."

"Unbelievable," said Escuté, and shook his head.

"You still have a father," said Nʉʉkaru. "This is something to be grateful for."

"Your father died well and he wasn't scalped," said Escuté. "He is already at the happy hunting grounds."

"Thank you, Escuté, and where is that, exactly? I've heard it's beyond the sun somewhere, in the west. You know it's strange, because sometimes I get the urge to ask my father's advice on various matters, or feel his hand on my shoulder, but everyone assures me he is in the west, just past the sun, though Tiehteti, who does not know our ways, tells me that if you follow the sun to the west you eventually reach a limitless expanse of salty water, rather than a land where horses run fast enough to fly, where it is neither hot nor cold, where game impales itself on your lance and is magically roasted and you eat everything with an accompaniment of the richest marrow."

"I'm sorry," said Escuté. "I have no right to complain."

"Ah. For once your lips move and there is truth."

"On a different matter," I said, "do you think it's likely I'll see Hates Work again?"

"Knowing my brother, no."

"Impossible to say," said Nuukaru. "But it would be an extremely bad idea to think about her at all, as Fat Wolf might be sensitive about it. That was incredibly generous, what he did, and he may have done it just to look good."

"She enjoyed herself, I think."

Escuté shook his head. "Be careful, boy."

"She enjoyed herself because her husband gave her permission. If it ever happens without his permission, or he even suspects it has happened, he will cut off her nose and ears and slash her face. And you will develop similar problems yourself."

"In your favor," said Escuté, holding up a hand, "your accomplishments notwithstanding, he still considers you to be extremely young, and not so much of a threat. So it is possible."

"You are better off thinking about her sister, Prairie Flower, who is unmarried."

"Also not as lazy. Or as good-looking, for that matter."

"But still very pretty. And intelligent."

"And thus pursued by plenty of men with more to recommend them than you have, who have killed more than one enemy and stolen many horses."

"Not to mention Escuté fucked her, so she almost certainly has a disease."

"Perhaps," said Escuté, "you should concentrate your efforts on your riding and shooting, which are known to need attention, and consider this as you might consider a visit from the Great Spirit."

"Scalps and horses, my son."

I didn't say anything.

"But if some other girl decides to come to your tipi at night, of her own free will, and manages to make it past Nʉʉkaru and I, which is unlikely, then you can safely fuck her. While the opposite situation—let's say you have been talking to a girl, and she has given you certain signals, such as letting you put a finger inside her while she is out gathering firewood, and, being certain she likes you, and being desirous of a respectable place to make love to her, you decide to visit her tipi one night—"

"You will be instantly killed by her father," said Nʉʉkaru. "Or some other family member."

"Who will then give Toshaway a horse in compensation for your death."

"In short," said Nʉʉkaru, "until they get married, the women get to be with whomever they want and are the only ones allowed to choose. Afterward, if they behave like that, they get their noses cut off."

"So what do I do now?"

Escuté was shaking his head. "Listen to the white one. He lost his virginity only eight hours ago."

"Horse and scalps," said Nʉʉkaru. "Horses and scalps."

Chapter Fourtee
Jeannie McCullough

I n 1937, when she was twelve, a man named William Blount, along with his two sons, disappeared from his farm near the McCullough ranch. The farm itself was dried up, the family living on relief flour and rabbit meat, and Blount's wife said her husband and two boys had gone onto the McCullough's property—which still had plenty of water and grass—to get a deer to feed themselves. Neither Blount nor his sons ever came home and his wife claimed to have heard shots from the direction of the ranch.

Everyone knew what happened if you trespassed on McCullough land. Both roads to town wound through its quarter-million acres and if your car broke down, you were better walking ten miles along the road than cutting through the pastures, where fence riders might e you for a thief. After the Garcia troubles, the ranch had been declared a state game preserve, which meant that in addition to the vaqueros, the McCulloughs had game wardens—technically employees of the state—as additional security. Some said they buried a dozen people a year in the back pastures, poachers and vagrant Mexicans. Others said it was two dozen. *Those people are just talking,* is what her father said. But she could see that her brothers, who treated the vaqueros as family, were not comfortable around the fence riders.

The day after the Blounts disappeared, Jeannie answered the front door to find the sheriff standing there alone. He was originally from up north; suspected of being a half-breed Indian, he was a tall thin man with a sunburned face and hawk nose. He had been elected over Berger, her father's man, by pandering to the Mexicans. Berger had hunted their land and borrowed their horses; Van Zandt only came when there was trouble. Or, said her father, when he needed money.

On the staircase landing, right under the big Tiffany window, was a daybed where you could lie and read. You could also hear downstairs without being seen. She lay there, with the sunlight coming through the window, the portraits of her family along the staircase:

the Colonel leaning on his sword, in the uniform of the Lost Cause; the Colonel's dead wife with their three boys. Both the wife and one of the sons (Everett, she knew) were illuminated by an otherwordly light; Peter (disgraced) and Phineas (whom Jeannie liked) looked normal. Also along the stairs were marble cherubs and busts. She listened to her father and the sheriff.

"I didn't want to call," said Van Zandt.

Her father said something she couldn't hear.

"Folks are saying we ought to be searching for these Blounts."

"Evan, if we let ten deputies on our land ever'time some greaser disappeared . . ."

"This is a white man and two boys and folks are pretty worked up, even the Mexicans. I haven't seen anything like it."

"Well, it is nothing new," said her father. "There are plenty around here who won't like me unless I lose money to them in every horse trade."

Relations between the McCulloughs and the citizenry had been strained for some time. A third of the town was out of work; a few months earlier it had come out that her father had blocked the construction of a new state highway through their lands—the road would have cut thirty miles off the trip between Laredo and Carrizo Springs. The *San Antonio Express* picked up the story. It was the same thing they were saying about the King and Kenedy ranches: Another Walled Kingdom. Common men not welcome.

"It's this goddamn Roosevelt," said her father. "You mark my words, that was the last free election we will ever see in this country. We are on the verge of a dictatorship."

The next day a crowd gathered at the main gate. They stayed there all day. Her father did not go down to talk to them; instead he distributed the ranch's half-dozen Thompson guns among the hands who knew how to use them.

"Stay off your porch tonight," he told her. "Stay away from the windows and don't turn on any lights."

"What's going to happen?" she said.

"Nothing. This has gone on plenty of times before."

She went to bed early, climbing the stairs to the east wing, where the children slept. All the bedrooms had their own sleeping porches and she turned out the light, debated a few seconds, then, disobeying her father's orders, went out to her porch and got quietly into bed. The stars were bright as always and she lay listening to the crickets, the hoots of owls, lowing of cattle, whippoorwills, a coyote. There was the creaking of the windmill that fed the house cistern, but she barely noticed. The tree frogs were thrumming, which meant rain. She heard a rustling from the next porch—her brother Paul.

"Is that you?"

"Yeah," he said.

"What d'you think's gonna happen?"

"I dunno."

"It's nonsense about those Blounts, isn't it?"

He didn't answer.

"Isn't it?"

"I'm not sure," he said.

"Are Jonas and Clint in bed?"

"They're with Daddy."

"Can you see down to the gate?"

"Stop asking questions."

It was quiet and then he added: "I can't see anything."

"What'll happen if they come through?"

"I imagine Daddy will shoot them. I saw them carrying the Lewis gun a few hours ago."

Her father must have called the governor because the next morning a company of Rangers drove down from San Antonio. The day after that he agreed to let the sheriff search the property, all quarter-million acres. The Blounts were never found, but she knew as well as anyone it would have been like needles in a haystack.

———

Of the four children, only she and Jonas liked school. Paul and Clint found it boring; their father had no use for it either; the compulsory attendance laws were another sign of the government reaching into his pocket. The school was in McCullough Springs, named after her great-grandfather. After the Blount incident her father set out to mend relations, agreeing to pay for a mural that had long been planned for the school, a pastoral scene showing Americans and Mexicans working together to build the town, but when the mural was finished, it showed skeletal Tejano farm workers stooped in an onion field, eyes bulging, a few ragged crosses in the distance. A *patrón* bearing a passing resemblance to Jeannie's father sat astride a black horse, keeping watch. The mural was painted over and Jeannie's father gave up trying to be nice to the townspeople.

The McCulloughs paid most of the school's expenses, though the Midkiffs and Reynoldses chipped in as well. The children of Mexicans attended free, though never for very long; they came and went throughout the year, a month here, a month there, the truant officer never went after them. There was no point trying to be friends; they would disappear for half the year and when they came back she would have to start all over. The children of the white farmers were better, but when they visited the ranch she could see how they wished they lived there instead of her, and an uncomfortable eagerness would come into their manner. Eventually she had stopped being friends with anyone. The only person she had much in common with was Fannie Midkiff, but she was three years older and crazy for boys. She was bound for a sorry end, they all said, Midkiff or not.

Before the Colonel died, so long as he had the energy, she was allowed to sit with him and do her studying. The Colonel spent his mornings on the west gallery, out of the sun, and his evenings on the east gallery, also out of the sun. The visitors never stopped: a man from the government (a Jew, they said) came with a recording machine and the Colonel would talk into it for hours. There were daybeds on the galleries so he might sleep whenever he wanted; he slept and slept, that was what he did mostly; *One day I will sleep forever,* that is what he told her.

He never slept for very long, though. He was always up in time to shoot a snake trying to get across the wide dirt yard, hoping to reach the cool under the porch. *Someday we will live in a house that doesn't have a damned dirt yard,* said her grandmother. *That will be the day we get snakebit,* said the Colonel.

If Jeannie happened to be nearby when the Colonel woke up, he would send her for ice. Or mint; he had planted a patch around one of the stock tanks. He seemed to live off juleps. She would crush the mint at the bottom of the glass and add three spoons of sugar and fill the glass with ice. Sometimes, before he added the whiskey, he would let her suck on the sweet minty ice.

When it was not too hot, she and the Colonel would go on walks, shuffling through the tall grass under the bright sky, stopping to rest in an oak mott, or a copse of cedar elms, or along the streams if they were running. She was always missing things: deer, a fox, the movement of a bird or mouse, a flower blooming out of season, a snake den. Though she could see twice as far as he could, she felt blind around him—she noticed practically nothing except the sun and grass. She often wondered if he were making things up, but every time they went walking, he recovered some keepsake—the bleached skull of a possum, a shed antler, a bright wing-feather off a yellowhammer woodpecker. He walked very slowly and often had to stop and lean on her for support. If it were not too dry when they came on a snake den, he would send her back for a jug of kerosene to pour down the hole, but it was dry most of the time. Sometimes when they stopped to rest he would

ask her to dig a thorn out of his hard yellow foot. He
didn't wear boots; he could no longer keep his balance
in them. He wore only Indian moccasins. Indians—the
real Indians from the reservation in Oklahoma—would
give him things like that, and when they left, he got a
sad look and would be short with her father or anyone
else who bothered him. Jeannie was his favorite, it was
plain to everyone, and her father pretended not to care,
though she knew he did.

If the Colonel was busy and she did not have schoolwork, her job was to gather the milch cows from the
pasture and milk them, smelling their sweet breath and
listening to the sound of the pail, tinny at first, then
soft as it filled with milk. Her brothers hated the job—
it was not proper work for a vaquero, being swished
in the face by the cow's dungy tail—but there was a
satisfaction at seeing the animal's relief, the sounds she
could make with the streams of milk, playing them
against the sides of the pail. It was not a song, but it was
something like one. The milk was taken to the kitchen,
strained, and either put into the icebox or left out for
the cream to rise and be skimmed off. The domestic
staff were allowed to have all the skimmed milk they
wanted, but everything else was for the family. They
always had more milk than they needed and often
entire buckets would clabber and one of her brothers

would carry it out to the bunkhouse for the vaqueros. It was something she missed later in life, clabbered milk with brown sugar and fruit. When pasteurization came along, they said clabber wasn't safe, though she'd been eating it all her life.

When she was not gathering the milch cows she was looking after the dogies; technically this was her brothers' job as well, but they rarely attended to it. When a calf was orphaned, the hands would drive it to the pens near the house. Jeannie would tie a cow to the fence, then splash the cow's milk on the dogie's head. She allowed the cow to smell her own milk on the orphan, then brought the dogie to the cow's udder. Usually the cow would kick the strange calf away, and Jeannie would have to wait a while before repeating the process. Sometimes the cow gave in immediately and allowed the dogie to suckle; other times it took days. Clint and Paul were always buying horses with their dogie money; no one knew what Jonas did with his. She gave hers to her father to hold, and when she was twelve she opened an account in San Antonio, depositing nearly ten thousand dollars.

When she could not sit on the porch with the Colonel, her other favorite place was the old Garcia house, which, though the Garcias were long dead, was still called the casa mayor. She had known from a young age what happened to them.

"Pedro Garcia didn't have any sons to work the ranch," her father said, "and his daughters all married bad men who ran Pedro into debt. The bad men started stealing our cattle and then they shot your uncle Glendale."

"So we went and shot them back."

"No, the Texas Rangers went to their house and tried to talk to them, and we went along with the Rangers. But the Garcias started shooting at the Rangers."

There was nothing higher in her mind than a Texas Ranger. "I am glad they are dead," she said about the Garcias.

"They were good people who had bad luck," he said. Then he added: "Bad things can happen to good people."

Daughters—that was one bad thing that could happen to you. Once she had overheard her father telling a reporter, who was visiting for the occasion of the Colonel's hundredth birthday, saying: "First you pray for sons, second you pray for oil. You look at the Millers over in Carrizo, they used to own eighty sections, but they had nothing but she-stuff to pass it to."

She went right up to her room and at supper she pretended to be sick. After that she had not minded when the Colonel talked bad about her father.

The Garcia house had been built in the 1760s, one of the first settlements in the area; it sat on a rise over the Nueces River valley where, even with the rest of the land dried up, a spring still flowed from the rocks. The house, which resembled a small castle, was built of heavy stone blocks. There was an observation tower, nearly forty feet high, for keeping watch over hostile territory, and the casa mayor's windows were tall slits, too narrow to climb through. There were plenty of gun ports as well, which she imagined had spit death at heathen Indians.

The roof was long collapsed and inside the casa mayor, mesquite and huisache grew up among the debris, along with a few oaks and hackberries that were already higher than the walls. From the outside, the casa mayor now looked like a walled garden, a safe and inviting place, though it was not. The floor was dirt and there were rusty nails and springs and bits of jagged wood, not to mention the thorns of the huisache. She was not allowed inside but she went anyway, picking her way carefully to the tower. After clambering over more half-burned beams and thorny brush, she could reach the stone staircase that wound around the inside of the tower, all the way to the top, though there was no longer any platform. She would stand on the narrow top stair, in the sun, looking out over the country as it descended to the Nueces River, then back toward her own house, and beyond that McCullough Springs, with its two- and three-story buildings and big stone bank. When the Colonel first moved here he had lived in a jacal, and then a house made from timber. That house had burned after the Colonel's wife died and he'd built another one from stone.

She had to squint to ignore the farmers and laborers like ants in the fields near the river, and she would avoid looking toward her own house and the town, and try to see the land as it had once been. A poor man's paradise—that was how the Colonel described it. But she preferred to imagine herself a princess, courted by all the sons of hacendados; there would be seven and she would have no interest in a single one and would lock herself in the tower and refuse to eat, until the poorest and ugliest of the seven revealed himself to be a prince in disguise, whereupon they would sail away to Spain, where it was cool and the servants would feed her plums.

Other times she pretended to be Mrs. Rosalie Evans, the Englishwoman her father always talked about who, just a few years back, had barricaded herself in a tower just like this one, and, in the name of democracy, had shot it out to the death with the Mexican communists who had come to take her land.

When she got too tired standing in the tower (there were only the narrow steps, a four-story plunge just beyond) or her eyes hurt from the glare, she would strip off all her clothes and sit in the spring, the best on the McCullough property. The vaqueros gave the casa mayor a wide berth and she knew she would never be discovered.

Mostly the spring ran down over the rocks toward the river, but it had once been dammed, and off to one side was a stone spillway that carried water to a cistern under the house. She could hang her head through the opening and smell the damp. From the cistern another stone trough carried the overflow to a bathing pool below the house and from there a third spillway diverted to a sink for washing clothes or pots, and from there the water would flow to a large earthen terrace, now overgrown with mesquite and persimmon, which had once been the kitchen garden. It was like the Roman ruins they showed in schoolbooks, but here she could walk along the edge of the old bathing pool, imagining it full of cool water, and sit in the shade of live oaks. In the distance were rolling hills and oak motts and buffalo, she imagined, grazing along the river. Though of course there would be danger; she would want a pistol for Indians. She could not imagine a more perfect life.

In the pasture below the house were more stone walls and rubble, the remnants of a church and other important buildings, the purposes of which were now a mystery. Many of the old *corrales de leña* still stood and the Garcias' spring still flowed, but someone had knocked out the dam so the water no longer reached the spillway. The casa mayor had gone dry like everything else. The stream now flowed in its original bed, down past the old church, where occasionally, especially after a hard rain, it would dislodge interesting things. Small bits of tin whose purpose she could not identify, uncountable shards of colored glazed ceramics, broken cups the Colonel said were for drinking chocolate. Antler buttons, brass screws, various coins and fragments of bone.

Only the children had interest in the casa mayor. The Mexican hands, if forced to fetch cattle from the pastures nearby, always crossed themselves. They could not help being ignorant Catholics. And the Garcias had not been able to help being lazy, cattle-stealing greasers and she felt sorry for them, even if they had shot her uncle Glenn.

Occasionally, it seemed strange to her that lazy greasers would construct elaborate stone houses, complete with cisterns, bathing pools, and various gardens, but on the few occasions those thoughts rose to the surface of her mind, she reminded herself that people often did strange, unaccountable things, like the Brenners, whose two sons had been shot robbing a bank in San Antonio, or the Morales family, who had worked for the McCulloughs three generations until their daughter ran off to become a prostitute. So Clint told her. He had scratched his name into the soft caliche walls of the casa mayor, C-L-I-N-T, in letters as tall as he was.

One scalding-hot day during the summer, when there was no school, and she was bored with swimming in the stock tank, she and Clint and Paul rode up to the hacienda.

They took a meandering route, passing along the way a spring none of them had ever seen before, not as large as the one by the casa mayor, but a spring nonetheless, which flowed into a stream lined with persimmons, grapes, and oaks. They rode to the edge of a swimming hole—where it was clear you might gig as many frogs as you wanted—noting the place so they could return to it later. There were streambeds all over the ranch, but they were mostly dry, filled with sand, their courses marked with the skeletons of dead trees. Irrigation, the Colonel said. It had dried everything up.

Which was another thing about the old Garcia place—all the springs there still ran, it was the best-watered section of the entire ranch.

Jonas, her oldest brother, was not with them. He was about to go away to college in the east, and as punishment, their father did not let him take a single day off the whole summer. Paul and Clint, the middle children, had decided not to work in the heat. Years earlier, she had asked Clint if he thought their father should get another wife, so they would have a real mother, and Clint had said we already had a mother, except you killed her. By being born, he added.

The only satisfaction she got was hearing Clint whipped for a very long time. Still she knew it was true. Their mother had died giving birth to her. God's will, her father said. Though another time he said it was because he hadn't gone to church.

She imagined if she had a mother, what that would be like. They would go burying things and digging them back up. Once, in school, she had buried a thick silver ring the Colonel had given her, as deep in the sandbox as she could put it. When she came back a little while later, Perry Midkiff was digging it up. Their teacher was standing there.

"That's mine," said Jeanne Anne, pointing at the silver ring.

"No," the teacher said, "he found it fair and square."

"But I put it there."

"Why would you put a ring in the sandbox?" said the teacher. She was young and fat and had no chin to speak of—she would die an old maid, everyone said.

"I wanted to discover it," Jeannie told them, but even as the words came out, she knew they made no sense. She had lost the ring forever.

There was plenty to dig for at the casa mayor, in the dirt inside the walls, or out in the yard, or down around the old church and the fallen-down jacals of the dead vaqueros. It was rare that some piece of treasure was not unearthed. There was a crumbling Spanish breastplate that her brothers broke into pieces trying to dig out. Plenty of old weapons, so rusted they were barely identifiable: a rapier, a lance head, hatchet and knife blades, a single-shot pistol with the lock broken off.

That particular day, walking along the streambed by the church, they came to a fresh cutbank where the earth had caved. There was a flat piece of wood lying just under the dirt, and Clint, sensing treasure, dug it out and flung it away before leaping back suddenly. Looking up at them, with the bright sun striking it directly, was a human skeleton draped with tattered cloth. Clint reached in and plucked up the skull. It was small—smaller than a muskmelon—and colored a deep yellow. She had thought all bones were white. There was a gold necklace that Clint removed as well. "It's a girl!" he exclaimed.

Clint made a show of looking at the skull for a while, then tossed it away into the grass. She wanted to touch it but could not. Paul put the skull back in its proper place, put back the coffin lid, and kicked dirt and rocks overtop.

"The animals will just dig it up again, jackass."

"There's nothing to eat in there," said Paul. "We're the only ones who care."

Back in the shade of the spring they stripped, though they were all too old now to remove their underclothes. They sat in the cool water, looking out over the pastures and the low crumbled walls of the old church, the Nueces far beyond.

"How old was she?"

"Half-grown," said Paul.

"Around your age," said Clint.

After a time they got cold; the temperature of the water never changed, no matter how hot the weather. They ate lunch and sat on the warm flat stones. Not far from the church, a group of cows had been standing in the shade, watching them, and now a bull came into the lower pasture, sniffing the air and following a particular cow. They watched the cow run, stop and look over her shoulder, then run again. Jeannie had a terrible premonition that the animals would step into the coffin, but they did not go anywhere near it.

"They are all like that, aren't they?" Clint was saying. "They run away but really they are begging for it. Soon he will get what he is after. And she as well."

Jeannie laughed nervously and squeezed her legs closed. Underneath the hair there were awkward flaps of skin and underneath those, a tiny opening that she knew a man was supposed to fit into, though she could not understand how or why she would ever let that happen, except by some strange agreement, the way she had once allowed Paul to borrow her horse.

"See," said Clint. He nodded at her. "She knows what I am talking about."

The cow had run partway up the hill toward them, then seen them and stopped. The bull caught up to her and she had not run and he quickly jumped on top of her.

"Look at that fuckin' hammer," said Clint.

They could not see well but it was clear the bull had put something into the cow and was moving it in and out. Finally he slid off her and stood panting and blowing.

"One of these days some big bull is gonna be doing that to you."

"Leave her be," Paul said.

Clint punched him but Paul just sat there. Poor gentle Paul. A few years later she would put his death notice on the dresser of his room, where his bed was still neatly done, his bookshelf still full of dime westerns, his school picture still dusted every week by the maids. *Small-arms fire, Ardennes Forest.* January and the snow waist-deep, and Paul, who had grown up in the Wild Horse Desert, had not even had a proper coat.

Clint had died first, but in Italy. Her brothers had both traveled a long way to die, but that evening, years before either of them had left the ranch forever, Clint had come to her and, without saying anything, had handed her the necklace from the young girl's grave.

Clint the Cruel. That was her name for him, though she knew it would have hurt him. He made a hobby of trapping birds and small animals, skinning and stuffing them until they did not resemble animals, they were like small lumpy pillows; he had them all over his room. At fourteen, he was an excellent hand, but her father cared only for Jonas. He was the oldest. Clint was a better rider, a better roper; he threw like the old Mexicans—overhand or under, no windup, no extra movement—and he rarely wasted a loop. He could pluck a calf from the herd before it even knew he was there. He was always first to tail a big bull or climb on a gut-twister; she had seen horses sunfishing, trying to turn themselves inside out; they could not get Clint off their backs.

It didn't matter. Jonas was the oldest and her father paid more attention to Jonas's various failings—too numerous to list—than to Clint's triumphs. One day the ranch would belong to her father, and after that it would belong to Jonas. Everyone knew it, including Clint, who had spent two days sick in bed after drinking a bottle of their grandmother's blackberry cordial.

But Jonas was leaving at the end of the summer and had told her, privately, that he was not coming back. Though she had not believed him at the time.

Technically Jeannie had another family, another set of grandparents from her mother's side. But the other grandmother had died long before Jeannie was born; she might as well have never existed. Her other grandfather died when Jeannie was eight. He was a farmer who had come down from Illinois to buy land the Colonel was selling on promotion. Maybe if his daughter—Jeannie's mother—hadn't passed Jeannie might have known him better, but the few times he had visited, he had been so quiet and deferential that he had seemed no different than a stranger. He had not tried to make any claim on her or any of her brothers, and once, after he left the house, her father called him a man who knew his place.

Much later, it had occurred to her that, scientifically anyway, she was a closer relation to this quiet farmer than she was to the Colonel, but she quickly put the thought from her mind. When he died, it was the last she heard of her mother's side of the family. She did not see much point to them; even the poorest vaquero was higher than a farmer. She was more interested in her uncle Glenn. He had still been a boy when he was first shot, and she imagined she would have done the same thing herself, bravely alerting her father of the Mexicans to their rear, then clutching her heart and dying painlessly. Of course, Glenn had not died. But she would have. They would have named the school after her, and put up a statue, and her teacher would be sorry for letting Perry Midkiff steal the Colonel's silver ring.

After the Colonel passed, her grandmother moved to Dallas, returning to the ranch a few times a year to make sure things were still in order. Jeannie had not expected to miss her. Her grandmother insisted that she wash and dress for supper—which her brothers did not have to do—scrubbing the dirt off Jeannie's hands, cleaning under her nails with a steel pick. Though she also threatened Jeannie's brothers with a quirt if they treated her improperly or said something a lady wasn't supposed to hear. But her grandmother was not home very often.

And so, as the only woman in the house, she was entirely unprepared for what happened when she was twelve, which had sent her running for her father and nearly stepping on a snake. He understood the situation so quickly, before the words had even come out, that she realized he must have known something like this would happen. He began ringing frantically for a maid. The two of them stood in silence. Her father, she saw, was more embarrassed than she was and she knew she was lucky this had not happened in front of her brothers, or in school, or in church; in fact it could not have happened at a better time, walking by herself, examining the tracks by the stock tank.

"Gramammy didn't say anything about this?" He called again for help. "Where is everyone?"

She didn't know.

"Well, from a scientific point of view you are a female. And your body is preparing itself so that eventually, many years from now, as a grown woman, you can get married."

She knew he did not mean married. As she looked at him, shifting his weight from one foot to the other, his white shirt stained with sweat, it occurred to her that she could no longer entirely trust him. The Colonel had been right; the only one you could depend on was yourself. She had always known it on some level or another and at this realization all the shame faded away from her; she was embarrassed only for her father, who despite his height and big hands was completely helpless. She excused herself and went into Jonas's old room and took an undershirt from his dresser, which she cut up to line her shorts.

When she went back downstairs a maid was waiting and, after inspecting Jeannie's handiwork and judging it suitable, explained as best as she was able, half in Spanish, half in a coded Catholic English, exactly what was happening, no, it would not stop, and then the two of them went to town to get supplies.

Chapter Fifteen
Diaries of Peter McCullough

SEPTEMBER 5, 1915

Glendale has been home two weeks, but he is pale, weak, and still fighting off some infection. Tomorrow they will take him back to San Antonio. Charlie's arm is better, though not entirely, and there is an image clinging to my mind, which is both of my sons laid out together in one casket.

After a long absence, the dark figure has returned. I see him in the shadows of my office; he follows me around the house, though he has not yet begun to call to me (I once saw him rise from the middle of the flooded Red, his arms open for me like Christ). I have unloaded all my pistols. No longer the energy to be angry at Pedro and my father. Visited the graves of my mother and Everett and Pete Junior (snakebite, which I cannot blame on the Colonel, and yet I do).

Of course he senses something wrong. Appears to not know what. A few times he has found me reading in the great room and stopped as if waiting for me to speak. When I did not—where would I even begin?—he shuffled on.

A man of Pedro's intelligence could not have overlooked it. So my father's voice—the one inside my head—tells me. The same voice says Pedro had no choice—his daughters had married those men, they had become his family, fathered his grandchildren. And if Pedro had no choice, then we didn't either. That is my father's logic—there is never any choice.

Meanwhile my old acts of cowardice continue to haunt. Had I married María (for whom I briefly harbored feelings), instead of Sally (my proper match) . . . who was thirty-two and twice jilted, who loved her life in Dallas, whose bitterness was apparent from the moment she stepped from the train, who came because her father and my father and her own biology gave her no choice. *I was so lonely when I met Peter,* that is the story she tells of our courtship. Our fathers arranging the breeding as if we were heifer and bull. Perharps I am dramatic; in truth our first years were quite pleasant, but then Sally must have realized that, just as I always said, I really had no intention of leaving this land. Many families of our stature, she rightly pointed out, maintain more than one residence. But we are not like other families.

There are moments I see José and Chico and (impossibly) Pedro himself on the other side of the river, shooting at us. Other moments I remember the event as it truly happened, a half-dozen riders in the dark, dodging into the brush, hundreds of yards away. Perhaps Mexican because of the cut of their clothing, perhaps not.

Being at the rear, higher on the riverbank, I had the best vantage. If I'd taken more time with my shooting, or dismounted . . . but I did not want to hit them. I thought I might push death aside, if only for a moment, so I held over their heads and emptied my rifle, nothing but sound and fury, the extreme range absolving me of marksmanship. Had I simply adjusted the ladder on my sight . . . one of the men I intentionally missed likely shot Glenn. The incident might have ended there. Though it is unlikely.

I cannot help having sympathy for the Mexicans. So far as their white neighbors are concerned, they come into this world coyotes in human form, and when they die they are treated like coyotes as well. My instinct is to root for them; they despise me for it. I see myself in them; they are insulted. Perhaps you cannot respect a man who has what you do not. Unless you think he might kill you. A preference for hardhanded authority seems bred into them—they are comfortable with the old relationships, *patrón* and *peón*—and any attempt to change these boundaries they find undignified, or suspicious, or weak.

To be a simple animal like my father, untroubled by consciousness, or conscience. To sleep soundly, at ease with your certainties, men as expendable as beef.

When I sleep I see Pedro, neatly arranged with his vaqueros in the yard. Eyes open, mouths gaping, the flies and bees swarming. I see him in bed, his daughter dead at his feet, his wife dead at his side. I wonder if he saw them shot down. I wonder if he recognized the men doing it as his friends.

SEPTEMBER 17, 1915

Sally has moved into her own room. Glenn continues to recover in San Antonio; we drive there alternately to be with him. Pilkington has no explanation. The vaqueros suspect dark forces, a *bruja* at work.

Today Sally began a conversation at supper:

"Colonel, what did you used to offer for a bounty on wolves?"

My father: "Ten dollars a pelt. Same for a panther."

"What would be a good bounty on Mexicans, you think?"

"Don't," I said.

"I'm just asking, Pete. It is a reasonable question."

"I don't think you'd have to offer a bounty," said Charles.

"So is ten dollars too much? Or not enough?"

"I would prefer not to talk like this. Today or ever."

"I do not even know if you are upset about this, Peter, I can't even tell. Can anyone else? Does Peter look bothered?"

Everyone was quiet. Finally the Colonel spoke up: "Pete has his own way of handling things. You can leave him be."

She got up and took her plate into the kitchen, with a furious look at my father. Me, she already hates.

Trying to console myself that we aren't alone in our suffering. Two weeks ago the railroad bridges to Brownsville were burned (again), the telegraph lines cut, two white men singled out from a crowd of laborers and shot in the middle of the morning. About twenty Tejanos killed in reprisal—twenty that anyone heard about. The Third Cavalry has been in regular fights with the Mexican army all along the border, shooting across the river. Three cavalrymen killed by insurgents near Los Indios and, across from Progreso, on the Mexican side, the head of a missing U.S. private was displayed on a pole.

In better news, the air smells sweet and the land is already coming back to life. The rain continues to fall and there are adelias and heliotrope, the hummingbirds everywhere in the anacahuita, bluewing butterflies, the scent of ébano and guayacan. The clouds glow at sunset and the river shimmers in the light. But not for Pedro. For Pedro, it is only dark.

OCTOBER 1, 1915

Woke up in a chair next to Glenn's hospital bed, thinking if I stayed there long enough my mother would come and rub my neck. I have always depended on other people to drive out the ghosts. When I shaved, the face I saw in the hospital mirror was not quite mine; it was as if there was some defect in the glass, my features crooked, out of proportion, like a dead man's.

OCTOBER 3, 1915

Back at home. Judge Poole visited from Laredo to tell me Pedro Garcia was eight years delinquent on his taxes. I knew what he was angling for. I was overcome with shame. I could barely hear what he said, my ears were throbbing.

The judge was looking at me.

"That doesn't sound right," I said.

"Pete, I hold the Webb County tax register and I have checked with Brewster in Dimmit."

"Well, I still don't believe it."

Poole sat there quivering like a bucket of clabber. He knew I was calling him a liar, but as I'm the Colonel's son he elected to overlook it. He repeated that the State of Texas was offering to sell us all the Garcia land, nearly two hundred sections, for back taxes. "Sheriff Graham has already taken possession of the property for the court."

"I thought notice of tax sale had to be posted."

"It *is* posted. It is on the courthouse door, in fact, but I do not think anyone will see it, as there are some other things posted on top of it. I do not see why any Yankee speculator ought to get into a bidding war over land that ought rightfully to belong to you."

Like all adulterers he is as passionate as a drummer, as sure of himself as Christ making his long walk . . . that the Yankee speculators were scared off long ago by all the shooting meant nothing to him. But there was no way out . . . I apologized and said my mind was still not right due to worry about Glenn. He nodded and patted my hand with his slippery claw.

I hoped my use of Glenn's name in such a mercenary fashion would not get me condemned to the flames, though if it allowed me to escape Poole's company, I might have agreed to it. I excused myself, but before I could leave (my own living room) Poole mentioned that a small consideration for his advocacy might not go unappreciated. I was thinking one hundred dollars but he read my mind. Ten thousand sounded fair, didn't I think?

Poole could have given the land to anyone, but Reynolds and Midkiff (along with all the other cattlemen in Texas) are known to be having money troubles and with the Colonel spending so much money buying up oil rights, we probably appear rich. Everyone loves the underdog. Until they have to take his side.

I am curious if Pedro did miss some tax payments. A year, maybe. Eight is not possible. He knew what happened to Mexicans who didn't pay their taxes, though he did not know that the same thing might happen to Mexicans who did. I can hear the Colonel—no land was ever acquired honestly in the history of the earth—but it does not make me feel any better.

Total price for the Garcia sections: $103,892.17. About what the land was worth when the Apaches lived here.

OCTOBER 27, 1915

The Colonel insisted I ride with him to the Garcia compound. When we dismounted he produced several jugs of coal oil from his saddlebags.

"I don't think so," I said.

"I should have done this fifty years ago, Pete. It is like killing all the wolves but leaving a nice den for other wolves to return to."

"I won't let you burn their house."

"Well, I won't let you stop me."

"Daddy," I said.

"Pete, it has been too long since we had a real talk and I know I am hard on you. And you are mad at me for the oil leases. I should not have gone behind your back. I am sorry but it was the only way I saw of doing it."

"I do not give two shits about the oil leases."

"Well, they were necessary," he said.

"We are surviving just fine. Unlike some of our neighbors."

"You know I was fond of old Pedro."

"Not fond enough, apparently."

It was quiet for a long time.

"I don't have to tell you what this land used to look like," he said. "And you don't have to tell me that I am the one who ruined it. Which I did, with my own hands, and ruined forever. You're old enough to remember when the grass between here and Canada was balls high to a Belgian, and yes it is possible that in a thousand years it will go back to what it once was, though it seems unlikely. But that is the story of the human race. Soil to sand, fertile to barren, fruit to thorns. It is all we know how to do."

"The brush can be removed."

"At enormous cost, which used to go into our pockets."

"And still we are not doing badly."

He shrugged. "Pete, I love this land, and I love my family, but I do not love cattle. You grew up with them. I will not say I grew up with the buffalo, because while it is true it is also an exaggeration, but I will say that to you there is something sacred in a cow, and in the man who raises and cares for them, but me, I can take them or leave them; it was a business that I undertook to support our family, and I have seen so many things disappear in my lifetime that I cannot bring myself to worry about this one. Which brings me around to my point. What were our losses this year, in one pasture, to the Garcias?"

"Daddy," I said again, a strange word to come from the mouth of a man who is nearly fifty, but the Colonel continued:

"In the west pasture alone, in this year alone, we lost forty thousand dollars. In the other pastures, maybe eighty thousand. And I would judge they have been robbing us for quite a while, at least since the first of the sons-in-law showed up. Now there has been a drought these four years, but does a drought reduce your calves fifty percent? Not if you've been feeding like we did. Do you suddenly lose thirty percent of your momma cows? No, you do not. That is the hand of man. You figure in the increase, they have stolen close to two million dollars from us."

"Don't forget the increase on the mules."

He shook his head and looked off into the distance and it was quiet for a long time. Of course I did not have to acquire this land, as he did. Of course I take it for granted in a manner that seems unthinkable to him. The Garcia sections will double the size of our ranch; this at a time when other cattlemen are struggling. It is an enormous coup, from a certain perspective, and I wonder if he is capable of seeing any other. Then he was talking.

"You've never had any problem standing up to your own family, Pete. But you have a hard time standing up to strangers. That has always been your problem." He wiped his forehead. "I am going to burn out this roach nest. Are you going to help me or not?"

"What's the point of having all this?" I said.

"Because otherwise it would be someone else. Someone was going to end up with this land, maybe Ira Midkiff or Bill Reynolds or maybe Poole would have gotten half and Graham would have gotten a quarter, and Gilbert would have gotten the other quarter. Or some new oilman. The only sure thing was that Pedro was going to lose it. His time had passed."

"It did not just pass of its own accord."

"We are saying the same thing, only you don't realize it."

"It did not have to happen that way."

"Matter of fact it did. That is how the Garcias got the land, by cleaning off the Indians, and that is how we had to get it. And one day that is how someone will get it from us. Which I encourage you not to forget."

He took up two coal oil jugs, one in each hand, and made his way slowly up the steps. The jugs were heavy and he was struggling; he nearly dropped them.

As I watched him I realized he is not of our time; he is like some fossil come out of a stream bank or a trench in the ocean, from a point in history when you took what you wanted and did not see any reason to justify.

I realize he is not any worse than our neighbors: they are simply more modern in their thinking. They require some racial explanation to justify their theft and murder. My brother Phineas is truly the most advanced among them, has nothing against the Mexican or any other race, he sees it simply as a matter of economics. Science rather than emotion. The strong must be encouraged, the weak allowed to perish. Though what none of them see, or want to see, is that we have a choice.

I heard my father knocking things around inside the house. On a horse he still looks like a young man; on the ground he carries the weight of all his years. Watching him shuffle with the jugs of kerosene I could not help feeling sorry for him. Perhaps I am insane.

I followed him into the house. I could knock him over and take the kerosene away. But it was too late. This was only a formality.

Inside everything was covered with dust that had blown in the open doors and windows, the tracks of animals were thick, the blood dried to an indistinct black stain. In the living room, my father had pushed the furniture into a pile and sloshed oil over it. I followed him into the rest of the house, into the bedrooms and then Pedro's office.

He pulled all the papers from their cabinets, old letters, stock records, deeds, certificates of birth and death for ten generations, the original land grant, back when this area was all a Spanish province, Nuevo Santander.

After everything was doused in coal oil, he struck the match. I stood watching the papers curl, the fire spreading across the desk and up the wall onto a large map of the state, drawn when all the sections had Spanish names. I heard someone calling my name— Pedro. Then I realized it was my father. I went to look for him and when I walked out of the office the entire house was filled with smoke; he'd lit fires in the other rooms.

I bent beneath the smoke, looking into Pedro and Lourdes's bedroom. Their bed was beginning to burn; the canopy caught and flared and the light filled the dark room. I wondered how many generations had been sired there and knew the Colonel must have thought the same thing.

Through the flames I saw a dark shape calling me forward and only with effort did I turn and make my way toward the sunlight. When I reached the outside my father was already limping down the hill toward the Garcias' stock buildings, a jug of fresh coal oil in each hand.

Chapter Sixteen
Eli/Tiehteti

The Buffalo

The Comanches owned all the territory between Mexico and the Dakotas, the most buffalo-rich land on the continent. The northern bands hunted them seasonally, but the Kotsoteka, whose home territory was the center of the range, hunted year-round. In summer they hunted the bulls, because they were fattest, and in winter they hunted the cows. Until the age of three summers, the meat of either animal was equally good; older than that and the cows tasted better. Old bulls were mostly killed for their hides.

The animals were hunted with either a lance or a bow. Using the lance required a bit more backbone; you had to match speed with the buffalo and drive the lance, one handed, through the ribs, through the lights and into the heart. At the first prick the animal would turn and try to gore you or crush you against the other running buffalo. The only safety was to go all in, give yourself totally to the lance, to use the animal's own weight to drive the point deeper. Unless you were crushed first.

The average buffalo was twice the size of a cow and as mean-spirited as a grizzly. They could jump over a man's head if they wanted, though they rarely did, and if your horse stumbled, or stepped in a prairie dog hole, you could lay money that there would be nothing left of you to bury, as buffalo, unlike horses, would go out of their way to trample you.

The bow gave more wiggle room, as the animal could be killed from a short distance, a few yards, shooting the arrow at a steep angle behind the last rib. Just the same, as soon as the buffalo felt it'd been stuck, it would turn and try to gore you. The best horses would veer at the sound of the bowstring, and this quarter-second gap was usually enough to keep you alive.

Until the big Sharps rifles came along, the buffalo had to be killed while running, from behind and to one side, and so a group of riders would whip the animals into a stampede, and then, by running their horses in front of the lead animals, turn the herd and force the buffalo into a mill, a running circle. Then the hunters would begin the killing.

When as many animals had been killed as could be cut up in a day, the herd was released from the mill and would disappear across the prairie. The fallen buffalo were butchered where they lay, though butchering is not the right word. The Comanche were like surgeons. The skin was cut carefully along the spine, because the best meat and the longest sinews were just underneath, and then the hide was peeled off the animal. If the village was close, by this point a group of optimistic children would have gathered and would be pestering the butcher for a piece of hot liver with the bile of the gallbladder squeezed over it. The stomach was removed, the grass squeezed from it, and the remaining juice drunk immediately as a tonic, or dabbed onto the face by those who had boils or rashes. The contents of the intestines were squeezed out between the fingers and the intestines themselves either broiled or eaten raw. The kidneys, kidney tallow, and tallow along the loins were also eaten raw, as the butchering continued, though sometimes they were lightly roasted, along with the testicles of the bull. If grass was scarce the contents of the stomach were fed to the horses. In winter, in the case of frostbite, the stomach was removed whole and the frostbitten hand or foot thrust in and allowed to warm; recovery was generally complete.

If water was scarce, the veins of the animals were opened and the blood drunk before it had time to clot. The skull was cracked, the brains stirred on a rawhide and eaten as well, being fatty and tender; the teats of any lactating cows were cut and the warm milk sucked directly from them. If the brains were not eaten immediately they were taken to tan hides; every animal has enough brains to tan its own hide, except the buffalo, which was too large.

Once emptied, the stomach was rinsed, dried, and used as a water bag. If there were no metal pots, food could be cooked in the stomach by filling it halfway with water and adding hot stones until the water boiled. Another popular water carrier was the whole skin of a deer, which, if it were to be used for that purpose, was cased and removed whole, and the ends sewn shut. But we are talking about the buffalo.

Once the organ meats were consumed, the hunters retired and the women took over the harder work of butchering. The meat was cut from the bones in three- to four-foot lengths. The strips were placed on the clean inner skin of the recently killed animal and when the animal's skin was completely full of its own meat, it was wrapped up, tied, put on a horse or travois, and taken back to camp to be dried. After which it was packed into *oyóotʉ*, or rawhide containers, and sewn shut with the animal's sinew. Once dry, the meat would keep indefinitely.

The tongue, hump, side ribs, and hump ribs were all choice cuts and were usually saved for barbecue. The bones were cracked and cooked and the buttery marrow, *tuhtsohpe?aipʊ*, scooped out to be used as a sauce alone, or, as previously mentioned, mixed with honey to make a sweet sauce, or cooled and mixed with pounded mesquite beans for dessert.

The shoulder blades were turned into shovels and hoes. The smaller bones were split, fire hardened, and whittled into needles or awls, or into knives, arrowheads, and scrapers. The hooves were boiled to make a glue used for saddle making, attaching sinew to bows, and nearly everything else. Every brave kept a small amount of this glue for emergency repairs. The horns were used as carriers for the fire drill, and, of course, for gunpowder.

The droppings, as a fuel source, improved every season they sat on the prairie, burning longer and slower and more evenly than mesquite. When dried and powdered, the droppings were also used to pack cradleboards for both warmth and moisture absorption, though cattail down, when available, was considered superior.

From the sinew along the spine, as well as the fascia under the shoulder blades, along the hump, and in the abdomen, all manner of thread, bowstring, and bow backers were made. Threads, ropes, and lariats were woven from the long tufts of hair on the head. Pipes were made from the thick ligament in the neck. Arrow straighteners were made from the center bone of the hump, though many preferred to use their teeth.

Scabbards were made from the tail skin, handles for knives and clubs from the tailbones; the trachea was cut and tied to make containers for paints, clays, and makeup. The hard yellow paste inside the gall was used for war paint, the udders dried to be used as dishes and bowls (pottery being fragile, heavy, and generally useless to horse-mounted people). Any unborn fetus was taken and boiled in its sac, and, being more tender than veal, was fed to babies and old people and those with bad teeth. While the pericardium was used for sacks, the heart itself was always left where the buffalo had fallen, so that when the grass grew up between its remaining ribs, the Creator would see that his people were not greedy and ensure that the tribes of buffalo were replenished, so that they would return ever after.

Chapter Seventeen
Jeannie McCullough

The Colonel died in 1936. Jonas left for Princeton the next year, returning only twice and fighting noisily with her father both times. He was no longer mentioned in the house. Her grandmother, too, had disappeared, but she had not died, only moved back to Dallas to be with her other family.

Her father and brothers took their supper in the pasture or ate it cold after working late. The three siblings would come home from school; her brothers would change quickly and ride out to meet their father; Jeannie would continue her studies. Every Saturday a tutor would drive in from San Antonio and assign her extra work. Her grandmother had insisted and her father agreed to anything that kept her occupied. One day she would rebel; she would do only half of what was assigned. She already knew what she would skip: it was Latin, it was definitely Latin, and the tutor would stare down his long sweaty nose while she triumphantly proclaimed she had not translated a word of *Suetonius*.

When her schoolwork was done, the silence in the house would begin to weigh on her, and she would put on her boots and clomp around just to hear the noise they made, then eat supper alone on the gallery. She would listen to the president's radio address and sometimes, if she were especially annoyed, she would leave it on so that when her father came home, he would have to go out to the porch and turn it off. It gave her satisfaction, knowing how angry this made him.

By that time she'd given up working in the pastures. She knew she might be good at it if she continued to try, but the work was hot and long and boring and besides, no one wanted her there. Even the Colonel, who had founded the ranch, had not thrown a loop in the last thirty years of his life—he saw no point to cattle except the tax breaks. Oil was what one ought to be interested in, and now, whenever her great-uncle Phineas came to visit—always with a geologist in tow—she would sit in the backseat while Phineas and the geologist rode up front, talking about shale and sand and electric well logging, which got the geologist very excited. He did not mind that Jeannie was only thirteen; he was happy to ramble on about everything he knew. She could see it pleased Phineas that she listened. The oil business was booming; there were parts of South Texas where you didn't need headlights to drive at night, there was so much gas being flared, the fire lighting the sky for miles around.

Her grandmother returned every so often, smelling of ancient perfume and peppermint drops, her stern face pointy above a black dress, it was always black, as if she were in mourning for something no one else understood. Nothing could be to her satisfaction: the maids were scolded, her father was scolded, her brothers were scolded; she went down to the bunkhouse and ordered the hands to wash their sheets. Jeannie would be prescribed a long bath to open her pores, which, according to her grandmother, were growing larger each month.

After she'd soaked her face, conditioned her hair, dried herself off, and dressed again, she would sit in the library on the couch while her grandmother cleaned under each fingernail, filing off the rough edges, pushing back the cuticles and rubbing cold cream into her skin. *We will make a lady of you yet,* she said, though Jeannie had not thrown a rope in over a year and the calluses were long gone from her hands. Every third visit she would bring her entire wardrobe to the library so that her grandmother might assess the fit of her dresses—*that one makes you look like a servant girl on the prowl.* The offending articles would be packed into a box that her grandmother took to Dallas for tailoring.

Her grandmother always had news from the city, which Jeannie found immensely boring, except for the stories of good girls being ruined, which had begun to feature prominently in her grandmother's lectures. Still, she no longer fell asleep during these talks; there was a comfort in being told to stay out of the sun—*your freckles are bad enough*—to watch what she ate—*you have your mother's hips*—to wash her hair once a day and to never wear pants. Then her grandmother would take up Jeannie's hands, as if something might have changed in the ten minutes since she last touched them, but no, there were her stubby inelegant fingers, which no amount of piano lessons could ever fix. Her grandmother's own fingers were knobby and arthritic and resembled the claws of an animal, but they had once been the hands of a lady, no matter how many years she had wasted on this ranch.

A month or so after she finished the eighth grade, her grandmother, after giving the usual news from Dallas, informed Jeannie that she had been accepted to the Greenfield boarding school in Connecticut. Jeannie

had not known she'd applied. *You leave in six weeks,*
her grandmother said. *Tomorrow we'll take the train
to San Antonio and get you some proper clothes.*

Her protests, which went on the rest of the summer,
meant nothing. Clint and Paul considered it pointless
to resist; her father was pleased that there might be a
better place for her, going so far as to invoke Jonas as a
reason she might be happy up north.

I'm not Jonas, she protested, but everyone knew
this was only partially true. Her grandmother gave her
pearls and four sets of kid gloves, but this did nothing to assuage her anger; she did not even look at her
father when he put her on the train north. She did look
at the pearls for a long time that evening, after closing
the curtains to her sleeping compartment. They were
worth twenty thousand dollars, her grandmother had
said; she would not have any granddaughter of hers
looking common.

Jonas was supposed to meet her at Penn Station but
was an hour late. In which time she stumbled in on
a man, his pants down and his rear end very white,
pushing up against a woman in a red bustle in the far
stall of the ladies' toilet. She rushed out but after five
minutes realized she had no choice and went back into
the same restroom, choosing the stall farthest from

the man and his friend. Miraculously, her luggage was not stolen. *I hate it here,* was the first thing she said to Jonas, who got her luggage properly stowed and then took her to lunch. They walked among the tall buildings. *Don't look up so much,* he said. *You don't want to be a tourist.*

But she couldn't help it. Pictures didn't capture the size of the buildings, which leaned ominously over the streets, ready to fall and crush her at any moment, if a taxicab didn't get her first. The din of all the trucks and shouting people left her ears ringing and she had a rushing in her heart that didn't go away until she was well north of the city, on the train to Greenfield, back among trees and pastures. There were a few stray cattle and sheep grazing in the distance, Holsteins and Jerseys, *at least I know about that,* she thought, it would be something to talk about with her new classmates.

There were numerous things that appealed to her about Greenfield. The old stone buildings with their steeply pitched roofs and tall ivy walls, the sunlight like a gauze across the landscape—what passed for summer was like winter in Texas—the dense forests and rolling fields at the edge of the campus. She had not known there were so many shades of green, she had not known there was so much rain and moisture on earth.

The campus was only forty years old, though it might have easily been four hundred, the way the vines had taken over the buildings and trees brushed the windows in the breeze. In the few moments she had to herself each day, it was hard not to feel like someone important, as if she were only steps away from being swept up by some prince, or prime minister's son, who, she now knew, would be English instead of Spanish, though other times she wondered if she did not want to be swept up at all, if perhaps she would be a prime minister herself—it was not inconceivable, times were changing. She could see herself behind a great wooden desk, writing letters to her loyal citizenry.

She did not have much time alone. The days were rigidly ordered: wake-up bell followed by breakfast and chapel, followed by classes, lunch, classes, athletics, dinner, and study hall. Lights out at eleven P.M., a monitor stalking the halls to enforce it.

Her roommate, a small Jewish girl named Esther, cried herself to sleep every night and at the end of the first week, when Jeannie returned from dinner, Esther and all her things were gone. Her father had owned factories in Poland, but he had lost everything to the Germans; the tuition check had not cleared. Jeannie was moved into a nicer room. Her new roommate was a girl named Corkie, who was shy but pleasant, and, unlike Esther, seemed comfortable at their new school. She knew everyone, though Jeannie sensed that she did not have many friends. Corkie had shoulders as thick as a cedar chopper's, and she was tall, and she went about everything with a kind of resignation: to her long face that would never be pretty, to the red bumps above her lip, to her split and frazzled hair. From the way she dressed—in drab, frumpy clothes—and the inattention she gave her appearance, Jeannie thought she must come from a very poor family, and so she went out of her way to be nice, bringing Corkie desserts she'd smuggled from the dining hall, as she had once carried the buckets of clabber to her father's vaqueros.

That Monday, when asked at lunch who her new roommate was, she told them Corkie Halloran.

"Oh, you mean the Mighty Sappho?"

That was Topsy Babcock. She was small and pretty with pale blond hair and skin to match, a smile that turned on and off like a traffic switch. Sometimes the smile meant approval, other times disapproval—she was not a person you wanted to disappoint. The others at the table laughed at Corkie Halloran, and Jeannie laughed with them, though she did not know why.

"She was at Spence but they say she was spending a little too much time with one particular girl, if you know what I mean."

"They should have sent her to St. Paul's—she would have fit in perfectly!"

Everyone thought this was hilarious. Jeannie just nodded.

The next weekend Corkie invited several people to her parents' house, which was only forty minutes from school. To Jeannie's surprise, many of the people who had made fun of her at lunch went along: Topsy Babcock, Natalie Martin, Kiki Fell, and Bootsie Elliot. Jeannie expected some old jalopy, or perhaps a truck, but instead they were picked up by a uniformed driver in a seven-seat Packard.

Kiki said: "You're the one who got stuck with that Jewish girl, aren't you?" She was the dark-haired version of Topsy, though her hair was cut just below her ears, almost as short as a boy's, and it was said she'd had a surgery to make her nose smaller. Since arriving at Greenfield Jeannie had spent more and more time in front of the mirror at bedtime, inspecting herself. Her nose had straightened considerably but her eyes had no character, they were the color of fog or rain. Her chin was pointy, her forehead high, and the scar across her eyebrow—which she had always been proud of because it was like the scars her brothers had—made her look like a man. It was a deep scar, you could not miss it.

"McCullough . . ." Topsy was saying. "That's Jewish, isn't it?"

The other girls tittered, except Corkie, who looked out the window.

"I don't think so."

"I'm kidding. Of course it's not."

Jeannie was quiet the rest of the drive. There were very few houses. The roads were small and winding and yet they were paved. There were tall hedgerows, red barns, the ubiquitous stone walls. Everything was in shadow, the sun came weakly through the trees and the sky felt small and closed in. There was a chill in the air, though it was only September.

Topsy and Kiki and Bootsie had gone to primary school together; the others seemed to know each other in the same ways, she guessed, that she knew the children of the Midkiffs and Reynoldses. The second silent girl in the car, Natalie, had long chestnut hair and a large chest that she slouched to conceal. She made a point of looking out the window, not making eye contact with Jeannie, though, like everyone else, she smiled at whatever Topsy said.

It was a relief when the car turned into a stone gate and made its way up a long driveway with big trees on both sides. There were acres of grass, she had never seen so much green healthy grass in her life; she tried to calculate the number of head you could support here (an acre per head? It seemed possible) but knew better than to say this out loud.

At the top of the hill the house appeared. She began to feel embarrassed. It was not any larger than the Colonel's house, but it was more grand, with arches and pillars and towers, dark granite, marble statuary, a look of weathering as if it had been standing since the time of kings.

"What does your father do?"

The girls all looked at her. Corkie gave her a look as well and she knew she'd made some sort of mistake. But it was too late. Corkie said: "He goes to his firm in New York and he plays racquets at the club and he rides and shoots a lot. And he works on his novel."

"What kind of firm is it?"

"You know . . ." Corkie shrugged.

Bootsie Clark said: "Poppy's father rides and shoots as well, I imagine." Poppy was what the others had decided to call Jeannie. "He's a cowboy. Isn't that right?"

"Cowboys are hired men."

"So what does your father call himself?"

"A cattleman." She was about to add, *but that's not where our money comes from,* when the other girls cut in:

"Does he go on those epic rides, then? Up to Kansas?"

"Those ended in the eighteen hundreds."

"That's too bad," said Bootsie. "They looked very exciting."

She was not sure if it was worse to respond or to let it drop. "They didn't really drive them like in the pictures. They had to walk them or they'd lose all their weight."

"How does Corkie's house look?" said Natalie, changing the subject. "I guess yours must be bigger."

"Not really."

"Of course it is. We hear everything is bigger in Texas."

She shrugged. "It's not as nice as this, though. It's not nearly as green."

"How many acres do you have?"

It was a rude question—the last thing you would ask someone in Texas—but she knew she had to answer. "Three hundred ninety-six sections."

"That's not so much," said Topsy.

"She said sections, not acres."

"How much is a section?"

"They don't even call them acres. An acre is too small."

"How much is a section," Kiki asked, for the second time.

"Six hundred forty acres."

For some reason this caused all the girls, with the exception of Corkie, to break into hysterical laughter. Corkie was watching the driver, waiting for him to open the door.

"Are you going to be a cattlewoman as well?"

"I don't think so."

"What are you going to be, then?"

"She's going to be someone's wife," said Corkie. "Just like the rest of us."

That afternoon, they went riding. Below the main house was a stable with twenty or so horses, an immense corral that they called an arena, and a large pasture. It was all set in a manicured wood but she did not ask where the property ended. There were men in the shadows, cutting branches and loading them into a cart.

She was wearing jodhpurs and knee-high boots borrowed from Corkie's younger sister. She felt ridiculous, but everyone else was dressed the same way. She presumed they were going for a long ride, four or five hours, and she wished she had eaten more at lunch.

"I imagine you must have horses," said Natalie.

"Yes," she said. "Do you?"

"There isn't really enough room for them in Tuxedo Park." She shrugged.

"There's room for Jews, though," said Topsy.

"Topsy and Natalie were neighbors with the girl you roomed with."

"Her father bought a house there ten years ago," said Topsy, "but they wouldn't admit him to the club, so his family couldn't so much as dip a finger in the lake. If they ever heard them splashing around down there, someone would call the police."

"Tell her about the wedding."

"They had a wedding last summer, and all the kids in Tuxedo Park went and turned the signs around, so none of the guests could find their house. Completely ruined the ceremony." She smiled. "The problem is when people think that just because they have money . . ."

Jeannie nodded. The horses were brought out. They were sorrels, smaller chested and longer legged than cow horses.

"I had them put my sister's saddle on this one," said Corkie. She handed the reins over. "You're about her height." The saddle was simple, without a pommel or high cantle, and when Jeannie climbed up, the stirrups felt short and awkward, as if they had been set for a child.

The horse was tall and long legged, near sixteen hands; it looked like a fast horse but it did not look nearly as fast as it really was. It was so much more powerful than a cow horse that it felt closer to an automobile. With a cow horse (quarter horse, these girls called it) there was a negotiation, there were times you let the animal have its way, but this horse was both fast and anxious to please; giving it its head just confused it, like letting go of the steering wheel of a car. It seemed— like everything else in these girls' lives—to have been created just to serve them.

She found she barely needed the reins; the horse responded if she even tensed her legs; he was so responsive, in fact, that he was difficult to ride at first. She wondered if she was a sloppier rider than she thought. She was uncomfortable in the saddle and when they hit a gallop she had a hard time maintaining her seat. They were going fast down a groomed path and there were a series of hurdles ahead; Corkie went over the first one and Jeannie got a bad feeling but followed anyway. There was nothing to worry about. The horse cleared the gate without any input from her at all.

After an hour the rest of the girls were tired and decided to return to the stables. She put her heels in and brushed through a small gap between Topsy and Bootsie, hoping to spook them, then passed Corkie as well. The horse was enjoying itself, so she did a hot lap of the corral (*arena,* she corrected herself), which was nearly a half mile in circumference. It was a good horse; it did not want to stop and she was overcome with sadness, for the life it lived in this corral and these few miles of manicured trail, ridden by these girls who spent longer getting dressed than they did in the saddle. A pointless existence.

By the time she'd cooled the animal down and walked back to the stable, the other girls were waiting and their horses were already being curried by the groom and his children.

Bootsie was saying: "She does ride like a cowboy, doesn't she?"

"Does it feel strange, not having a handle to hold?"

"You don't touch the saddle horn," said Jeannie. She knew she'd looked awkward at first, but she thought she'd recovered well. It was plain she was a better rider than any of them, perhaps even Corkie. It was equally plain that none of them would admit it. Or they would find some way to turn it into an insult. She had an impulse to get back on the horse, gallop into the woods, and begin her long journey back to Texas. Certainly no harder than anything the Colonel had done. Her father would pay for the horse.

"Then why is it there?" said Bootsie, still talking about the saddle horn.

"It's for holding your tools. Tying your rope to and such."

"Well, you looked uncomfortable. I'm sure you'll get used to it."

"I'm a better rider than all of you," she said. She felt her face get hot; she had been pressed into saying something she wasn't sure of. "Except Corkie," she added.

"Still," said Bootsie. "You looked strange."

"That was nothing compared to what we do at home."

"Because it's bigger down there, I'm sure."

"Because we're roping big animals and trying not to get gored by their horns."

"I believe she said we'd be gored," said Topsy.

"She meant bored. To actual death."

"I'm going inside," said Corkie. She was standing against the stall door, looking tired. "Dinner will be ready soon."

That night, she couldn't sleep, and after a good deal of wandering down dark hallways, she found her way to the kitchen for a glass of milk. She had just gone into the icebox when she heard someone behind her.

"You're not supposed to be in here," said a voice. It was one of the maids.

"I'm sorry."

The woman's face softened. "You just ask, sweetie. We'll bring you whatever you need."

After drinking her milk she decided to go outside. It was dark, but there was a light on at the stable and she made her way down the hill in the wet grass—wet, everything here was wet—she was not sure what she had in mind. To talk to her horse, sneak him out for a night ride, to ride away and never come back. As she approached the stable she saw the light was coming from an upper window, in what she had presumed was the hayloft. There was a person moving behind a thin curtain, the faint sound of music. She was close enough to smell the stalls. The person passed behind the curtain again and she realized it was the groom. He lived with his family above the horses. She watched as he sat down in an armchair and appeared to close his eyes, listening quietly to the radio. She could not believe it. Even the lowest hands, who did nothing but stretch fence all day, slept in the bunkhouse. They did not live with animals.

She felt very tired and turned to go back to the house, her legs cold and damp from the dew. It was only September, it was just the beginning. *Things will get better*, she told herself. She thought of the Colonel being held by the Indians; if he had survived that, she could survive this, but even that did not feel true, it was just words, it was a different time.

Back in the main house, she heard a noise and saw a light at the end of a corridor and made her way toward it. It was a library or study of some sort; a fire was going and there was a person sitting in a leather chair, smoking a pipe. She approached and when she got close enough the man looked up at her.

"Excuse me," she said.

It was Corkie's father. He looked almost like a boy in the dim light; he must have been very young when his children were born. He was very handsome. Much more so than his daughter. He took off his reading classes and she saw his eyes were wet, as if he was upset about something. He rubbed them and said, "You're the gal from Texas, right?"

She nodded.

"How are you finding it here?"

"It's green. The grass is nice." It was all she could think of and then she was afraid to say anything else.

"Ah, the lawn," he said. "Yes, thank you." He added: "My great-grandfather spent some time in your state before it was admitted to the Union. In fact he was instrumental in that process. But then we had the Civil War, so back he came. I've always wanted to go and see it myself."

"You should."

"Yes, one of these days. It seems to be where everyone goes to make money now. I suppose I should
see it."

She was quiet.

"Well." He nodded. "I ought to get back to work."
He put his spectacles on. "Good night."

The next morning, after breakfast, Corkie whispered
that she ought not talk to her father while he was
working in the library.

"He's finishing his novel," she said. "He's been
writing it a long time and he can't be disturbed."

She nodded and apologized. She was trying to recall
if she'd ever seen her own father crying. She hadn't.

The next weekend she took the train to see Jonas at
Princeton. The ride was pleasant and she felt very
grown-up, in a strange land traveling by herself. She
did not think she could ever get used to how green everything was. And yet everywhere you stopped, there
was a faint odor of mold, of decay, as if no matter what
you did, the trees would come back, the vines would
grow over, your work would be covered up and you
would rot into the moist earth, no different from anyone who had come before you. It had once been like

Texas, but now it was just people, endless people; there was no room for anything new.

Jonas met her in the train station and she hugged him for a long time. She was wearing her pearls and a nice dress.

"How are you doing up there?"

"Oh, fine."

He fingered the pearls, was on the verge of commenting, then decided against it.

"You'll get used to it," he said. "It's better that you're here than being stuck in McCullough or Carrizo. You're not going to learn anything down there."

"The people are cold."

"They can be."

"I sat on the train with two men and neither of them even said hello to me. It was like that for a whole hour."

"It's different here," he said.

Later they spent time with Jonas's friends: Chip, Nelson, and Bundy. It was only two in the afternoon, but they had all been drinking. Chip burst out laughing when he heard Jeannie's accent. He was soft around the middle, not exactly fat, just soft everywhere, with a deep sunburn and a confidence out of proportion to his appearance.

"Goddamn, McCulloughs. You two *are* from Texas. For a while we didn't believe you—this one hides it so well." He pointed at Jonas. Then he cocked his head and narrowed his eyes, assessing Jeannie. "Bundy, this one doesn't appear to have a drop of the tar baby, either. We must be sitting with the only pure-blood southerners who ever lived."

She reddened and Bundy touched her shoulder. "Don't worry about him. We're all so inbred we don't know how to act when someone new comes in."

Chip was not through with her: "What are your opinions on this war, Mizz McCullough? Should we send in the Marines or wait?"

She must have had a blank look.

"The one Hitler started? Last week?"

"I don't know," she said.

"My God, McCullough. What the hell are they teaching you at Greenfield, anyway?"

"The blessed M-R-S," said Nelson.

"Dump that bunch of slags and go to Porter's." He waved his hand. "We'll get it arranged. You are not going to learn a goddamn thing at Greenfield."

It had gone on like that for hours. She knew nothing the older boys hadn't heard before, nothing they hadn't already considered. Finally she and Jonas went for a walk around campus.

"They're just kidding around, Jeannie."

"I hate them," she said. "I hate everyone I've met here."

She had thought they would spend the evening together but Jonas had work to do. Next time, he said, she could stay in his room and meet more of his friends. They were good people to know—it would be nothing to get her into Barnard when the time came. But for now he was exhausted and behind in his studies. *Because you have been drinking all afternoon with your friends,* she thought.

She considered mentioning that she had spent three hours on the train coming to see him, and would now have to spend three hours going back to Greenfield, but she was too angry to say anything. When she got to New York it was already dark and the train to Connecticut did not leave for some time. She walked around outside the station, looking in the pawnshop windows, getting bumped by all the people walking, men staring at her in ways that would have gotten them shot or at least held for questioning in Texas. The newspapers were all screaming about the war, the Germans had taken Poland. As miserable as she'd been at Greenfield, she'd only faintly registered the war's existence, and, even now, it seemed more important that she make her train.

She did not get back to Greenfield until just before lights-out and as she'd forgotten to eat, she had to go to bed hungry. The next morning Corkie let her know they'd announced the fall dance. She would need to invite a date, preferably several. Even Corkie, who did not care about those things, had already drawn up a list of two dozen young men, intending to write invitations to all of them. Jeannie excused herself, then went to the library and spent the day there.

It would be a disaster. Not only did she have no one to invite—the only boys she'd met here were Jonas's friends—but the previous weekend, when the girls had gotten into Corkie's parents' wine and danced afterward, she had not known any of the steps. Charleston, hat dance, waltz, box step. She had not known any of it. Corkie had tried to show her, but it was pointless, utterly pointless; it would take years, years to learn these things, it would be utter humiliation. Even riding with these girls—the one thing she had nearly mastered—had been somehow degrading.

Meanwhile, the rest of them were already talking about the dances they would attend later, the big ones around Christmas; at fourteen they were now old enough. She realized that her classmates had spent their entire lives preparing for this moment; while she had been off visiting Jonas, they had spent the day shopping for dresses with their mothers. And of course they all knew dozens of eligible boys, who would all have to come several hours from other schools.

That Saturday she packed a small overnight bag, telling Corkie she was going to visit Jonas again. She took the train into New York and went looking for a bank—she did not have enough money to make the trip she wanted to make—but it turned out that banks were closed on weekends. All of them? Yes. Finally she walked into one of the pawnshops near the train station. The man inside was in his fifties, looked as if he didn't eat much or see the sunlight, and spoke in a heavy foreign accent. She had never seen a Jew like him. She handed over her grandmother's pearls.

"Are they real?"

"Of course," she said. He looked past her, to the street outside, to see if anyone was waiting for her. Then he put the pearls in his mouth as if he planned to eat them. Instead he rubbed each one against a front tooth. Afterward, he looked them over with a magnifier.

"Did a policeman send you in here?"

"No," she said.

"I am interested in why you brought these here."

"I saw the window." She shrugged.

"They're yours to sell."

"Yes."

He looked at her, but he didn't say anything.

"What sort of hat is that?" she asked, trying to be polite.

He said something that sounded like *hichpah*. "I'm Jewish. Unfortunately a bad one, working on the Sabbath. Don't worry, I won't eat you. But I can't buy your pearls, either."

"I don't have any money. I went to the banks but they're closed and I have to get home to my family."

"I'm sorry."

They stood looking at each other and finally he told her: "I'll go wake up my brother. But he is just going to tell you the same thing."

Another man, much more nicely dressed, came in from the back. He looked over the pearls, and ran them over the edge of his teeth, then looked at them with another loupe, then under a very bright light, and then under what appeared to be a microscope.

"Obviously these are worth several thousand dollars . . ."

"They are worth twenty," she said.

"They are worth eight," he said. "On a good day, to the perfect buyer."

"That would be fine."

He smiled. "I can't buy them from you. You're too young. I'm sorry."

She felt her eyes get wet. She wanted to take the pearls back and run out into the street, but instead she made herself stand there so they could see that she was crying.

"You're too young," he repeated.

"I don't care. I'm not leaving."

The two of them looked at each other and began to discuss things in a foreign language. Finally the better-dressed one said: "We can give you five hundred dollars. I'd like to offer more, but I can't."

Through her tears she said: "I will take a thousand."

That night she was on a train to Baltimore. Four days later, when her grandmother picked her up in San Antonio, she told her the pearls had been stolen.

It was not a story she had told many people and even Hank had never grasped its significance. It had been the turning point of her life, in some sense its most important moment; she had seen the world and re-treated, while Jonas, for all his other failings, had not. There were times she imagined how she might have turned out had she stayed in the North. Like Jonas, she knew, settled and comfortable, she would have been someone's wife. And that was not who she had wanted to be.

And yet Jonas had four children who adored him, a dozen grandchildren. Her houses, all three of them, were empty. Pointless monuments. Her life's work would pass to a grandson she barely knew—who would likely crumble under its weight. *It is not fair*, she thought. She wanted to weep.

She looked around her. She was certain now. There was a smell in the room, it was gas.

Chapter Eighteen
Diaries of Peter McCullough

NOVEMBER 1, 1915

Phineas came down from Austin. We are the darlings of the capital for killing nineteen of our neighbors and getting two family members shot in the process. Phineas talking about a run for lieutenant governor.

Glenn is home, but still sick. He and my brother talked for a long time. The boys have always liked Phineas; to them he is a younger version of the Colonel, the pinnacle of manly attainment. Of course I do not dare tell them what I suspect, though I am not sure he would extend me the same courtesy, were the situation reversed—he would probably take me out to a pasture and shoot me.

How two men from the same stock might be so different . . . my father likely reckons my mother snuck off for congress with some poet, scrivener, or other near-sighted sniveling half-man. I have always seen myself as two people: the one before my mother died, fearless as his brothers, and the one after, like an owl on some dark branch, watching the rest move about in the sunlight.

How he and Phineas can stand in front of a hundred men and never once wonder what they are thinking—I can barely eat dinner without considering if I've been talking too much or not enough, drinking too much or not enough, making as little noise as possible with my knife and fork, paying mind to the clunk as I set down my water glass. And yet when I crossed the wall at the Garcias', I forgot myself.

Have been tending their grave, unbeknownst to everyone. That day, after I left, they were all buried in a single pit: mother, father, daughters, grandchildren, assorted employees. No marker and, owing to the caliche, the hole was not very deep so I have been piling rocks and dirt on top. Old Pedro, who sent a priest to his vaqueros after every miscarriage, who always paid for a lined casket and a Christian burial. I still imagine the house as it has always been; each time I am freshly shocked, the charred walls, the birds flying freely where there was once a roof. The wood was old and seasoned and the fire burned hot. Little left inside but nails and bits of glass and metal. Even staring directly at it, part of me believes it is an illusion.

Perhaps this is why I am constantly disappointed—I expect good from the world, as a puppy might. Thus, like Prometheus, I am unmade each day.

Phineas and I rode out to see what was left of the casa mayor; he explained he had already been talking to Judge Poole about the Garcias' "tax problems." I waited for him to acknowledge the chicanery, but he did not. He does not trust me entirely. No different from the Colonel.

When we reached the house Phineas was shocked. He sat there on his horse while I dismounted and went to pay my respects at their grave. He must have realized what I was doing so he left me alone. As I passed their spring I saw that someone had thrown a dead dog into it. I roped the animal and pulled it out.

"See clear to the goddamn border, can't you?"

It was an exaggeration but I got the meaning.

"You know, Pete, you might want to stay away from here for a while. I don't like looking at this myself and you . . ." He shook his head.

"Pedro Garcia was a friend."

"That's what I mean," he said.

I walked off behind the house, where I could sit on the patio and look over things. A few minutes later he came and found me.

"You shouldn't hold this against Daddy."

"How would that be possible?"

"This would have happened anyway. And of course, Pedro wasn't eight years behind in taxes. But there are things he could have done . . ."

"Such as?"

"Marrying his daughters right? I guess he thought he was making them happy, but . . ."

"If they'd married whites, you mean."

"Why not? All the old families did it. They saw the writing on the wall and married their daughters off to the proper people." He shrugged. "It's Darwin at work, Pete. Dilution is what the situation called for, but Pedro decided to double down."

I thought about Pedro encouraging me to call on María. I began to get a sick feeling.

"You and Daddy see eye to eye on a lot of things."

"There is not a moment of my day I am not thinking about this place."

"You are here twice a year," I said.

"You think a bank in Austin wants to lend a half-million dollars to a ranch it's never seen, and doesn't know anything about except it's already mortgaged

out its asshole? Or Roger Longoria in Dallas? You ever
wonder why your credit comes on such good terms from
him? Or why it even comes at all? Or how it might be
that the cattle business is collapsing all around Texas
but somehow money comes easy for us?"

I decided to change the subject. "Meanwhile Daddy
goes and spends the money on oil leases."

"Daddy can smell a change coming like a buzzard
can smell a dry canteen. He's got more sense than both
of us put together and if he had any ambition, he'd be
governor."

"That I highly doubt."

He shook his head. Any word against the Colonel
is like a word against God, or rain, or white men—the
good things of the earth.

"I have spent most of my life trying to figure out
what goes on inside your mind," he said. "First I
thought you were slow and then I thought you might
be red. Finally it occurred to me that you are just a
sentimentalist. You believe in the open range, the code,
the nobility of the sufferin' cowpoke and the emptiness
of bankers' hearts—all stuff you picked up from Zane
Grey . . ."

In fact I have not read Zane Grey, though I do not
mind Wister, but explaining these distinctions to my
brother is pointless.

" . . . you know in the old days, when Daddy needed stock, he found them in the bushes or paid some half-breed a dime a head to steal them. If a slick calf was found, it got branded, if a piece of land caught his eye, it got fenced. If there was someone he didn't like, he ran them off. And"—he looked at me meaningfully—"if someone stole your cattle, you crossed the river, burned their entire fucking village, and drove all their animals back to your pastures."

"That does not appear to have changed much."

"It *has* changed. You now need an adding machine just to figure out if you're getting enough beef per acre to cover your payroll. You've got a quarter of your labor going into brush, another quarter into screwworms and fever ticks. And when you're worrying about that kind of piddling bullshit . . ."

I put up my hand to stop him. "This is what we have, Finn. We can complain about it or we can keep working, and I would rather keep working. Daddy wants to think we are sitting on a sea of oil, but we are not; we are sitting on a bunch of expensive and utterly worthless leases on land we don't even own." I thought it was well played but he was smiling. Through sheer willpower I forced myself to stay where I was.

"When did they find oil in North Texas, Pete?"

Something they have always done: call me by name, as if disciplining a child. And yet still I feel compelled to answer them, as if, despite decades of evidence to the contrary, I might explain my point of view.

"Twelve years ago," he said, when I didn't respond. "And now half of our oil comes from there. Spindletop was only two years before that. The biggest fucking oil well in human history, before which the Rockefellers, Mellons, Pews, all those eastern cocksuckers, they made hundreds of millions in Pennsylvania. Pennsylvania! There are two buckets of oil in that entire state. Christ, Pete, the Hughes bit, what was that, 1908? Before that, a drilling rig was not so different from what the Romans used. Do you follow?"

Looking over the grave of the Garcias I did not tell him that 1908 was also when they found the caves at La Chapelle, when they found an apelike man, a Neanderthal fifty thousand years old, who had been carefully buried in a sepulcher, a haunch of meat and several flint knives left to protect him in the afterlife. That is how long we have been hoping for a next world. Since before we were truly men.

" . . . this is like the cattle business in 1865. There's nowhere to go but up. We find oil in even a couple of acres, our costs will be covered."

I walked back to my horse, silently, and he did the same. We made our way down the hill, through the old Garcia hamlet, the ruined church and old graveyard, the burned tower of the casa mayor still the highest point on the land. We drifted slowly toward the river, not speaking, my brother riding a few paces behind.

Finally he caught up: "You know, I've always been glad you like living here. When you left for the university I thought I would be stuck taking care of this place, but then you came back. And I have always been grateful for that, because this place is too important to have someone running it who isn't family. That is what I wanted to say. I am grateful you are here."

"Thank you."

"Just remember that you are not out here alone, and that I am thinking about it same as you."

I did not say anything. Phineas inherited my father's great ability to make any compliment sound patronizing. Then I said, "What's going on with Poole? I am trying to figure out how this land deal won't come back to bite us."

"Back taxes."

"Tell me."

"Back taxes," he repeated. "And possibly the judge has an itch to leave Webb County; we're looking into a position for him on the Fifth Court. But you can dig all you want. The Garcias owed taxes, and if it was not in the books before, it is there now, and there is nothing more to it."

Other neighborhood events:

October 18, a train attacked by sixty insurgents near Olmito (five killed).

October 21, army detachment at Ojo de Agua attacked by seventy-five insurgents (three killed, eight wounded).

October 24, second attack on the Tandy Station railroad bridge.

October 30, Governor Ferguson rejects calls for more Rangers. Reason? They are too expensive. Raising taxes out of the question.

Which is perhaps for the best—for every insurgent they kill, a hundred more are converted to the cause. The Tejanos do not mind the army, but they hate the Rangers.

NOVEMBER 15, 1915

Now that we have clear title to the Garcia land, it is just as my father supposed—we look like benevolent kings. Where Pedro was tightfisted, we employ half the men in town. Anyone who wants work now has it: clearing brush, digging irrigation, rounding up twenty years of maverick longhorn bulls. Two men have been gored and Benito Soto died of heatstroke but people are at the gate every day wondering if we are hiring. Despite the sheriff's warnings, I am allowing some of the Mexicans to be armed. Just working for a gringo can get you shot by the *sediciosos*.

How we can appear to have clean hands, despite what happened, I find baffling. And depressing. As if I alone remember the truth.

Mood must improve. Record year for rain—twenty-one inches already. The faster we get the brush out, the more grass will start. There is a pall of smoke over the town from all the brush being burned, and in that smoke I see nothing but good. The ashes will fertilize the soil and it is well known that the bluestems and gramas germinate best if they are heated.

Some bitterness in town (among whites) that no one else was offered the Garcia land. Bill Hollis's widow was one of the lead rabble-rousers. She has no real means—she could not have afforded to buy even a quarter section, let alone two hundred—but she senses the unfairness of it. Dutch Hollis, Bill's brother, apparently has not been sober since his brother died.

Will suggest to the Colonel that we offer Marjorie Hollis a generous price for her house, just to get her out of town. And perhaps we know someone a few counties over who might be induced to offer Dutch Hollis work. Certainly it cannot be good for him to remain in this town, our big white house on the hill, his brother's grave . . .

Such is the way I deal with things. But the Colonel has never had any trouble knowing people dislike him.

JANUARY 1, 1916

Sally has decamped to Dallas with her father and sisters, taking Glenn and Charlie with her.

After they left I went to the graves of Pete Junior, my mother, and Everett. Seeded with rye to keep them green. The birds will probably get most of it. Not sure if cemetery so close to the house is good or bad.

In the afternoon went to the casa mayor. The Garcias' grave has sunk in quite far. Spent three hours scraping dirt to fill it; did not return until well after dark.

Meanwhile the bandit raids continue: three ranches hit in the Big Bend. The Twelfth Cavalry, after several months of heavy losses, crossed the border and burned two Mexican towns.

JANUARY 4, 1916

Sally and the boys are back. She accused me of feeling more for the Garcias than she did for our own son. Asked me why I go back there so often.

"Because no one else will."

"Those greasers shot Glenn," she said. "I want you to think on that."

"Well, we killed them. All nineteen of them, not one of whom was present when Glenn was shot."

"That doesn't make us even," she said.

"You're right," I said, "but we do not have that many family members, do we?"

"I wonder if I am beginning to hate you. But then I wonder if you would even notice."

"If you hate me it is because I have morals."

That left her speechless. I went to my office and put a few logs in the fireplace and pulled the sheets over the couch.

It is only now, since we have been sleeping apart these three months, that I wonder how I ever managed to have any feelings for her at all. She is still pretty, charming in her way. But if she has ever had a thought that did not in some way involve herself, I have not heard of it.

Chapter Nineteen
Eli/Tiehteti

1850

By summer we knew that the Penateka, the largest and wealthiest of all the Comanche bands, had been mostly wiped out. The previous year's smallpox epidemic had been followed by cholera—all spread by the forty-niners, who shat into the creeks—and a hard winter had finished off the survivors. By the time the first meadowlarks appeared, the Penateka—with the exception of a thousand or so stragglers—were rotting into the earth.

We moved our camp far north, into what was then still New Mexico, to get away from the sick Indians and the disease-carrying whites still crossing along the Canadian toward California. We were now in the territory of the Yap-Eaters and I had a hope I might run into Urwat and be able to pay him back, but I never saw him, as the Yap-Eaters had gone even farther north, into Shoshone territory.

Despite the extermination of ten thousand Comanches, the plains had never been more crowded. The displaced tribes—from the easterners like the Chickasaws and Delawares to the more local Wichitas and Osages—continued to be resettled in our hunting grounds. The buffalo were scarcer than anyone could remember and the spring hunts had not yielded enough meat or hides to carry us through the year. Toshaway and the other elders decided to put in all our chips; planning the largest raid in the band's history, which would bypass most of the settlements in Texas and go straight down into Mexico. Because of the size of the raid and the long distance, a number of women and boys would go along to keep the camps, and three hundred people in total, including Toshaway, Nuukaru, and Escuté, rode out in July and did not return until December.

I was left in the main ranchería, where, with the men gone and the buffalo scarce, the younger boys, whether they had gotten scalps or not, were kept patrolling and hunting all the time. There was a sense things were changing for the worse. The camp felt empty, everyone was missing a family member or two, and a general downheartedness had settled. The only good news was that the market for captives had improved—a white person could be sold back to the government at any of the new forts, sometimes for three hundred dollars or more. We bought several whites from the Yap-Eaters and took them to sell to the New Mexicans, who eventually sold them at the forts.

Hates Work never came back to my tipi, but gradually other girls began to, because their *notsakapʉ* or lovers were off raiding, and I was known to be a solitary type who didn't talk to the other young *tekʉniwapʉ*. Scalp or not, I was still a captive, and the other men saw nothing to gain by talking to me.

So the women would find me while I was out hunting or taking a nap and tell me things they didn't want anyone to hear. Who was sleeping with her friend's husband or with the *paraibo*. Who was planning to defect to the Yap-Eaters or start a new band. Who was going to elope with her *notsakapu* because his parents couldn't afford her bride-price, who was tired of being the third wife of some fat old subchief—who, by the way, was lying about something he'd done in combat—who had caught *pisipʉ* from a married man, was it worth paying for a cure?

One night someone came into the tipi and sat by the opening, looking for my pallet in the darkness. There was a sweet smell I didn't recognize, like honey, or maybe cinnamon.

"Who is it?" I said.

"Prairie Flower."

I poked the embers to get some light. She was possibly not as pretty as her sister, Hates Work, but she was so far above my bend that I guessed she had come to talk.

"I'm tired," I said.

She ignored me and took off her dress. She fell asleep so quickly afterward, nestled into me, that I wondered if that was all she wanted in the first place, someone to sleep next to while her boyfriend was off with Toshaway and the others. I fell asleep but only halfway. It was too dark to see her face, but she was warm and sweet-smelling and her skin was smooth. I lay for a long time breathing into her neck. I wanted to rut but I did not want to wake her up. Then I must have fallen asleep because later she was shaking me awake. She was putting her clothes on.

"Don't expect this ever to happen again, and don't tell anyone, either."

I wondered if I'd done a bad job. "That's also what your sister told me," I said.

"Well, I am not a slut like she is, so you can expect I'm telling the truth."

"She was also telling the truth."

"Then you are one of the lucky few who has only had her once."

"Huh," I said.

She adjusted her dress. "That's not true, really."

"You can get back under the robe," I said. "We don't have to do anything."

She thought about it, then did. I gave her as much space as I could.

"Good night," I said.

"It's been hard for you, with everyone being gone?"

"It's been hard for everyone."

"But you especially. Nʉʉkaru and Escuté are your only friends."

"That's not true."

"Who else, then?"

I shrugged. "What do you smell like?" I said, trying to change the subject.

"This? Cottonwood sap. The bud sap, you can only collect it in spring."

"It's nice," I said.

It was quiet.

"People are stupid," she said. "Everyone is from captives."

"I guess not everyone looks like it."

"What about Fat Wolf?"

"No, not really."

"Poor Tiehteti."

"Poor nothing," I said.

"Okay, I'm sorry."

"Time to sleep."

"I wonder when you'll stop being so nice."

"Time to sleep," I said again.

"You are nice," she said. "It's obvious. You don't order people around, you mostly skin your own animals, you—"

"Ask that *papi bo?a* how nice I am." I pointed above the pallet, where the scalp of the Delaware was hanging.

"It's a compliment."

A short while later she put her hand on my thigh. I was not quite sure what it meant. She moved her hand slightly higher. "Are you still awake?"

"Yes."

She pulled me on top of her and hitched her *kwasu* up. As usual it was too quick and then it was awkward as she tried to keep moving. I started to roll off but she held me.

"It's okay," she said. "Everyone is quick with me at first."

I was annoyed at how sure she was. Then I decided I wasn't. I fell asleep. When I woke up she was gone, but she came back the next night.

During the day we wouldn't speak but at night, after the fire had died to nothing, I would hear her rustling at the tipi flap and then she would be in my bed. By the third night I had memorized every inch of her, as if I were blind as a pup, though there were moments, if her hair was different, or her smell was different, when I was not sure it was her. The Comanches took this uncertainty for granted, which worked mainly to the advantage of the women, who could satisfy their needs without risking their standing, and less so for the men, who were often not sure who they'd conquered, or if maybe they had been conquered themselves and had done it with someone they hadn't wanted to. All skin was good at night, blotches invisible, crooked teeth straight, everyone was tall and beautiful and it was a fine kind of democracy; the women would not admit their names, and so a breast or ear or chin would be kissed to determine its shape, or the curve of a hip or collarbone, the softness of a belly, the length of a throat, everything had to be touched. The next day we would make a shape from the pictures we had gathered with our hands and mouths, watching the girls go by in the sun, wondering who it had been.

It had always been this way. There was a story about a beautiful young girl who was visited every night by a lover (which, as men, we were not allowed to do, but this had taken place in a different time) and, as her passion turned gradually to love, she began to wonder who this lover was; she knew every part but not the whole, and as time passed she became obsessed with knowing, so she might be with him during the day as well as night, that they might never be separate. One evening, just before her lover came to her, she blackened her hands with soot from the fire, in order that she might mark his back and have her answer. In the morning, when she rose to get water for her family, she saw her handprints on the back of her favorite brother, and she cried out and fled the tribe in shame, and her brother, who had never loved anyone more, ran after her. But she would not slow down, and he could not catch her, and the two of them streaked across the earth until finally she became the sun, and her brother the moon, and they could only be in the sky together at certain times and were never again allowed to touch.

As for Prairie Flower, she had something serious with a boy named Charges the Enemy, who was five or six years older than me but had gone on the long raid with Toshaway, Pizon, and the others. She was around sixteen, which the Comanches considered a marriageable age, but the fifty-horse price set for Hates Work had scared off most of Prairie Flower's suitors, which she considered a temporary advantage, as she knew that no men in the tribe could afford her, though she also knew that as soon as we became prosperous again, she would be purchased by some fat old chief, and her life as she knew it would be over.

Most of the girls quietly worried about this. Prairie Flower's hope was to remain unmarried until the age of twenty, a year longer than her sister, before some old man decided he would buy her as a wife. Charges the Enemy did not have fifty horses, or even twenty—he had about ten, she thought—and his family did not have many more; her father would never consider him a suitable match. In fact there were no young warriors with the capital her father required, Toshaway's generosity being an unheard-of exception, and so Prairie Flower was doomed to be the third or fourth wife of someone she would never love, the lowest in the domestic order, and once married she would live out her days scraping hides like a common *na?raiboo.*

Meanwhile, I had made friends with the bow. With buffalo in short supply, I was killing a deer, elk, or antelope every other day for camp meat, though like everyone else, I was riding farther and farther to find the animals. At one point in August I was gone for nearly five days and realized I could simply ride east until I reached the whites, but as I sat there looking out over the plains on my horse, leading a mule loaded with meat for the tribe, it occurred to me that I had nothing to go back to, no family except perhaps my father, who, if he was still alive, had made no effort to find me. Many of the white families were actively seeking their children and news of rewards spread quickly among the tribes. A month earlier, a free Negro from Kansas had ridden into the camp, taking everyone so completely by surprise that it was decided not to kill him. His wife and two children, also Negros, had been taken, and he was hoping to buy them back.

We did not have them but we knew they had been seen with another band to the west, and, after feeding him and allowing him and his horses to rest two nights, we directed him toward the *Noyʉkanʉʉ*. The only non-Indians we universally hated were the *Tʉhano*, or Texans, whom we always killed on sight. Other whites, or Negroes for that matter, were mostly judged on an individual basis, and if a man did something especially brave or clever—like surprising a camp full of Comanches in broad daylight—he would not only be allowed to live, but be treated as a guest of honor as long as he wanted to stay. Toshaway's father informed me that before the *Tʉhano* came, the Comanches had

had nothing against the whites—we had traded with the French and Spanish for hundreds of years—and that it was only the arrival of the *Tuhano,* who were greedy and violent, that had changed this. The whites knew this and a Texan, if caught by the Indians, would claim he was from New Mexico or Kansas. Coming from Texas would get you roasted over a slow fire. Even a knife was considered too quick for a Texan.

I stood there watching a blue front blow across the plain and decided to make my way back to camp. It occurred to me that I had not thought about going back to the whites in several months, and what I would be returning to was most likely an orphanage, or a job as a servant, and while the tribe considered me a grown man, the whites would have not thought any such thing. And of course there was Prairie Flower, who denied there was anything serious, but still came to my tipi every night. If I saw her carrying water, I would carry it for her, or help her collect firewood, or skin a deer I had killed for her family. Her father did not approve of me, though I was technically Toshaway's son, he preferred Escuté, who was older, and not white, and not a captive.

Most of the boys were embarrassed for me, especially because they knew that the moment Charges the Enemy returned, Prairie Flower would forget I existed, and Charges the Enemy, while he would probably not kill me, would certainly hurt me badly, a likelihood they repeatedly reminded me of, urging me, if not to stop seeing her, to at least not humble myself in public. But if I'd once thought her the inferior of her sister, I now thought the opposite. Prairie Flower was as light on her feet as a fawn, her eyes and cheeks and chest not as exaggerated as her sister's, but much finer, as if the Creator decided there ought to be nothing extra. I didn't mind humbling myself.

In the end, there were other things to worry about. We had enough to eat but it was the same every night; we were short of all our trade goods, of sugar, corn, and squash as we had no spare horses or hides to trade for them. We were short of lead and powder and screws to repair our guns; we were in cold, dry, unfamiliar country. The sense of order continued to slowly break down, as young boys who ought to have been playing were depended on to hunt, and old men were stuck doing the work of women. And perhaps it was this general lowness that had led Prairie Flower to first visit my tent. Or perhaps it was because in June, when it was presumed the raiders had reached Mexico, she had a series of dreams in which she had seen Charges the Enemy's scalped corpse, which was not something she could have told any other Comanche, as it was very bad medicine. If for some reason she had decided to share her dreams, many of the older people in the tribe would have blamed her for being a *bruja* and she would have been driven from the band or killed. Of course if anyone had witched Charges the Enemy it was me, though I did not believe in those things, and besides felt bad for him, as he had taken me hunting a few times, so I did not want to see him scalped, maybe just captured by the Mexicans, and put in prison, and kept there forever.

All in all, it was the greatest summer I had ever had, and despite everyone's blue mood, I was content in a way I had never been. I might be killed any day, by whites or hostile Indians, I might be run down by a grizzly or a pack of buffalo wolves, but I rarely did anything I didn't feel like doing, and maybe this was the main difference between the whites and the Comanches, which was the whites were willing to trade all their freedom to live longer and eat better, and the Comanches were not willing to trade any of it. I slept in the tipi when it was cool and in a brush arbor when it was warm, or under the stars, went hunting or wandering when I wanted, and had a girl, even if she also considered herself the girl of someone else. The only thing I really missed was fishing, as the Comanches would not eat fish unless they were starving. Though even on my hunting trips, when I could have fished, I didn't.

In October the older men of the tribe decided we ought to move south, into familiar territory, as winter would be much worse here, and food more scarce. Despite the fact the raiders had not yet returned, which was beginning to worry everyone, we packed the camp and left detailed instructions, in the form of hiero-glyphs carved into a tree, about where we were headed.

We set up close to our old campsite, ten miles north of the Canadian, expecting it to be occupied, as it was close to several well-known Indian trails, but it was empty and the grass was tall. It had been a wet year and there was plenty of forage to get our horse herd through the winter, which was a good sign, but no other horses had been grazing there, which was a bad sign, and the tribe went further into a depression, the con-sensus being that an enormous number of Comanches must have been destroyed, not just the Penateka, for a campsite this good to have gone unoccupied since we had left it.

When the raiding party finally returned in December, the only good news was that Toshaway, Escuté, and Nuukaru were still alive. They were all so pale and had all lost so much weight that when they first rode up, everyone thought they were spirits. Toshaway had nearly lost a foot to frostbite. Escuté had taken a ball through the shoulder early in the raiding and spent three months riding with it broken. He could barely raise his bow arm.

In June, they had captured eight hundred horses but there had been an ambush—the army and the Mexicans were working together now, instead of killing each other as they had always done—and nearly half the Kotsoteka warriors were killed or scattered. The army, along with several Ranger companies, had chased the remaining warriors deep into New Mexico.

While this was happening, the women's camp, which had been waiting for the warriors to return from Mexico, had been attacked by Mescalero Apaches, and either wiped out entirely or carried away as captives. The remaining bodies were so scattered by animals it was impossible to count them. Toshaway's daughter was among the lost, and of the three hundred Kotsoteka who'd ridden out, less than forty had returned, and, while no one would mention it in the same conversation, nearly a thousand horses had been lost as well, which meant that we had no surplus to trade and the winter would be even worse than expected. From that day until early spring, all the other noises were drowned out by crying and wailing, and half the women in camp had cuts on their faces and arms, many of them clipping off whole fingers to honor their dead family members.

Prairie Flower stopped seeing me for a while, as Charges the Enemy was known to have been killed, but had fallen behind the enemy lines so quickly that his body had not been recovered and was presumed to have been scalped and desecrated. She barely ate or left her tipi, but as they were not married, she could not even mourn in public, or tell anyone she had known when it happened, that she had witnessed his death just as clearly as if she had been there to see it.

Chapter Twenty
Jeannie McCullough

1942

Phineas called her to Austin a week after she finished high school. It was May and already hot,
one hundred in McCullough, ninety in Austin, it would
be nice to make a trip to Barton Springs, to lie in the
grass and watch the people swimming—flirting cou-
ples, young men and their footballs—to spend the day
by herself in a place she was not known. She wouldn't,
of course. There were people you could never figure—
her great-grandfather for instance—but that was not
her. *I am boring,* she thought. *Predictable. But brave
in my own way, brave despite* . . . she did not like to
think of the North, she did not like to think of her time
there. She had been miserable and she had left. She did
not mind taking risks when she wanted something,
though no one else understood this. When she wanted

something, she was truly brave. And yet no one else knew. So it didn't matter.

The train made its way to Austin. There were more cars on the highway, double or triple what she had seen in her childhood, most Texans now lived in cities, they said. You would not have known it in Dimmit County. She watched a truck with a half-dozen Mexicans in the back, their knees scrunched around a pile of scrap iron, the driver weaving and changing lanes, one miscalculation and they would all be spilled to the pavement. She wondered why they allowed themselves to be treated that way. They're animals, is what her father said. On Election Day he would take her down to the south end of McCullough, dusty streets, tin shacks, wreaths of chilies and goat meat hanging with the flies buzzing everywhere. Her father would hand out slabs of beef from an ice chest in the back of his truck, cases of warm beer; he would pay their poll taxes and show them how to mark the ballot. *Gracias, patrón. Gracias.* They were more gracious than niggers—that was another thing he always said.

The windows in the train were open and her face was cool in the breeze but she was sweating under her dress, under her arms. It was the time of the year the heat became its own entity, a creeping misery. No. It was like a sledgehammer on the head of a steer. It would only get worse until September. From the other side of the car, three soldiers were stealing glances, one of them was much older, the other two were Mexican, barely her age, afraid to look. Most draft boards had not yet begun to call up whites, though some, like her brothers, had volunteered.

She studied her reflection, imposed as it was on the dry rushing landscape beyond the window. *I am pretty,* she thought. There were prettier, but she was well above average. *Phineas will offer me a job.* A sort of special adviser, a confidante. But that was not possible, either. She was not even qualified to be a secretary; you needed shorthand for that. There was nothing she really knew how to do, nothing she did well, she was a dabbler. Pointless. If she vanished from the earth that instant, it would not have made a lick of a difference to anyone.

Maudlin, maudlin. She leaned her head against the glass and felt the shaking of the train. *That's not even your word,* she thought, *that's from Jonas.* She could see the hills to the north, the Llano uplift. The Colonel had known those things: this rock is ten million years old, this other two hundred, here is a fern contained in stone. The soldiers were staring at her openly now. When she was young, a year or two ago, she would have turned and stared them down, but now she let them drink her up, have their fantasies, or so she imagined. In a few months they would be off to war, and many would not come back, their final rest in a foreign place. Perhaps all three of them, their lines come to an end. She wondered who would survive, she guessed the bigger one, though you could not tell. It was not like the old days, it was a falling bomb and a hundred dead at once, all mothers' sons. An emotion came over her, and she wondered if she might give them something, cigarettes or a soda pop, but those were just tokens, money would not help them. There was only one thing and she allowed herself to think about this for a while, shifted her legs and adjusted her dress, it was just a thought, out of the question, she had never given herself to anyone. But what did it matter, truly? There were times she was desperate, absolutely desperate to be shed of her virginity, but no, she thought, impossible, it could not be some pimple-faced soldier, or that older, more scary one with the patch of razor burn along his neck as if chafed by a rope. He will be the one to die. She felt it instantly. It excited her. It was all very dramatic.

Then she felt guilty. She thought of her brothers, who were still in America, training in Georgia. Clint would do something to show off and be killed. Paul would be more careful, though easily convinced to do something risky, especially if a friend were in trouble. She prayed he would have no friends. Otherwise he would surely be killed. It was Jonas: he was the only one among her brothers who acted like a rich man's son. He would not take any risk if someone else might do it instead. And he was an officer.

Outside, the grass was already brown from the heat. To the south, the flat Texas plain stretched down to Mexico; to the north the escarpment began. A yellow tint of summer haze. A mule pulling a plow. She did not know why, it was plain to see there would be no rain for weeks, the dryness made you wonder if it would ever rain again.

Her uncle Phineas was a powerful man, head of the Railroad Commission, more powerful than the governor, they said. He was not really her uncle, but great-uncle, and he determined how much oil could be pumped in all of Texas. Somehow that controlled the price. She supposed it was like cattle. In a drought everyone had to sell quickly so the price went down, though when beef got scarce the price went up again. Except the packers were now interrupting this—buying cheap from distressed ranchers while raising the price on the other end—telling the city buyers, who did not know better, that a drought meant scarcity. The packers were where the money had gone; it was no longer made on grass, but in cement buildings. Armour and Swift. Her father hated them. Meanwhile Texas made more oil than anyplace on the earth. You did not hear people who made oil complaining very much.

She opened her eyes. She was on the floor of the great room, watching the fire. Her arm, the skin old and so thin the light seemed to pass right through it, the watch askew on her wrist. Perhaps she might inch just one finger? No. Her eyes moved around the room and settled on a globe next to the divan. It was no older than she was, but many of the countries had already ceased to exist. No hope for a single person. She could see that the mortar had begun to crumble in the fireplace; the stones would soon come apart. *When did that happen?* she wondered, and then she thought: *I did not expect to live this long myself.* Except that was lie. She had always known it was the others who wouldn't make it.

Death the common companion; it was not like the settled places of the North. Jonas sensed it and saved himself. *You did not know better. Or did and thought you could escape it.* She watched the ember on the hearth. She wondered if she had really known that about Paul and Clint, or if it was another trick of the mind, the memory recording something that had never been true, like a magnetic tape that had been tampered with.

Phineas had been good to her. It was hard to imagine the power he'd had: as OPEC would years later, the Railroad Commission controlled the price of oil in the entire world. Phineas had become enormously wealthy. He could make or break any oilman in the state, any politician—you might drill all the wells you wanted, but you could not pump a drop without his say-so.

The commission's offices were in a drab state office building; the only thing giving it away were the cars—Packards, a Cadillac Sixteen, Lincoln Zeyphrs, and Continentals. Phineas had a corner office, the walls lined with his trophies, the Colonel's Yellowboy Winchester, a brace of Colt Peacemakers, plaques from the Southwest Cattle Raisers and the Old Trail Driver's Association. There were pictures with elephants and lions and antlered game of every description, he had hunted on five continents. There were pictures with Teddy Roosevelt in Cuba, Phineas smiling broadly, more sure of himself than the old man.

He was seventy-five now and, when seated, still gave off an impression of power. He looked nothing like the

Colonel: a tall man with thick white hair, expensive suits, beautiful secretaries. He did not wear cowboy boots or a bolo tie—those were affectations of a later generation—he was more like an eastern banker.

But his health was failing. His legs were swollen, his heart unsteady. He would never live to see his father's age, that was plain.

Jeannie watched the secretary as she left coffee and a tray of kolaches. A brunette with violet eyes, high cheekbones, a perfect figure—she would never be pretty enough. Phineas asked about the news from Paul and Clint, congratulated her on finishing school. Did she have plans? Not really. She settled into a chair overlooking the capitol and downtown Austin. She was only five hours from the ranch but it was a different country entirely.

When the secretary had closed the door, something in Phineas's manner changed and she knew he meant to talk business.

"I suspect it is obvious to both of us that the ranch is losing money."

She nodded, though it had not been obvious: beef had been climbing steadily since the war began.

"I lived on that land before it was settled," he continued. "I buried my mother and father and brother there. And now my nephew—your father—is running it into the ground. He is content to burn through our money as if a fresh supply will come up like grass in the springtime. Why the old man left him majority holder, I have no idea." He leaned back in his chair. "Have you seen the books?"

"I don't think so," she said.

"Of course not." He beckoned her around to his side of the desk, where a ledger was sitting open. He pointed to a number: a little over four hundred thousand dollars. "Last year's cattle sales. It seems like a large number, and it is, because your father sells a lot of cattle. But the next thirty-seven pages are debits." He skipped forward, first a page at a time, then two or three at a time, until he reached the end. He pointed to another number, just under eight hundred thousand dollars. "The ranch's expenses are nearly double its income."

There is some mistake, she thought, but she kept quiet. Instead she asked: "How long has it been like that?"

"Oh, twenty years, at least. The only thing keeping us in the black is the oil and gas, but the wells are old and shallow and the Colonel, quite wisely, leased only a few thousand acres, trusting that we would lease the rest at higher prices. Which we have not yet done."

He paused again.

"For reasons I do not quite understand, our state has a club of wealthy children who like to play at being cattlemen. As if the term can even exist today. Bob Kleberg has put it in your father's ear that with technology, better bulls, and a few bump gates, he can make money selling beef, which is a feat Kleberg has not even managed on his own land. As you may or may not know, the King Ranch, all million acres of it, was on the verge of bankruptcy until Humble Oil loaned them three million dollars. Which was a pity, because I had made Alice King a very generous offer. And I have always liked the coast."

He looked for her reaction but she sat quietly, so he continued.

"Your father is counting on the fact that I will not be around forever, because he thinks that once he gets my money, his problems are over. What he does not seem to realize—or care about—is that even *with* my money, the ranch will still go bankrupt—it is just a question of how many millions your father will go through until it does."

She knew then why she had been called: he wanted her to betray her father. To her surprise she did not object to this as much as she might have hoped. Her father, for all his rough-and-tumble image, was a dandy. She had always known this, perhaps because the

Colonel was always pointing it out. Earning money was the furthest thing from her father's mind, he wanted to be on magazine covers, like the Colonel had been. She had always known that the Colonel did not respect him and now she saw that Phineas—the other famous member of the family—did not respect him, either.

"Shall we get lunch? Or can you handle a little more business?"

"I'm fine," she said.

"Good. Tell me what you know about the depletion allowance."

"Nothing," she said.

"Of course. That's what your father knows about it as well. The depletion allowance is one of the things that makes the oil business as far from the cattle business as the North Pole is from the South. At the moment, it says that if you drill for oil, you can write twenty-seven point five percent of your proceeds off as a loss."

"Because you spent money to drill the wells?"

"That is certainly what we tell the newspapers, though in general we have already written off about sixty percent of those costs as intangibles. The depletion allowance is something entirely different. Every year a well produces oil, even though it is putting money into your pocket, it is simultaneously reducing your tax burden."

"You're making a profit, but calling it a loss."

She could see this pleased him.

"It sounds dishonest," she added.

"It is the opposite. It is the law of the United States."

"Still."

"Still nothing. The law was put there for a reason. People will raise cattle even though they will lose money doing it—you do not need to incentivize the cattle business. Oil, on the other hand, is expensive to find and even more expensive to get out of the ground. It is an enormously risky enterprise. And so if the government wants us to find oil, it must encourage us to do so."

"So we should drill."

"Of course we should drill. How your father can still be thinking about cows is a mystery. Every bit of profit we made in the old days was based on overstocking, on using up a thousand years of grass in a decade. The way we used to fill those pastures, it was like those file cabinets there, touching on both sides, it was mining for grass. But, as you must know from listening to me this long, facts are boring, especially to men like your father. Because what does every coonass wildcatter do when he makes his first million? He buys a ranch and stocks it with Herefords, in the same way he acquires a Packard or a beautiful wife.

Though he does not expect any of them to be profitable investments.

"In the meantime, the rest of us have no choice but to exist in the present. I'm getting calls from the secretary of the navy, who is telling me he does not want a single production control in place. He wants drilling, drilling, and more drilling—the only thing we have over the Germans is our oil—they are building a pipeline from here to New Jersey, where all the refineries are, and they want every goddamn drop we have."

He was looking out the window; he was talking again but she could not follow the thread—it was more taxes—and she was beginning to feel sick, she could not bring this up to her father, it was out of the question. *This war won't last forever,* that was what her father was always saying, *things will go back to the way they were.* She wondered what it must be like to be her father, taking himself so seriously, imagining himself a kind of royalty, though from a country no one had heard of. Of course, in his defense, people had lately begun to agree with him. The Colonel had been dead long enough that her father was now interesting to reporters; they would visit and he would tell them the Colonel's stories, jumbled together with his own, the time he and the Colonel had charged a house full of Mexican horse thieves during the bandit wars of 1915. It was said he had once shot a man in cold blood.

Regardless, her father *was* part of a dying breed, for better or worse, most of the old-time ranching families had gone bankrupt. Most people now lived in cities— she could still not get her head around that one—the days of the frontier were gone, long gone, though there were those who preferred not to admit it. As for her father, with his heavy face, his big hands, he had finally become what he had hoped for since childhood, the representative of a bygone era, an emissary from a lost time. That he himself had not lived during this time was irrelevant—he would take the reporters out to the corrals and put on a show, rope and cut for them, he had begun to keep older, gentler horses just for visitors, which would have been unthinkable in the old days, because horses cost money and they were for work, not play.

An automobile horn on the street brought her back. Phineas was still talking.

" . . . even if most of the Hill Country still doesn't have electricity, even if one does encounter the occasional bucktoothed child on a donkey, this war has dragged the rest of the world into the modern age. The Polish cavalry smashed itself against German tanks, every cannibal in the South Pacific has now seen a

Zero, and if there was doubt in any mind that the era of the horse was over, that question is now settled."

She nodded. It was obvious even to her.

"Jeannie," he said, "it will not be long before we look back on this time and think we barely used any oil at all. Which is why we need to get some wells sunk on that land. I am tired of lending your father money."

The next day she took the train home. It stopped for a long time in San Antonio, the air still, the sun beating against the car. She lay against the window, trying to breathe slowly, thinking of cool things, the stock tank, the spring at the casa mayor. There were soldiers everywhere, Mexicans sweating through their uniforms, heads hanging numbly, sweat pooling, their only hope that the train might move again, they were like steers on their way to Fort Worth. Thousands had been abandoned to the Japanese, who were cutting off their heads with swords. Though MacArthur himself had escaped. A little too proudly, she thought.

She searched their faces but they were all looking down. The walking dead. How many were not even men yet? She was tired of being alone, she imagined her father's angry face, *I gave it to a soldier*, the great burden carried away. Clint and Paul had gone to a house in Carrizo. Her father had known about it beforehand. *But I am not allowed.*

When she was younger and found her father working in his study she would sit next to his chair and read, or hang around his neck and look over his shoulder, and finally he would turn and silently give her a kiss, the signal to leave him alone.

That was all he had. A hug and a kiss. Though he would kiss a horse as well, give months to understanding it, more than his own daughter.

Phineas was just using her, that was true, but he had always made time for her, even when she was young; she must have been tiresome and yet he'd made a point of teaching her things. To her father, she was just in the way. An inconvenience. A thing that might have been a son.

It was all an exaggeration, it was not the entire truth, but it made her furious, the nights she'd spent alone in the house, her father and brothers in the pastures. Things had improved since Clint and Paul left, but still. *He loves you,* she thought, *but he prefers not to think about you.* What did he prefer? Horses. Cows. Women, perhaps, though if so she hadn't heard about it. She decided if she ever had children, she would not leave them alone for a single minute.

"I won't have children anyway," she said out loud.

The Negro porter in the doorway looked up, then looked away, embarrassed. The train began to move. She wondered what she would say to her father.

When she was sixteen she had kissed one of the vaqueros, out in the stables he was supposed to be cleaning; they had stood there for ten minutes, she could feel his tongue move lightly inside her mouth. She spent the whole night thinking about him, his cheekbones and soft eyelashes, but when she went to see him the next day, he would not let her near. A week later he was gone. She knew they had not been seen; it was as if her father had merely sensed it—as if he had sensed something was making her happy—and ruined it.

Meanwhile he did not care if the family declined. He cared only for himself. Eventually they would be bankrupt and all they had ever done would be forgotten; they would be no different from the Garcias, the children of strangers in their ruined house, a young girl in a grave. She leaned against the train window and listened to the tracks rumble beneath her, it would all come to an end.

No. She would not let it. She did not know how she would stop him, but she was as sure of this as she had ever been of anything; Phineas was old, her father was a fool, and Jonas cared only about himself. Paul and Clint were happy savages, running around without a thought in their heads. *It is up to me,* she thought. *I will have to do something.*

Jorge picked her up at the station in Carrizo. She didn't feel like talking so she rode in the backseat, which she didn't normally do, she wasn't inclined to make people feel like servants. But Jorge wasn't bothered. He seemed relieved, even. He liked being alone with his thoughts just as she did, going for a drive to think, his own life, same as her, working through problems in his mind. Somehow this embarrassed her.

As they came up the caliche driveway, the house appeared at the top of the hill, the sun blinding white on the limestone, the dark green oaks and elms, the sky a hot pale blue. The third floor would be unbearable, the second floor only slightly better: she would be sleeping on her porch tonight, ice water on the sheets and two fans blowing. There was a black coupe parked in front that she recognized as her grandmother's. The driver, a white man, was sitting on the porch by himself, far away from the vaqueros who were noisily taking their supper.

The curtains were drawn against the sun; the house smelled of hot stone. She went upstairs and changed out of her sweaty dress, fixed her hair and face, then went down to join her father and grandmother in the dining room.

Her father smiled and got up to kiss her hello and she knew immediately something was wrong. She wondered if one of her brothers had been hurt, then reminded herself they had not even left the country yet. Of course that meant nothing: one of their vaqueros had lost his son in basic training, run over by a jeep on a military base. It all went through her head in an instant; she dismissed it just as quickly. They would not be sitting for supper if something had happened to Paul or Clint.

Her grandmother, weaker even than Phineas, did not get up; Jeannie greeted her and kissed her cheek.

"How was your trip?"

"Hot," she said.

"And Phineas?"

"He's well."

Her father, who had no use for Uncle Phineas, said, "Your grandmother was just telling me she's spoken to the people at Southwestern in Georgetown."

She nodded.

"You can start there in August."

"Oh, I'm not interested in that," she said cheerfully, as if they were asking her opinion.

A look went between her father and his mother and he said: "Jeannie, it's unpleasant, but we all have our jobs in life. Mine is to make sure this ranch stays above water. Gramammy's there is to make sure I don't make any mistakes." He smiled indulgently at her grandmother. "Yours is to get a proper education."

He does not respect her, she realized. All the air went out of her; her talk with Phineas was just talk, it meant nothing. She felt cold. She would end up at Southwestern; she would make the best of it.

"You won't have to go so far away this time," her grandmother was saying.

Later she would not recall making any choice, the words seemed to come out on their own: "I am not going to be a secretary."

"You don't have to," said her father.

"Or a teacher."

"We all have our obligations, Jeannie."

"Phineas and I were just talking about that same thing," she said brightly. She took a drink of water.

"Well, it is true," he said.

"He showed me the ledger."

Her father was beginning to say something else but then her words caught up with him. She intended to stare him down but couldn't and instead she spoke to her plate. "In fact, the ranch is not above water. It is quite the opposite."

She looked up; her father's face showed nothing. Out of the corner of her eye, she saw her grandmother trying to get her attention.

"I know what we lose on the cattle."

"Well, you shouldn't spend so much time listening to old Phineas," he said. He tried to smile again, but couldn't.

She began to feel sick; she wondered if she had caught a fever on the train.

" . . . this ranch is not the right place for a young lady with your talents," her father was saying. "You'll report to college, which is an opportunity I myself never had, at the end of summer."

"Your life is no harder than mine," she said. "You ride a twenty-thousand-dollar horse but you act like we live in the poorhouse. We lose four hundred thousand dollars a year on your cattle. Phineas says he's tired of lending you money. Something will have to be done."

There it was: she'd declared her betrayal. He was saying *you will leave the table, you will leave the table right now* and she said: "I will not." She couldn't have anyway; she was sure her legs would not hold her. "Every day you pretend you are supporting the family, when all you are doing is spending the family's money."

"It is my money," he said. "It is not your money; you have no say in this, you are a child."

"It is the Colonel's money. You did not earn a dime of it."

"You will stop."

"We have not had supper in two weeks. Why? Because you are playing with your horses. Before that it was almost six weeks. The oil is the only thing allowing you to do this."

She expected to be slapped, but her father seemed to calm down and he said, "The oil pays for improvements to the land, honey. It pays so we don't have to sleep in the mud at roundup, so we can just drive home and sleep in real beds at night. And that airplane, because we can't hire enough men to check those pastures from horseback anymore."

"Then perhaps we should stop doing roundup altogether," she said. "As it would save us a great deal of money."

Then he got up. He squared himself and stepped toward her, but nothing happened. He turned and walked out of the room. She could hear his footsteps slow as he reminded himself the house was still his, his boots went down the hall, past the parlor and into the foyer, then out the front door, slamming it behind him.

"That was very stupid," said her grandmother.

She shrugged, wondered if she'd destroyed every-thing she knew; then had a feeling it had never mat-tered anyway. The day before, an hour before, to speak to her father, to speak to anyone like this would have been unthinkable.

"I didn't realize you were afraid of him," she said. "Is it because the Colonel didn't leave you anything?"

Her grandmother ignored her. "You can't stay here, Jeannie. Especially after this."

Jeannie had a feeling she would be content if she never spoke to her grandmother again, or to anyone else in the family.

"Your father is not going to let you run this ranch."

"There *isn't* any ranch. We're living on minerals and borrowed money."

"Did Phineas write you that little speech? Because if you think a woman will have any place in his schemes, you're mistaken." She got a nasty look. "In more ways than one."

"I guess we'll see." She was thinking about her father, how thin he was; she knew he no longer slept through the night.

Her grandmother set down her knife and fork, arranging them carefully and smoothing the tablecloth, and took a sip of her sherry. "I have always known that you find me tiresome," she said. "You think it is my nature, or my disposition, or you have likely never thought about it. But when I decided to move here, I found I had a choice between being liked and having a say. That's the choice you'll have to make as well. They will either love you and not respect you, or they will respect you and not love you."

"Things are changing."

"It may appear that way, but when the war is over, the men will come back, and it will go back to the way it has always been."

"I guess we'll see," she repeated.

"This place," said her grandmother. She waved her hand, dismissing not only Jeannie but everything else, the house, the land, their good name. "I'm a member of the wealthiest family in four counties, but they still give me dirty looks when I vote."

It was quiet. It occurred to Jeannie that for years she had wanted nothing more than this—for her grandmother to treat her like a confidante, a real person—but now she wanted nothing of the sort. She guessed she ought to feel privileged; instead she was embarrassed. Embarrassed that her grandmother was bullied by her own son, embarrassed that she would complain about her sex; what should have been sympathy somehow turned to anger, her grandmother ought to be out among the right people, solving the social problem, for if not her, then who? It was weakness, the entire family, and she felt a lifetime of fear and respect burn off as quickly as it had for her father. She sat up straight, smoothed her dress, she would be alone in life, that was clear, but right now she did not mind.

"You are not going to find a husband here who understands that we are halfway through the twentieth century. Do you understand?"

"I'll end up like you, you mean."

"That's exactly what I mean. Married to men like your father or your grandfather or your brothers. To the sort of men who would choose to live out here, you will just be a place to get warm."

"That's not going to happen."

"You won't have a choice, Jeannie."

Chapter Twenty-one
Diaries of Peter McCullough

MARCH 10, 1916

Yesterday Pancho Villa crossed the border into New Mexico, killing twenty. Today, hardly a white man to be seen without a pistol or slung rifle, even to buy groceries.

The Germans have promised to reinforce Mexican troops with German infantry should they choose to cross the border. Whole town in a frenzy; we are only ten miles from the river.

I do not point out there is little likelihood of the Kaiser sending troops to McCullough Springs when he is losing them ten thousand a day in France. I do not point out that the number of Americans killed in Columbus is the same as the number of Tejanos shot in bar ditches on any given night in South Texas. I do not point these things out because everyone seems happy with the news of this new threat; neighbors who didn't speak are suddenly friendly, wives have new reasons to make love with their husbands, disobedient children do their schoolwork and come home early for dinner.

Four Mexicans found shot outside town, all teenagers. No one is sure who they are or who killed them. The vaqueros think they are *fuereños*, men from the interior of Mexico, though how they can deduce this from a bloated corpse is beyond me. Incident not mentioned in newspaper. If it were four dead mules, there would have been an investigation, but there is nothing except general grumbling about the burial costs.

MARCH 14, 1916

Yet more blood on our hands and Charles has been taken to Carrizo. He was in town buying supplies when he ran into Dutch Hollis. Though it was only noon, Dutch was quite drunk and in front of a lunchtime crowd of onlookers accused our family of various crimes (of which we are certainly guilty), including engineering the death of the Garcias to gain their land.

After a short struggle Dutch got the better of him; Charles went to the truck and returned with his pistol. Dutch may or may not have reached for his knife (a folding jackknife in a pouch, same as all the men here carry). Charles shot him in the face.

Our caporal Garza arrived in time to see the final act: *Madonna, you should have seen it, his hand did not even tremble.* He related this expecting I would be proud.

Shortly after getting home, Charles saddled his horse and rode for Mexico. The Colonel and I caught him a few miles short of the river and convinced him to come back.

"It'll be all right," I said to him, as we returned.

He shrugged.

"We'll muddle through." He did not say anything. I felt the old impotence rising within me—what was the point of my even existing—or so everyone else seems to think.

"He had it coming," said Charles. "He's been talking like that all over town."

"With his brother dying . . ."

"His brother? How about *my* brother?" He kicked his horse and caught up to the Colonel, who was riding ahead of us. They nodded to each other, did not speak, some wordless understanding, the same as my father and Phineas. My skin began to tingle . . . it occurred to me that I was the one who ought to be fleeing to Mexico. . . .

Was he right? He and Sally seem to think the same way . . . is a near death equal to a death?

When we returned to the house, Sheriff Graham was waiting. Charles, bluffing over, turned white. Graham told us there was no hurry. He was thirsty.

The four of us spent the rest of the evening on the gallery drinking whiskey and watching the sunset, the three of them sitting together and chatting easily about how to best handle the incident, the sky going its typical blood red, which to me alone seemed symbolic, as I was sitting off a small distance from the others.

To listen to the three of them talk about the death of Dutch Hollis, you might have thought there had been some accident, a lightning strike, flash flood, the hand of God. Not my son's. *Had to do it, acted on instinct,* the sheriff just nodding away, sipping our whiskey, my father refilling his glass.

Considered interrupting them to note that the entire history of humanity is marked by a single inexorable movement—from animal instinct toward rational thought, from inborn behavior toward acquired knowledge. A half-grown panther abandoned in the wilderness will grow up to be a perfectly normal panther. But a half-grown child similarly abandoned will grow up into an unrecognizable savage, unfit for normal society. Yet there are those who insist the opposite: that we are creatures of instinct, like wolves.

Once darkness had fallen and all were convinced of my son's righteousness, Graham drove Charles back to Carrizo, all agreeing it was best if Charles spent a night in jail for appearance's sake. Glenn meanwhile has been keeping his distance. He is confused by Charlie's actions, to say the least.

MARCH 15, 1916

Went to see Dutch Hollis's body before they bury him. He was lying in Graham's back shed with several blocks of ice. He was unshaven, had not been washed; his face and clothes were filthy and clotted with blood and, like all the dead, he had lost control of his waste. Not long ago, twenty years maybe, he was a child reaching for his mother . . . a boy becoming a man . . . I had a sudden memory of him playing the fiddle, together with his brother, at the Midkiffs' house. I peered into the dark spot, just at the edge of his eyebrow, an intricate machine, broken forever; there had been words and music . . . we had put a stop to that.

There was something shiny inside his shirt, a woman's locket . . . I lifted it but could not quite make it out in the dimness. I broke the chain, jerking his head in the process. Then I left the room quickly and walked back into the light.

When I got home (heart racing the entire time, as if I'd committed some great felony, as if the crime was not killing him but taking his locket), there was no picture, no message, no piece of hair: the locket was empty. I took it to the Garcias' and buried it there, along with our other victims, the whole time expecting I was being followed, the criminal feeling lingering. There are those born to hunt and those born to be hunted . . . I have always known I was the latter.

MARCH 16, 1916

Charles has returned, but he is not allowed to leave any of the four counties in which our property extends. He strides about with his chin up; I find it difficult to look at him. Judge Poole assures us there will be no indictment. In fact he and the sheriff and my father went calling at the homes of those likely to be empaneled.

Would like to report I have been torn between a hope he might receive punishment and hope he'll be exonerated. I have not. I want only for him to be acquitted.

And yet his crimes multiply . . . this the son I raised with my own hands.

Have been in to buy supplies, keeping my hat pulled low, terrified the entire time I would run into Esther Hollis, Dutch and Bill's mother, but this evening, with enormous relief, I remembered that she has been dead several years.

No one seems particularly bothered, least of all the Mexicans. The *coraje*, they say, the heat and dust and thorns. Even horses get it. For the grandson of a great *patrón*—a man with blood—to get the *coraje*, it is only to be expected. Especially when a man slanders his family. And in public . . . In truth it was the only reasonable action.

Meanwhile both Hollis brothers now lie rotting. Impossible to believe we are truly in God's image. Something of the reptile in us yet, the caveman's allegiance to the spear. A vestige of our time in the swamps. And yet there are those wish to return. Be more like the reptile, they say. Be more like the snake, lying in wait. Of course they do not say *snake*, they say *lion*, but there is little difference in character between the two, only in appearance.

MARCH 24, 1916

Grand jury refused to indict.

APRIL 2, 1916

Despite Dutch Hollis, despite the Garcias, our name carries more weight than ever. Where I expect bitterness, I receive respect; where I expect jealousy, I receive encouragement. Do not steal from the McCulloughs—they will kill you; do not slander the McCulloughs—they will kill you. My father thinks this the proper state of affairs. I tell him this is the tenth century of the second millennium.

In the end it is as he says—they think we are made of different stuff. If it ever occurred to them that we eat and bleed the same as they do, they would run us down with torches and pitchforks. Or, more accurately, holy water and wooden stakes.

In news of the broader suffering, Villa's men attacked the barracks at Glenn Spring yesterday. My sympathies for the Mexican people aside, my father and I are both anxious for the arrival of our Lewis gun, which fires ten .30-caliber rounds per second. A true blessing for the few holding out against the many. Due to war in Europe they are running a severe backlog.

Serious talk that the Mexican government is planning an assault on Laredo—Carranza's troops are massing across the river. The Mexicans believe we ought to hew to the original border (the Nueces). Texans believe the border belongs another three hundred miles south, somewhere around Durango.

Sally wants to move to San Antonio or Dallas or even Austin—anywhere but here.

"We are perfectly safe," I told her. "Neither the Huns nor the Mexican army will be approaching our gate anytime soon."

"That is not what I care about," she said.

"Is this about the boys?"

"It's about all three of them. The two living and the one buried."

"They will be fine."

"Until they do something like this again. Or until someone's brother finds them."

"There are no more Hollises left. We have seen to that."

"There will be someone else," she said.

Considered mentioning this was her reward for marrying into the family of the great Eli McCullough, but said nothing. All the energy had left me.

"My nephews in Dallas have guns," she said. "They use them to hunt deer. They go to school, they chase after the wrong sort of girls, but . . ." She choked up. "I went to see the boy . . ."

"Dutch?" I said gently.

" . . . they had him laid out in a shed behind Bill Graham's office. It was a disgrace."

I did not say anything. Things have been so bad between us for so long and every time I have had hope, she has smashed it. I looked away from her and closed myself off.

"You might be staying here alone, Pete. I have lost all the sons I care to lose."

Chapter Twenty-two
Eli/Tiehteti

Spring 1851

To white ears, the names of the Indians lacked any sort of dignity or sense and made it that much harder to figure why they ought to be treated as humans rather than prairie niggers. The reason for this was that the Comanches considered the use of a dead person's name taboo. Unlike the whites, billions of whom shared the same handful of names, all interchangeable in the end, a Comanche name lived and died with a single person.

A child was not named by his parents, but by a relative or a famous person in the tribe; maybe for a deed that person had done, maybe for an object that struck their fancy. If a particular name was not serving well, the child might be renamed; for instance, Charges the Enemy had been a small and timid child and it was thought that giving him a braver name might cure these problems, which it had. Some people in the tribe were renamed a second or third time in adult life, if their friends and family found something more interesting to call them. The owner of the German captive Yellow Hair, whose birth name was Six Deer, was renamed Lazy Feet as a teenager, which stuck to him the rest of his life. Toshaway's son Fat Wolf was so named because his namer had seen a very fat wolf the previous night, and being an interesting sight and not a bad name it had stuck. Toshaway's name meant Bright Button, which had also stuck with him since birth, but that seemed a strange thing to call him so I thought of him as Toshaway. Spanish-sounding names were also common, though they often had no particular meaning—Pizon, Escuté, Concho—there was a warrior named Hisoo-ancho who had been captured at the age of seven or eight, whose Christian name was Jesus Sanchez, and, as that was all he would answer to, that was what he was called.

Many Comanche names were too vulgar to repeat in print and thus, when the situation required, were changed by whites. The chief who led the famous raid on Linnville in 1840 (in which a group of five hundred warriors sacked a warehouse full of fine clothing and made their escape dressed in top hats, wedding gowns, and silk shirts) was named Po-cha-na-quar-hip, meaning Cock That Stays Hard Forever. But neither this nor the more delicate translation, Erection That Will Not Go Down, could possibly be printed in newspapers, so it was decided to call him Buffalo Hump. He was thusly referred to until he died, many years later, attempting to learn farming on a reservation, having lost both his land and his good name to the whites, though in his own mind he remained Cock That Stays Hard Forever.

The medicine man who, along with Quanah Parker, led the entire Comanche nation against the whites in the Red River War of 1874 was named Isahata?i, meaning Coyote Pussy. The newspapers called him Ishtai, Eshati, and Eschiti, no translation offered. Toshaway had a nephew called Tried to Fuck a Mare, a name acquired in adolescence, and Hates Work, as previously mentioned, was originally called Single Bird. The Comanches were a good-natured sort and names were accepted with humor, though after Tried to Fuck a Mare got his first scalp and it was decided to change his name to Man on a Hill, he was not heard to complain.

By February the tribe was starving. There had not been a big buffalo kill in over a year, and most of the local deer, elk, and antelope had been hunted down over the winter. The few animals still alive moved only at night, surviving on twigs and dry brush. By then we had taken to tracking packrats back to their nests and eating their stashes of dried fruits and nuts, along with the rats themselves if we could catch them, and everyone in the tribe knew that the very young, the very old, and the sick would soon begin to die, and they would have, had we not discovered a buffalo herd beginning to drift north.

Everyone took this as a sign that our bad luck had ended, and the Creator-of-All-Things had forgiven us. By the time the first Spring Beauties appeared we had replenished our stores of meat and hides and begun to look forward to the summer, when the weather would be warm, though this also meant that the women in the band were put to double work preparing all the hides, so that they would be ready by the time the Comanchero traders arrived.

In May it was time to go raiding again. A third of the band had been killed the previous year, most of its horse wealth lost, and if this summer's raids were not successful, it was not clear how much longer we would survive. Toshaway would go again, though Escuté, who still could not quite draw his bow, was ordered to stay in camp, and I would be sent in his place. Nuukaru was also going but, unlike the other young braves, he was quiet about the deeds he would commit.

"Don't look so down in the mouth," said Escuté. "You can bring back a beautiful Mexican girl and listen to me fuck her."

Nʉʉkaru shook his head.

"Let me guess. You have a bad feeling."

"Stop," he said, indicating me.

Escuté looked over: "This one always has a bad feeling. Don't listen to him."

"I had it about the last one, too."

"Ah, the great *puha tenahpʉ*. I had almost forgotten."

"Things are changing," he said. "Whether or not we admit it. The Penateka . . ."

"Fuck the fucking Penateka. They were the white man's *tai?i* and they got what was coming to them."

"They were four times our size."

"And they were the white man's bitch and got all his diseases."

"Ah, of course. The ones who make the greatest-ever raid on the whites were also his bitch."

"Ten winters ago."

"They had horse herds as thick as buffalo."

"Nʉʉkaru, we had one bad year, and you are a gloomy cocksucker, and you might ask to stay behind because if you continue to talk like that, instead of singing the *woho hubiya,* someone will shut your mouth with a tomahawk."

"If we have another raid like last year," said Nɯɯkaru, "there will be no one left to shut my mouth at all."

"Ignore him, Tiehteti. This is what gets people killed." He shook his head. "You will bring back a thousand horses and a hundred scalps and fifty Mexican slaves. That is what you will do. Talking about it is a waste of time."

"All right," said Nɯɯkaru.

"My arm hurts so bad I can't sleep but you don't hear me whining like a child. Kill some Mexicans, die a hero, I don't give a fuck, but this talking is pointless, you might as well cut your own throat, and the throats of your people while you're at it."

"We are planning to avoid the whites," said Toshaway, "but . . ."

"You don't have to worry about me," I told him.

"Good." He looked out across the village, noticeably smaller than it had been the previous year. "I wish you had been born twenty years ago, Tiehteti, because those were real days. The buffalo wolves used to follow us on our raids because they knew they'd get something to eat." He scratched his chin. "But perhaps those times will return."

We descended from the plains and the land became mesas and canyonlands again, there were trees, mostly cottonwoods and oaks, the grass was tall and the blanketflowers were thick, patches of color going on for miles.

Toshaway had relatives along the San Saba headwaters and while looking for them we found a freshly raided Comanche camp, around seventy bodies, all scalped. There were a few warriors, but mostly it was women and children and old men. Toshaway had found his relatives. They were a splinter band of the Kotsoteka. Many of the women and girls had been treated the same as my mother and sister, cut up in the same way as well. We spent the day burying them.

"Their men must still be out," said Pizon.

There were boot prints everywhere, boots made in Austin or San Antonio or somewhere in the east. There was a strange litter of musket balls on the ground and the hoofprints of shod horses. The tipis, weapons, and camp equipment had all been thrown into a fire and burned. I was dauncy with shame, but the other Comanches kept their faces hard, and the only thing said was that a few years earlier, the nearest white settlements has been hundreds of miles away, and it was a bad sign that they had found this camp.

"How many whites are there?" said Toshaway. "Do you know?"

"They say about twenty million."

He grunted and looked at me.

"Come on."

"It's a fact."

"Okay, Tiehteti."

We rode in a wide circle around the camp, taking a break from digging. It could not have been a Ranger squad because twelve men could not kill seventy-three Comanches, even women and children. Toshaway guessed three hundred riders, but there were so many tracks on top of each other, as they had spent at least a day raping and sacking the village, it was hard to be certain.

I thought about my father's tracks, he had a strange duck-footed walk and his left foot stuck out more than his right, and for a tall heavy man he had very small feet. I decided not to look.

At the top of a hill we found ruts as if a pair of wagons had been parked. The grass was burned down to the dirt.

"Strange," said Toshaway.

"Those were cannons," I said. "That's why the grass is burned."

"Those are very heavy, no?"

"A mountain howitzer can be pulled behind a horse. The army used them against the Mexicans all the time."

The hill was maybe a furlong from the village and I knew the musket balls littering the ground must have been canister. A mountain howitzer loaded with canister was like two hundred rifles firing at once, or as my father used to say, like the hand of the Lord Himself.

"Tiehteti, it is very strange. For instance, how did they get into position without being noticed? And why would they have brought cannons all this way unless they were sure that Indians would be here? That is what I find strange." He shook his head. "Someone was leading them."

"They put the guns in place in the dark."

"Of course in the dark. But still. They knew Indians were here." He stood looking down at the ruins of the camp.

"Unfortunately most of the men seem to have fallen into their cooking fires and I could not tell if my cousin was among them. Though I did recognize his wife and two daughters."

By then the other men were washing the ash and gore off in the river. Before we left, we hacked a flat place into a cottonwood and carved a note in hieroglyphics, telling what had happened, and how many we had buried, in case there were other members of the band who had not yet returned.

The next night we saw campfires in the distance, fires as only the whites made them, twice as large as they needed to be, nearly two dozen in all. It could only be the army, as there were not that many Rangers in the entire state of Texas.

There was discussion about whether to steal their horses but we decided to keep going. It would be safer to get them from the Mexicans, and instead of sleeping we rode all night to put distance between us and the soldiers. We crossed the Pecos without seeing anyone else, though there were recent tracks of shod horses, a small party of travelers. There was a debate about following them but the army was still close and it was again decided to wait. Climbing out of the Pecos Valley, the land became flat and dry. Long patches of caliche, clumps of oaks, mesquites, and huisache, the occasional cedar. We didn't relax until we'd reached the Davis Mountains, where there was another debate about using the standard route past the old Presidio del Norte, which was well watered and had good grass and involved the least climbing, or going farther east into the mountains, where it was steeper and less watered but also less traveled. The younger men—who needed scalps—were annoyed we hadn't taken on either the army or the travelers whose tracks we'd crossed, so it was decided to go past Presidio.

We stayed at a distance from the town, dropping gradually into the valley, then the river itself, and then back up into the mountains. A day's ride from the border was a latifundio that was known to have a thousand horses.

There was a small village attached to the latifundio and we left the remuda with a half-dozen young Indians to guard the animals. Most were better hands than I was at riding and shooting, but that did not matter, because I had gotten a scalp and they hadn't.

The rest of us picked the best horses, covered our faces and bodies with red and black and yellow paint, put on silver and brass armbands and bracelets, and tied feathers to the manes of our horses. Toshaway made sure I got a medicine hat with a large brown shield and I spent a long time painting it. I emptied my bowels three times, though the last time it was all water. I kept my eye on Toshaway and Nuukaru. Toshaway was laughing and joking with various people, making sure everyone was ready; Nuukaru was keeping to himself, and looked serious, and I also saw him go into the bushes and then a second time a few minutes later. I tried to eat some pemmican, but my mouth was too dry. I decided that was fine. If you were hit in the guts you did not want them to be full.

The sun was close to setting when a bell in the hacienda began to ring, probably the supper bell, but the Comanches thought we'd been spotted and then everyone was on their horses, moving toward the village and the ranch. Shields were adjusted. A few riders carried cut-down shotguns or repeating pistols, but most had their bows ready with a half-dozen arrows clenched in the hand that held the bow, the seventh arrow nocked, quivers adjusted so they could get to more arrows when they needed them. Reins were tied short so they would not be in the way. You were expected to steer only with your knees.

We came at them with the sun behind us, making our way quietly through the brush until we were nearly at the edge of the village. Then we kicked the horses into a run. There was a small open area to be crossed and there was whooping and ululating as if we were celebrating a great occasion, white-clad Mexicans fleeing for the chaparral, a general cry of "*Los bárbaros,*" a single puff of gunsmoke from between two houses, another musket pointing from a window. I aimed just to the left of the barrel but the horse was running too fast and I missed. I fumbled away my rifle and took out my bow and we were into the village, a wide main street with white adobe houses on either side; I wondered how many people there were and saw more puffs of gunsmoke but all I heard was the whooping and ululating and I started to think I would not be hurt. Everything was moving slowly. I could see each stone and clod of dirt, arrows falling toward men on rooftops or behind walls, a boy holding an escopeta sprinting down the street in front of us, his hat fell off, his arm went back to reach for it and an arrow stuck into him, then a second arrow hit and then he turned suddenly and dodged between two houses.

Then we were at the end of the village. There was only one street so I turned around and went back down it. An old man stepped out with a pistol; he was pulling a careful bead and I felt the wind as the ball went. Before I could get my bow aimed the horse changed course and ran him over and I could tell by the sound that he would not be getting up. Then I was going by a long adobe wall and there were puffs of clay the whole length and I realized people were shooting at me. Somehow I was at the front, but the arrows were still going past on both sides and then I reached the end of the village again.

A man wearing the black coat of a hacendado was crouched behind a mesquite, calmly letting off a repeater. I shot two arrows but they went rattling off the branches and then another arrow came from behind me and cut through a small opening and the man fell backward. There was a *whoopwhoopwhoop* and Toshaway shook his bow, then turned away to look for more people. I realized I had not been shooting enough. I stopped to situate my arrows. My shield popped me in the nose; there was a white-shirted man surrounded by a cloud of gunsmoke and I shot a quick arrow. He dropped his musket and took a few drunken steps, then ran into the chaparral with the arrow wagging in front of him. I shot another into his back, which didn't slow him down either. He disappeared. I noticed I'd been standing still. I kicked the horse and we went back down the street.

There was no longer a charge as much as a general melee. Arrows kept flying past me; people kept falling over; I would look at someone—they would get hit by an arrow—I would look at someone else—they would get hit as well. I was beginning to feel like the hand of God Himself, then remembered my shield and got it up and moving just as it was knocked into my head again. I tried to wipe my eyes and kicked the horse just as the shield was hit a third and fourth time. I was rowing it in huge circles; I crouched and reached the end of the village and charged directly into the chaparral to gather myself up.

A woman with a child appeared in front of me; she was running blind and the horse turned to trample her. I kneed him away, missing her, then made a big circle in the brush and headed back to the village. By now the street was nothing but bodies and dismounted Comanches taking scalps. Most of the riders had gone somewhere else. There was shooting a few hundred yards away, at the main ranch house. A person with a musket came out from behind a wall, looked around, and sprinted for the chaparral. I cut his shirt with an arrow but he kept running and I knew I'd been missing most of my shots. I sat there a minute and nothing happened. I rode toward the shooting.

A dozen Indians had surrounded the house and were shooting arrows and occasionally a rifle toward it. The inhabitants were alive and well as there were regular puffs of smoke coming from the gunports and windows. On a stone patio, two men were lying next to a stub-barreled cannon, a ramrod and barrel of powder turned over next to them.

The main body of Comanches was off rounding up the horses, and I got a strange feeling watching the siege of the house so before I could be recruited I rode off to help gather the animals.

We rode all night but everyone was in a good mood, a thousand horses stretched out in front of us, enough to get our band back on its feet. I thought about the man I'd shot in the back and stomach and the other man I'd run down with the horse, and the others I had shot at but was not sure if I had hit. I figured it was possible they were all dead. None of them had given me the feeling of the Delaware and I wondered if I would ever have that again. I told myself they were just Mexicans and they would have done the same to me. My father always said the Mexicans had as much fun torturing people as the Indians.

Around midday we were into the foothills, driving the horses up a dry streambed. At the top of the hill, opposite the side we'd climbed, we stopped to collect our thoughts. I rode to find Toshaway and found him standing with Pizon, refilling his waterskin at a stream and cursing the Indians who had driven the horses through the water instead of along the banks.

"Ah," said Pizon. "The Great Tiehteti."

"He who charges at the front."

I started to grin.

"Oh, that was quite beautiful, Tiehteti, you charging through the middle of them like that, missing with every arrow you fired, then meanwhile every single one of them was trying to kill you, and they were missing as well." He chuckled and shook his head. "It was something to behold."

"I did hit one of them," I said.

"Are you sure?"

"Yes, in the stomach. And in the back. And I killed another one with the horse."

"Did you scalp them?"

"No, I kept going." I couldn't quite remember why I hadn't scalped them. "The one had a musket," I said.

"Oh, a musket."

"Pizon and I were maybe ten paces behind, but it was as if all the rays of the sun were shining only on you, you were like the prize that every man in that village wanted and they had no eyes for the rest of us."

"And you were riding so fucking fast."

"That's what you said to do."

"If you are attacking, you don't ride faster than you can shoot."

"Don't worry, we killed them all for you. And Saupitty and Ten Buffalo killed the ones we didn't see. What a beautiful fucking massacre."

"How is it possible I missed?" I said.

"I would say that you shoot like a woman," said Pizon. "But it would not be fair to the women."

"Tiehteti, if you are charging directly toward someone, it does not matter that you are moving. But if they are off to your side, it matters a lot. If your horse is running, you aim one step behind your target if he is close, so the arrow will be carried into him, but if he is far away you might aim five steps behind, though of course it depends on the angle, and on the wind, and how fast you are moving. When the horse is running, you have to remember the arrow is falling both down and forward. Last night you shot ahead of every target, as if you were aiming directly at them."

"I was," I said.

"Fuck it," said Pizon, "he deserves a scalp anyway. I have never shot so many people in my life who did not even know I was there." Then he added: "You are fucking brave, Tiehteti. I was very worried for you. And Toshaway is right, you cannot shoot for dogshit." He saw the look on my face. "At least not from a horse. I have seen you shoot from the ground, and you are okay. But perhaps for the rest of this year, when we return, you will practice only from horseback and only at targets that are to one side of you."

"And perhaps we will make sure you have a few pistols in the future. The white men all have them now anyway. It is not such a crime to use them."

"I've been trying to ask for one."

"If I had given you one, where would you be with the bow?" He shook his head. "You are very good with the pistol, we all know that, but there is no point practicing what you are already good at."

We stood there. I filled my *pihpóo* with the muddy water. To the north we could see the river and the mountains rising up from it, blue and purple with the distance. Then Nʉʉkaru came bounding over the rocks, followed by another young *mahimiawapi*.

"We are followed. Maybe a hundred men, maybe more."

We stood looking at him.

"Did you hear me?" he said.

"You are like a little girl, Nʉʉkaru."

"We need to get moving," he said.

"Where the fuck did a hundred men come from?" said Pizon. "There are not one hundred horses left in this entire province."

"A hundred, fifty, there are a lot of men. I am not sure how else to explain it."

"First it's one hundred. Now it's fifty. Soon it will be five old men herding goats."

"Toshaway," Nʉʉkaru said, "bring your spyglass, but you won't need it."

He ran back up the hill.

Pizon looked at the boy who'd come down with Nʉʉkaru. "Is he just being a woman?"

"I can't see if it's men or horses, but there was a lot of dust." Then he added: "His eye carries farther than mine, though."

"Probably some asshole driving cattle."

"They are following our route."

"It's a dry riverbed through chaparral. With a spring at the top of the hill. Every animal within five miles is going to use this path."

"I think they are men, Pizon."

Pizon dismissed him. "Do not let yourself become like this, Tiehteti. There are many things to worry about, but when you think every bush is hiding something, you soon become tired, and then you will not see the man who really is waiting to kill you."

He spat into the dirt.

"*Yee*, this is making me crazy. When we get to Presidio, it will be time to worry."

No one said anything.

"You fucking kids."

Toshaway came back.

"*Tʉyato?yerʉ*, the young ones are right. When we reach the river, you'll take the horses and the north trail, the rest of us will make tracks going west."

Pizon looked at him.

"They are right. It is far and the dust is thick, but they are men, and they are chasing us for sure."

When we reached the river it was dark and we were barely a few miles ahead of them.

The water was shallow; the summer rains hadn't yet come. That was lucky and the moon was not up yet, which was also lucky.

Pizon and twenty or so others took the horse herd downriver, directly through the middle of the water. They would ride that way before turning into the Texas mountains. The rest of us rode up and down the banks trampling their tracks, leaving obvious sign pointed upriver and also directly up the opposite bank, any direction except the one they'd taken. Then we headed upriver.

"We're the bait," I said.

"If they are stupid they'll presume we crossed directly and they will enter the rocks on the Texas side and become confused about where we went. If they are smart they will presume we went upriver."

"What if they go downriver?"

"Let us hope for the sake of our band that they do not do that."

"So they will follow us."

"Most likely."

When we reached a point where the ground was rocky, we climbed out of the water in single file and, after a brief discussion about where to meet, split into three groups heading in different directions. Toshaway and I continued west, along with a few others.

"If they are Mexicans, maybe they do not follow us," he said.

The moon had finally come up and we could see where we were. Then there were sounds and a dozen riders were coming upriver and then another group came out of the brush and the shooting started and didn't stop. I took off into the chaparral. When I looked back the only one still mounted was Toshaway; he had another Indian riding double behind him. I stopped in a thicket with my rifle pointed toward a gap, watching as the men approached the opening and squeezing the trigger as they passed. One of them doubled over and I turned and rode straight into the thorns; there was a lot of shooting and bullets cracking branches all around but they couldn't see me and I didn't slow down. After a few minutes I couldn't hear anyone. It was a miracle my eyes had not been torn out by the brush. I continued uphill another half mile or so, then circled and waited.

There were a few shots down toward the river and I stopped to recharge my rifle then rode toward the noise. Then I saw a man crouched in the brush. It was Toshaway. He was naked and his breechcloth was tied around a wound on his leg. All he had was his bow and a handful of arrows; his knife and pistol were gone. He mounted behind me and kicked the horse and we were moving again.

"Are you shot?"

"I don't think so."

"Then your horse is."

He was right. Its flank was streaked in blood, which I had mistaken for sweat. "You're a good horse," I said.

"Use him up, but do it gently."

"How's your leg?"

"It must have missed the artery or I would not be alive."

We rode for two hours, climbing into the barren mountains, keeping to the drainages to stay hidden. Whatever water had carved them was long gone; the streambeds were as dusty as the flatlands. We stopped at a ridge top. While I was watching our backtrail, Toshaway slashed the needles off a pear pad, split it, and packed it into his wound. I tied the poultice on with his breechcloth. The muscle was badly bruised. Behind us the mountain dropped steeply toward the river; we had not made much distance but we had climbed a lot.

I could see riders moving where the moon came off the water and I knew they could see us against the pale rocks.

"Now we ride."

"Does it hurt?"

"Does it hurt. Oh, Tiehteti."

There was shooting along the river—they had found someone from the band. The noise slowed and then stopped. I wondered who it was.

"Keep going," said Toshaway.

By the time the sun came up, the horse was nearly dead. Toshaway was pale and sweaty and we were looking north into a dry basin that went on for dozens of miles.

"How is your water?"

"The *pihpóo* was shot at the river."

"Very bad," he said.

The horse was lying on its side. There was no hope for it.

He cut a vein on the animal's neck and drank for a minute. Then he made me do the same. The horse didn't protest. Toshaway began to drink again. My mouth was full of hair and my stomach was full of blood and I wanted to air my paunch. He made me drink some more. The horse's breathing got quicker.

"Now we walk," he said. "And hope the buzzards don't lead our friends to the *tusanabo*."

I inspected my rifle and saw the lock was wrecked so I threw it into the brush.

"Those were fucking Indians leading them," he said. "Lipans. And there were white men as well." He shook his head. "The Apaches sucking the cocks of the Mexicans who are sucking the cocks of the whites. The world is against us."

By afternoon we had dropped into the basin. From the top we could see a tree line farther north—a stream—but to reach it we would have to cross miles of open ground, no cover but cane cholla and giant dagger. Anyone looking would see us right away.

"Unfortunately I do not think I will make it if we skirt the edge."

"We'll cross the flat."

"No," he said. "Give me a few of your arrows. You will take the long way and stay hidden."

"We'll cross the flat," I repeated.

"Tiehteti," he said. "It is good to give your life, but not for a dead man."

"We're crossing the flat," I said.

By late afternoon we were in the shade along the creek. It was not much more than a muddy trickle and as gyppy as I'd ever tasted, but we both lay drinking for several minutes. I left Toshaway and went off with my bow to see if I could find a deer or something we might eat and also we needed a stomach for a water carrier.

I had been sitting in the willows, hoping to see some game, when I noticed a man on a bay horse picking his way up the stream. He was leading a small paint that was saddled and covered in handprints, similar to the horse Ten Buffalo had been riding.

The man was white and wearing new buckskin and there were scalps on his belt. I began to shift my weight. Then he stopped. He was staring at my footprints in the mud. I had been drawing my bow so slowly he would not have seen it even if he'd looked directly at me, and the way the light came through the leaves there was a pattern all over him and I found a bright spot and popped my fingers. He saw the arrow and then his horse turned and pitched through the bushes. There was more crashing. I moved about another ten yards and nocked another arrow and waited. I thought I could see his horse just past the trees. Finally I circled around.

He was lying in the grass in the shade. He had pulled out the arrow and it was still in his hand and something made me think of my father, but there was only a slim resemblance, dirty black hair and bloodshot eyes and pale skin under his hat. He looked right at me but it was an illusion; I counted the scalps tied to his saddle and then rolled him onto his belly to take his.

In addition to the two horses, he had a pair of brand-new Colt Navys, a .69 rifle, a nearly new gun belt, a powder flask, a knife, a heavy bullet pouch, three water gourds, and a wallet full of food. I notched the arrow with an X, then stripped off all his clothes and bundled them in case Toshaway wanted them.

The paint was grazing at the edge of the stream. I nickered and it came immediately. I was no longer sure it had belonged to Ten Buffalo but it was wearing a Comanche saddle and there were red and yellow handprints all over it.

I was looking out over the mountains to the north where I could see trees and good grass; it would be nothing to ride away, there would be no more ambushes, I could reach Bexar in eight days. But the feeling soon passed and I went to find Toshaway.

We sat eating the man's dried beef and drinking his clean water and eating the dried plums and apples he'd been carrying as well. I was starting to feel good about things when Toshaway decided it was time to cut the bruised parts out of his leg. He had split and cut more pear pads and gathered up creosote leaves for a poultice and mashed them with water and soaked two clean pieces of the man's shirt. Then he sat down near the stream.

"Don't be a fucking butcher," he said, "but don't take your time, either."

He put a stick in his mouth and I took up my scalping knife and cut around the bullet hole. His eyes rolled and the stick fell out of his mouth. I finished cutting, then rolled him over and cut out the bruise from the other side. Then I pushed the pieces of the man's shirt through the wound and drew them out. I was packing it when he woke up. Piss continued to run out from between his legs, but he did not seem to notice. The wound was bleeding freely and he told me that was a good sign. When I had packed it full and covered it with the split pear pads, we tied a tight bandage with another piece of the scalp hunter's shirt.

As we were sitting there he told me he knew on the night I was captured that I had been the one to shoot Skulking Bear, but he had not told anyone else in the tribe.

"It did not make sense to me, either," he said. "I knew you had done it and yet I did not tell anyone."

I was quiet.

"I knew what you had in you," he said. "Now everyone else will see it as well."

I wasn't really listening. I was thinking about the night I was captured, about my mother and brother and sister. He saw something in my face and told me that his grandfather had been a captive Mexican—the tribe was all from captives—it was the way of the Comanche; it had kept our blood strong all these years.

We continued to ride and change his poultice. A few days later we found a honey tree and filled our wallets from it, eating some but saving the rest to pack his wound, resting while the sun was up and traveling only at night.

By the time we reached the plains, two weeks later, there was still a gash in his leg, but the redness and swelling were gone. In another two weeks we were back in camp.

Chapter Twenty-three
Jeannie

Spring 1945

It was a bad storm, a gully washer, the rain coming so fast the ground had no time to absorb it, the clouds so heavy they blotted out the light. By noon it was completely dark. The lightning was echoing through the house and she was sure it was a gunnery raid, a mission from the Kaufman air base gone off target. She watched fire leap through a patch of cedar close to the house, entire trees erupting ahead of the flames; a great sheave of rain put it out.

Her father had been out in the far pastures. He did not return for supper but a few hours later his horse showed up at the gate, alone and still saddled. It was even darker now; she could barely see her own feet. There was no chance of going after him, but it was not cold, and he was resourceful, and she expected he would show up sometime in the morning, soaked and footsore but otherwise intact.

Still, she slept in fits, waking every hour or so until at some point she looked out and saw the moon. The vaqueros were all waiting downstairs; her horse was already saddled. At first light they followed the dim tracks of her father's grullo, nearly obliterated by the rain but, when she put herself in the right mind, clear enough to follow.

The tracks led to a big arroyo but they did not continue on the other side. The light was spreading across the horizon and the birdcalls were starting up as if nothing had happened. Jeannie and the older vaqueros continued the search, the horses and most of the men held back so as not to trample any sign, but even later, with the sun risen, there were no tracks.

Her father, upon reaching the arroyo, must have dismounted. Or more likely, he had come upon it at speed, blinded by the rain and dark, and been thrown. There was only a thin trickle of water now, but high along the banks, fresh grass dangled from the sycamores. A man might have been carried miles. Dozens of miles.

Four days later, one of the Midkiff vaqueros found him at a water gap, the white sole of a foot showing under the brush and flotsam. No one told her; the telephone rang and then Sullivan got into his truck and went to town and when he returned, there was a box on the front seat with her father's clothes. They were filthy and torn but she recognized his shirt. She picked it up, thinking to bring it to her face, then dropped it. It was crawling with blowflies.

Clint had died at Salerno, Paul at the Battle of the Bulge, even though she had prayed every night, even though she had not missed a Sunday of church. When Clint was killed she had continued to pray for Paul and Jonas, and at some point, months before his death, she had begun to pray for her father as well. Now she wondered if she had somehow killed them. One seemed as likely as the other. She decided she would stop praying for Jonas, and he had lived.

Because of her father's condition, the funeral was planned for the next day, and as she lay in her bed that afternoon, exhausted but unable to fall asleep, it occurred to her that the ranch still needed to be run, that there was no one left but her.

She allowed herself a few more minutes, then drew a bath, scrubbing herself thoroughly, though without wasting any time, as she imagined a mother might wash a child. She put on her black dress, then decided against it; she could not afford to be worrying about her clothes. She changed into blue jeans and old boots and knew her grandmother would not have approved, though of course she was gone as well, dead the previous year. She put on a bit of makeup—almost as bad as the pants. But her eyelashes were blond, like the rest of her—they made her look too young. *Where is Jonas?* she thought.

No work had been done in four days; everyone had been looking for her father. Now all thirty of his employees—vaqueros, fence riders, the windmill monkeys—were gathered around the bunkhouse, sitting on the porch or under trees in the shade, speaking quietly and wondering what was going to happen.

She told them nothing would change, that if for some reason she were not around, their paychecks would be distributed by Mrs. Wright, the bookkeeper. Everyone will be paid for the past four days, she continued, and tomorrow will be a day off. But between now and then, the water gaps need tending, the Midkiffs have some of our stock, and anything else the storm broke, you just get to fixing it, you don't have to ask.

She did not tell them that she did not have the authority to sign their checks. She spent the rest of that day and night alternately worrying that no one would attend the funeral and wondering where her father kept his will. Their lawyer tore his office apart but found nothing; around midnight Jeannie found the document in an old file cabinet. It had been updated several times: once for Clint and once for Paul, but the newest version, dated only a few months previous, which had doubtless caused her father much anxiety, named her sole inheritor of his share of the ranch. Jonas got a share of the minerals but that was all.

A feeling of happiness overtook her; she could not help smiling, then laughing, and then felt terrible. Still, Phineas would be overjoyed—the entire property was now split between them. Jonas would not care too much; he was trying to make his way back from Germany, though the flights were infrequent and always full and a ship would take weeks. She went back to worrying about the funeral.

Outside several fires had been built, calves and goats and hogs set to roasting. Trips had been made to Carrizo for beans, corn, coffee, and two dozen store-made cakes. A hundred cases of Pearl beer and four cases of whiskey. The house felt more alive than it had in years; the cooks were up all night, doing whatever it was they did, and the maids were as well, changing all the linens in the guest rooms, getting the folding cots out of storage, making the house ready for company.

Phineas arrived with a sizable entourage; there was a trickle, then a flood, of people from Austin and San Antonio and Dallas, from Houston and El Paso and Brownsville, the other South Texas ranchers, newspapermen, nearly five hundred people in total, which at first caused her to weep—her father had been more appreciated than she had ever realized—but as the day went on she saw that most had come out of politeness, not for her father but for her, or for the family, for the idea of the McCulloughs. The local Mexicans, who had mostly hated her father, and not without cause, they all came as well, because that was what you did when your *patrón* died.

The last time the house had been so full was at the Colonel's funeral, but that had a different feel altogether, of genuine misery, the end of something, of grown men who could not stop crying. The faces now were somber but not troubled, the conversation easy. Her father had not mattered. It was not fair but the more she thought about it, the more condolences she accepted, the more she heard the circumstances of his death whispered around the room, the more furious she got. He had died stupidly. From stubbornness and poor judgment. The vaqueros had all lit for home as soon as the storm blew in—lightning killed more cowboys than guns ever had—but her father, with his notions, had wanted to finish his count. *I don't mind getting a little wet*—those were his last words.

She circulated through the house, hundreds of people, thanking them for coming and insisting they eat, the smell of beef and cabrito and roast pig, unending dishes of beans and sauce and tortillas, gallons of beer and sweet tea. She was in and out of the kitchen; yes, another calf should be knocked in the head—on the coals immediately—yes, another run was needed to Carrizo—no telling how long people would stay. Sullivan periodically appeared and pressed a cold glass of tea into her hand. She had sweated through her dress. She went up to change but there was nothing else; of course she had only one black dress. She hung it in front of the fan in her bedroom, wiped herself down with a wash towel, then stood in front of the fan herself. She made a note to check Sullivan's salary; his people had worked for the family three generations; her father had been stingy. She was tempted to rest but knew she would fall asleep.

Back downstairs she continued to move through the crowd, barely hearing what people said. There was Uncle Phineas in the corner, leaning on his cane, holding forth with a group of young men. He was so clearly enjoying himself that she turned away when he called to her.

The vaqueros and the Mexicans from town stood deferentially, speaking quietly, but the men from the cities—all in riding boots and stockman's hats— clomped and talked noisily like they were family. It made her feel weak. The Colonel would not have stood for men like that. She wished that one of his old friends might show up—as a few still did, once in a while— and, for the sake of the Colonel, empty a six-gun into the ceiling to clear out the house.

But even that was a fantasy. From what she had known of cowboys, even the old ones, they tended not to do well in crowds, they tended to be polite and deferential, and most could not have even looked these new men, these city men, in the eye.

Jonas missed the burial but came home from Germany anyway, where the war, for all practical purposes, was over. She practically smothered him when she picked him up; she was not sure what to expect—a thousand-yard stare, deep scars, a limp—but he looked fit and healthy and had a confident stride.

The first thing he said, when he walked into the house, their steps loud in the cavernous great room, with its stone walls and thirty-foot ceilings, was, "We need to get you the hell out of here. You won't have a normal life. The war will be over in a few weeks and I could get a job for you in Berlin. It would probably be as a typist or something but we could live together."

She was not sure how to respond—it was appealing but also entirely wrong—she was not going to be a typist. It was her brother who ought to be coming home, not her going to some foreign country.

"Or hell," he was saying. "We've got money. You don't have to work at all, just come live."

"How is it there?"

He shrugged.

"I guess you've seen terrible things?"

"No worse than others."

She wanted to ask if he had shot anyone, or seen anyone shot, but he seemed to sense the question was coming and stood abruptly, walking to the other end of the room, looking at the old drawings, the marble statues and figurines, shaking his head, picking things up and putting them down.

"Would you like something to eat?" she called.

"We probably better go to the grave. I can't stay long."

This didn't make any sense—he had traveled a week to get there—and she decided to ignore it, not being sure he was in his right mind.

"Do you want to drive or ride?"

"Let's ride. It's four years since I've been on a horse."

Over supper, which he was now calling dinner, he had asked, in a way that struck her as too direct: "Are there any men around here you like?"

No. In fact the year before there had been another vaquero, less handsome than the others, with a squishy sort of nose; they had kissed behind one of the brush corrals and later lain together by the springs at the old Garcia place. He had been more aggressive than she wanted—the few men left seemed to get their way far too quickly—but that night, when she was reflecting on it alone, she was sorry she'd stopped his hands. These chances only seemed to come at great intervals, and so a few days later, when they agreed to meet again, she had carried an ancient condom—found in Clint's room, of course—tucked into a pocket in her dress. She had waited an hour, then two, lying by herself under the trees, in the soft grass overlooking the old church.

Her vaquero had not shown up. Again it was no mystery what had happened: the young man's friends, afraid of her father, afraid for their own jobs, had warned him off. She had cried for days—even for this man, whom (snobbishly, she knew now) she had considered below her, she was not good enough. She had always thought herself a prize: blond, petite, not as shapely as some but certainly with a woman's shape; her button nose had straightened out, her eyes had gotten bigger, and in a certain light she wondered if she might be beautiful. But most of the time she was at least pretty, far above average, and while it was true that there was a Mexican girl in Carrizo who was prettier, that girl was very poor.

And yet . . . she was nearly twenty, she was supposed to be out living, she was supposed to have suitors and she did not, with the exception of a few men from town who may have thought they were courting her, but, so far as she was concerned, weren't. She did not think of herself as rich, but she knew that other people did; she did not trust any of the whites from town; they saw her in the wrong way. The vaqueros she knew and trusted well enough—it was against their interest to damage her reputation—though apparently they did not trust her, or they did not respect her, or perhaps they sensed her desperation.

As for Jonas, she barely recognized him. His face had filled out, his frame as well; there was no longer anything of the boy. He spoke too fast, like someone raised in the North, and he cursed constantly, like someone raised in the North; he seemed entirely too sure of himself. Over dinner he got drunk on whiskey and they talked and built an enormous fire, of the sort their father would have found wasteful, but when they finally decided to go to sleep, Jonas refused to go up to his old room—making a show, she thought—and instead he took a blanket to a couch near the fire. She went to her bedroom and as she sat there in her nightgown, she knew she would be responsible for losing everything. Jonas had absolved himself—he cared nothing for the house or their legacy. Though of course he had been cut out of much of it. It must have stung him, their father's final insult, though he had still left Jonas half his minerals, which, in the end, mattered more to her brother than the land ever could have.

The next morning they took their breakfast in the great room, where they could listen to the radio.

"Will you stay here until the fighting is done?"

He shook his head. "I remember Daddy turning that off every time FDR came on." Pointing to the radio.

She wondered if she would have to defend her father for the entire visit. Though as it turned out, it was for the rest of their lives. "He didn't do that once the war started," she said. "On D-day he let everyone off and we all sat here and listened, and he drew a big map, and he would say that is Paul's division, the Eighty-Second Airborne, who have landed there, and that is Jonas's division. He made all these notes for everyone to see. He was proud of you."

"Well, he was wrong because I didn't land until the second day. And Paul didn't land on a beach at all, he dropped in by parachute in the middle of all the Germans."

"I don't remember all the details," she admitted.

"Do you remember him saying that FDR's election was the end of American democracy? Or that the Dust Bowl was a communist invention?" He shook his head. "I don't know how we came from him."

"He wasn't so bad." She had not remembered her brother as so cold, but then maybe she had never really known him. She closed her eyes.

"I remember him saying that we lived on the Frontier," Jonas continued, "Frontier with a capital *F*. I told him the frontier had closed before he was even born, and then he would lecture me about the tradition we were carrying on. I would tell him there *was* no tradition, there could *be* no tradition for a thing that had lasted only twenty years. Anyway . . . I don't know what this place will become, but right now I can't see the point. It's not settled enough to have any culture, but it's not wild enough to be interesting. It's just a province."

She didn't answer.

"You should sell it. Keep the minerals but make a clean break. We could get you into Barnard easy as that."

"I'm not moving to the North," she said quietly.

"You were a kid then."

"I'm happier here."

"Jeannie." He put his hand to his forehead as if what she had said was the stupidest thing he'd ever heard. "Everything we were taught was either a lie or a bad joke. It was always Yankees this or that, the worst sort of people, all full of shit, and then one day it occurred to me that if Daddy hated them so much, that was probably where I belonged. Meanwhile he was worse than anyone I met at Princeton, born into money but always complaining about how poor and put-upon he was. And the way he was with the Mexicans?"

She didn't say anything.

His eyes were closed. "I was so fucking stupid when I got there."

He stayed another week, until they were both sure the estate was in order. By then all the anger had gone out of him. He changed his will to leave her everything in case something happened; he signed a power of attorney. She felt closer to him than she ever had; she had lost her father but regained her brother. And then he got on the train east, toward the war, and she did not see him for three more years.

Starting the day Jonas left, and continuing for how long she didn't know, she kept hours like a cat, sleeping three-quarters of the day, waking in the middle of the night, pacing the empty house, crying herself to sleep on the sofa only to wake a few hours later with the sun in her eyes. Going back up to her room with its heavy curtains, finding breakfast or dinner on a tray outside her door, cold eggs, cold meat, visiting the bathroom.

There was nothing for her to do. No job, nothing useful to which she might attach her mind. Once a week, on what she knew must be Thursday, she found a clipboard on the dining room table with all the employee paychecks attached, which she signed individually and left by the door. She thought of her father and cried, she thought of her brothers and cried, she was vaguely aware that time was passing, she wondered why Phineas wasn't calling her, why he hadn't invited her to live with him. Often she could not tell if she was crying about this, or about her father, or her brothers, or even her great-grandfather, gone almost a decade but more tender toward her than her father had ever been.

A month might have passed. It might have been two. But she woke up one morning as the sun was rising, and accepted, with total certainty, that no one would ever look after her again.

A week later a man from Southern Minerals showed up, wanting to talk about her future.

"I've been stopping by awhile, but they always said you were indisposed."

He acted as if they were old friends but she crossed her arms and stood square in the door. He promptly offered a million dollars plus 12.5 percent to lease her property, with the exception of the acreage that Humble had already drilled. He knew her entire story. He knew her brothers had died in the war, that her father had died in the accident, that Jonas had gone back to Germany.

"You can move to the city." He quickly adjusted: "Or raise your steers. Life won't have to be hard anymore." He gave her a sympathetic look.

She was not looking at him; she was hoping one of the vaqueros would ride past.

"You sound like a minister," she said.

"Thank you." He smiled and went back to talking about grass, and the weather, and how the cattle were doing, and after a time, when she had thought of what to say, she interrupted him.

"Do other people still sign at eighth royalties or is it just widows and orphans?"

He smiled again, saw right through her, saw the planning that had gone into her rudeness. He was standing closer now and she resisted the urge to step back—that would mean giving up the threshold—and then there was the heat; the natural thing was to invite him out of the sun. She decided she did not care how close he stood; she would not budge. But at the same time she wondered if this was stupid, if she was misjudging the situation entirely. She wondered if all the maids had left; she wondered how he had gotten through the gate.

He was so close she could smell his breath, and she felt a growing alarm at how alone she was. All the hands were out in the pastures—miles from earshot—and Hugo, the cook, had gone to Carrizo for supplies. She was alone and this man thought nothing of her whatsoever.

"I believe I'm getting tired," she said.

He nodded but kept right on talking; he took off his hat to mop his forehead and she saw he had no tan line: an office man. He mentioned for a second time that it was no place for a girl to be alone and a tingling began in her neck and spread to her fingers; perhaps it was too late. He would take whatever he wanted. Her mouth went dry and she summoned up the effort to say, "If you do not leave I will call the sheriff."

He stood as if this statement required further consideration, or maybe just to show that he was only leaving because he felt like it. Then he reached forward and squeezed her shoulder and wished her a good afternoon.

After closing the door she went straight to her father's office, passing dozens of open windows, French doors with useless locks—there were any number of ways to get into the house—he was likely going around the back.

In her father's drawer she found his Colt pistol, but after pulling back the slide in the manner she'd been taught, the magazine fell out onto the floor and bounced under the desk.

She unlocked the large closet where the rest of the guns were kept and found the .25-20 she had hunted with as a kid. Her brothers thought it weak medicine but she had killed two deer. She found the proper shells, prepared the rifle, and went back to the hallway. It had taken minutes. It was ridiculous. If the man really had followed her, he would have gotten her ages ago. She felt a fury building at Jonas, at her father, at . . .

There was something outside—the landman's Ford—it was already at the front gate. She watched him, a distant speck now, open the gate and drive through. She felt very tired. She wanted to lie down.

Instead she loaded several revolvers (the automatic she no longer trusted), put them into a basket, and walked around the house distributing them as if they were flowers: one in the big vase next to the front door, another on a shelf in the kitchen, a third next to her bed, the fourth next to her favorite couch in the great room.

She went out to the gallery—where she could see a long way over the hills, nearly to the main road—and began to analyze what had happened. Calling the sheriff was wrong. It was the vaqueros you would call. The thought of someone killing the landman made her heart light, cleared her mind in a pleasant manner. She sat and watched the clouds and thought of what it might look like. He would go down like a steer or hog, right on his chin. She wondered why her hands were shaking. *I am going crazy*, she thought. She left the gallery and wandered through the house, stopping in front of the hall mirror. It was a joke, the guns were a joke, she was a child playing at grown-up things. She wondered again if she was going crazy.

It was a relief when she heard the cook come in and begin chattering to one of the maids. She was not sure if she had been talking to herself or not, if the maids had heard her. Everyone had been right—Jonas, her father, her grandmother—she did not belong here.

She saw the first of the vaqueros' trucks crest a distant hill, trailering the horses from the pastures. Then the second truck, and the third. She felt everything get lighter. It was as simple as that. She would tell them. What would come of the landman, she didn't care—*I don't,* she thought, *I really don't*—this was not the North, where you went around accosting people. Even loading the guns had been wrong; she needed a wall of armor around her, of men, like her father had kept.

Sullivan, the vaqueros, they would all know what to do. She decided to act before any further consideration weakened her; he was probably not such a bad man, she had probably misread the entire thing, she was young and alone (*he accosted you,* she reminded herself). Yes, that was it. The man would pay some price. Even Jonas would agree with that. He would not be killed, but it would be something unpleasant. She was not sure what. She didn't care. She reminded herself of the way he had grabbed her and then, before she could change her mind, she was out the front door, ignoring Hugo's calls about supper, making her way down the path toward the bunkhouse.

Chapter Twenty-four
Diaries of Peter McCullough

MARCH 25, 1917

Drought is back but cattle remain high due to war. Woke up after a night of vivid thoughts, pulled the curtains expecting the green country of my youth and of my dreams. But with the exception of the area immediately around the house, there was nothing but sparse brittle grass, thorny brush, patches of bare caliche. My father is right: it is ruined forever, and in a single generation.

Meanwhile he has hired promoters to bring in northern farmers. The trains are specially chartered and the Yankees will be shown the best farms (irrigated), the best houses (ours, as it is the most ostentatious), and offered used-up hardpan at five hundred times what the current owners paid for it. I have been ordered to make myself scarce.

For two months the Colonel has been diverting water from the stock tanks onto our lawn (we now have one, instead of a dirt yard) and the stream that runs below the house, past Everett's pasture, has been dammed to flood the lowlands one looks over from the gallery. Ike Reynolds came to complain that his water dried up, but the Colonel explained his reasons and Ike left convinced.

Even the springs at Carrizo are barely flowing; it is said this is a result of the irrigation. The resacas have all gone dry. The entire earth, it seems, is being slowly transformed into a desert; mankind will die off and something new will replace us. There is no reason that there should only be one human race. I was likely born a thousand years too early, or ten thousand. One day those like my father will seem like the Romans who fed Christians to the lions.

April 6, 1917

Heard Charlie and Glenn and my father talking this evening, walked into the great room to see what was about, they all three looked at me and went silent. Of course I left. The generations pass, nothing seems to change, the silent understanding between the others and my father, wordless looks that have always excluded me. Wilson declared war on Germany today.

APRIL 9, 1917

Charlie and Glenn came to me. They have both decided to join the army. I told them it would be better to wait until the end of the year when it would be easier to find hands to replace them. They were unconvinced. "We have plenty of money to hire people," said Charlie.

Sally has been in her room all day, unable to get out of bed.

They could not have picked a worse war to join. Machine guns and half-ton shells. I had always thought the Europeans returned to the Stone Age when they landed in America, but apparently they never left it. Seven hundred thousand dead at Verdun alone.

What we need is another great ice to come and sweep us all into the ocean. To give God a second chance.

APRIL 12, 1917

The boys took the train today to San Antonio. Sally is packing a bag to stay with her family in Dallas. Told me this is the reason she wished we had daughters. I told her I agreed with her.

"Come with me," she said.

Could not explain to her why I could not survive Dallas.

An ominous sign: immediately after seeing Glenn and Charlie off, received a call from the postmaster. The Lewis gun has arrived. After several mint juleps with the Colonel, decided to test the gun.

We took the largest drum—nearly one hundred rounds—and after laboriously loading it and figuring out the winding mechanism, which is much like a pocket watch, we were ready to send some prickly pears to the next world when the most unfortunate group of javelina on earth walked into view.

They were nearly a quarter mile away but the gun was advertised as effective at three times that distance for "area fire." The Colonel could barely make them out so he suggested I do the shooting while he looked with field glasses. I was lying on the ground behind the gun while he stood next to me. I saw a shadowy figure waving in the distance.

We elevated the sight and I fired a quick burst, perhaps five rounds.

"Son of a bitch, Pete, you missed 'em by near thirty yards."

"Must be the wind." My ears were ringing. I pretended to adjust the sight.

"All right, they're back to rooting. You gonna shoot or piss your pants?"

I aimed into the sounder of pigs—which at that distance looked like a brown patch against the green of the brush—and pulled back the trigger. It was like holding on to a locomotive. One does not aim so much as direct the gun like a fire hose.

"Left," he was shouting, "right, right, walk 'em right . . . now left, more left, left left *left left!*" I did as he asked, seeing the bullets kick up dirt among the running brown shapes.

"Put on that other drum, there are some still kicking."

I attached the second drum.

"Son of a whore," he was saying, "I wonder is that really four hundred yards . . ."

I drowned out his talking with the noise of the gun.

When we went to pack our things, my mare, who is used to me shooting deer, quail, and turkey from her back, was bug-eyed. She knew something unnatural was afoot. My father's horse was nowhere in sight and it took nearly half an hour to find him.

Before heading home, we rode out to inspect the damage. The javelina were spread over a large flat section of caliche, splayed in all manner of disassembly. It looked as if someone had put dynamite inside them.

"Good," my father said, surveying the damage. He rode around nodding. Then he said: "You think the Germans have these?"

"They have thousands," I told him.

The Lewis had cooled enough to strap it to my saddle. Of course the Germans have machine guns. But it is not my father's nature to look to that side of things. We began to ride back to the house.

"I remember when a five-shot Colt was a weapon of mass destruction. Then you had maybe twenty years and there was the Henry rifle, load it on Sunday and shoot all week. Eighteen shots, I think."

"Life gets better and better," I said.

"You know I always thought those books would take you somewhere. I was sad when they didn't."

"They have," I said.

"I mean away from here. You think I don't *sabe* but I do. My brother was exactly like you. It runs in the family."

I shrugged.

"Wrong place, wrong time . . . wrong something."

"I like this family and I like this place," I told him, because for some reason, at that moment, it seemed true.

He started to say something, then didn't. As we rode back through the sun and the dust, toward our great white house on its hill, he seemed to relax, to settle into his saddle; I could tell his mind was wandering, doubtless over the many things he has done for which the entire world admires him.

I began to think of how often he was home during my childhood (never), my mother making excuses for him. Did she forgive him that day, at the very end? I do not. She was always reading to us, trying to distract us; she gave us very little time to get bored, or to notice he was gone. Some children's version of the *Odyssey*, my father being like Odysseus. Him versus the Cyclops, the Lotus Eaters, the Sirens. Everett, being much older, off reading by himself. Later I found his journals, detailed drawings of brown-skinned girls without dresses . . . My assumption, as my mother told us that my father was like Odysseus, was that I was Telemachus . . . now it seems more likely I will turn out a Telegonus or some other lost child whose deeds were never recorded. And of course there are other flaws in the story as well.

APRIL 13, 1917

This morning, Sally found me in my office, where I had slept. She had brought a tray of coffee and kolaches. I presumed she wanted something. She has not yet left for Dallas.

"How was your new gun?" she said.

"I guess the Colonel is quite fond of it."

"Is it the one we use or the one the Huns use?"

"Ours, of course."

"But the Huns have them too."

"Of course," I said again.

"Well, I hope you had a good time with it." She shook her head. "The whole time I was listening to that gun I could only think about Glenn and Charlie."

"I know."

She stood there, and I noticed the lines around her eyes, deeper every year, like my own. She looked like my mother in that light, her pale hair and skin . . . but unlike my mother, there is always a wheel turning somewhere in her mind. Though today she looked tired of thinking. I went forward and held her.

"I'm not sure I can stay here anymore."

"You've been saying that."

"I really mean it."

I shrugged and released my grip, but she pulled me tighter.

"We have to stick together," she said. Then she added, "You haven't touched me in weeks."

"You haven't touched me either."

"I have. You just haven't noticed."

"Our children will be fine."

"Pete," she said, "is there anyone you ever have honest conversations with?"

I wasn't sure what she was getting at. "There isn't anyone else."

"So start with me," she said. "Tell me exactly what you're thinking. Not what you think I want to hear, but the truth."

"You are talking crazy."

She looked at me. "I know I don't do much for you. I know I never have."

What would I tell her? That I have always known I belonged here? That one day some action will be required that will prove my life's value? A forty-six-year-old man, waiting for fate to take over . . . it likely already has.

"You promised me a place in the city when the children left."

"I know," I said.

"I still have a few years I could salvage. A few men still find me attractive. If you want me to move to San Antonio by myself, tell me. Otherwise I am willing to split our time between here and someplace civilized, if you will just come with me some of the time."

"This place will fall apart without me," I said. "And the Colonel cannot be left alone."

"You are worried about your father."

"He is eighty-one years old."

She shook her head. She looked out the window for a long time.

"Is that your final decision?"

APRIL 15, 1917

Sally departed for the train station. We have made love four times in the past two days, more than the past year in total. Deep depression when I dropped her off, pointlessness of living alone . . . several times allowed the car to wander without my hands on the wheel . . . but that was not it, either. Somehow this was required. The greater plan. Strange tingling along my scalp, as before we rode on the Garcias, as on various days in my younger life, such as when Phineas stepped forward to take the halter of that black horse. My father had wanted me to do it, but in front of all those people, I could not touch it.

When I got home it was dark and the house was also dark, quiet, and empty. Added another item to the list I began in Austin, originally titled "The Seven Types of Loneliness" (a man and woman sitting close, boy holding his mother's leg, a cold rain, the sound of crows, a girl's laughter down a stone street, four policemen walking, a thought of my father); of course the list has reached several hundred now. I ought to have burned it years ago, but instead I add another item: "A quiet house."

Tomorrow will release all the staff except Consuela and one or two of the maids. They should have no trouble finding work—men are being drafted left and right—I will give them three months' pay.

I tried to fall asleep but after a few hours I got up and walked around turning all the lights on. I could hear the wind rattling windows on the other side of the house. Finally I couldn't stand it and walked out to see if my father was still awake.

Chapter Twenty-five
Eli/Tiehteti

Fall 1851

P izon and the others, driving the thousand stolen horses, had reached camp a week before us, and stragglers continued to trickle in. We had lost eleven members of the band but the raid was quietly considered a success. Though we knew that if we continued to have these sorts of successes, there would be no Indians left to ride the horses.

Smaller raids continued all summer, mostly put on by young men who needed horses and scalps, both for marriage and because otherwise they had no status. The army had nearly finished a second line of forts—from Belknap to Abilene to Mason—but many settlers had already leapfrogged this second line. To the old-timers, the most ominous sign was the bee trees, which seemed to precede the line of settlement by a hundred miles or so and now reached nearly to the edge of the Llano. We were happy for so much honey, but we all knew what it meant.

The Comancheros had figured out we were prosperous again, and I convinced Toshaway to double the price of the horses we traded. Previously, a good horse might be traded for a handful of glass beads or a few yards of calico, but now we wanted more ammunition and gun parts, more steel arrowheads, and more food. I stayed in camp and hunted and broke horses, but mostly I spent time with Prairie Flower, who was no longer embarrassed to be seen in public with me, as my stature was now equal to Nʉʉkaru's or even Escuté's, even if my abilities were not.

The most important event of late summer was the capture of a young buffalo hunter, who, along with the rest of his party, had misjudged the degree to which the army and Rangers could protect him. We caught them in the lower reaches of the Palo Duro and after a brief fight his companions were all killed. He crawled out from under their wagon with his hands raised and, knowing what would happen to him, I immediately nocked an arrow, but Pizon shoved me and it went wide.

The hunter was in his late twenties, with blond hair and beard and blue eyes and an innocent sort of look. I was happy to get his rifled Springfield and Minie ball molds, but the real prize was the man himself. Because he was alive and uninjured and so close to our camp, it was decided to bring him in to be tortured.

This caused great excitement and all work was stopped for the day. It was as if the circus had come to town, or a public hanging called among the whites. He must have seen what was going to happen because he begged me to help him but there was nothing I could do, and a few of the newer captives, whose position was less secure, stomped on his face to show their loyalty.

The torture of a captive was considered a high honor for the women of the village and all the female elders were gathered along with the younger ones. Prairie Flower was upset that she had not been selected. After stripping him naked, tying his hands and feet to stakes, spread-eagled so he was just barely suspended in the air, they poked fun at his pale hair and his privates, which were shrunken with fear; one woman sat on top of him and pretended she was going to rut him, much to the delight of everyone. Most of the village was gathered, with children sitting or standing on shoulders, the same as would witness a hanging in town. The women built four very small fires, one each at his hands and feet. Fuel was added carefully, keeping the flames to a minimum, only building them hotter when he stopped shouting, which indicated the nerves had died. They would increase the heat by adding one very small stick, at which point he would begin to sing again.

He shrieked himself hoarse and the children mimicked him with great joy. By late afternoon he was barely making a sound and I wondered if he'd ruptured his vocal cords. At supper he was given broth and water, which his body accepted gladly, though he must have known why we were giving it to him. Later they fed him again. I walked by, thinking he was in a stupor, but he recognized me and begged me to kill him—one Christian to another. I stood there thinking, knowing what I would want done for me, and then Toshaway caught me as I was returning to the tipi.

"I know what you are thinking, Tiehteti. Everyone will know and the penalties will be severe. More than you think, probably."

"I'm not thinking anything," I said. "He's killing our buffalo."

"All right," he said. "All right, Tiehteti."

Prairie Flower was on fire that night. I did my best but after the second time I was less interested. She was rubbing herself against me and finally I stopped her.

"Usually I can't get rid of Nʉʉkaru and Escuté," she said. They were out on a raid, so we had the tipi to ourselves. "But now the one time I could use them . . . "

"I'm sure others are still awake, if that's what you really want."

"You know I don't." She cuddled against me. "What's wrong?" she said.

"Nothing."

"It's the white man, isn't it?"

I shook my head.

"Okay," she said. "I apologize for my horniness."

"Just give me a minute."

"Don't worry."

"I'll try," I said. But I couldn't.

In the morning, just after breakfast, they cut off his hands and feet because the nerves were all dead, and when the screaming began to abate, they moved the fire under the stumps where the nerves were still fresh. Fewer people were watching now, and though the sound of the man's screaming filled the camp, it had already started to seem normal.

Toshaway told me this had once been a regular event, but over the years, as they began to raid farther and farther away from camp, the risks of bringing back a full-grown male prisoner just to torture had not been worth it.

"I am going out to hunt," I said.

He looked at me.

"I'm fine," I told him.

When you don't want to see snakes you find them everywhere and when you want one you can't find it. Certain men milked rattlesnakes for war arrows, but I fumbled my equipment so much I had not wanted to risk it. Still, I had milked snakes, and after spending most of the day looking, I finally found a big *wutsutsuki* late in the afternoon, on a high rock in the sun. When he had stopped thrashing I cut off his head and wrapped it in a piece of buckskin.

The second night, the buffalo hunter was given broth and more water. By then he had only fifty or so fans, sitting around eating and watching him. I went to bed like normal and then waited until I couldn't hear any more talking. The night was overcast and nearly black, which I took as a sign. I made my way quietly to where he was staked out.

He made a sound when I approached; he might have been saying please; he might have been saying anything at all.

It was a stupid plan; it was dark, there were small sharp teeth, and it was messy, but I used the back of my knife to milk the snake's head over his mouth. It was only a drop or two but he began to kick. "Let it pass through you," I said. "You don't have to hold on to it." I made a cut on his throat and milked the rest of the venom into that. I could tell I'd nicked my hand.

His breathing was already starting to change.

I walked away and washed myself in the stream. When I got back to my tipi, Prairie Flower was in my bed, as excited as the night before.

When we were done, she said: "Where were you?"

"Just walking."

"You were wet," she said.

My arm was tingling. Finally I asked her: "That didn't bother you, what they did to that man?"

It came out louder than I wanted.

"It's just because he is white."

"I don't know."

"It is not good to discuss this with anyone."

"I'm not. I wouldn't."

"Even me," she said.

It was quiet.

"I know you're not weak. Everyone knows you're not weak." She was measuring her words. "Toshaway says you'll be chief one day. They're making you a buffalo robe, but it was supposed to be a surprise."

"I was just asking how you felt."

"They're making a robe that shows how you killed the Delaware, how your magic protected you from his arrows, and then how you saved Toshaway from the soldiers. It's supposed to be a surprise, though." Then she said, "That man was white. You need to think about that."

"We didn't do those things where I grew up."

She rolled away. "You know I was not always Kotsoteka," she said.

"No."

"When I was *tuepuru,* maybe six years old, the Texans attacked my band. My brother made my sister and me go into the river and swim away. They shot my brother's head off in the water, and they shot at me but missed. The next day my sister and I went back to our camp and found my mother, along with one hundred other dead women and dead old men and dead children. The Texans had cut off my mother's head and put it on a stick in the ground and they had taken a *tutsuwai* and put it all the way up between her legs, and there was so much blood we knew they had done it while she was still alive. But there was no blood around her neck so we knew that was not done until after. That is why I grew up *Pena tuhka* but now I am Kotsoteka."

"The same thing happened to my mother and sister," I told her. "And my brother."

"Tiehteti," she said, "this cannot happen." She reached for her things and began to dress and I decided I didn't care. And of course she was right: she was allowed to talk about her family, I was not allowed to talk about mine, because unless your family was Comanche, it was as if they had never existed.

"You can stop me if you want," she said.

I didn't say anything and I heard her make a little sob and then I grabbed her and pulled her back down.

"I won't talk about it anymore," I said.

She shrugged. She slipped out of her clothes but we just lay against each other and eventually she fell asleep.

I stayed up thinking, trying to figure if the tingling in my arm was spreading to my side or if I was imagining it. Then I was thinking about my father. In the early forties, there had been so few victories over the Comanches that when they occurred, the news spread to the entire state. In all those years there had only been one fight in which so many Comanches had died, which was Moore's expedition on the Colorado. Moore had claimed that over one hundred fifty braves had been killed, but there had always been talk that it was mostly women and children, that the braves had been out hunting when the raiders hit the camp. My father had ridden with Moore, and sometimes talked about the raid, but no differently than he'd talked about anything else. It was just something that had happened. Little Indians became big Indians. Everyone knew it.

Prairie Flower kissed me in her sleep. "You are good," she murmured. "You are honest and good and you are not afraid of anything."

The next morning the buffalo hunter was dead. His face and neck were bloated, but no one seemed to notice. Mostly they were disappointed. It was another sign the old ways were being lost: in the past, a captive might have been kept alive two or three days longer.

But if anyone suspected me, nothing was said. Prairie Flower and I spent every night together and Toshaway said if I wanted to borrow some horses to offer as a bride-price, they were free for the taking. He cleared his throat then, and mentioned, in a quieter tone, that fifty horses would be far too high. Times had changed.

I was given the buffalo robe they'd made for me, and my own tipi as well. It was turning out to be a good year. Fall had come and the rains were heavy and the heat had left the plains. The nights were crisp and the days sunny, the hunting good, and I began to make my plans with Prairie Flower.

A few weeks after the buffalo hunter died, people began to get sick.

Chapter Twenty-six
Jeannie

Summer 1945

V E-day came and for a few weeks it seemed everything would be different and then it wasn't. Her
brothers did not return, the vaqueros went about their
business without her—she did not see the point of
helping them lose money. Several times she packed a
suitcase, feeling desperate enough to take up Jonas
on his offer, but she could never reach him before she
changed her mind, she was sure that if she found him
in Berlin, it would be no different from Princeton, he
would abandon her some way or other.

Mostly she was bored. She made runs to Carrizo for
the cook (always managing to forget a thing or two),
she made trips to San Antonio, where a few dressmak-
ers knew her and promised to introduce her to young
men, but never did. She visited with Phineas, always

expecting an invitation to stay with him, in his grand house overlooking all of Austin. She thought they might sit on his gallery and talk long into the night, but he was a private man (*you are a grown woman,* is how he put it) and so she roomed at the Driscoll instead.

It was a good year for the land. The grass had stayed green. With so much good grass she knew she ought to buy a few hundred stocker animals, but the cattle were a luxury, the horses were a luxury, even the grass was a luxury: the poorer ranches now looked like patches of dirt. Anyway, she preferred grass to cows.

Once a week she would saddle her father's horse, General Lee, and take him out on the land. Sullivan objected—he'd wanted to shoot the animal—and he was probably right. A few times General Lee had nearly gotten the best of her. He would stand quietly, allowing himself to be saddled, and then, just as she mounted, he would begin to kick. He did tend to buck a straight line, but he had thrown her more than once. You ought to be grateful, she told him. I am the only reason you are still alive.

But he was not grateful. He must have known she did not appreciate him, or that her feelings were mixed, or maybe, like her, he was simply bored, because he had no job and no prospects and when you went on like that too long, habits tended to grow on you.

Texas had once been full of wild horses, five million, ten million, no one knew. But they had mostly been rounded up and shipped to the British during the Great War. Between the war and the rendering plants, Texas had been just about cleaned out of ponies. In her childhood, most of the old cow horses still went to East Texas to become plow horses, but the tractors had changed that. Old horses now became feed for other animals.

Oil was what mattered. The Allies had burned seven billion barrels during the war; 90 percent of that had come from America, mostly from Texas. The Big Inch and Little Big Inch: they could not have invaded Normandy without them. The Allies had sailed to victory on a sea of Texas oil.

She sometimes wondered about that—if the pipelines had not been finished—if the liberation of Europe had been canceled—maybe Paul and Clint would still be alive. Or maybe the war would still be going on. Maybe Jonas would be dead as well. That was what they always said—if this or that terrible thing had not been done, the war would never have ended.

She was not sure she believed them. They sounded like men who'd been thrown from horses because they'd wanted to get off anyway. And as for the war ending, it turned out the Russians were as bad as Hitler.

No, she would not go to Europe. She would not follow her brother around like a stray. Something would change, she could feel it.

Since the vaqueros had done their work on the landman, there had not been any other callers, but one day there was a letter from a manager at Humble Oil. He wanted to take her to lunch.

They met in town and he was nicely dressed with fine features and gray hair that was neatly parted. He was handsome and tan and she liked him immediately and right after they ordered their steaks he offered four million plus 25 percent royalties.

It was double the offer from Southern Minerals but after pretending to think it over carefully she said: "What else will you give us?"

He held the same sweet expression.

"I know that you put in bump gates for people, but we already have them."

"What else would you like?" he said.

"What if I asked you to clear all the land within"—she thought of a large number—"five thousand feet of each well?"

"You want us to root plow your mesquite."

She nodded.

"You want us to root plow five hundred sixty-eight acres of mesquite around each well."

Was that the real number? She had no idea. She had no idea how he'd calculated it without pen and paper. But she knew she couldn't reveal her ignorance so she said: "Actually we want you to clear the acreage around each drilling site, whether it's a good well or not."

He laughed, reminding her of Phineas. "Honey, you realize there's a lot of proven land in South Texas, and no one else is asking for these improvements."

"I know you paid three and a half million plus royalties for the King Ranch," she said. "And that was ten years ago, with nothing proved, and I know all the work you've been doing to their land, because we are friends with Bob Kleberg."

It was quiet and it continued to be quiet. Outside it was busy, people dressed in city clothes, shopping or out for lunch. She started to apologize, she'd pushed too far, but of course this man wanted something from her, same as the other one, and she made herself sit as if the silence was perfectly natural. She could sit without talking for a hundred years. The man was looking out the window. She took note of his bright eyes, his small features—a man's features, but finely done—he had clearly taken more from his mother. He was quite a striking man. It occurred to her that he was just as aware of this as she was. He seemed to decide something. Now he was judging.

"I wish we could do better, but . . ." He put up his hands.

"What if we just connected to your pipeline?"

"That is funny," he said.

"Well, there is very little oil going through it at present. It will likely rot."

"If you're planning on drilling your own oil, Ms. McCullough, let me assure you there is no faster way to go bankrupt, and you'll end up living in one of these houses with the niggers and the never-sweats. If you take our offer, that land will be supporting your family for the next few centuries and you will not have to dirty a finger except to sign the lease."

She knew he was wrong but she didn't know why and she knew if she said another word her ignorance would be laid bare, if it had not been already. She collected her purse and shook his hand and walked out of the restaurant before their food even came. It was a three-dollar steak and she wondered if she ought to leave money. No. She slowed her pace, making her way down the street in the town named after her family, the shade of the awnings, parked cars, the sky looking bright between the brick storefronts. Four million dollars. It did not seem meaningful to her. In truth she felt more guilty about the three-dollar steak.

Then she began to feel stupid. She was not a grown-up at all, she was a girl, the accountant said she would owe the government five million dollars in estate taxes—that had not seemed real, either. They could get an extension but they would have to drill, and soon; it was a question of finding the right people. Phineas had told her not to worry, but she had not been worrying anyway.

The road turned back to dirt. She passed the houses of the Mexicans, their filthy alleys, doors that didn't close properly, people living ten to a room, slabs of meat hanging in the sun, collecting flies. She was sure she ought to turn around, to catch the man from Humble before he left.

But she was still walking. It was brush and farmland. Her feet, in her good shoes, sank into the dust; they would be ruined. It was stupid talking to people without Phineas around. It was stupid what she'd said about the pipeline. She should not be taking these meetings alone. But that made no sense, either. Phineas would not live forever, he was no different from her father.

Ed Freeman was in his onion field, tinkering with his irrigator. Did he still owe her father money? She waved and he looked as if something might be wrong—as if he might be required to help her. She continued along the bar ditch, sweat running down her back now.

Her father had allowed her to hate mathematics; he'd told her it didn't matter if she were good at it or not. He had been wrong about that as well. It did matter. What had the man figured—five thousand times five thousand? No, it was a geometry problem. *I haven't the faintest,* she thought.

She watched a car pass, roiling up the dust, a white man taking four Mexicans to work. License number 7916. Seventy-nine times sixteen. It seemed impossible. She did not see how the man had done it. And yet he had.

As soon as she got home she had called Phineas and told him what happened, including what she'd said about the pipeline. He told her not to worry: she hadn't said anything they weren't already thinking. She felt relieved but Phineas was still talking. He was inviting her to Austin. He had someone for her to meet.

Chapter Twenty-seven
Diaries of Peter McCullough

APRIL 17, 1917

"Would you ever go into farming yourself, Colonel?"

"Sure," he says. "Natural progression of the land."

There are perhaps fifty of them, all in their Sunday best, eating tenderloin and drinking claret in the great room, listening to the Colonel expound on the wonders of our southern climate. I consider leaving my shady spot on the gallery to tell them that his policy was to shoot at any farmers who tried to toll us on cattle drives. And has said his whole life that grubbing in the dirt is the lowest form of human existence. He blames this on his time with the Indians, though it is common among all horse people, from landed cattleman to poorest vaquero.

" . . . the winter garden of Texas," he is saying, "two hundred eighty-eight growing days . . . you'll never lift a hand to shovel snow again." Scattered applause. "Further," he says, "you will find the proportion of advanced females greatly reduced compared to what you are used to in Illinois." Laughter and more applause. I close my ears; I decide to go for a walk.

Naturally they will only show the farms that are doing well; none whose water was too salty for irrigation, none of the farms on the old Cross S land, subdivided less than ten years ago, most of which are reverting to the lowest class of scrub rangeland. The soil as dead as anything you might find in Chihuahua.

April 18, 1917

Ran into Midkiff's son Raymond at the store. He was driving a few critters along the road after the hailstorm this afternoon when he saw the caravan of Illinois farmers pulled over under some trees.

They were standing in the road examining hailstones the size of oranges, remarking how they might have been killed. One of them called to Raymond to ask if this weather was unusual.

"Sure is," he told them. "But you should have been here last year, when it rained!"

When the Colonel returned he was furious and told me we needed to fire the limp-dicked droop-eyed son of a bitch who was driving brindle calves on the lower road.

Explained we could not fire Raymond Midkiff. He said that was fine—we would shoot him instead. Reminded him the Midkiffs are our neighbors.

Naturally, all the farmers thought Midkiff was joking. The irrigated fields are quite lush. They have no mental ruler to understand the country here; a few of them were overheard repeating the old saw "if you plow, the rains will follow." I wonder what century they are living in.

All of it, for some reason, makes me feel almost unbearably lonely . . . but I have always been a keen student of that emotion.

APRIL 19, 1917

The entire Pinkard Ranch—over one hundred sections—has been sold and divided. The family is moving to Dallas. I went to visit with Eldridge Pinkard. He could barely look at me. We are nearly the same age—his father settled this country not long after the Colonel.

"The bank would have taken it one of these days, Pete." He shrugged. "Even with beef where it is, this drought . . . I had to pull the money out before there was none left."

"Heard you bought a little in the cross timbers."

He chuckled bitterly: "Two whole sections."

"Probably run a few head."

He shrugged and scuffed the dirt, looked out over what had been his pastures. "Before you get to thinking I am too badly looed . . ."

"I don't," I lied.

"You do, but I appreciate it. I wasn't going to say this to any of you who's staying, but you and me have known each other since there was Indians."

"Sure," I said.

"I was mighty down in the mouth about this until I got to talking to Eustice Caswell. On the draft board?" He shook his head. "Pete, a year from now all the good men'll be overseas. I can't even take a piss without some bond salesman drumming me for ten dollars. And . . . truthfully I am jealous of some of those boys who are shipping out, because by the time they get to France, they will have seen more country than I've seen in my whole life. And once I realized that, I got to seeing this as the last clear swing I'd ever get. And that I was a fool if I didn't take it."

"I guess."

"It ain't like our daddies grew up here, Pete. It ain't like people have lived here long. This is just the place they happened to stop."

"The fences got all of us," I said.

He looked as if he might cry, but he didn't, and then I saw that he was not happy, but he was not sad, either. The idea of moving away from here appealed to him. "You know if I was staying, I'd build roads through the whole place, get to where I could run it with a quarter of the hands, drive ten minutes instead of riding four hours, eat home every night, do the feeding out of trucks. You could get it pretty well oiled, if you put your mind to it. But even so . . ." He lifted his boot and ground it down on a mesquite seedling. "Let's face it, Pete. This land is niggered out. I wish they'd taken pictures when we were kids, because I want to forget it ever looked like this."

When I got home, my father revealed he has known about it for months—he picked up half the minerals underneath the Pinkard land. I asked how we were going to pay for it.

"I decided to sell the pastures across the Nueces."

"Where are we going to keep the bulls?"

"After the promoter's cut we're clearing $31.50 an acre. We can fence off whatever we want. This pays for the minerals under the Pinkard, plus half the Garcia acquisition."

"You can see those pastures from every high point on our property," I said.

"So what? We'll look at the pretty farmer girls."

"What if I refuse to sign the deed?"

"You can refuse whatever you want," he said.

Except I cannot. I signed as he knew I would. I console myself with the fact that the Nueces pastures were not exactly convenient, anyway. The Colonel consoled me by pointing out we kept mineral rights. "Anymore, the surface ain't worth two shits," he said. "Luckily them ignorant Yankees were too busy carrying on about their college to figure that out."

Fine except the Nueces pastures were the only sensible place to keep the bulls. It will be much harder to control breeding now, more work for us, more work for the vaqueros, and much more expensive.

As for the minerals, there has been a good deal of drilling along the big river; trucks and roughnecks no longer garner any notice. Lease prices have tripled. But still the closest strikes are at Piedras Pintas, far to the east, which produce only a few hundred barrels a day under pump. The rest is just gas, which for now is useless.

APRIL 26, 1917

The Colonel, who has been gone a week, returned today from Wichita Falls with a nearly new rotary drilling rig on several old trucks. He claims to have gotten a good price. *Feller who owned it went bankrupt,* he told me, as if this were a selling point.

Accompanying the Colonel is a very drunk man who claims to be a geologist. A second drunk who claims to be a driller. Drunks number three through five are the floor- and derrickmen. They look to have been sleeping in hog wallows.

"Where did you get all that?" I asked him.

"Wichita Falls," he said, as if I didn't know where he'd been.

"We puttin' in more windmills?"

"Don't you worry about it."

He and the geologist went to explore in the sandy Garcia pastures. The rig builder, toolie, and driller retired to the Colonel's porch to drink.

MAY 4, 1917

Having come up with nothing better, they have located a spot to drill, barely half a mile from the house, based on a foggy recollection of a seep my father might have seen fifty years ago, which has not been seen since.

"That's an interesting spot," I told him, "where we can see and hear it from the house. I guess you couldn't find anywhere else in almost four hundred sections."

"That's what the doodlebug told me. Always listen to the doodlebug."

There are times I can't tell if he thinks I'm a simpleton, or if he really is one himself.

MAY 27, 1917

Panic sweeping through the Mexicans. Six of our top hands, including Aarón and Faustino Rodriquez, informed me they are resigning and returning to Mexico—they do not think it will be safe for their families.

Reason: The good people in Austin just approved funding to expand the Ranger force. Number of Rangers on border will increase to eight hundred (currently forty).

I tried pointing out to the vaqueros that Mexico is a war zone. They don't care. Safer than here, they say.

Freddy Ramirez (our segundo who first caught the Garcias stealing cattle) also put in his notice. The factories in Michigan are still hiring Mexicans. Or so he has heard.

I tried to make a joke about it: "Michigan? *Muy frío!*" Rubbing my hands on my arms.

He did not find this funny. "The cold we can survive. The *Rinches,* maybe not."

My father does not care that we are losing seven of our best hands. After putting half our employees to work assembling the derrick and getting supplies to the drilling site, the real work has begun. Din is oppressive. Where there was once the sound of cattle, a creaking windmill, it now sounds like a train station, though the train never gets closer, or farther, or quieter. Because of the heat all the windows are open. I walk around with cotton stuffed in my ears.

JUNE 19, 1917

Drilling continues and so far nothing but sand. Meanwhile, because of the sale of the Pinkard Ranch, and other smaller ranches like it, the town is nearly unrecognizable. Trucks and vegetable pickers instead of horses and vaqueros. Gilbert's store selling fertilizer by the ton. Went there to buy some digging bars, a few shovels, and a case of .30-cal gov't for the Lewis gun.

"Is that my price as well?" Everything was three times as expensive as it had been.

"Nah. I figure the few of us left ought to stick together." He pretended to do some figuring on a pad and reduced the bill by half. It was still a 20 percent increase over the previous month. I decided not to mention it.

"Who's left?" I said.

"Far as the greasers, none of them. About ten families, Vargases, Guzmans, Mendezes, Herreras, Riveras, I don't even fuckin' know who else—all happened the same day, it seemed like—they sold their lots to Shaw who owns the rooming house, bought a few old trucks, and headed to Michigan, forty or fifty of them in one caravan. Cleaned me out of coats and blankets. They say Ford hired two thousand Mexicans in one factory. Which is pretty funny when you think about it, greasers building cars and all."

Considered mentioning that several of the "greasers" (Vargas and Rivera, at least) had gone to college in Mexico City while Gilbert and his cross-eyed brothers were diddling heifers in Eagle Pass.

"Even old Gomez sold out. Everything in his store for cost. I got crates and crates of metates, chorizo, horsehair bridles, and hide ropes. Plus his *curandero* shit. You believe that? You are looking at the new town *curandero*, right here."

The thought of any Mexican trusting Niles Gilbert to sell them medicine was depressing. I paid the bill and tried to hurry out, but not before he added: "Funny thing is, I do miss all those people, which I never thought I would say, given all the trouble they caused."

Fine sentiments for a murderer. I suppose I am no better.

Despite the disappearance of the last of the original Mexican families (many of whom have been here five or ten generations—longer than any white), a new crop has arrived to fill their places. They speak no English and will be easy prey for men like Gilbert. Still, it is better than northern Mexico, where a state of open warfare persists. *Dunno what they're complaining about,* said my father. *At least there's no taxes.*

After I got home, I rode out to help rotate the beefs off the number 19 pasture. We are getting everything cross-fenced, and as Pinkard said, this place *is* beginning to run like a well-oiled machine. But when does the soul go out of it? That is what no one seems to know.

June 20, 1917

Need a new truck. Have settled on a Wichita. The 2.5-ton would be a dream. Cannot decide between the worm drive and the chain drive.

Considered a Ford (they now make the Model T cars in Dallas) but everyone who owns a Ford has had a shoulder dislocated (or broken) when the starting handle kicked back. You can judge a Ford driver by the cast on his arm—that is the old joke.

You cannot build junk and expect to survive in today's world. People want things that last.

June 21, 1917

A poor Mexican woman came to the door today. Was surprised she was bold enough to come through the gate. She looked familiar but I could not place her, presumed she was the wife or sister of one of the hands. She was thin and pale, wearing only a shift and a thin shawl over top, and when the wind blew her dress against her body I could see her legs were nearly skeletal.

"*Buenas noches*," I said.

There was a pause.

"You don't recognize me." Her English was perfect.

"I guess not," I said.

"I am María Garcia."

I stepped back.

"I am Pedro Garcia's daughter."

Chapter Twenty-eight
Eli/Tiehteti

Fall 1851

At first it was just a fever but then the spots appeared and everyone panicked. A quarter of the band struck their tipis, gathered their horses, and left the camp within a few hours. A few days later, the people who'd first taken sick were covered in boils, their faces and necks, arms and legs, the palms of their hands and the soles of their feet.

The medicine men built sweat lodges along the stream; people were dunked in the cold water, put in the sweat lodge, then dunked again. It wasn't long after that that people started to die; soon all the medicine men were sick as well.

The whites had been variolating their children for a hundred years, but by the time of statehood, you could find the vaccine in most cities. The Germans had paid a doctor to come to Fredericksburg and my mother had taken us there to get our shots.

Prairie Flower was one of the first to get sick. She hadn't touched the dead man, but I had. I hoped it was just a fever, but then her mouth felt strange, there was a kind of roughness around her lips, which I tried to smooth away.

A few weeks into the epidemic, a pair of young Comanches in their best war paint rode up to the camp calling out that the raiding party, including Escuté and Nʉʉkaru, had won a great victory, many scalps and horses, not a single man lost.

The messengers stopped at the edge of the village and Toshaway, who had the first of the red marks on his face, limped out to meet them, carrying his bow and quiver.

"The band is sick," he said. "You have to go somewhere else."

The messengers protested; they didn't want to be denied their victory, and finally Toshaway told them he would shoot anyone who came into the camp, including his own sons, as it would be a more merciful death than the *tasía*.

Later that day the raiders appeared. They rode to within a few hundred yards of the camp and the people who were still able came out to wave their good-byes. Toshaway stood leaning on his bow. Two riders broke from the group and everyone squinted to see who they were. It was Nʉʉkaru and Escuté. They came within fifty paces and then Toshaway nocked an arrow and fired it into the ground in front of them.

"We'll wait for you in the Yamparikas' territory," said Escuté.

"We will not see you there," said Toshaway. "But I will see you in the happy hunting grounds."

Another young tekʉniwapʉ came forward.

"I have stated my mind," said Toshaway. "I will kill any man who comes into this village."

"Where is Gets Fat?" said the young man.

"She's sick," said someone.

He continued to ride forward.

Toshaway shot an arrow past his head.

"You can kill me if you want, Toshaway, but either way I am going to die in this camp with my wife."

Toshaway thought about it. Then he aimed his bow at the other raiders.

"The rest of you will leave now," he said.

A few of the other tekʉniwapʉ, not sure what they ought to do, not wanting to look like cowards, began to ride forward, but Escuté and Nʉʉkaru held them back. Even the very sick had come out from their tipis; they gathered at the edge of the camp and began to call out to the young men, first telling them to stay back and then telling them things they wanted them to know, family news, old secrets, things they should have said a long time ago, things that had happened since the raiders had gone.

Finally, after all the messages had been shouted across the distance, the riders kicked their horses and began to ululate and the entire band, for the last time, called back with their own war whoops, until they filled the air, and the riders shook their bows and lances, and turned their horses, and disappeared across the prairie.

By the fourth week the boils covered Prairie Flower's entire face—there was nothing left I could recognize, she had become the sickness itself. Each morning our pallet would be soaked from her breaking sores; but finally the boils began to shrink and scab and it seemed she would heal.

"I am not going to be beautiful anymore," she said. She was crying.

"You'll still be beautiful," I told her.

"I don't want to live if my face is ruined."

"You'll heal," I said. "Don't pick."

That night her fever broke and she began to breathe easily. I watched her for a long time. When the sun woke me up my arm was numb—all her weight was on it—and when I tried to wake her she wouldn't move.

It was a clear warm day but only a few people were about. Toshaway was lying in his hammock, eyes closed, face to the light. The bumps on his skin were just starting to swell.

"Do I look bad?" he said.

"I've seen worse."

"Yes. And soon I will look worse." He spat. "Tiehteti. What an absurd way to die."

"The strong always survive."

"Is this known among the whites?"

"Yes."

"You are lying."

"Maybe not," I said.

"Now it's only maybe." He closed his eyes again. "It's not dignified."

I wasn't sure if he was talking about my lie or the sickness.

"When I was younger," he said, "the son of our *paraibo* became very sick. He had always been small but he was growing thinner every day, and no matter what medicine was made, he did not get better. Finally the *paraibo* asked if I might do him a favor. He made a purification ritual, washed and dressed his son for battle, gave him his own shield, the chief's shield, and then we all went to a mountain, and my friend and I did battle with the chief's son, just the three of us alone, and we killed him. And in that way, we took a pointless death and made it into a brave death."

"I'm not going to kill you."

"You could not anyway," he said. He grinned. "At least not yet."

"But someday." I didn't mean it, but I knew it was what he wanted to hear.

"Come over here, if you don't mind touching me."

I sat on the ground.

"You smell," he said.

"Prairie Flower just died."

"Ah, Tiehteti." He took my hand. "I am so sorry. And meanwhile you have been letting me talk." He began to cry. "I am so sorry, my poor son. I am so sorry, Tiehteti."

After I buried Prairie Flower I began to go to the other tipis. There was a surplus of the dead. Pizon died that afternoon and I helped his son bury him. A week later I buried his wife and two weeks later I buried his son. Entire families passed in the same night and now I went tipi to tipi, tying the flaps shut if I had buried everyone. I buried Red Bird, Fat Wolf, Hates

Work—whose dead face I kissed, imagining the scabs were not there—Lazy Feet and two of his slaves, Hard to Find, Two Bears Walking, Always Visiting Someone, Hisoo-ancho and his three children, whose names I never learned, Sun Eagle, Big Fall by Tripping. Black Dog, Little Mountain and her husband. Lost Again, who died in the arms of Big Bear, who was not her husband. I buried Hukiyani and In the Woods. Humaruu and Red Elk. Piitsuboa, White Elm, Ketumsa. The other names I didn't know, or had forgotten.

I slept in my own tipi but spent my days with Toshaway. He and his two wives were all sick, the three of them on one pallet. There was a good supply of firewood and it was warm.

"Come over here, Tiehteti," said Situtsi.

I did. I sat with my back against their pallet, and my feet near the fire, and she stroked my hair. I began to close my eyes. Watsiwannu was asleep, closer to the end than the others. Toshaway was murmuring. I couldn't tell if he knew I was there. But a little while later, he said: "Tiehteti, the next band you go to, if this happens to them, I want you to ride to the whites and tell the army where their camp is, and tell them to bring the mountain howitzers. Do you understand?"

"Yes."

"That is an order," he said. "From your war chief."

I nodded.

"Will you go back to the whites now?" said Sitʉtsi.

"Of course not."

"Do the whites get this disease?"

"Yes, but they make medicine on people who do not have it, and it keeps them from becoming infected."

"This was done to you?" said Toshaway.

"When I was a child."

"So what do you think of the Comanche medicine?" he said. Then he began to laugh. Then Sitʉtsi began to laugh as well.

"You will lead our people to a good place," she said.

"Do not let him get ahead of himself," said Toshaway. "First he must dig." He lifted his head to look at me. "That is your only job. You must dig."

Many of the captives had begun to flee, stealing horses and disappearing across the plains. No one was strong enough to stop them.

As for me, I dug. I wore out all our bone shovels and then I dug with lance shafts, tipi poles, and anything else I could find. I might have dug for weeks, or months, it got colder, the nights were freezing but the daytime sun kept the soil soft, and so I dug. Some of the Comanches who'd recovered from the sickness began to dig alongside me, the color gone from their faces in patches. Some of the survivors hunted so we could keep digging, others did nothing, still waiting to die with their families, until they did not, and so they joined us.

While digging the grave for Toshaway and Sitътsi, in a place far from the camp, an overlook I'd spent weeks thinking about, I found a small black-and-white cup. It was made of pottery and beneath it, as I dug deeper, I came to a flat stone and beneath that was another stone, and the more I dug, the more stones I found, until the stones turned into a wall, and then a corner of two walls, and then I stopped.

Neither the Comanches nor the Apaches before us had ever built houses of stone, and no horse people would have made pottery. The Caddo and Osage had never lived this far west, and neither had the whites or Spaniards, and I realized I had come on the remains of some ancient tribe that had lived in towns or cities, a tribe so long extinct no one remembered they had ever lived.

I decided to take the cup to ask Grandfather but he was dead, and then I thought I would ask Toshaway but he was dead as well, and I nearly put it down but couldn't, I couldn't stop turning it over in my hands, and then I knew why, because it had lain there a thousand years or more and it made Toshaway and all the others seem very young; as if they were young and there was still hope.

Chapter Twenty-nine
Jeannie McCullough

1945

The man Phineas introduced her to looked like a sharecropper—a deep tan, high cheekbones, and a raw, underfed look—except for a widow's peak he might have been a half-breed Indian. He was leaning against the file cabinets in Phineas's office, trying to act older than he was, and when she came in, he nodded as if he had not seen anything interesting and turned back to her great-uncle. There was something in his manner that made her wonder if this young man had some private relationship with Phineas, if maybe he was part of the reason she was never allowed to stay at her great-uncle's house. She decided she didn't like him.

"Hank is a driller," said Phineas. "And Hank is looking for work."

Hank nodded to her again but didn't offer to shake her hand. He and Phineas continued a conversation they were having about rocks and well logging or something equally boring. She half listened and walked around the room, but they continued to talk and she began to wonder why she had been invited, she looked at pictures of Phineas with her family, Phineas with various famous people. The driller wore a white shirt and dark trousers, which were clean but had seen better days; leather work boots, because, she guessed, he had no proper shoes. Still, she found that she wanted him to notice her; he was not properly handsome but there was something. *You have been living by yourself too long,* she thought.

On the other hand, there were few men whom Phineas treated as equals; for some reason this driller was one of them, though she could not understand exactly why. As for the driller (Hank, she thought), he continued to take no notice of her at all. A secretary walked in, a beauty like all the girls who worked for Phineas, dark hair and creamy skin and all her assets on display in a tight green dress; she went out of her way to touch Hank's hand as she filled his coffee, but Hank acted as if she didn't exist, and Jeannie forgave the girl her good looks and became sure that there was something between this young man and her uncle.

Finally they finished talking and Phineas swiveled his chair.

"We're hiring Hank," he said. "He'll be heading down to the land with you today."

They drove back to McCullough Springs in Hank's old truck. It was hot and noisy; she hoped he wouldn't notice how much she was sweating. *He is just a driller,* she reminded herself. And not all that good-looking, either; she was far out of his league. He had a flat nose that might have come from being punched, or might always have been that way. A bit of the cur dog in him, her grandmother would have said, and yet he had a sort of physical confidence that could not be faked, she had seen it in the best vaqueros, there was a swagger about him as if, despite his size, whatever you or anyone else could do, he could do it better. He reminded her of Clint: the sort of man to whom things came easily, who was good at everything he tried.

Hank was twenty-four and had spent the war (and all the years before it, back to early childhood) looking for oil with his father, who was now dead. They had been worth several million at one point, but their last few gambles had not paid off, and then his father was killed in a blowout, leaving Hank in a tight spot.

He owned his own Cummins power rig and six-wheel-drive International, knew of dozens of good rough-necks looking for work, but at the moment he barely had money for gas.

"I could rent my rig out," he said, "but then what would be the point?"

He wasn't looking for a reply.

"You got brothers or sisters?"

"Three brothers," she said, "but two died in the war."

"I've got two sisters."

Something must have occurred to her because he said: "In case you're wondering, I tried to enlist in '42, but they turned me down for color blindness."

She nodded and looked out the window, watched the brush and baked earth pass outside. Everyone who hadn't served felt compelled to give you their tale of woe.

"Meanwhile I never knew I was color-blind, I see the same as anyone else. A few months later I went to the station in Houston, but I still couldn't make out the numbers in the test, so they flunked me again, only this time I went back and borrowed the book when they weren't looking." He looked at her. "I figured it didn't cost much."

"Probably not," she said.

"Anyway I memorized the numbers and had to drive to New Mexico so they wouldn't remember they'd already seen me. This time I passed the test, but I must have done it too quick, because they started showing me the pages in a different order and I didn't get a single goddamn one of them. They knew what I'd done and told me if I ever tried again they were going to have me arrested for interfering with the war effort."

"That is some story."

"Interfering with the war effort, you believe that?"

"I believe it was a blessing."

"Try going four years where everyone thinks you're a communist or some other type of shirker. I was about to go to Canada and join up there. I probably should have but Daddy talked me out of it."

"A lot of men in oil and gas were exempted," she said. "We couldn't have won the war otherwise."

"Well, I didn't intend to be one of them."

She started to say something else, but he rolled down the window so all the wind came in.

By then they were south of San Antonio, into the great flat plain. She squinted against the glare; the noise made it hard to think. Hank kept the needle at eighty and she wondered what would happen if they lost a tire. She watched the way he drove, the muscles in his arms going tight and then loose again, his jaw working; it was plain he was a man whose mind was always running. She thought about her father, who thought he was a good driver, but was not. Hank kept the truck on a very straight line; he was going too fast but they were not jerking around the road. She wondered about her brothers, what they might say if they could speak, if their opinions might have changed on the war. She supposed it would not be any different. Once men got an idea, they did not seem to care if it killed them or not.

"Well, I am glad you are here," she said, once he rolled up the window. He nodded; perhaps he no longer remembered what they had been talking about. Or perhaps he did not agree. Long before they reached McCullough Springs she was wondering what it might be like to live in the big house with him. Her suspicions of his relationship with Phineas did not seem to be correct; he seemed entirely masculine. But otherwise nothing special. She was not sure why she felt so drawn to him. *You do not meet enough men*, she decided again.

Still, she pretended to sleep so that she could watch him without his knowing it. She could not help the feeling that she had been waiting for him, not someone like him, but him exactly, that she had been waiting without even knowing that he existed. And then, a minute later, she would resolve to get an apartment in Dallas or San Antonio so she would not be so alone. She supposed this man reminded her of her father and brothers; he had that sort of confidence, though he did not have their vanity—he'd worn work boots into the office of the most powerful man in Texas. *He is like the Colonel,* she told herself. The Colonel had not come from anything, either.

When they reached the ranch, they sat at the gate until she realized that he expected her, as the passenger, to get out and open it, even though she was a woman. Then they were climbing the hill. The enormous white house appeared; she wondered if he would find it too much. He didn't seem to notice. He might as well have been pulling up to an old shack. They parked in the shade and went inside, though she saw him check his boots at the threshold.

"I'll have someone get your bag and show you to your room. Then we can have supper."

"I'd like to study the maps your uncle gave me," he said. "While that drive is still fixed in my mind."

"There are lots of tables in there," she said, pointing to the great room.

She went upstairs and read in the sun with the noise and cool of the air conditioner blowing. Her father had been against them. She had a pleasant feeling and then she thought she was kissing one of the vaqueros; when she opened her eyes she could still hear the peculiar sound their lips had made. Then she was awake. She went downstairs and found Hank eating alone in the kitchen; Flores had fixed him a steak.

"You might have called me," she said.

"I figured you wanted to eat alone."

"We consider it normal to eat with company."

"I didn't know if I counted as company."

"Well, you do," she said.

"All right. In that case I am sorry I missed dining with you, Missus McCullough."

She turned her back on him and got a glass of milk from the icebox.

"I will make it up to you."

"You will indeed," she said.

She didn't want to look at him but she could tell he was grinning. "I will show you to your room now," she said.

She took him upstairs, past the enormous dark paintings of the Colonel and his children, past the Roman busts and drawings of Pompeii and silver knickknacks on all the marble, finally to the guest rooms on the opposite side of the house. Something told her he was used to sleeping in his truck and she said, "I hope you find the accommodations adequate."

He shrugged and she got annoyed again.

"Well, good night," he said. "You are not as bad as I first thought." He smiled and she found she didn't like it; it was too direct. She hurried away down the hall.

The next morning he laid out the maps in the dining room. "From what your uncle said, the most obvious faults are over here on the eastern part of the property. That is where we'll want to start."

"Then the easiest way will be to ride. Otherwise we will be walking through a lot of brush."

He did not react to this.

"I'll find you some proper boots," she added. "I doubt yours will fit in the stirrups."

"I will be honest," he said. "Horses don't like me much. And I guess I have never cared for them, either."

"That is very strange."

"I suppose it is for you. But I prefer my truck. It doesn't make my eyes itch and I know it won't kick me."

"Where are you from again?"

"The moon."

"I am going to teach you to like horses."

"You can try," he said. "But if I am kicked, it might decrease my affections for you."

He looked away and cleared his throat noisily.

She looked away as well. She had never met anyone so direct. She felt a prickly sensation. She worried that Flores had heard, then she decided she didn't care. "You will not be kicked," she whispered. "Nor will your affections decrease." Her neck got even hotter.

"You are probably right," he said.

"About which?"

"I guess we will find out."

But once they were driving, he seemed to lose all interest. He looked straight ahead and off to his left and off to his right but never at her; he was looking at things outside. She thought about what she had said: it had been too much. She had been too direct. A despair came over her, yes, she had been too forward, she had not known what to say. Now he thought she was a different kind of girl than she really was.

"I have never been with a man," she said. "In case you were getting the wrong idea."

He began to laugh, then stopped himself.

"I didn't want you getting the wrong idea," she insisted.

"You aren't used to talking to people, are you?"

She looked out the window. For a moment, idiotically, she thought she might cry.

"It's all right," he said. He reached over and squeezed her hand, then took his own hand back just as quickly. "I'm the same way."

They spent the entire day driving the ranch's dirt roads. He would skid the truck to a stop, then climb out and stand on the roof.

"What are you looking for?"

"The escarpment," he said. "But there is so much goddamn brush."

"There's brush everywhere."

"That's what I just said."

"It's not just on our land."

He continued to look. "I forgot my binoculars," he said. Then he added: "For someone who owns this much country, you are one sensitive individual."

She didn't answer.

"But at least you have good roads. Half the time I drill in Texas I have to bushwhack through three miles of mesquite."

"We ought to just drill near the Humble fields."

"That is a good idea," he said, "except they have been tapping them for twenty-five years. And if we find something they will just have incentive to get those wells reworked, and take even more oil, and your uncle will be mad at me."

"So we're just going to start drilling in the middle of nowhere?"

"You know how you are with horses?"

"Yes."

"I am that way with oil."

"So you have convinced my uncle."

He grinned. "We'll get a shot truck in here and narrow things down."

"I suppose that will be expensive."

"It will be a lot less than a dry hole."

She slept in her bedroom and he slept in his. She did not want him to get the wrong idea, though on the other hand she did. She left her door open, just a crack, just in case he came. Which of course was ridiculous. He didn't even know where her room was and he was not going to come find it in the dark. "You are a slut," she said out loud. Though of course it had been two years since any man had touched her. And compared to her mother, who was already having children by now . . .

She was awake most of the night. She saw herself marrying him, she saw him using her and throwing her away. She decided she didn't care as long as he wasn't rough. Then she was thinking about the glorious life of men—to go off and have whatever experiences you wanted, whenever you wanted to have them—meanwhile here she was, nearly twenty and still a virgin, her only prospect asleep on the other side of the house. He acted as if he liked her but then suppose he didn't. It was too awful to contemplate. She looked out the window and waited for the sun to rise.

Chapter Thirty
Diaries of Peter McCullough

JUNE 22, 1917

I stood there with the door open, expecting her to draw a pistol, or rush with a knife, but she didn't move. She was smaller than I remembered, her clothes ragged, sun-beaten, beyond worn, her skin leather over bone, scabs on her face where she had fallen or been struck. Her hands hung at her sides as if she did not have the energy to lift them.

I tried to recall her age, thirty-three or -four, except she would be older now . . . I remembered her as a pretty girl, small with dark eyes; she now looked her mother's age. Her nose had been broken and it had set crooked.

"I came to see our house," she said. "I was hoping to find my birth certificate." She shrugged. "Of course they assume I'm not a citizen when I try to cross."

I looked away from her. There was something troubling about her accent—she had spent four years at a women's college—compared with the way she looked.

"You may have trouble finding it," I said quietly, referring to the birth certificate.

"Yes, I saw."

Still I could not look at her.

"I'm very hungry," she said. "Unfortunately . . ."

Every time I tried to lift my eyes, they wouldn't. It was quiet and I realized she was waiting for me to say something.

"I'll try at the Reynoldses'," she said.

"No," I said. "Come in."

She has been living in Torreón for two years with a cousin, but the cousin was a Carrancista and the Villistas had come to his house and killed him, then beaten up María and the cousin's wife, perhaps done worse. What money she had was long spent and she had been on the road for nearly a month. Finally she'd decided there was nothing else to do but come back here. She reminded me, several times, that she was an American citizen. I know that, I told her. Though of course she looks as Mexican as anyone else.

Was it polite to offer condolences for her family? Probably the opposite. I didn't say anything. We stood in the kitchen as I heated beans and carne asada, some tortillas Consuela had made, my hands shaking. I could feel her eyes on my back. The beans began to burn and finally she pushed me aside. I smiled at her, I didn't usually do this sort of thing, but she didn't smile back. As the beans were stewing she cut some tomatoes and onions and a few peppers and mixed them together.

"If you will excuse me, I am quite hungry."

"Of course. I have a few things to do upstairs."

She nodded, not taking her eyes off me, not touching the food until I'd left.

I sat in my study as if all the life had been sucked out of me . . . all the energy I'd once had, my years at university, smashed against the rocks of this place. I nearly picked up the phone to call the sheriff to come remove her, though what my reason would be, I couldn't say. We had killed her family, burned her house, stolen her land . . . she ought to be calling the sheriff on us . . . she ought to have shown up at our door with a hundred men, rifles cocked.

I considered climbing out the window onto the roof of the gallery—it was only fifteen feet to the ground—I could drop to the grass and walk away, never to come back.

Or I could simply wait until someone, perhaps my father, more likely Niles Gilbert, would take her outside, walk her into the brush, snip the last frayed end. I see Pedro, the tear weeping from beneath Lourdes's eye, I see Aná's head tilted back, her mouth wide as if trying to scream even in death.

I decided I would tell her. I had done my best— perhaps she had been watching? I had stood between the two lines and the shooting had begun anyway. I went to the safe and counted out two thousand dollars and put it into my pocket. I would drive her to the hospital in Carrizo or wherever her birth had been registered, procure the necessary papers, and help her on her way, polite but firm; there was nothing for her here.

She was trimming the skin off a mango.

"What are your plans," I said, as gently as possible.

"Right now I am planning to eat this mango. With your permission, of course."

I didn't say anything.

"Do you remember the times we sat out on our portico?" She continued to peel the fruit. The knife slipped but she continued as if nothing had happened.

"Do you want a bandage?"

"No, thank you." She put her thumb into her mouth.

I looked at the table, then around the room, at the patterns in the tin ceiling. Her shoulders were shaking;

her head was down and I couldn't see her face. But there was nothing I could say that wouldn't be taken the wrong way.

It was like that until I decided to put the dishes in the sink.

"Of course I shouldn't be here," she said.

"It's not inconvenient," I told her.

"It was inconvenient to my cousin."

"Do you have other family?"

"My brothers-in-law. I'm hoping they're dead but they are the type to survive."

Of course it was obvious what any normal person would do. We had provided a place to live for numerous of my father's old friends, decrepit herders from another age, men who had no families, or who no longer had anything to say to their families; dozens of them had lived out their last days in our bunkhouse, taking their meals with the vaqueros, or with us, depending on how close they had been to my father. But this was a different matter. Or so it would be said.

"I live here alone," I told her. "My father has his own house a little ways up the hill. My wife has left me; my remaining sons are in the army."

"Is this your way of making a threat?" she said.

"It's the opposite."

"I imagined you might shoot me," she said. "I imagine you still might."

The sympathy began to go out of me. I continued to wash the dishes, though they were already clean. "Then why did you come?"

No answer.

"You're welcome to stay the night. There are plenty of spare rooms on the second floor, just go up the stairs and turn left and pick one."

She shrugged. She was sucking at the pit of the mango, the juice had run down her scabbed chin. She looked like she belonged on a stoop in Nuevo Laredo, the old combination of hopelessness and rage. I began to hope more than ever that she would turn me down, that a meal in the house of her enemy would be enough.

"Okay," she said. "I will stay the night."

JUNE 23, 1917

My bedroom did not feel secure so I lay back down in my office, door locked. I loaded, unloaded, then reloaded my pistol. I listened for her footsteps in the hall, though the runner was thick and I knew I would likely hear nothing.

Around midnight I unloaded the pistol a second time. Of course I am no different from the others, the same dark urges inside me. I was not afraid of her physically. It was something much worse.

Around first light, I drifted off. Then the sun was coming in; I rolled over and fell back asleep. In the distance was a sound I had not heard in a long time; when I realized what it was I woke up immediately and got dressed.

Downstairs, Consuela was standing at the entrance to the parlor, watching. She saw me and walked away as if I had caught her at something.

María was sitting at the bench, playing the piano. She must have heard my footsteps because her back went straight and she missed a few notes, then continued playing. Her hair was down around her shoulders, exposing her neck; I could make out the vertebrae easily. What she was playing, I didn't know. Something old. German or Russian. I stood a few paces behind her; she continued to play without turning. Finally I went to the kitchen.

Consuela looked at me. "Should I prepare breakfast for her?"

I nodded. "Is there coffee?"

"In the pot. *Frío.*"

I poured a cup anyway.

Consuela busied herself chopping nopales, tossing them into the pan with butter.

"Does your father know?"

"He will soon enough."

"Am I to treat her as a guest or . . . ?"

"Of course," I said.

I wondered how well she had known the Garcias. But of course the Garcias were wealthy and Consuela is a servant. The sun had been up two hours and was filling the house, the warm air coming through the windows. I was four hours late for work. I went to the icebox and pulled out a few chunks of cabrito, then wrapped them in a cloth with a tortilla.

"Let me heat that," she said.

"I better go," I said. "I'll see you at dinner."

"Should I watch her?"

"No," I said. "Just give her whatever she wants."

I didn't get home until well after dark, when I knew Consuela would have gone back to her house. I could smell that someone had been cooking, but the plates had all been cleaned and put away. María was at the table, reading a book. *The Virginian*, by Wister.

"Do you like this one?" she said.

"It's not bad."

"The strong white man comes to an unpopulated wilderness and proves himself. Except there has never been any such thing."

We sat there with nothing to say. Finally I decided to bring it up.

"Everything happened pretty fast that morning."

She went back to the book.

"I think it's best we talk about it."

"Of course you do," she said. "You want to be forgiven."

The night air was blowing through the house. There was a screech owl outside and the windmill, and, in the distance, the sound of my father's drilling rig. I sat and listened.

"I'll leave in the morning. I'm sorry I came."

I felt myself relax. "All right," I said.

Lay awake several hours. Am courting disaster, some cataclysm I cannot imagine; I feel it as the old man knows rain is coming. I want only for her to disappear . . . the thought itself relaxes me. All my noble thoughts vanish—when kindness is truly needed it is scarce as the milk of queens. It seems that any moment a company of *sediciosos* might kick down the door, carry me off to the nearest adobe wall . . .

But that was not what I was really afraid of. I had a memory of Pedro and I sitting on his portico. Aná came out and brought us sweet tea, but when Pedro drank, the tea ran down his shirt and onto his lap;

there was a hole under his chin I had not noticed. Then I was standing with my father and Phineas, on one side a deep green pasture, the smell of huisache, the shrubs all around us dotted with gold. In front of us an old elm tree . . . a man on a horse, a rope slack around his neck, people expecting something of me; I could not do it, though it was a simple enough action. Finally Phineas slapped the horse across the hams and the man slid off the back, twisting and kicking, his legs searching for purchase, but there was only air . . .

Humiliation of failure, jealousy of Phineas. And yet I knew I could not have done it, no matter how many chances they might have given me. They were trying to harden me; all wasted effort.

I opened my eyes. I was cold. The wind was blowing through the house, two or three A.M., the windmills creaking, coyotes yipping. I thought of a fawn running in panicked circles, then went to the window and stood looking, there was enough moonlight to see far out over our pastures, ten miles at least. Nothing in sight that did not belong to us.

Finally I got dressed. I made my way to the hall-way in the west wing of the house, stepping quietly, as if meeting for an assignation, though it did not matter . . . we were alone. I noticed that my breath was foul, my hair and face greasy, the smell of old sweat, but I continued down the hall. A prowler in my own house. Past the busts on their pedestals, the drawings of ruins . . . another portrait of my mother, past Glenn's room and Pete Junior's room and Charlie's room . . . finally I heard a fan blowing behind one of the doors. I knocked softly.

I knocked again and waited and then knocked a third time. Then I opened the door. The bed was empty but the sheets were mussed and it was dark. I went to the window and she was standing on the roof of the gallery, at the very edge.

"Come back from there."

She didn't move. She was wearing a nightdress Consuela must have given her. For a moment I thought she was sleepwalking.

"Come here," I repeated.

"If you're going to kill me . . ." she said. "I don't care but I am not just going to walk out into the *brasada* with you."

"You should stay here," I told her.

"Imposible."

"Stay until you're well."

She shook her head.

"I wanted to stop you before you left. That's all I wanted."

"In order that you will have done something kind."
She looked at me, shook her head, then looked out over
the land. She was looking toward her old house, I realized. I worried she might step over the edge. She said,
"Today in the kitchen while your back was turned, I
thought about how I might put the chopping knife into
your throat. I thought about how many steps it was and
what I would do if you turned around."

"Stay," I said.

She shook her head. "You don't know what you're
asking, Peter."

JUNE 24, 1917

In non-Garcia-related news, the vaqueros complain
that the noise of the drilling is ruining the cattle. They
do not see this year's calf crop being a good one if the
animals are subjected to all that noise.

I went to my father to ask how deep they intend to
drill. He told me to the center of the earth. I ask if he
knows that our aquifer is shallow, and our water some of
the best in this part of Texas, and that if he leaks petro-
leum into it, we are done for. He tells me these men are
experts. He means the ones who sleep in hog wallows.

It occurs to me that we are entering an era in which
the human ear will cease to distinguish sounds. Today

I barely heard the drillers. What other things am I not hearing?

When I returned to the house for dinner, there was the sound of the piano before I even reached the door. I removed my boots and left them outside so she would not hear me enter, opened and closed the door very softly, then lay on the divan listening to her play. When I opened my eyes she was standing over me. For an instant I imagined her as she had been ten years earlier: her round face, dark eyes. Then I looked at her hands. They were empty.

"I am going to eat."

"Alone?"

"I don't care," she said.

She heated up what Consuela had left for us. When we finished I asked her again what had happened that day.

She acted like she hadn't heard. "Would you mind if I cooked a little more? I can't stop thinking about food."

"There are always things in the icebox," I said.

She took some cold chicken and began to eat. She tried to be dainty but I could tell it took a lot of effort, I was full but she was starving.

"Tell me."

"You think that talking about this will allow me to forgive you."

"I haven't forgiven myself," I said quietly.

"Telling you changes nothing," she said. "Just so we are clear."

I nodded.

"Fine. So, when they came into the house, they shot everyone, whether they were already on the floor or standing up. Someone shot my niece, who was six, and then, like a coward, I went into my room and hid in my closet. After that I remember sitting on my bed and someone removing my shirt and realizing they are going to rape me before they kill me, then I saw it was you. I thought you were going to rape me and somehow it was much worse.

"Then you walked me through the house. I saw into my parents' room, my mother and father dead, my sister lying with them, then in the *sala* were Cesár and Romaldo and Gregorio, Martin and my nephew, and their families. I could see the front door was open, and the sun was coming through it and I began to hope I might live, but when we reached the portico I saw the entire town had gathered. Then I wished I hadn't hidden in the closet. I nearly took your gun.

"After that I was at the Reynoldses' house. They thought they were rescuing me, they thought they were doing me a favor. They fed me, allowed me to bathe, gave me clothes, a room with clean sheets. Meanwhile, my own house, with my own bed and my own clothes, was just a few miles away. But it was already not mine."

"No one wanted it to happen."

"These lies come out of your mouth so easily," she said. "You yourself, I believe you had reservations, perhaps a few others . . . the Reynoldses, obviously . . . but not anyone else."

She looked at the plate in front of her. "And still I am hungry. That is what I cannot believe."

It was quiet and finally she said, "Can we go outside? I get spells of hot and cold, and now I am very hot."

We went onto the porch and looked over the land. It was an unusually cool day, a pleasant evening, with the sun just going down. I considered remarking as much, then decided against it. I could hear the drilling going on from the other side of the hill.

After we'd sat awhile, she said: "I've spent a long time thinking about what happened. And the longer I thought about it, the more I began to think that things had just gone very badly wrong, of course the shooting of your son—it was Glenn?"

"Yes."

"And how is he?"

"He is alive."

"I am glad."

I felt my face get hot. For some reason this—Glenn still being alive—embarrassed me.

"One of yours hurt, eleven of mine dead . . ." She put up her hands, as if balancing scales. "We have all suffered, the past is the past, it is time to move on."

I didn't answer.

"That is what you think, isn't it? Your child injured, my family exterminated, we are even. And of course you are the best of them; the others think okay, a white man was scratched, there is no amount of Mexican blood that can wash out that sin. Five, ten, one hundred . . . it's all the same to them. In the newspapers, a dead Mexican is called a carcass"—she held up her fingers—"like an animal."

"Not all newspapers."

"Just the ones that matter. But of course I'm no better; for a long time, I had fantasies about nearly every white person in town, burning them, cutting them. I remember very clearly Terrell Snyder staring at me with a grin on his face and the Slaughter brothers as well . . ."

"I don't think the Slaughters were there," I said.

"They were, I saw them clearly, but that is irrelevant. I decided I would stop being angry and perhaps accept that the entire situation, everything that had happened, was bad luck. In fact I became certain of it. We had known your family for decades, it didn't make sense. You in particular we knew very well; I could not imagine you plotting against us. I began to think that perhaps I overreacted by fleeing from the Reynoldses' house.

"And so when my cousin was killed, I decided I would come back. I crossed the river and reached our pastures and felt more alive than I had been in months. I decided to walk all night. I had a story prepared if I met one of your fence riders, though I hoped I would not, as I knew that, depending on their mood, my story would not matter. But . . . there was no one. This I also took as a sign.

"I knew what condition the house would be in. The stuffing would be pulled out of chairs, bird droppings, dirt everywhere, our papers shredded by mice, and of course the old pools of the blood of my family would not have been cleaned and the bullets would still be in every wall. It would look exactly as I had left it, except that it would have aged two years.

"When I reached our lower pasture, by the old church, the sun was coming up and I could see the house had been burned. But still I thought no, empty homes are often vandalized, lovers go to them, the poor occupy them, the dry climate—even a cigarette might have started a fire. I went through one of the doors, made my way through the rubble to my father's office, where I knew all our papers were kept, in metal cabinets that would have resisted any fire. The cabinets were buried under debris, like everything else, but after some time I uncovered them. My birth certificate, perhaps some money, stock certificates, things like that. But do you know what I found?"

I looked away.

"Nothing. They were empty. The papers were gone. Every single document and letter, every record had been removed. And then I knew it had been intentional. It was not enough to exterminate my family; it was also necessary to remove every record of our existence."

"No one wanted that," I told her.

"Another lie. You of all people, you have already forgotten that you are lying. Your lies have become the truth."

I decided to study a green lizard scuttling across the porch. Sometime later I heard a sound; her breath was rattling like a dying man's. I had a terrible feeling but I watched her and she continued to breathe; she was asleep. I watched her for a long time after that and when I was sure she was not going to perish, I went inside and got a blanket and put it over her.

Chapter Thirty-one
Eli/Tiehteti

Late Fall/Early Winter 1851

After we buried the last of the dead, the fifty of us still alive had gathered the few remaining horses and were making our way southwest, mostly on foot, hoping to find the buffalo, or to at least cut their trail. There was no fresh sign. It was clear the *nʉmʉ kutsu* had not been in the area for over a year.

No one knew where the good grass was or where the buffalo might be headed. Later we found out they had stayed north, with the Cheyennes and Arapahoes. Meanwhile, the snow was beginning to fall and there was not much to eat.

With the exception of Yellow Hair, myself, and a few old Comanches who'd been exposed in previous epidemics, there was no logic to who had survived. The *tasía* had killed the weak and the strong, the smart and

the stupid, the cowardly and the brave, and if the survivors had anything in common, it was that they had
been too lazy or fatalistic to run away. The best of us
had either fled or died in the plague.

No one spoke. There was nothing but the wind,
creaking of packs, the travois poles scraping over rocks.
If we did not see enough deer or antelope, we would
kill a horse, further slowing our progress. There was
no plan except to find the buffalo; we did not know
what we would do if we ran into the *Tuhano* or the
army; there were less than ten of us who could still
fight; many of the children had gone blind.

One day, as we watched another norther blow in,
the sky behind us the color of a bruise, a cold I knew
would cut through my robe, it occurred to me that I
had missed seeing many of the children at breakfast. I
could not recall seeing them the previous night, either.
I looked behind me and made a count of our long slow
column and it was true. Half the children were missing. Their mothers had taken all the blind ones out
onto the prairie and killed them, so that the rest of us
would have enough to eat.

That night we ran into a group of Comanchero traders who saw our fire in the storm. They were loaded
down with cornmeal and squash, powder and lead,
knives and steel arrowheads, woolen blankets. We had

nothing to give them. Apparently all the other bands were decimated because they decided to keep us company a few days. They gave us a few sacks of cornmeal but we had no hides and our few remaining horses could not be traded.

As they began to repack their mules, a sense of despair came over everyone; a few people sat down in the snow and refused to be consoled. The night had cleared and I walked away from the fire to look at the stars. There did not seem to be much point in continuing. The few people like me, who could still hunt, could simply ride away, but that was out of the question. I was standing there thinking when our surviving chief, Mountain of Rocks, came up next to me.

"I would like to speak quickly, Tiehteti."

"All right," I said.

"Obviously," he said, "we may not make it through the winter."

"I can see that."

He looked out over the prairie, now covered with a light dusting of snow, which would soon turn into several feet.

"There is a way for you to help."

I knew what he was getting at. The government was still paying high prices for returned captives.

"You yourself may survive this winter here. Most of us will not. Maybe none of us will. But if you return to the *taibo* . . ." He shrugged. "You can simply come back once the traders are paid."

I didn't look at him.

"It is your decision, of course. But there is talk that you might volunteer to do this, especially given the sacrifices that many of the families have already made." He meant the children. "Still, you are one of us and we would prefer if you stayed."

For the German girl and me, the Comancheros left twenty bags of cornmeal, forty pounds of *piloncillo*, ten bushels of squash. Twenty pounds of lead, a barrel of powder, some gun lock screws, a thousand-pack of steel arrowheads, a few rough knife blades with rawhide handles. It was considered quite generous, though the traders had no doubt they would make a large profit, as I was still young, and the German girl still pretty, her face unmarked. Many captives, especially women, were returned with ears and noses cut off, faces branded, but Yellow Hair looked unscathed, and it was obvious that she would be beautiful once cleaned up. I was asked a few questions in English, to see if I still knew how to speak it, which I did. After nearly three years living among the wild Indians, that was not common, either, and by any measure our return would look like a great success and the Comancheros would be well paid.

Mountain of Rocks asked me to leave him my Colt Navy, one of the two I'd gotten off the scalp hunter, but it was out of the question. I had buried the other with Toshaway. And I did not like the look of the traders, or Mountain of Rocks, for that matter.

The first night Yellow Hair stayed close to me, away from the Comancheros.

"Don't let them touch me," she said.

"I won't."

"Make them think I'm your wife."

"They're trying to get money for us," I said. "I don't think they'll do anything."

"Please," she said.

The next night I knew she was right: one of them kept sitting closer until finally he put his arm around her. He was a big man with a large gut; he looked like an unwashed version of St. Nicholas. I stood up and pulled my knife and he put up his hands, laughing at me.

"You look a little young, but I won't fight you."

"We don't have to fight for her," I said. "We can just fight."

He laughed some more and shook his head. "Boy, I can see you are holding on to her like death to a dead nigger. I already said I won't fight you. I'm going to sleep." He got up and went to his pallet under the wagon.

That night she slept in my robe. I hadn't touched a woman or even myself in nearly two months, because all I could think about was Prairie Flower, and her ruined face when I put the dirt over her.

But spooning with Yellow Hair, part of me seemed to forget all that. I could smell her sweet unwashed hair, and finally, when I couldn't stand it, I began to kiss her neck. I wondered if she was asleep but then she said: "I won't stop you, but I don't want to do that right now."

I kissed her behind the ear and tried to make out that I had just been being brotherly. She moved my rutter so that it was not poking into her. We fell asleep.

The next night she said: "We can make love if you want to but you know I was raped by maybe ten men in our band. I tried to talk to you about it many times."

I felt so ashamed that I pretended to be sleeping.

"It's okay," she said, patting my hip. "I doubt they would have let you into the tribe if you'd been nice to me."

"I'm sorry."

"Just don't let these men rape me. I don't think I could stand it."

On the third night I asked her: "Do you think I am not attracted to you because you slept with all those men in our band, or do you just not want to sleep with me?"

"I don't want to sleep with anyone," she said. "But especially not these Comancheros. St. Nicholas showed his cock and balls to me and they are covered with a disease."

On the fourth night I persisted: "But what about me?"

"Would you kill these Comancheros if I asked you?"

"Yes."

"In that case I'll sleep with you. But we have to be quiet so they don't hear us or you might end up having to kill them."

"I'll kill them," I said, though in truth I thought it was unlikely, as we represented a year's wage for them.

She looked at me. She was a sensitive one. "Forget it. I'll sleep by myself." She got out of the robe. "I'd rather be raped than have sex with a liar."

"I'll protect you," I said. "Let's not do anything. I'm sorry I mentioned it."

The last time I asked her anything about sex was: "Did you ever get pregnant?"

"Three times, but they all came out after a couple of months."

"How?" I said.

"I beat myself in the stomach with rocks. Also, no matter how hungry I was, I would not let myself eat."

"If you'd had a baby, they might have made you a tribe member."

"That would have been great except every night I was there, all I dreamed about was going home."

"To where?"

"Anywhere there were white people. Anywhere I wouldn't have to live with men who'd raped me."

I should have felt sympathy for her, but it just made me angry. I missed Toshaway more than I missed my own parents and the thought of Prairie Flower made me so empty that I wanted to put my gun to my head. I rolled over and went to sleep.

We rode together for three weeks, sharing the same robe so the Comancheros would think we were married, and every night I expected we would make love, as we slept spooning in the same robe, but it was true what she had told me, she had no interest at all. Even the one night we drank whiskey with the traders and she let my hands wander more than normal and I thought this is the night I might get inside her, but soon realized she was breathing very deeply and was no longer awake. I let my hands wander over her a little longer. The Comancheros knew their buyers, they were feeding us four or five times a day and Yellow Hair was looking healthier every minute, her ribs softening, her breasts and hips filling out, though still she cried every night in her sleep.

"I guess if I had a fantasy," she told me, "it would be to rape all the men who raped me. Bring them back from the dead and rape all of them, over and over. With a big jagged stick, I mean. I would push it in and out and I would not stop until I was good and ready."

I didn't say anything. I thought about Toshaway and Nuukaru and Pizon, and Prairie Flower and Fat Wolf and Grandfather, and Hates Work, who was really Single Bird, Escuté and Bright Morning, Two Bears, Always Visiting Someone; I guessed I might kill Yellow Hair quite happily just to have a single one of them back.

But she did not appear to notice. "I've actually thought about it quite a lot," she said. "I mean raping them. It was what got me through the day sometimes."

She was smiling.

"But now I don't have to think about it anymore."

I didn't talk to her that night, or the next day, either.

The last week we spent on wagon roads, passing villages, settlements, the first white people I'd seen in three years who hadn't shot at me. Yellow Hair waved at everyone. But the whites did not think it was a special occasion, seeing other white people. The land was settling up.

When we reached the Colorado, close to Austin, I could not believe the roads; they had doubled in width and the ruts were all filled. Yellow Hair was happy, unusually talkative, and she had kissed the traders on their cheeks and thanked them and cuddled very close to me during supper. I could see their looks of jealousy, but St. Nick kept them in line. He knew what we were worth. He offered me a spare cylinder for my pistol if I would let him wash and cut my hair, which had grown halfway down my back. I thought about it, then agreed.

When we went to bed that night, Yellow Hair allowed me to put myself partway into her but she was very dry, and after moving around for several minutes she got no better, and I was so ashamed I removed myself.

"Go ahead and finish," she said.

"I can't with you not wanting to."

She shrugged. "I really don't mind. You kept your word."

I thought about it and then got out of the robe, stood up, looked at the sky, and finished myself off. The grass was not even covered with frost, it was so much warmer in the hill country than on the plains. I got back into the robe with her.

"You're a good man," she said. "I've never known anyone like you."

The next day we rode into Austin. We were taken to the house of a merchant the traders knew and then to the state capitol. A bunch of white men came and asked our names. It took most of the day but eventually three hundred dollars each was raised for us; the traders were paid and rode off without a word to me, though they tried to kiss Yellow Hair good-bye. She turned away from them. Now that we were in public, she would not even allow them to touch her.

Her real name was Ingrid Goetz. The word spread and various wealthy women adopted her. When I saw her the next day she was wearing a blue silk dress, her hair washed and braided and pulled into a bun behind her head. Meanwhile I had refused to let them touch me—I was wearing buckskin leggings and a breech-cloth, no shirt, and while they had insisted on holding on to my revolver, I would not let them take my knife, which I kept tucked into my belt.

And so I slept on a spare cot at the jail while Yellow Hair stayed at a plantation east of town, the home of the U.S. representative and his wife. After a few days there was a reception for us at a judge's house, a Georgian-style mansion near the capitol with a nice view over the river. The judge was a big redheaded man who could have hoisted a barrel in each arm, though his hands were soft as a child's. He'd been educated at Harvard in his youth, then became a senator in Kentucky, then swore off politics entirely and moved to Texas to increase his fortune. He read a lot of books and his words ran eight to the pound, but he had a good spirit and I took to him right away.

Yellow Hair and I made quite a pair. She looked like she'd lived in town all her life; I'd taken a bath and lost my long braids but otherwise I looked like a feral child. Several reporters gathered and they asked if we were husband and wife and looking at her, with her hair washed and her face clean, she struck me as even more beautiful than I had ever thought and I wanted her to say yes.

Everyone else wanted her to say yes as well, as it made a good story, but Yellow Hair was a selfish creature. No, we were not connected in any way, I had simply protected her honor from the Comanches, she was returning with her honor intact thanks to me, honor honor honor, she still had it, that was all.

I was speechless. No one except the Yankees believed a word of it. The Indian's appetite for his female captives was well known to all Texans.

We were fed big meals with fresh bread and beef and a roasted turkey, which I would not touch, as the Comanches thought that eating turkey made you a coward, and staring at the bird I was reminded of Escuté, who liked to tell the joke, *if eating turkey makes you a coward, what does eating pussy make you?* There was also roast pig, which I would not touch, as the Comanches knew it was a filthy animal. I ate about five pounds of beef and two rabbits and it was commented what a good appetite I had. Yellow Hair ate a small amount of bread and turkey and, looking at me directly, helped herself to several servings of pork.

That night, despite the breezes flowing through the house, it felt so hot and still, and the beds so soft and smothering, that I went outside and slept in the judge's yard. Yellow Hair, meanwhile, was already telling people that she had come from an aristocratic German family, though, as they had all been killed, there was no way to verify it. I was certain she was lying, as I knew where her family had been living, and the others doubted her as well, but no one was going to say anything. They had never seen a female captive returned in such good condition. You did not look a gift horse in the mouth.

A few days later, the judge gathered several of the town's influential people in his yard for a barbecue, along with a few reporters from the East. I was asked to dress in my garb and do some tricks. Of course most of what an Indian knows cannot be shown in a circus, like how to follow game, or read a man's mood from his footprints, so I asked for a horse and galloped it up and down the yard bareback, while shooting arrows at a hay bale. The judge had first suggested I shoot a stump but that was out of the question, as it would ruin my arrows, and as both they and my bow had been made by Grandfather, I had no desire to damage them except on a living target. I sat there on the horse and people gave suggestions. The judge pointed out a squirrel that was high up in a live oak and I shot it off the branch and then shot a dove off a different branch. The onlookers applauded. Not far from them was a black eye in the grass that I knew belonged to a rabbit so I put an arrow through that as well. Several of the eastern reporters looked sick at the rabbit shrieking and flopping itself into the air but the judge laughed and said, *He's got quite an eye, doesn't he?* Then his wife gave him a look. He called an end to the demonstration. The Negroes stomped on the rabbit to quiet it and trampled the divots in the lawn as well.

We sat and drank tea and finally they got to quizzing me about Yellow Hair, or Ingrid Goetz, as they insisted on calling her. During my demonstration she'd claimed to have a spell and they'd taken her back to the plantation. Of course I knew better.

The judge, who was sitting in, said: "Did you know her well?"

"We were captured at the same time," I said.

"So you did know her."

"Somewhat."

"And it's true she wasn't misused?" said the reporter. He was from the *New York Daily Times*.

I considered throwing her under the wagon, because she clearly wanted nothing to do with me, but I couldn't. "For sure not," I said. "They never touched her. She was a member of the tribe."

"That is somewhat unlikely," said the judge. He looked embarrassed but continued: "If that is true she would be the first case I have ever heard of, as most female captives are misused by the entire tribe. And often by any visitors to the tribe as well." He coughed into his hand and looked at the ground.

"That is not what happened to her," I said. "A lot of the braves wanted to marry her but she wouldn't allow them. She was kept separate from the men."

The judge was giving me a strange look.

"I guess there was one young chief who wanted to marry her but he was killed in a battle with the army and maybe that broke her heart."

"Was she ever attached to this chief, matrimonially or otherwise?"

"No," I said. "The Comanches are real strict about that stuff."

"Poor girl," said the reporter. "She might have ended up a queen."

"Probably would have."

The judge was staring at me, as if trying to deduce why I would tell such an outrageous lie.

"I guess that proves the red man can be noble if he wishes it," said the reporter from the *Daily Times*. He looked at the judge. "Contrary to what I am told."

The judge didn't say anything.

"It is as plain as day," said the reporter. "If the Indians were left in peace . . ." He shrugged. "There would not be any trouble with them."

"May I ask where are you from?"

"New York City."

"I know that, but what tribe are you from? The Senecas? The Cayugas?"

The reporter shook his head.

"Or perhaps you are Erie, or Mohawk, or Mohican, or Montauk or Shinnecock, or Delaware or Oneida or

Onondaga. Or, my favorite, Poospatuck? I suppose they are your neighbors. Do you attend their scalp dances?"

"Come off it," said the reporter.

"There are no Indians left in your part of the country because you killed them all. So we find it interesting you have such a fascination with making sure we treat ours humanely. As if, unlike the savages your grandfather wiped out, ours are thoughtful and kind."

"And yet look at this woman. She was taken as a prisoner, but not mistreated."

The judge began to speak, then thought better of it. After a time, he said: "So it seems."

Two weeks later, Ingrid Goetz was traveling east with that same reporter. I never saw or heard from her again.

Around that same time Judge Black came to me and told me my father was dead. He had been killed somewhere near the border, riding with a Ranger company. A woman claiming to be his widow, who had seen the announcement of my return in the newspaper, had written the judge and offered to let me stay with her.

From what anyone knew, my father had signed back with the Rangers after coming home to find his house burned and his family dead or missing, and while he had survived his first two years, he had been killed the third. The Texas Rangers in those days had a 50 percent fatality rate per tour; they lay buried all over the state, three or four to a grave. My father had been killed by Mexicans. That was all anyone knew.

I took my bow and a pair of trousers the judge had bought for me, so I would not be mistaken for an Indian, and went walking by the river. I expected to blubber, but nothing came out, and then I wasn't sure if I was betraying Toshaway or not and I decided to stop thinking about it. That night I had a dream in which my father and I were standing together by the old house.

"You couldn't have caught us," I was telling him. "No one could have."

But then he was gone and I was not sure if I was saying that to him or to myself.

The judge claimed it was no problem but I could tell I was disturbing his household, as his three daughters had taken to painting their faces and making war whoops and practicing their ululations. His wife suspected this had something to do with me. She was the type who liked saving people but she had so many rules I couldn't keep them straight.

I took to excusing myself after breakfast and spending the day along the river, looking for things to shoot.

The judge made me promise to wear the white man's clothing. He was worried I'd be killed by a citizen.

I was careful to hunt the birds I knew his wife liked and one afternoon I returned and laid out four ducks and a pheasant for the servants to pluck.

"Good day at work, I see." The judge was sitting on the gallery, reading a book.

"Yessir."

"It will be difficult to get you into a proper school, won't it?"

I nodded.

"I have always found it interesting that white children take so quickly to Indian ways, while Indian children, when brought to be raised in white families, never take to it at all. Not that you are a child."

"No sir."

"Of course there is no doubt that the Indian lives closer to the earth and the natural gods. There is simply no question." He closed his book. "Unfortunately there is no more room for that kind of living, Eli. Your and my ancestors departed from it the moment they buried a seed in the ground and ceased to wander like the other creatures. There can be no turning back from that."

"I don't think I'm going to school," I said.

"Well, if you stay around here, at some point you will have to. Especially in m'lady's house. It's not quite proper to have wild Indians sleeping under one's roof."

I considered pointing out that I had two scalps under my belt, that I was a better hunter, tracker, and horseman than any white man in town. The idea of putting me in a school, with children, was ridiculous. But instead I said: "Well, maybe I should go check in with my father's new wife." She lived in Bastrop, which had never really settled up.

"No hurry," he said. "I enjoy your company. But even there, if you want to have a future, you'll have to acquire some education, however painful that might be."

"I could sign with the Rangers right now," I said.

"Of course. But I think it might be in you to do something more important than living among outlaws and mercenaries."

I got sore at this but kept quiet. I tried to consider by what measure I might be thought to need further education. It was just that the whites were crazy for rules. And yet they were in charge. And I was white myself.

One of the Negroes brought us cold tea.

"Something's been bothering me," he said. "Ingrid Goetz wasn't really treated any differently than any other captive, was she?"

"She was treated just as you thought she was."

"So you made that story up to protect her?"

"Yes."

He nodded. "Glad to see your time with the savages has left your humanity intact, Master McCullough."

"Thank you, sir."

"One other thing."

I nodded.

"M'lady's favorite Persian cat is missing and she is worried you might have had something to do with it."

"Absolutely not."

"How are the Indians on cats?"

"I never saw one. Plenty of dogs, though."

"They eat the dogs, don't they?"

"That's the Shoshones," I said. "A dog or coyote is sacred to a Comanche. You would be cursed."

"But they do eat human beings occasionally?"

"That's the Tonkawas," I said.

"Never the Comanches."

"A Comanche who ate a man would be killed by the tribe immediately, because supposedly it becomes an addiction."

"Interesting," he said. He was scratching his chin. "And this Sun Dance they all talk about?

"That's the Kiowas," I said. "We never did that."

Shortly after Ingrid left, two more captives, sisters from Fredericksburg, were brought in by traders.

There was a big fuss until people got a look at them. One had her nose cut off. The other seemed normal but her mind was gone. There was a big announcement in the paper but no one knew what to do with them; they were not talkative and very upsetting to be around so they ended up living in the spare house of the minister, behind the church. I went and visited them at the judge's request, to try to communicate with them, but as soon as I spoke to them in Comanche, they didn't want anything to do with me. They both drowned themselves a few weeks later.

Which, of course, saved everyone a good deal of trouble, as proper society now regarded them to be roughly the same as whores, being they'd been raped by buck Indians. And, unlike a whore, who might renounce her immoral choices and properly redeem herself, these women had no power over what had happened to them, and thus had no power to undo it, either.

I was already getting tired of the judge's house and had taken to sleeping outside. I'd gotten in small trouble for borrowing a neighbor's horse and for shooting various of the neighborhood hogs full of arrows, not to mention that all the other petty larcenies, which had nothing to do with me, were now attributed to my presence.

I admitted to the judge that the Comanches hated swine and I guess I'd inherited that from them. I was severely understimulated. I had no idea what white children did to occupy themselves. They go to school, he told me. I told him the slaughter of the pigs would look like nothing if I was put into school. Which of course was an exaggeration—I would simply walk out. Meanwhile the judge told the neighbors that the state would reimburse them, as I was still adjusting back to civilized life.

One afternoon he sat me down: "Master McCullough, I don't mean to suggest you aren't welcome in my house, but it might be time to pay your father's new family a visit down in Bastrop. M'lady believes this might do you some good, if you know what I mean."

"She doesn't like me."

"She admires your spirit greatly," he said. "But one of the Negroes discovered a few items that he believed to be human scalps and reported as much to m'lady."

"The niggers went into my bag?"

"They are naturally curious," he said. "My apologies."

"Where is it now?"

"It has been deposited above the stables for safekeeping. Don't worry, I told them they would be whipped if even a single item was missing."

"I guess I will leave today, then."

"No need for that," he said. "But soon."

I gathered my things and asked the Negroes to return the scalps they'd stolen, along with my madstone.

Then I went and found the judge in his study and thanked him and made him a present of my butcher knife and beaded sheath. I had liberated a better one, a fine bowie knife, from one of the judge's neighbors who had kept it in a glass case: supposedly it had been owned by Jim Bowie himself. I would have given it to the judge, but I did not want to get him in trouble. As for my Indian knife, the judge asked: "This ever raise any hair?"

"Some," I said.

He raised his eyebrows.

"Only Mexican and Indian," I lied.

He looked at the knife.

"I'll have a display case made for it. I know just the man to do it."

"Whatever you like," I said.

"I'm honored to meet you, young man. You're headed for great things if you don't get yourself hanged. I think you'll find that not all servants of the law are as liberal minded as yours truly; that judge in Bastrop is a real prick, in fact, he's one of my greatest enemies and I would not mention our friendship to him if you can avoid it."

That night I left for Bastrop, over the judge's objections, as he said I ought to catch a wagon in the morning. I could see the mistress felt guilty about having me removed, and the children, when they found out I was leaving, wept and could not be consoled; their eldest daughter jumped on me and began kissing my neck and crying hysterically.

But I felt free again, as the judge's forty acres, though he was quite proud of it, seemed to me like a postage stamp; I was used to having twenty or so million at my disposal. And Austin was overrun with people, five thousand and climbing; it was impossible to walk along the river without being interrupted by the clinking of horsebells and the cries of boatmen. Anyone could see there were too many pigs for the tits.

Chapter Thirty-two
Jeannie McCullough

It was near first light when she fell asleep and sometime later she heard him calling. She opened her eyes. By the sound of it he was right outside her door and though she'd been thinking about him all night, she found herself afraid and not sure what to do so she stayed quiet. She could hear him there in the hallway.

Finally she got the nerve to call out, "I'll be down in a minute. Tell Flores to make you coffee."

She heard him go downstairs. Then she was sorry. She told herself it was only because she didn't want him seeing her like this, puffy faced and without makeup, but she knew that wasn't true. *I'm a coward,* she thought. She washed and put her hair back and made herself up. Then she went to the kitchen.

"How'd you sleep?" she said.

"Pretty good, I guess."

If the comment hurt her, she didn't show it.

After breakfast, he went to fiddle with the maps and as she was carrying the lunch basket out to the truck, her eye caught on the serving cart with its bottle of whiskey and silver cocktail shaker. She put them into the basket, chiding herself the entire time, wondering how she might explain it if she were somehow caught, or if he objected, but it occurred to her there was no one to catch her, and this made her feel both better and worse, and then it seemed to her that as far as Hank was concerned, things could not move quickly enough. She went back to the kitchen and wrapped a block of ice in some towels and she needed sugar as well. She could always get rid of it if she changed her mind.

As they were driving away from the house, she said, "Pull up next to that stock tank."

He complied. She got out and picked a big handful of mint and put it in the basket. "What is that for?" he said.

"Refreshments."

"I will take your word for it."

A few hours later, when he was satisfied he had seen enough of the country to take a break, they ate lunch at the stream by the old Garcia house. Along the stream were a few young cottonwoods; she excused herself and picked her way down the steep embankment and plucked a handful of the buds, then walked back up to see him. She scraped the sap of the buds with her fingernail.

"Here," she said.

"What is it?"

"Just smell it."

He gave her a skeptical look and then she put her hand near his face.

"Whoa," he said. He seized her arm and pulled her whole hand in and they sat like that. She could feel his breath on her wrist.

"I wish I could smell that the rest of my life."

"It's the sap of the buds," she said. "You can only get it a few times a year."

"What's it taste like?"

"Try it."

"Off your fingers?"

She shrugged. She watched him . . . hoping for . . . she didn't know. But he put only the tip of her finger into his mouth, then removed it quickly.

"Smells better than it tastes," he said, and laughed.

She sat there hoping he would kiss her, but he didn't move, in fact he let go of her wrist.

"This is country," he said, looking out over the savannah.

She forced herself to nod. Something had settled over her which blotted out the light.

"The company is not bad, either."

She nodded again. They could hear the stream running and the locusts.

"And if you are telling me that I am hard to beat as well, I agree with you."

"I didn't say anything at all," she said.

"That is what I am choosing to hear."

"Well, you have not said anything like that to me." Thinking, *He is an idiot.* She was in no mood for clever talk, the moment had passed, it was ruined.

"You are a beautiful girl." He reached his hand toward her cheek, then stopped. "But . . ."

"I am going to make us those refreshments," she said, though she was not sure she wanted to.

"We ought to get moving," he said. He sat up and began to gather his things. "It might be difficult for me to explain how bad I need this work."

He started to stand but she took his hand and pressed it to her mouth.

"You do not know very much about your uncle, do you?"

She shook her head and kept hold of him.

"He will have me hanged. After I am shot and stabbed."

"He will not," she said. "You will remain on the blanket." She felt jittery; she hoped it didn't show.

"I am the dumbest man alive." But he stayed where he was.

She retrieved the julep fixings from the truck, mixed the mint and sugar and a good deal of bourbon in the shaker, crushed it all together and added the ice. She had forgotten to bring glasses. She supposed he would not mind. She sat down again and passed him the shaker.

"That is a rather large refreshment," he said. She noticed that in her absence he had spread the blanket out neatly, and moved it farther into the shade, and she was jittery again.

"I forgot the cups," she said. "We will have to share."

"I have no objection."

"I doubted you would. This is my great-grandfather's recipe," she added.

He took a big sip. "That is a delicious julep." He coughed. "My Lord. Be careful it doesn't put hair on your chest."

"I have been drinking these since I was a child." She took a sip, and then another, and felt it go to her head instantly.

"Oh my," she said. She lay back.

"You okay?"

She nodded.

"You look to be in distress."

Still, he hesitated. He wasn't like the others. She felt the annoyance coming back and then she decided she liked it. She took his hand and pulled him over. They kissed for a long time, in what she thought was a very considerate way; he mostly stayed to one side of her. Then she was waiting and wanting for his hands to wander but they didn't. She began to move her hips and then he stopped kissing her and the feeling of embarrassment came back; she had somehow gone too far again.

"What's wrong?" she said.

"I believe we should continue our search for oil and I also believe that your great-uncle will kill me."

He does not mean kill, she thought, *he means ruin,* and it was depressing to hear people worrying about money; she felt herself get cold inside. She did not want to look at him. She decided that if she never saw him again, she would not mind. Maybe that wasn't fair. She made herself say, "He won't hear a word about it."

"Thirdly, though it is against my own self-interest to mention this, I can take one look at that house and see I am not right for you."

She knew what he meant but she pretended not to. She felt tired, enormously tired, she was tired of these men being nice to her, she wanted him to lift up her dress or push her against a wall, she wanted him to stop asking and stop talking. "Do you have a bad reputation?" she made herself say.

"I have no reputation. I've spent my life chasing oil instead of chasing tail." Then he added: "Unfortunately, and my dad was more the type to dip me in the water than send me to the whorehouse."

"It decreases your risk of a disease."

"Yes, though it increases my risk of losing a limb."

"Is it really that dangerous?" A stupid thing to say: obviously it was dangerous, he'd just lost his father. But she found she did not care at that minute, she did not want to go in this direction, she did not care about his father or anyone else.

"It's getting safer all the time."

"You could do anything you wanted," she said, "it is plain to see just watching you."

"I happen to like doing this."

It was quiet.

"Just so you know, my being broke is a temporary situation. Though fortunate for your family."

She pulled him over and kissed him again. They stayed like that for a while, but still his hands didn't wander, it was frustrating, she was ready to give herself to him, she had a feeling she might not ever see him again, she wondered if there was something about her, about her body or about her face or just something else entirely, that men didn't like.

Perhaps they sensed her inexperience, perhaps they thought she would not be good at it, or that it would mean too much to her; *it means nothing,* she wanted to tell him, *it feels like a curse to me and I want to be rid of it.* Or perhaps they did not think about her that way at all. Perhaps she was simply someone nice to talk to. She began to feel cold again.

"I guess we have to get back to work?"

"We should," he said.

"Okay," she said. "Great. That is a great idea." She sat up and gathered her things quickly and walked to the truck ahead of him. She could feel his eyes on her, he did not know what he'd done wrong, but she didn't care. She wanted to go home.

They spent the rest of the day driving, stopping every so often so he could make marks on his maps.

"How do people find their way around here?" he said. "It all looks the same."

"It doesn't look the same at all," she said.

"Perhaps I'll get used to it."

"How long will you be down here?" She did not care, she was just asking.

"If we find oil? It could be years if I am not hanged from that oak tree in front of your house."

"That is a cedar elm," she said.

"We will see."

"Do you always talk so much?" she said.

He blushed and looked out his window and it got quiet and awkward again. She considered asking to be dropped off at the house but instead she said, "Did you ever go to school?"

"To a certain extent."

"What does that mean?"

"I am a proud graduate of the sixth grade."

"I guess it's better than nothing."

"Even that is an exaggeration, unfortunately."

"You seem to be able to read and write."

"As we say back home, there are coonasses and then there are coonasses. I am the first type."

That night they took supper with the vaqueros. Hank spoke to them in Spanish. She could tell they liked him, though they were suspicious, and also, she could see, jealous, which surprised her. Her feelings came back. But when supper was over and all the maids and Flores and Hugo were cleaning up, he excused himself. "We need to get an early start tomorrow," he told them. "Good night." Not a word to her. She went to bed furious.

————

The next morning they were driving and she ordered him to stop to collect more mint.

"You are intent on making sure we don't get any work done, aren't you?"

"You'll be here a year."

"If your uncle doesn't throw me off."

"Fine. I don't care what we do."

"Don't sound disappointed."

"Too late," she said.

"Are you really?"

"Yes, I am."

"I didn't know."

This made her furious. "You are quite stupid."

He reached over and tried to take her hand. At first she didn't let him.

That afternoon they laid a blanket out in the shade. She encouraged his hands to wander, which they did, but then there was the natural pause and it seemed to not go any further. She felt her interest peak and decline, all the heat seemed to go out of her, as if she were already feeling a disappointment that had not arrived. She decided to think about it mechanically, a problem she might solve, and she made herself sit up and unbutton Hank's shirt, though she was not sure exactly how to get it off his back, and then she undid his belt and the buttons of his pants. He didn't stop her but he gave her a questioning look. She nodded. Then he took over and a few seconds later he was entirely naked. And then she was as well. He was suspended in the air over her, looking at her breasts, at the rest of her body, she guessed he was enjoying it but he might also have been judging, either way it was uncomfortable and she pulled him on top of her.

They lay there, sliding a little, then more, and after a time it was unbearable, she began to push against him much harder, she was not sure how to get what she wanted, she lifted her hips, and then again, and then suddenly he was inside her. It had not hurt at all. In fact it was the opposite. She pulled him closer and then it hurt, though it stopped again immediately. It was like a paper-thin wall between what pinched and what felt exactly as she'd hoped. Then he began to take over and she forgot herself for a moment, then remembered again and began to wonder if the only reason they made such a big deal about the pain was to keep you from doing it every minute of your life.

She could see the trees above her, then she was not sure, it did not seem like she was any particular place at all, she wondered if she was bleeding, *there will be blood*, they said, *blood blood blood*, as if this were the worst thing on earth, she wanted to laugh, she must not laugh, it would not be taken the right way. She was in and out of her body, in and out of sleep, here and then somewhere else, and then here again. On a blanket with a man on top of her, a rock or stick or something hard in her back. She pulled him tight against her. It went on a long time until he pulled out of her suddenly. She knew why but she was still sorry.

Then he said, "Sorry," as well.

"For what?" She kissed his neck.

"It'll be better next time."

"I liked it."

"It will be better."

"Go back in," she said.

"Give me a few minutes." He rolled off and lay next to her with his leg over her.

She began to move her hips. It felt like she was breaking some rule and she was happy. "Can you use your hand?" She had a feeling she was being greedy, but he happily complied.

She could feel it building, it was much better than anything she'd tried herself, but before she finished he climbed on top again.

"Go slower and take longer strokes," she told him.

He did and she felt a sort of heat washing over her, like someone had dipped her in a warm bucket (*red paint*, she thought, *it feels red)*, she could feel it spreading from her waist.

Later it began to feel very good again and he pulled out of her just as suddenly. She held him so he wouldn't go away. He tried to lift his head to kiss her neck. She could see he didn't have the energy. He was like a person drunk or asleep, he moved his mouth from her ear to her shoulder without actually kissing her. He had nice breath. She held him tighter.

"Did you?" He said, after a minute.

Had he really not been able to tell? She was hurt and then no, she was just being sensitive. It was likely normal.

He was talking again, "Do you think . . ."

"Shhhhhh," she said. "Shhhhhh shhhhhhhh shhh-hhhhh." She still felt like she was underwater, or in a warm bath. She woke up a short while later, her heart was beating strangely, it was not hers, but his. *Blood,* she thought again, she found this hilarious, people were stupid, she could not believe it, *silly,* she thought. She began to stroke his back, she kissed his hair. He sighed but didn't wake up. There was a breeze and she could hear the trickling of the water from the spring where it ran down the hill past the old church, where her brothers had found the grave, *all gone,* she thought, *all dead,* she watched the sun flickering. *If I died . . .*

A short while later Hank was inside her again but now her bladder was full. He continued to move but she wanted to get up. She was not exactly sure what to say to him and she began to wonder if she'd given away something valuable, the most valuable thing she had, without asking for a single thing in return, without even asking for a promise. She wanted to stop him and be reassured, but this was not a good idea, he might say anything now.

As if he'd been reading her thoughts, he seemed to wake up and all his weight came off her.

"Was I smothering you?"

"No," she said.

He rolled off slightly, she sighed as he came out. They lay together, legs entangled, for a long time, until finally she had to get up or there would be a real accident, there was no getting around it.

"Where are you going?"

"I need a minute alone," she said.

"For what?" Then he realized.

She slipped her dress on and her shoes and scooted off to the other side of the house.

When she came back to the blanket he was still naked, lying with the sun spotted all over him. It was nice in the shade. She ran her hands over his chest. It was bony, though he had muscle there, his shoulders were thin as well, though ropy, there was just nothing extra anywhere on his body. She traced the thin line of dark hairs from his belly button down below his waist, his . . . (*penis*, she thought), there were a variety of words but she was not sure which was correct in this situation, it was lying against his leg, much darker than the rest of him. It was covered with a dried-up film, and there were spots of that on his belly as well. She touched him and he flinched.

"Does it hurt?"

"Surprised me, is all."

It seemed small now. Very small. She nearly said something about this, then decided against it.

"What do you think Phineas would say?" she asked.

"That is a very scary thought."

"I think he will be happy," she said.

"You are probably the only person in Texas who thinks so. But . . ." He shrugged. "I imagine he knew this would happen. Or something like it."

"Though maybe not so soon."

"I cannot see how he would approve of me for you, but he is no dummy, either. I was surprised when he asked me to drive you home. That did not make sense to me. I took one look at you and thought . . ."

"What," she said.

"I thought you would never speak to me, that's all."

"Why would he have sent us down here together?"

"I think the main reason was I am willing to work cheap."

"He is not stupid," she said.

"Oh, he is definitely not stupid. I have no doubt about that."

"I mean he likes you. He does not like many people."

"Huh."

"And maybe because we're both orphans."

"I'd never thought of it that way."

"Really?"

"No," he said.

It was quiet.

"It's up to you how you're going to feel about that stuff," he said. "People have it a lot worse."

"You don't really like me," she said.

"You're right. I can't tell if I like you or not."

She pushed him.

"You look nice in the sun."

"I feel nice," she said. She had taken her dress off again. The sun was nothing but spots on the other side of her eyelids. "I could lie here forever."

They made love again that night and then went off to their bedrooms on opposite sides of the house. She did not want Flores suspecting anything, though why this concerned her, she wasn't sure, she lay there and felt slightly guilty, again wondering if she'd made a mistake.

But when morning came her first thought was of him, of why he was not in bed with her, and she hugged her pillow toward her and lay half on top of it, then kissed it, imagining it was his neck. Then she got a strange feeling. She wondered if she ought to stay home today. To lock herself in her room and not come out . . . it was an extravagance, something she might use up, she should not waste it all at once. Yes, it was certain, she should not see him. It would not do to get used to him.

Time was passing and she realized that he must be waiting for her downstairs; she got a nervous excited feeling and made herself up quickly and hurried to meet him.

They ate breakfast slowly, both struggling for things to talk about while staring intensely at Flores's back and willing her to leave as soon as possible. Finally Jeannie had told her, in what she hoped was an innocent voice (though it was not, it could not be), that she and Hank would clean up.

When Flores was gone they pulled each other's clothes off in the pantry, they tried it first standing up, but it was not satisfying and finally she was on the floor, among the bags of beans and flour, she felt a brief cold flash as if her father was seeing and judging her and then she decided she would do as she pleased.

Six months later the first drilling rig was up and running. After all the shot testing, Hank decided the best place to start was in one of the old Garcia pastures. He insisted (disgustingly, she thought at first, then endearingly) on putting the samples of rock into his mouth; he plucked them right from the shale shaker. They were starting to taste like oil, he claimed, and if she wanted to learn the business, she would have to learn how it tasted. He offered her a crumbly piece of limestone from several thousand feet below the earth. It was wet with drilling mud, she smelled it, it was sulfurous and disgusting. She touched it to her tongue and wanted to gag immediately; it did taste like oil, but it tasted like other things as well, like something bitter or rotten, it had been in the damp earth for eighty or a hundred million years.

Near the end of the day the big Cummins diesel had suddenly changed pitch, the drill string gave a little hop and then dropped into the hole and then the derrick, the entire steel superstructure above them, gave a loud groan as if suddenly burdened.

"Not good," Hank said.

The engine was running with less strain, it was quieter, but the hands were suddenly moving with purpose. There was a movement high in the derrick; the derrickman had come off the monkey board; he was half jumping, half sliding down the ladder. He brushed past her, running down the stairs toward the mud pits; a short time later, the mud motor got louder.

Nothing seemed to have changed but everyone was running around like a circus. It was amusing. She leaned back against the railing.

The piperacker and tongman were cutting sacks of yellow barite powder and dumping them into the mud pits; the derrickman was pumping mud from the reserve.

Now she could see a change: the return mud pipe, which had been flowing smoothly out onto the shale shaker all day, began to burp and sputter. The drilling mud was what kept the drill string in the hole; the drilling mud was the only thing keeping gas from blowing out of the wellbore.

She began to get nervous. A minute later there was a popping noise and mud blew out over the top of the traveling block. There was a sulfur smell and Hank pointed at her and said: "Get out of here."

"Why?"

"We're getting kicked."

Then he stopped paying attention to her again. She was not sure if he was treating her like a girl. She decided she would not be treated any differently. She stayed where she was. She would never learn this if she went running off every time things got complicated.

"Get off the rig," he said again, but she didn't. He declutched the drill string and dropped the rams. More drilling mud blew out over the traveling block, spattering her dress and shoes.

"Get the fuck off the rig, Jeannie." He shoved her roughly to the edge of the stairs. She looked back at him and finally went down. He was ignoring her again. She sat on a rock a few yards away. She was scared, though she was not sure of what. On the other hand if something happened . . . it was fine. She would be there with him.

After ten or fifteen minutes, the burping stopped. Mud began to flow into the pits again. The men began to laugh and the way they were clapping each other on the back, all talking very fast and grinning uncontrollably, she knew they had all been afraid. There were hundreds of empty Baroid sacks blowing around in the wind.

Hank waved to the motorman to shut the engine down and the hands all sat by the doghouse. One of them lit a cigarette, but Hank reached over and plucked it out of his mouth and crushed the ash carefully into the dirt.

"Maybe we can hold off on that cowboy shit, you think?"

The man nodded.

Then he turned to Jeannie: "Next time I ask you to leave, you leave."

"How am I going to learn if I leave when things go wrong?" she said.

"You would not have learned anything. This would have been a fireball they would have seen from town."

The roughnecks were slumped on a bench in the doghouse. The derrickman was pacing back and forth, cursing the mud pumps.

"What about the rams?" she said.

"Sometimes the gas is coming up no matter what. You can do everything perfect but you can't always stop it."

After that she did not want to be away from him. If he was on a well that blew out, she would be on it as well. She would not be alone again.

Chapter Thirty-three
Diaries of Peter McCullough

JUNE 25, 1917

Tonight she found me in my office. I had given her one of the trucks to take to Carrizo, half expecting she would never return.

"Did I scare you?"

"A little," I said. I realized I had indeed been expecting her to disappear, which had made me feel both relieved and depressed.

She looked around. "All these books. And you sleep here?"

I nodded.

"Because of me?"

"I got in the habit before my wife left," I told her, which was not entirely a lie.

She took a seat on the sofa. "Look at me," she said, holding out her hands. "I'm like a dead person. I can't stand to even look in the mirror."

"You just need to eat and rest."

"I can't stay that long," she said.

"I already told you I don't mind."

"But I do."

It was quiet and she looked around again.

"How old are you?"

"I am eleven years younger than you are," she said. "Though I now look older."

"You are still very pretty." It was not true, not really, and yet all the blood went to my face. If it is possible to make an improvement in four days, she had. Her skin was no longer dry, her lips less cracked, her hair washed and shining. But she didn't appear to notice my compliment.

"You know I imagined telling you all these things for years now, but when I see it hurts you, I feel guilty. Then I am angry at myself for feeling guilty. And yet the past two nights, I have slept very well here. Which also makes me feel guilty. I guess I am the coward after all."

"That's ridiculous," I said.

"You're not in a position to judge."

She continued to look around the room, at all my books, floor to ceiling, and her eyes got soft again but I could not help the feeling she was not long for this earth; I had seen dead people with more weight to their bodies.

"There are many farmers here now?"

"Yes."

"And the other Mexican families? The ones who were here?"

"Some of them went to Michigan to work. Some disappeared. Some are dead."

She asked which ones. I opened my journal and told her what I had written, though I mostly knew it from memory.

Killed in the riots: Llewellyn and Morena Pierce, Custodio and Adriana Morales, Fulgencio Ypina, Sandro Viejo, Eduardo Guzman, Adrian and Alba Quireno, all four of the Gonzalo Gomezes, all ten of the Rosario Sotos except the two youngest, who were adopted by the Herreras.

Fled during or after the riots: the Alberto Gomezes, the Claudio Lopezes, the Janeros, the Sapinosos, the Urracas, the Ximenes, the Romeros, the Reyes, Domingo Lopez, unrelated to Claudio, Antonio Guzman, unrelated to Eduardo (killed), Vera Florez, the Vera Cruzes, the Delgados, the Urrabazes.

"There may have been others I have not heard about."

"Well, you wrote them down," she said. "That is something."

"There are more," I said.

The ones who had moved to Detroit for work: the Adora Ortizes, the Ricardo Gomezes, the Vargases, the Gilberto Guzmans, the Mendezes, the Herreras (including the two daughters of Rosario Soto), the Riveras, Freddy Ramirez and his family.

"Do you own all our land," she said, "or was it split with the Reynoldses and Midkiffs?"

"Just us. And some farmers from the North." Which was true, but also a lie, and I was sorry I'd said it.

"For taxes, I guess."

"They said your father was in arrears."

"He was not. Obviously."

I looked out the window.

"There is so much anger in me," she said, "that I sometimes cannot understand how I still breathe."

JULY 1, 1917

María Garcia has been here ten days. According to Consuela, when I am gone she wanders the house or sits on the gallery staring out over the land that used to be her family's or plays the piano that used to be my mother's. When I come back from the pastures she is usually playing the piano—she seems to know it is a kind of present for me.

After supper I find her in the library. We both like the same places in the house—the library, the parlor, the west side of the gallery. The small protected places where you can see a long way, or hear if someone is coming.

When I ask about her plans she says she would like to continue to eat, and when she is done eating she will make other plans. She is already looking better, gaining weight, the years dropping off.

"When it becomes inconvenient," she tells me, "I'll be on my way."

I don't tell her it is already inconvenient, that my father has already demanded that she leave. "Where would you go?"

She shrugs.

Then I say, "How's old Mexico these days?" as if I don't know the answer.

"They pick you up on the street, or when you are coming out of the movies, or from a cantina, and say here is a gun, you are now a Zapatista or a Carrancista or a Villista, depending on who catches you. If you protest, or if they find out you were on another side, they kill you."

"You must have friends from university?"

"That was fifteen years ago. And most of them left when things got bad."

"Michigan?" I regret saying it immediately.

"Those are not my people." But she shrugs and I can see she forgives me.

I look at the light coming in on her hair, which shines, and the line of her neck, where there is the faintest hint of sweat. It occurs to me that she has very nice skin. She leans back into the stream of air from the fan, kicks her foot up and down, looking at the slipper on it, which she must have gotten somewhere in the house.

"I'll be fine," she says. "It's nothing for you to worry about."

July 2, 1917

Went to see my father to discuss the matter further. The drillers have run out of coal for their boiler and the silence is a relief. Forgot what silence sounded like.

The Colonel was sitting in the shade on the gallery of his house, which is more like a jacal. It does not have nearly the view of the main house, but it is in a copse of oaks, with a live stream running past it, and is ten degrees cooler than any other place on the ranch. He still sleeps in a brush arbor at night (though he has run an electric wire and keeps his Crocker fan blowing) and refuses to use an indoor toilet, preferring to squat in the bushes. Walking around his house is a bit like walking through a minefield.

"This heat," he said. "We should have bought on the Llano."

It was 110 at the big house, 100 at his jacal.

"We'd have to shovel snow," I said.

"That is the problem with having a family. Take a man like Goodnight, does whatever the hell he wants, moved himself right up to Palo Duro when the Comanches left."

"Charles Goodnight has a family. A wife, anyway."

He looked at me.

"Molly."

"Well, he never talks about them." Then he changed the subject: "There is a man coming here in the next few weeks, name of Snowball. He's a Negro I knew from the old days. He may be here awhile."

I cleared my throat and said: "There is also the matter of this Garcia girl."

"She is not as good-looking as her mother. I will say that for her."

"She is pretty enough."

"I want her making dust as soon as possible."

"She's sick."

"It's not in the best interest, Pete."

"The best interest."

"There are three events regarding this woman. The first is her brother-in-law shot your son. The second is that, with a half-dozen law enforcement officers present, we went to capture the guilty parties. Unfortunately things did not go as hoped."

"That is an inaccuracy, at best."

He waved his hand furiously, as if my words were a stale odor. "The final thing is her father's land was put up in a tax sale by the State of Texas, which would have happened sooner or later, whether they were living on the property or not, as they had not been paying their taxes."

I snorted.

"It is in the records."

"Which makes it all the more likely to be a lie."

"Pete, there are many things I have wanted to save: the Indians, the buffalo, a prairie where you could look twenty miles and not see a fence post. But time has passed those things by."

How about your wife, I thought, but I remained silent.

"Give her some money and get rid of her. By the weekend."

"She will leave over my dead body."

He opened his mouth but nothing came out. By his color, he must have been very hot.

"Now don't go getting up on your ear," I heard him start, but I was already walking away, my hands hidden in my pockets as they were shaking. They did not stop shaking until after I got back to the house.

Called Sally, hoping she might be a voice of reason. We had not spoken in a month—she does her communicating through Consuela—and she was surprised to hear from me. Says she has no interest in returning to McCullough Springs. Greatest mistake of her life. We discussed Charlie and Glenn, who are still in training. We both agreed it was unlikely they would ever make it to the war. I suspected Charlie would be disappointed by this, but I did not say it.

After a time she mentioned that she spent two weeks in the Berkshire Mountains in Massachusetts with a "friend." She wondered if I had heard anything of it, if perhaps that was the reason I had called. Ridiculousness of asking her opinion about María Garcia suddenly apparent; I became annoyed at myself for calling her, annoyed at my own desperation. But she thought I was annoyed at her tryst and immediately became conciliatory.

"I'm sad you're not here," she said. "It would be more fun if you were."

"I'm just working."

Silence.

"Are we separated?"

"I don't know."

"But we are taking some time away from each other."

"I don't care what you do," I told her.

"I'm just asking. I'm trying to figure out our status."

"You can do whatever you want."

"I know you don't care, Peter. You don't care about anyone but yourself and your sadness. That is what you care about the most, making sure you are as unhappy as possible."

"The things you do haven't bothered me before," I said. "I don't know why they would now."

"I am trying to figure out how it's possible that I still love you, but I do. I want you to know that. You can still save this whenever you want."

"That's nice," I told her.

Silence.

"Say," she finally said. "How is that drilling going?"

Went down to see about dinner.

"Your father says I am not to cook for her," said Consuela.

I shrugged.

"I'll make extra for you," she said.

Of course there is no one to talk to, even Consuela; I know what her answer will be. What anyone's answer will be. The right thing is to get rid of her. Perhaps for her own good.

After a ten-minute search I find her in the library. The nicest spot in the house, as most of the windows face north and there are a few seeps hidden among the rocks to keep the view green.

"What's wrong?" she says.

I shrug.

"I saw you walking back from your father's house."

I shrug again.

"Of course. Consuela's given me a few things, I'll get them together."

"Didn't your family have a bank account?"

"They did," she said, "and what little I could withdraw I used to live."

"Is there really nowhere else?"

"Don't worry about me."

"He's always done this," I say, referring to the Colonel.

"The land makes people crazy."

"It's not the land."

"No, my great-uncle was the same. A person to him was an obstacle, like a drought, or a cow that would not do what he wanted. If you crossed him he might cut your heart out before he came to his senses. If his sons had lived . . ." She shrugs. "Of course we didn't belong here, my father was two years into university when his uncle died. But . . ." She shrugs again. "He was a romantic."

"He was a good man," I say.

"He was vain. He loved the idea of being a hidalgo, he was always telling us how blessed we were to live on the land. But really, there was no *we*. It was only him. He could not accept that his neighbors might one day kill him, and so he kept us all there, despite the risks, which we were all aware of."

It gets quiet.

"You don't belong here, either," she says. "You've probably always known it and here you are."

Not always, of course, but perhaps since my mother died. Though I cannot tell her that story; it does not compare to her own. Instead I tell her another:

"I remember when I was a kid, we caught this boy who my father thought had stolen cattle from us. He was maybe twelve or so, but he wouldn't tell my father anything so my father threw a rope over the top of the gate, put it around the boy's neck, and tied the other end to a horse. When they let him down he started talking. He scratched a map in the dirt and said the men we were looking for were white, that they'd made him come along because they didn't know the land."

She nods. I can't tell if I should continue or not. But I do:

"I was taking the noose off him when my father slapped the horse and the boy went back up in the air."

"And then?"

"He died."

"Did they catch the others?"

"He hanged the ones he didn't shoot."

"The sheriff?"

"No, my father."

There were nine of them but the last four gave themselves up and my father stripped the saddles off their horses and found a proper cottonwood and hung them with their own ropes. I held the camphene lamp while Phineas put the nooses on. At first Phineas was nervous but the last man he noosed he told: *It'll all be over in a minute, partner.*

That is real kind of you, said the man.

My father said: *Either way you're hanging, Paco. It's just whether it's now or in a few weeks in Laredo.*

I'll take the few weeks. Spit popping in his mouth.

You ought to be happy we aren't skinning you, said my father.

María has come to sit next to me. The sun is going down, the light in the room is dim. She brushes a hair behind her ear and I swallow. Her eyes are soft. She touches my hand. "You should stop thinking about it," she says.

I can't. But that is difficult to explain to people, so I don't say anything.

Phineas stood beside one of the horses and slapped it, then moved down the line to slap the next one. When the last man dropped it was quiet except for the ropes creaking and the men gurgling and shitting as they pedaled their legs. They were still kicking when my father said: *There's some nice saddles here.*

"Peter?"

Her hand is covering mine and I am afraid to move.

"That is in me somewhere," I say.

We sit there like that and I wonder if something might happen but we both know there is nothing right about it.

Chapter Thirty-four
Eli McCullough

Early 1852

I arrived in Bastrop and found the address of my new home, a rickety frame house with multiple rooms added, built before statehood when materials were thin. But there was a large front yard with flowers and grass and a whitewashed fence.

My stepmother was in her forties, with a harsh expression and a tightly tied bonnet. She looked like she'd been raised on sour milk and when the Indians thought of white people, she is the person they imagined, from the look she gave, she did not exactly think me nickel-plated, either. Her two sons were both taller than me and they smirked. I made up my mind to bash their heads.

"You must be Eli."

"Yes," I said.

"Well, we found some clothes for you. You can change out of those things. You better give that pistol to Jacob."

The taller one was reaching for my Colt. I slapped his hand away.

"We lock our guns up here," she said.

I slapped his hand away again.

"Mother."

She looked at me for a long time and then said: "Let him be."

I had a pallet in the same room as the other two boys, who were eyeing my bow, knife, pistol; everything I owned. As soon as I'd been given the tour I went on a walk, and, after losing my stepbrothers, who were trying to follow me, I buried the pistol and everything else I cared about in my bag, taking only my bow and arrow and a small wallet of things I did not think would interest anyone.

On the way back I saw my stepbrothers walking in circles, trying to cut my trail, considered ambushing them but decided against it, and made my way back to the house.

That night we had salt pork, which I would not touch. I ate most of the corn bread and all the butter, though. The family was originally from East Texas and did not believe in buying wheat. The fact they had butter was a small miracle.

I could not fault my stepmother as she had bought me a new set of clothes, including shoes, and the next morning I was dressed up like her sons, tripping over my shoes the first time I walked in them, which inspired great hilarity in everyone but myself.

The state was paying for my schooling, on the judge's orders, and there was one room and a very young teacher trying to teach two dozen children of all ages. After sitting a few minutes I stood up so I would not fall asleep. I felt sorry for the other students, who could not imagine saying no to this teacher or anyone else; they were going to spend entire lives doing things just like this. I felt so sorry for them I nearly burst out crying. The teacher forgot how nice she was and came after me with a paddle and I let her chase me awhile before going out the window.

I spent the rest of the day building snares and setting them, walking in and out of people's barns. I stole a mare, rode her for an hour, and returned her to her stall. I watched a pretty older woman reading a book on her back porch, her fine brown hair going gray, just wearing a shift on account of it being warm. She adjusted one breast and then the other and then reached up under her shift and left her hand there, which was too much. I ran off and had a few moments to myself. I thought I could probably make it in Bastrop.

When I got back home, my stepmother was waiting.

"I heard you left school," she said, "and I heard you were seen on Mr. Wilson's horse and I heard you were walking around the yard of the Edmunds, looking in their windows."

How she had learned this I did not know. I expected her to check my hands for the mark of Onan. Then I noticed a strange smell. Something was burning and I went to the fireplace and saw that some person had put my moccasins, bow, arrows, and loincloth into the flames.

"The man who built that bow is dead," I told her. "It cannot be replaced."

"You need to put those days behind you, Eli."

If she had been male I would have killed her and not thought another thing about it. Later I would consider this and decide we were both lucky.

"Jacob and Stuart brought your shoes back for you."

"I'm not wearing those fucking things," I said.

I went to my pallet and took the wool blanket off it, then went into the kitchen. I took a knife and some things I found in the drawers, a ball of sisal, a needle and thread, a half loaf of corn pone.

"Eli, you may take whatever you want," said my stepmother. "It all belongs to you. This is your home now."

It was a queer way to act. She was either softheaded or a Quaker.

I was sure I'd be followed by my stepbrothers so the trail I left them led right to a patch of quicksand. From there I made some footprints that led to a rattlesnake den. Finally I went to the tree where I'd buried my things and dug up my bag, which contained my revolver and various other pieces of gear, all in fine condition.

After walking another hour I found a high overlook with a stream running in front of it and plenty of shade. I made a fire and fell asleep wrapped in the blanket, listening to the wolves howl. I howled back and we went on for a while like that. I kept my Colt under my knees, Indian-style, but I knew I was not going to need it for anything, the country was too settled up.

The next morning I hacked down a bunch of saplings with my stolen bowie knife, which was indeed a very good knife, heavy but nicely balanced; even after batoning through some of the saplings it was not dulled at all. I wondered if Jim Bowie had actually owned it but by then for him to own all the knives attributed to him he would have had to live a thousand years. I made a drying rack and a frame for a brush arbor. But there was not much point in working so hard. I lay down in the sun and looked out over the green hills; I had forgotten how warm it was in the lowlands. I thought of all my friends buried up on the snowy Llano, cried for a while, and fell asleep.

That afternoon I shot two does and skinned and flayed out the meat and hung it on the racks to dry. I teased out the long sinew from the backbones and cleaned and washed the stomachs. One of the legbones I sharpened into a passable scraper and fleshed both the hides. By then the sun was almost down so I built a fire and had a fine supper of venison rubbed with cedar berries, and marrow mixed with dried sugarberries. The next day I decided to find a bee tree.

After a week I'd built another bow and a dozen arrows so inferior to the one Grandfather had made me that it put me into a conniption every time I drew it. I made a new pair of moccasins and a breechcloth, then went back into Bastrop. I walked directly to the backyard of my stepmother, where my stepbrothers kept the hogs they had threatened to feed me to. I shot all the hogs full of arrows.

Their mutt was easily converted with the gift of a bloody piglet, after which we were friends for life. He followed me back into the countryside where my brothers were afraid to go, as they'd been told they would be stolen by Indians. Of course the Indians would not have stolen them; they were more the type to be knocked on the head.

I stayed out a month, missing Toshaway and Prairie Flower and all the others. I guessed Nʉʉkaru and Escuté were out there somewhere in the snow, but how I would find them, I had no idea.

I went back to town often, mostly to steal things that seemed interesting, like horses, which I rode for a while, then left them tied wherever I got tired of them. I let myself into people's houses and enjoyed fresh-baked pie and roasted chicken and all the other bounties of civilization, but when the sun got low I always headed back where I belonged.

It did not take long to figure out that the nicest house in town belonged to a judge by the name of Wilbarger, who was the enemy of my friend in Austin. I would sit in the trees overlooking his backyard, listening to the stream there. Occasionally his wife would come out and read books on the porch. She was the woman I'd seen in the shift, very pretty, somewhere in her forties, but very thin and sad. Everything about her was pale. Her hair, skin, eyes. I did not see how a creature like her might survive in such a sunblasted place, and the servants must have agreed because they were always looking in on her, as if they expected her to die or run off at any moment.

A few times a week she would go walking by herself in the woods, which was safe for someone with sense, but probably not for her, so I would follow at a safe distance. She would walk a stream until she guessed she was alone, then strip naked and swim in some convenient hole. She had a few favorites but they all got more traffic than she supposed. The first time I saw her go under she held her breath so long I nearly dove in to pull her out. She and the judge had as much in common as a Thoroughbred and a cross-eyed donkey.

After swimming she would lie on the rocks in the sun and I would squint to get my look. There were wisps of gray in the hair she had, which was something I had not thought about. I felt certain the judge had not been in there recently. All thunder and no lightning.

At the edge of town one afternoon I was stopped by a man who identified himself as the sheriff's deputy. He was not pointing his gun but he said he needed to take me in for some questions. I could have slipped him but I was bored and I wondered what jail would be like.

It was not bad. The judge's wife came and cooked for me every day, three meals with pie. Of course I recognized her and she was even prettier up close than from a distance. She was tall and thin with gray eyes and delicate bones and a pleasant manner; one look and you knew she was an import. The local women, most of whom could have wrestled a razorback hog, must have hated her. She had an accent that made her hard to understand but I knew my brother would have liked it. She was English, they said.

Judge Wilbarger, whose Thoroughbreds I'd been riding some nights, came and gave me a lecture on morality.

"I understand you have been through a hard time," he said. "But we cannot have you stealing horses and killing people's livestock."

I nodded.

"I've hanged men for stealing horses."

I nodded again. I hadn't actually stolen any horses, just borrowed them and returned them, probably better behaved than they'd been before I got to them.

"If you are caught breaking the law again, you will be severely punished. This is your only warning. Tell me you understand me, boy. I know you speak English, you were with those Indians not even three years."

"The wind blows softly through the flowers," I said, in Comanche. "Also, you smell like a buffalo's cunt."

"Speak English," said Wilbarger.

"I have stimulated myself to your wife over thirty times."

"English, boy."

Then I didn't say anything.

Finally he got up. "You're smarter than you act, boy. You can be tamed and I will do it if you make me."

They held me three more days but after Wilbarger left, the sheriff let me out of the cell to walk around.

"Don't piss him off," he said. "They told me you came in with scalps but you are gonna get yourself in a tight you can't get out of."

I shrugged.

"Those *were* Indian scalps, weren't they?"

"One was a white man," I said, in English. "But he had been living in Mexico."

He looked at me and burst out laughing. I started laughing as well.

"Is it true all they had you doing all day is riding and shooting?"

"There was a lot of rutting as well," I said.

"Some old fat squaw, I imagine."

I shook my head. "You are only allowed to do it with the young ones. Once they get married they are off-limits."

I could see this idea appealed to him but he did not believe me.

"The one who popped my cherry was twenty and the others were even younger."

"Son of a bitch," he said. "Maybe they will kidnap me."

Then I felt low speaking that way about Prairie Flower. And Hates Work, Big Water Falling, and Always Visiting Someone. It occurred to me that they were the last people in the world who had actually loved me. I got up and went over to the window. I could feel myself getting dauncy.

I heard the sheriff go back to his desk and move some things around and then he came up next to me. He handed me a glass of whiskey.

"So what the hell happened?" he said. "Why'd you come back?"

"Everyone died," I said.

Thinking about the Indians had put me in a state and when they let me out I went back to my stepmother's house, thinking I would make good with her, but no one was home. I felt low and I was tired of being by myself. Still no one came home. I got restless. I went to my stepbrothers' room, where I found several nice steel fishhooks, which I pocketed, and a large collection of wrinkled pornographic postcards, which I left in the kitchen for my stepmother. Then I took all their gunpowder and percussion caps and headed back into the woods.

I slept under the brush arbor or under the open sky, set traps, caught raccoons and tanned their hides, killed deer and tanned them as well. I found a pool by an old beaver dam where the water was brown from oak leaves and I buried the hides in the mud under the water. After a few weeks the hair slipped and they were nicely tanned, just stiff.

Among the whites in town I was as popular as the tax collector. I knew they wouldn't put up with much more horse stealing and stock-killing so I mostly stayed where it was natural. But eventually it got to where the deer and wolves did not cut through my lonesome, not to mention I was in a fierce rutting mood, so I went back to check on the judge's wife.

Eventually she came out on the porch. One of the Negroes brought her tea. I was in dire need of stimulation and afterward I fell asleep. When I woke up she was not on the porch and the sun had sunk a good ways. The judge had a few shoats and piglets in a pen and looking at them I got very hungry, I had forgotten to eat for nearly a day. I arrowed one of the piglets but despite all the squealing no one came, I took my time and went into his smokehouse and got a big helping of salt and carried the piglet back to camp.

A few hours later I was lying there, my belly full of the crispy meat, watching the sun go down from my perch. I could not remember why the Comanches hated pork so much. It was likely the best thing I had ever tasted. The wolves howled and I howled back and they howled back at me.

The next morning the wife went on her daily walk to the swimming hole, but instead of following her I waited until her two Negroes went out on an errand, likely to hump, then slipped into the kitchen. I liberated a bottle of sweet wine and several cigars, smoked one of the cigars and nearly threw up. I was sure I would be sick. I lay there on a couch while my head spun. It was a nice house with wood paneling, thick rugs, paintings everywhere. The couch was firm like no one had ever sat on it.

When I opened my eyes someone was standing over me and I was running before I even woke up. I was nearly to the door when I stopped.

It was the judge's wife.

"You don't have to run," she said. "You looked so peaceful that I didn't want to wake you."

I didn't say anything.

"It is nice to see you again," she said. "I mean, not behind bars. Though I've also seen you out in the yard."

I didn't want to evidence against myself, but I didn't want to lie, either. I stayed quiet.

"So. How is the wild Indian?"

"I am fine," I said.

"People say you're very dangerous."

"Only to hogs."

"Are you responsible for our missing piglet?"

"Depends who's asking."

"We were just going to eat her anyway. Or was it a him? I can't remember." She shrugged. "You can sit down, you know. I'm not going to tell anyone you were here."

"That is all right," I said.

"Did you eat it? They say you just like to kill them."

"That one I ate."

"Well, I am glad."

I didn't say anything.

"You really should have a seat. I can see you were smoking one of Roy's cigars. They're awfully strong."

At the mention of the cigars, I began to feel green at the gills again. I decided I would stay a few minutes. If the judge came home, I would kill him and go back to the Indians.

"What are you doing here?" I said.

"This is my house."

"I mean in Bastrop."

"The judge was the business partner of my first husband."

"Did he pull stakes?"

"He caught the fever in Indianola. The heat here was quite a shock. As were the insects."

"They are worse in Indianola," I said. "Along with everything else."

"I suppose you could slather yourself with mud."

There was something about the way she looked at me and I went and sat on the couch. She sat down as well.

"Are you going to call for the sheriff?"

"I'm thinking about it. You're not going to scalp me, are you?"

"I'm thinking about it."

"How old are you?" she said.

"Nineteen." Of course I was only sixteen but on account of being in the sun I never had carbuncles.

"Did they treat you badly?"

"The sheriff?"

She thought this was funny. "The Comanches, of course."

"They adopted me."

"But you were of a lower caste than a natural-born, no?"

"I was mostly the same. I was a member of their band."

"That is very interesting."

"My Comanche family died," I said. "That's why I came back."

Her face went all motherly. She really was a sweet woman. But before we got too far down the path of righteousness I said, "I'm going to drink some of the judge's port wine and then I'm going to steal one of his horses. Do you want some or not?"

"I could have a drink with you," she said. She wrinkled her nose at me. "But would you object to a bath?"

"Are you gonna give it to me?"

She acted surprised but I could tell she wasn't.

Chapter Thirty-five
Jeannie McCullough

They heard it before they saw it, but when it finally appeared over the trees, it was clumsy and ponderous and not much to look at and most wished they had not taken off work. The sheriff and his men backed everyone out of the way, and, when it was safe, the helicopter dropped through the air until it settled in the dirt next to Hollis Frazier's spinach field.

A tall man with a big nose uncurled himself from the machine and, once the dusty crowd had formed around him, stood on a wooden box and began to speak. Someone else distributed peaches from the Hill Country. The man insisted that Coke Stevenson was giving away the state to big ranchers and northern oilmen, with nothing left over for the workingman. It occurred to her that she would have been nervous to speak in front of four hundred strangers, but it was plain he was not nervous, he was enjoying it, and he turned his megaphone on a group of people at the out- skirts of the crowd and urged them to come in and hear him. Bullshit Johnson, they called him.

Watching him shake hands with all the shorter men around him, she knew Phineas was right. She had met Coke Stevenson, a nice man who did not particularly care what your opinion was. He had his own moral compass; a do-gooder, the sort of man you hoped your children would become. The man she saw in front of her was so happy in the crowd, so happy to be watched and paid attention to, there could not be room inside him for anything else. There wasn't an oilman in the state who didn't back him.

"I have something for the future senator," she told the aide, hoping he would notice this flattery.

He didn't. He looked her over and said, "You can give it to me." He was sweating in his black suit, a northerner, with thick plastic glasses, a man no one had ever liked, who was beginning to come into his own. It was a look she would take for granted among people who worked in Washington.

The man took her envelope and she thought of his boss and she thought of Coke Stevenson, and then she thought about what Phineas had told her before she sat down to write the checks. *The problem with most people is they don't give enough. They all want to be ambassador, but when it comes to giving money they think a hundred bucks is plenty and are surprised when they never hear back.* In her envelope were four checks for five thousand dollars each. One from herself, one from their lawyer Milton Bryce, one from their foreman Sullivan, and one from a vaquero named Rodriguez. Sullivan and Rodriguez made less than five thousand a year put together; she'd had the money deposited in their accounts the previous day. Any one of the checks would have bought a new Cadillac and the aide read each one carefully, making sure they were properly filled out. Then he led her over and whispered something to his boss.

Johnson's face lit up; he was a natural. He nudged a few people and the crowd parted, big ears, big nose, bushy eyebrows, he towered over everyone else.

"You must be Phineas's niece." He hadn't stopped smiling since he landed.

"Yes," she said.

"Well, he has spoken about you often and I am pleased to meet you. Tell him I miss those fishing trips."

"Yessir," she said again.

Someone was grabbing at his sleeve.

He grinned at her. "Back to work. But I will be seeing you again, young lady."

After the congressman was back in the helicopter, the aide found her and said: "Since you're at your limit, next time pay cash. It's going to be a tight race and we need all the help we can get." He handed her a peach.

She considered it as she walked back to the car. It was runty and bruised, barely fit for hog feed, and dozens more just like it lay scattered in the dirt.

When was that? Forty-seven or -eight. She couldn't remember exactly. To say he was elected was not exactly accurate. Though at least Box 13 had come from Jim Wells County, not Webb or Dimmit. Those years had blurred together. They'd gotten enough wells sunk on the ranch to start a capital flow, then agreed there ought to be no more drilling there. She and Hank had bought a house in Houston. Rented a small office. Then a bigger one. Then they bought a bigger house. The way the economy was going it was impossible to lose money no matter what you did.

In the three years she and Hank had been together, she had expected they might settle into a pattern, boring but stable, they would begin to track like tires settled into ruts. But that had not happened. Their lives were changing too quickly, their business growing five- or tenfold each year, it was hers as much as Hank's. She was not surprised at her own abilities, which she had always taken for granted, but his, which seemed to have no limit, and she was beginning to wonder if he might surpass her—a thought that was liberating and disturbing at the same time. She'd never considered that she might be looked after, that she might have a normal life and not have to worry so much.

Most of the men she'd known were fools like her father and brothers, their lives shaped by a willful ignorance they mistook for pride. That ignorance guided every moment of their existence and until now, she had never doubted that she saw more clearly, more honestly, than any man she had ever met, with the exception of the Colonel and perhaps Phineas. And now there was Hank.

Though he was not perfect. He had no patience for things he found foolish, even if those things were important to others. There was a coldness about him that was almost northern. That awful writer from New York had come to visit and she had not wanted to meet the woman alone, but Hank had made sure he was out of town. Jeannie, meanwhile, had stupidly agreed to meet the writer at the ranch, an eight-hour drive from Houston—they didn't own a real plane yet—instead of insisting on meeting at the office. The woman was writing a big novel about Texas; she had already seen the Klebergs and the Reynoldses and had just come from the opening of Glenn McCarthy's hotel. And she had won the Pulitzer Prize; it seemed a good idea to be in her favor.

They sat down for an early supper; Jeannie instructed the maids to put out the good plates and silver. She noticed the woman appraising those things, she was taking in everything, like a poor relation about to come into an inheritance. She was tall and gangly as a teenager but her hair was gray and frizzy like birds had made a nest of it, and like many northerners, her confidence was out of step with her appearance.

"You're the millionaire teenager."

"I'm twenty-two," she said.

"But you got the money when you were a teenager."

"That's true," said Jeannie. "Though I never thought of that as being of any consequence."

"Oh, it is," said the writer. "It most certainly is." Then she added: "How very Texan."

She could not tell if this was meant as a compliment.

"Were you very lonely out here?"

"I have a husband now," said Jeannie, "and most of us don't live on our land anymore. We're all city people now." She wished Hank was with her; he would know the proper way to deal with this woman; she worried she would end up saying something she did not mean.

"The house is decorated unusually for this area," said the writer.

Jeannie shrugged.

"Very tastefully, I'd say. It looks as if it's been here forever."

She shrugged again. She was not going to feed the woman any more gossip. "My great-grandfather was a brilliant man."

The woman nodded. Jeannie could not understand what was so important about her. Even her hat was ridiculous. Everything about her screamed she was from somewhere else, she was obsessed with how much money and land all the families had, with whatever dirt might be scraped up on them.

The maids brought supper out. Jeannie had considered carefully what ought to be served and, after ruling out anything elaborate that might imply she was seeking the woman's approval, had decided on fajitas.

Flores was a good cook; she'd rubbed the steak with salt and hot pepper, charred it over mesquite, and served it with heaping sides of guacamole and salsa and fresh tortillas.

When they finished, the hands were getting in from the pastures and taking their places at the long table behind the main house. Flores began to carry out their meal, chatting with them in Spanish. The author watched through the window.

"Do you want me to introduce you?" said Jeannie. "Those are the people who do the work these days."

"I don't think I speak their language, darling. But I do think I'll go out for a cigarette."

"I need to freshen up," said Jeannie.

When she returned from the toilet, she found the writer standing next to the window in the dining room, a strange look on her face. "Jeannie," she said, indicating the vaqueros with her chin, "they are eating the same thing we did."

The woman's book had come out and later was made into a movie starring James Dean. It was one long exaggeration. It made everyone look like clowns, as if they had stumbled dumbly into wealth, as if the state was nothing but backwoods tycoons without two brain cells to rub together.

And yet most of the oilmen had liked it. They began to invent over-the-top mannerisms, throwing silver coins out of the windows of their limousines, taking twenty-thousand-dollar baths in champagne. Maybe it was no different from any other time. The frontier was not yet settled when Buffalo Bill began his shows and the Colonel always complained about the moment his cowboys began to read novels about other cowboys; they had lost track of which was more true, the books or their own lives.

Johnson lost by a few hundred votes. But he became senator anyway and Jeannie began to expect his calls. He called on the Murchisons, on Cullen, Brown, and Hunt. There were very few oilmen he did not call on. Sam Rayburn was House Speaker; Rayburn and Johnson were the only thing keeping the Yankees from overturning the depletion allowance and as they would later need Congress to be Republican, the oilmen of the time needed Johnson and Rayburn in charge, they needed the House to remain Democratic, and they gave generously to keep it that way.

They were all gone now: Hank, Johnson, Rayburn, Coke Stevenson, Murchison, Cullen, and Hunt . . . soon she would join them. She supposed she ought to be happy: nearly everyone she had ever known had passed over to the other side. But she was not happy at all. She was going into a darkness from which she would not return. That others had gone before her did not make any difference.

She was not a good Christian; that was the problem. The true believers all had their motives, things they had wanted, but not gotten in this world—money, happiness, a second chance—but she had those things or did not need them and had always known that the greatest of her gifts was her ability to see things just as they were. To see the difference between her desires and reality. And the reality was that her life would end just like Hank's. She would not see him again: what made him Hank had stopped existing the moment he died. They now said that even the tunnel of light was just a trick of the neurons. There was only the body. She hoped she would be proved wrong, but she doubted it.

She looked around at the ancient carved furniture and the high cold ceiling and the logs burning without any heat. It might be a sort of purgatory. She would not mind that, remaining like this forever, reliving pleasant memories. She closed her eyes and she was in Washington visiting Jonas. There was someone he wanted her to meet and they had spent the afternoon on his boat in the Chesapeake Bay.

Her legs were tan, not a vein to be seen. She was wearing a white-and-yellow sundress and sitting in a wooden Chris-Craft; Jonas was driving and the man, pale and thin-haired and going pink from the sun, was flirting with her. A pleasant feeling. Not something she would have indulged back home, but here on the bay, under a sky that was blue but not hot, on the water that was clean and cool, she did not mind it.

It was the first time she'd been away from her children in over a year. Though she sensed she was carrying one inside her. Benjamin, probably. She was not showing—the pleasant man had no idea. He was short, soft in the gut, the opposite of Hank, but he was funny and she found him attractive. Though it might have simply been that she was treated better; women still had their place here, but it was not quite as small as in Texas. A Yankee might forget to hold the door, but he might also forget (or pretend to forget) that he was your superior. She began to imagine a life.

Then something passed between the man and Jonas and then he turned to her and was not smiling.

"I hate to get down to business, Jeannie, but I fear our friend the driver"—he indicated Jonas—"has some pressing business back in the city."

She shrugged as if she didn't care, though she would have been content to spend the entire day out on the water, away from her children and the telephone.

"What do you know about Mohammad Mosaddegh?" he said.

"I know we should have been more careful of him."

"What if I told you that he is not long for the throne?"

As he allowed her to process this she realized she might say any number of things. She decided to say nothing. She was glad Hank was not with her.

"Anglo-Iranian will get back some of what they lost," he continued, "but it won't be like before. Times have changed."

She sipped her drink.

"The majors will get the biggest piece, but right now we're trying to assemble a coalition of the willing. We need good people who have resources available immediately."

"Because it won't look good if you give it all to the majors."

"That is correct," he said. "And this is America. We like to look out for the little guy." He went back to looking over the water. "Nice day, isn't it?"

She knew that Hank would have pressed the man for numbers, for percentages, but that was not the right approach; she simply had to agree and to trust in this man and in Jonas.

"We'll take as much as you can give us," she said. She considered asking him what the time frame might be, but that would be even worse than asking for the size of the piece. She felt another wave of relief that Hank was not with her.

"You know Sedco?"

"I know Bill Clement."

"Get with him when you get back to Texas. Tell him I sent you."

Jonas turned the boat toward Annapolis; Jeannie and the man went on talking about other things. Their knees brushed, then brushed again. She expected he might ask her for a drink when they reached the dock, decided she would turn him down, but was hurt when he didn't. Of course it was for the best. She called Hank from her hotel and told him in a coded manner that they ought to free up as much cash as possible. They were both used to calls like that, they both knew better than to ask for details over a telephone.

By then it had been clear for decades that the future was overseas. The first well drilled in Iraq, in 1927, when it was still called Mesopotamia, had come in at ninety-five thousand barrels a day. A big Texas well, even then, produced five hundred, maybe a thousand, and everyone knew it was only a matter of time. The Persian Gulf was where the real oil was. If that well in Iraq had come in ten or twelve years earlier, the Ottoman Empire would not have collapsed. The world would be an entirely different place.

By the 1950s, domestic drilling was a tough business. It cost a fortune, the wells produced less, and once you found the oil, there was no guarantee you'd be allowed to remove it from the ground. The government was planning a war with Russia and they wanted plenty of domestic oil in storage if that happened. The best way to store oil was to leave it where you found it. Strategic reserves, they called it. Good for the government, bad for the oilmen.

There was no good answer. The hot oil days of the '30s—filling tankers at night and running them over the border to avoid production quotas—were long over. You had to go overseas. All over the old Ottoman Empire, you could pull oil out of the ground for pennies a barrel. There wasn't much infrastructure yet, but that was just a matter of time.

Chapter Thirty-six
Diaries of Peter McCullough

JULY 4, 1917

When I am in my office I leave the door open so that I might hear the faintest noise of her footsteps around the house. If I hear someone on the stairs I walk casually down the hall to see whom it might be, heart rushing . . . but it is generally Consuela or her daughter.

Have not been out to pastures in several days. Told Sullivan I was buried in paperwork. Since then have been inventing tasks for myself so I can remain in the house.

When I do hear footsteps I rush for my door. If she is not in the west hallway (I am at the end of the east hallway, on the other side of the staircase) I will walk to the middle, hoping to catch her on the stairs or in the foyer below. Then I will stand, pretending to investigate the stained-glass window I have been looking at for thirty years, as from this vantage I can see anyone who passes the main entryway or goes from one side of the house to the other.

María's footsteps are easily discerned from the vaqueros' but I am constantly fooled by the light feet of Consuela and her daughter Flores. And by Miranda and Lupe Jimenez. If they see me, they look away— they all now suspect I have designs on them, though in fact I am hoping they are someone else.

If several hours (which feel like weeks) pass in which I have not seen her, I'll pick up a few worthless papers and stroll around the house as if on an errand, and, if the door to the library is open, I will go and pretend to find some book or pamphlet, for instance, *The Record of Registered Brands (1867)*—or something equally useless—but of course María does not know better. She thinks I am being diligent, and we'll speak for half an hour, and then she'll apologize for interfering with my work and take her things and go elsewhere, while meanwhile all my blood, or whatever vital force that is in me, sinks down into the earth.

Today I was in the kitchen, eating a plum, and she walked in and asked what I was doing and without answering, I impulsively offered her the plum, from which I had already taken two bites, and without hesitation she took it and had a dainty bite, looking at me the entire time. Then she abruptly left. I put the plum to my mouth and held it there until common sense forced me to eat the rest of it.

I cannot imagine making love to her. It seems disrespectful somehow. Every evening she plays the piano; I have moved the divan into the parlor (it properly belongs there, I lied to her) so that I can close my eyes and feel how close she is. She seems to think this a proper time for us to keep company, as she never tries to escape. Cannot stop reliving the moment in the library (her hand on mine), I curse myself for not responding, for not returning her touch or even leaning against her—this is likely the reason she has not done it again. Or perhaps she was simply being sympathetic, and the world I have invented for us exists only in my own mind. Just the thought leaves me hollowed out.

July 6, 1917

My father's deadline for María to leave has come and gone. Was beginning to feel better until he found me this morning.

"Pete, I am going to Wichita Falls. I will be back in one week, at which point the Garcia woman will have made her absquatulation. I have always let you do whatever you want, but this . . ." He looked around my office, as if the right words might be found among my books. " . . . this is not adjunctive to the forwarding of the design."

"What are you doing in Wichita Falls?" I said.

"Don't worry your head over it."

"There is nothing she can do to us."

"This has gone on long enough. There is one person on earth who cannot be here and you have brought her into this house."

"You are not going to change my mind," I said.

"Every day I see you now you're out on a dike. You think I don't notice that for ten years you don't bother to wash and now you're wearing collars?"

I didn't say anything.

"This ain't a grass widow you get to tap free, son. This one will cost us the ranch."

"You may leave now," I said.

He didn't move.

"Get out of my office."

Later I come across María in the library. I am pretending to look for a book, when she says, apropos of nothing: "How is your work going?"

"I'm not really working," I say.

She smiles, then gets serious again.

"Consuela tells me things."

"Whatever she is telling you, I won't let it happen."

"Peter." She shrugs and looks out the window, past the trees. I look at the skin along her neck, her collarbones, the edge of one shoulder, I look at her arms, still thin. " . . . I shouldn't be here anyway. This is the last place I should be, in fact."

"I'll take care of my father."

"That's not what I mean."

"Where else do you have?"

She shrugs and it is quiet and I watch her face changing. After a moment she decides something. "Do you have time to sit? If you are not really working?"

She is on her chair facing the window. I go to the couch.

"Don't worry about my father," I say.

She stands up and comes over and sits next to me. She touches my wrist.

"Sooner or later, I'll have to leave. Days or weeks, it doesn't matter."

"It does to me."

She touches my cheek. We are so close and I wait for something to happen, but it doesn't. When I open my eyes she is still looking at me. I lean forward, then stop myself; she is still looking at me, and I kiss her, just barely. Then I lean back. I am seeing spots.

She puts her fingers through my hair.

"You have good hair," she says. "And yet your father is bald. And he is short, and you are tall."

I can feel her breath.

"You will forget me," she says.

"I won't."

I wait for something to happen. We're leaning against each other. I work myself up and turn to kiss her again, but she only gives her cheek.

"I want to," she says. But then she stands up and walks out of the room.

Chapter Thirty-seven
Eli McCullough

1852

A few weeks later Judge Wilbarger's wife and I were lying naked on her couch, in my mind to spite the judge, in her mind because she was high on laudanum and being naked on the couch was a comfortable place to be. She had sent the Negroes to Austin on errands. She had the sort of face you saw in old books; it was pale and very delicate and I guessed that at one point she'd been the kind of woman that men would have killed to be with. And I guessed that she knew this, and knew it was not true anymore.

"How old are you, really?"

"Nineteen," I said.

"I don't care, you know. I just want to know more about you."

"Seventeen," I said.

She looked at me.

"Sixteen."

"Will the number keep going down?"

"No, it's sixteen."

"I'll take that. It's the perfect age."

"Is it?"

"For you it is."

She was quiet. I wondered how it was that a woman like her would ever end up with a man like the judge. I wondered if she had loved him. Then I was thinking about the Comanches.

"Are you mad at me?"

"No," I said. Then I said, "Why don't you go back?"

"To England? I'm very respectable here." She laughed. "No, of course I'm not. But what would I do there?"

"Better than Bastrop, probably."

"Probably."

I was looking at her smooth belly and wondering if she'd ever had children, but something told me not to ask, so instead I said, "I don't understand why you won't go back. Even I don't like this place."

"It's complicated," she said. "I can't explain it."

In the meantime, being in town so much, I began to see the same kid over and over until I was sure he was following me. I knew his name was Tom Whipple; he was thirteen or fourteen, but barely five feet tall and lazy eyed to boot. Finally I caught him waiting for me around the judge's house, which I took for a bad sign. I followed him home and waylaid him in the woods behind his house.

Though I had him on the ground, for some reason he didn't look afraid. "You're the wild Indian," he said.

"I am."

"Well, the Indians killed my father. I guess now you'll kill me, too."

"You have been following me," I said.

"They say you go around stealing horses from people."

"I borrow them."

"They say you kill people's chickens and hogs."

"I quit doing that weeks ago."

"They say that someone is going to shoot you."

I snorted. "Well, I would like to see them try it. I could whip every one of these alfalfa desperados."

"My Daddy was a Ranger," he said.

I'd been in town long enough to know this wasn't true; his father had been a surveyor, and the whole party had been killed by Comanches. Or so it was told. Most people couldn't tell an Apache from a Comanche from a white man dressed in buckskin.

It was quiet.

"Show me how to steal a horse," he said.

The next day I told Ellen about Whipple lurking around the house. We went out her back door and cut through the woods until we were out of town, then went to a swimming hole I knew about. I brought a pair of deer hides for us to lie on.

"These have a smell to them," she said. "Are they very fresh?"

"A few weeks."

"My little savage." She was lying with the sun on her, her legs spread, her arms at her sides. There was a breeze but the rocks underneath us were warm. I could see the waving green of the cypresses and the bare branches of the oaks, and the sky in the narrow place above the stream. It had been like this every day for a month, and it would stay like this until the summer. It was not a bad life.

"Have you ever had another affair?"

"You *are* a man, aren't you?"

"I guess."

"Men always want to know."

"Why shouldn't we?"

"Do you want the real answer or the nice one?"

"The real one," I said.

"You're my first. I have never felt as good as the way you make me feel."

I got up.

"I'm sorry," she said. "I thought being half Comanche you wouldn't mind it."

"I don't care."

"Come back." She patted the ground next to her and I did what she said. After we lay awhile longer she said, "You know there are times I think I might open my legs for nearly anyone, just to keep from going crazy. There are times when I think I would open my legs for Henry."

"They will sure as shit lynch you."

"Over a black man, yes. Do you know he won't even look at me?"

"He's a Negro," I said.

"But still he won't look at me. He knows they would kill him for it, so he's afraid of me. I feel sick about it all the time. He is more scared of me than Roy."

I was quiet.

"If I ever move back to England, that will be why."

I slid up next to her and lifted one leg and eased inside. Then I had the urge to stop and hold her. She wanted me to continue with the rutting. When we finished she fell asleep. I sat up and looked around, watching the stream going over the rocks. There was a mockingbird going through its songbook.

When I opened my eyes it was late.

"When are Cecelia and Henry getting back?"

"I don't know," she mumbled. "I sent them to Austin."

"We should get dressed."

She didn't move. Her long hair, which wasn't quite gray and wasn't quite brown, was tangled all around her.

"You know if you keep sending them on errands like that, one day they will run to Mexico."

"I certainly hope so."

"And you know they know about us."

"I certainly hope not."

"Of course they do."

"Well, Roy will shoot us both."

"They'll never tell."

"Why not?"

"Well, they like you better than him, for one. And for two, they're niggers."

"What does that mean?" she said.

"You know." I watched as she put on her underthings.

"Not really, I'm afraid."

I knew I was in the right but still I felt my bristles go up.

"If you don't like the judge, why don't you just leave him?"

She was shaking her head.

"It's not as hard as it sounds."

"Sure," she said. "I suppose we could run away together."

"We should."

"You don't know what you're saying, honey."

She pulled back her hair and tied it and then went into the bag for her laudanum.

"You think you're a bit superior to me, don't you." She held her fingers together. "Just a tiny bit."

I shrugged.

"Well, you're right."

She offered me the laudanum. "Would you like to try some?"

"Not really."

"Good," she said. "Good for you."

She took the trail back to town and I waited half an hour or so then walked out after her. There was another set of footprints across the rocks.

The judge's Thoroughbreds knew me so well that it was not really stealing. Tom Whipple knew nothing about horses. The first time I took him into the stables, they nearly kicked him through the wall. I helped him onto the saddle, then got up behind him.

When we got back, Whipple was so excited he couldn't stop talking, and, as we snuck away through the woods, it occurred to me that he was going to do something stupid. I watched his feet as he walked ahead of me.

A few days later he tried to catch his neighbor's horse, a hog-backed Belgian draft animal, and instead caught a load of turkey shot. Luckily the barn door stopped most of it. But that did not stop him from blabbering.

I expected Ellen to see me in jail but she didn't. When I mentioned her, the sheriff just shook his head.

"Son, I am tryin to figger how you could have picked a worse person to connubiate with."

I didn't say anything.

"Were you drunk?"

"Sometimes."

"Them aborigines must have scrambled your head, boy. I really had my hopes for you."

"Is there gonna be a real trial, you think?"

"If there is," he said, "it will be the shortest one in history."

Chapter Thirty-eight
Jeannie McCullough

She was sitting on the couch, watching Susan suck her blanket and Thomas, with his cowlick and overalls and fat little arms, his red bandanna, she wanted to eat him up. He was trying to make a tower from blocks. The sun was on him and she continued to watch and after the tower collapsed for the twentieth or fiftieth (or hundredth) time, she winked out. Later she came to. Thomas was arranging the blocks; Susan had fallen asleep. It seemed that the rest of her life, before she'd had children, had been a dream. Did she even have a mind at all? She was like an animal chewing its cud.

Now she was awake. She was bored but there was something else, a restlessness so intense that she could not physically sit still any longer, she got up and paced the room and then, glancing behind her quickly—the children still in place—she went out the glass door to the backyard and walked a lap around the high wooden fence. The grass was thick; it was humid under the trees. She could make a drink.

She returned to the patio and watched her children from the other side of the glass. Of course she loved them, but there were times, she did not want to say it, there were times when she wondered what would happen if they simply stopped existing. *There is something wrong with you,* she thought. *There is something very wrong.* She'd tried to broach the subject with Hank, but it had not gone anywhere; he'd had no idea what she was talking about, and she'd ended the conversation before indicting herself any further. Hank spent only fifteen or twenty minutes a day with them alone. Though in his own mind, he looked after them from the time he got home until the kids went to sleep: his idea of looking after them was simply being in the same house. She spent as much time with the kids in one day as Hank spent in an entire month. She could not help doing the calculations.

She'd been low since the birth of Thomas, their first. She'd gotten lower when the doctor insisted, six months into the pregnancy with Susan, that she stay home as much as possible. She had begun to wonder about the point. The same as when her father died. Something was wrong with her, here she was surrounded by her growing family, her beautiful healthy children, asking about the point of being alive.

It was beautiful, it was natural, but of course it was something else, something you could never say or they would lock you away forever, it was another creature taking the blood right out of you. She was there in the hospital and then it was as if some malevolent spirit had settled inside her, something had risen and taken hold, one minute she was herself, the next she'd been snatched and pulled under, she had no say, she had never understood how small she was. It was not something you could explain to other people. She had survived.

A feeling of being tricked came to her constantly, betrayed by her own body, she had thought it existed for her own enjoyment and she was angry and jealous of Hank, who had paid no cost, who, as she lay in the hospital bed, held her hand and looked lovingly into her face and told her to *breathe, breathe;* meanwhile she was on a plane that had lost its engine, plummeting toward open water, toward annihilation, breathing was the last thing on her mind. She had not stopped being angry about that, either. His sure advice on matters he knew nothing about.

She was being unreasonable. There was no point thinking about it. She stood on the patio, watched her children through the window a few moments longer, wondered what she would say if a neighbor saw her or the nanny came downstairs or Hank came home. She went back inside. She called the nanny on the intercom and asked her to pack a bag for Susan. Thomas was old enough to be looked after; Susan she would take to the office. She still went in a few times a week to visit her old life. *You are being a baby,* she thought.

She put Susan in the front seat of the Cadillac and felt an immediate relief, even before she left the driveway. Susan began to cry. Jeannie lifted her and held her in her lap as she drove. Twenty minutes later they were in front of the office, and after a long elevator ride she handed Susan off to the secretaries, who were happy to have her, happy to hold a child, happy to avoid work, she didn't know and didn't care, she only wanted to be alone.

She went into her office and shut the door. It was hot, pleasantly so—it was all windows. It was a green view over the city, which was growing, growing, the East Texas country was lush and wet, it was the Deep South. Hell in the summer. She loved her children. She had expected something different. She had expected them to be like her brothers, or like foals or calves, helpless at first, but quickly capable of looking out for themselves.

What she had not expected was so much need. They said it was love but it was not love at all, if she was honest, they had taken far more than they could ever give. Perhaps they had taken everything. "That is wrong," she said out loud. "I am wrong for thinking that." She sat there, not daring to breathe, looking out over the skyscrapers, filled with people, she could see them bustling, sitting in their offices. There was no one like her. *You are pathetic*, she thought, *think about your own mother.*

In the other room, she heard Susan begin to cry; the sound brought her out of the chair, she was moving toward the door before she even knew what was happening. But of course the girls could handle it. She went back to her desk—stacks and stacks of papers—it was ridiculous, she had no context for any of it, she began to read at random. A landman's report, a geologist's report, a deal long gone bad. It was hot. The questions were pointless. She'd known what she was getting into (*except I did not,* she insisted, *I did not know*), her life was ruled by the needs of others; the only need she could not indulge was the one she felt nearly every day, to get into the car and begin driving and never stop.

Sometime later she woke up sweating. The sun was still coming in. She wondered if the air-conditioning was on. She shuffled the papers, throwing out the old ones, but it was pointless, it would take her months to catch up. She went to the divan and fell asleep again. Then it was past five. Nothing had been done.

She checked her face in her compact: puffy, the fabric had marked her, there was a pretty girl in there somewhere, with good cheekbones and perfect skin and a nice mouth, but it was not visible in the mirror; all the color was gone except for under her eyes. Her teeth were yellow, her hair was like something dried up in the sun.

She winked out again. When she came to it was dark. She touched herself up and she went back out into the office.

Susan was asleep in the remaining secretary's lap. Everyone else had gone home and the girl was not moving, just sitting there, looking helpless.

"I'm so sorry," said Jeannie.

"Oh no, I love her," said the girl, and she did. She was perfectly happy to be sitting there with an infant on her lap; she looked as angelic as the child and somehow this made Jeannie feel even worse.

"Thank you for looking after her. You have no idea what a relief it is."

The girl just looked at her. It was true—she did not have any idea. She would be happy if she had a baby like this, happy to have a husband to go along with it.

Luckily, Hank was up in Canada again. At least she was spared him seeing this. He, along with Herman Jefferson, their geologist, and Milton Bryce, their lawyer, was always telling her she didn't have to worry about coming in. Things had been running fine without her, running fine for two years. They were too delicate to say it, but what they meant was, *You are not needed. Our world has continued without you.*

Though hers had not. *I might as well be dead,* she thought.

When Hank got back from Alberta, she told him it was time to add a second nanny, and maybe even a third, if they were to have another child.

"That's silly," he said. He buzzed about the kitchen, fixing himself a sandwich, moving with his usual efficiency, everything put back in its place.

"Why does it matter?" She thought he was talking about money.

"It matters," he said. "I don't want our kids being raised by people they won't know when they get older."

"So stay home and raise them."

He looked at her to see if she was being serious.

"You don't have to work," she said. "We will never need money."

He was annoyed. He took a bite of his sandwich and washed it down with milk.

"I can't do this by myself anymore. I'm serious."

"That's ridiculous."

"Then I guess I'm ridiculous."

"No, I mean it's ridiculous to say you're by yourself. You have Eva all day and I am home by six every night."

"What if I were to point out that they are half yours," she said. "And that you might take half care of them."

"I do my share," he said, and by the funny way his voice broke she could tell he really believed it.

"You do," she said, "but it is not half, or even a quarter, it is more like one percent. I appreciate that you leave your door open but that is quite different from sitting all day with them, alone."

He didn't say anything.

"We will get another nanny. Nothing will change for you."

"Out of the question," he said.

"I will not be leaving the business."

"You already left it," he said. "You barely know anything that is going on."

It occurred to her then that he was no different from her father, which was maybe an exaggeration, or maybe not, maybe he just put a nicer face on it.

"I don't feel like a person anymore," she said.

"Well, that is nice to hear from the mother of one's children." Now he would not look at her.

"I feel like it's me or them," she said.

"I don't know what's gotten into you." Even through his tan she could see his neck was red. He put down his sandwich and walked out of the room, then out of the house.

She heard him start the car and pull out of the driveway.

Of course she began to cry. The truth was much too far. She should never have said it. She went out into the yard and sat in the green darkness. What he wanted, what everyone wanted, was that she stay at home and never have a meaningful thought again while they all kept doing exactly as they pleased. It was insane. Hank, Jefferson, Milton Bryce—she hated all of them, actually hated them at that moment—she didn't care what they thought of her.

The decision was made. She was not going back. An arrangement would be figured out, she was worth fifty million dollars and it was insane, actually insane, that she should be trapped here, or anywhere else, by children, her husband, this situation, she was not sure how to properly describe it, but it was all of those things, and it was over.

She heard the car pull into the driveway. She stayed in the yard where it was dark. Inside, she watched Hank come down the steps into the living room, past all the new furniture, two hundred thousand dollars' worth—her money—she watched him go to the bar and pour a whiskey and stare into his glass. Then he went to the window and looked out. It was too bright in the house for him to see her; he was looking only at his own reflection. His coarse sharecropper's face and his thick hair and the lines already around his eyes, yes she loved him, but she stayed where she was. He would have to choose.

He was a good man. But in the end, the money was hers, and without that, she was not sure he would have given in.

It did not seem right, having to bargain with her own husband, having to manipulate him, but maybe he'd been doing it to her the entire time, even if neither one of them had realized it.

They hired two more nannies, and she went back to work. They thought she was a bad mother. She overheard the secretaries, of course they were all un-married, of course they were all jealous, of course they would have slept with Hank in a heartbeat—a wealthy, good-looking man. Women pretended sister-hood until it counted; they acted as if they cared noth-ing for men they were actually in love with. Naturally, she made sure that every girl they hired was so un-attractive that Hank would have to be extraordinarily drunk to even consider them. *We have the ugliest sec-retaries in the world,* he always said.

Still. They thought she was a bad mother. She tried to forget it.

Chapter Thirty-nine
Diaries of Peter McCullough

JULY 7, 1917

Slept only a few hours, thinking of her on the other side of the house. She did not report for breakfast and if she left her room at all, she must have done it quietly as an owl. When I went for lunch I found dishes in the drying rack, freshly washed; she had been there, I had missed her. Lost interest in eating and returned to my office.

Picked up and set down at least two dozen books. Considered, then dismissed, calling Sally. Overcome with need to tell someone about this. If I could climb to the roof and announce it with a bullhorn . . .

But I am happy simply knowing she is in the same house. If there is any question of whether it is better to love or to be loved . . . the answer is obvious. I wonder if my father would agree. I wonder if he has ever felt this way; like all men of ambition I suspect he is incapable of it. I want to weep for him. I would trade everything in this house, everything we own, to keep feeling this, and at this thought, I do begin to weep, for my father, for María, for the Niles Gilberts and the Pedros.

Fortunately or not, I was pulled from this morass of emotion by events that required my action. Around two P.M. there was a loud noise. When I got up to investigate I could no longer see the top of the derrick sticking up over the brush.

As it turned out, the driller had hit a gas pocket and lost control of the rig. One of the hands rode the derrick to the ground; by some miracle he is still alive (they say drunks fall better). By a second miracle the gas did not ignite and by a third miracle (from the common perspective) there is oil now flowing steadily into our pastures, down the hill and into the stream.

By evening the entire town had arrived, looking at the fallen derrick where it lay in a swamp of oily mud. It was plain this was a coup of monstrous proportion, that what few worries we might have had are now over, we are even further removed from the daily lives of the citizenry. But the townspeople did not seem to understand this. They almost seemed to think it was *their* good fortune. People were dipping cups into the mud to taste the oil as if it were coffee.

It is as my father says. Men are meant to be ruled. The poor man prefers to associate, in mind if not in body, with the rich and successful. He rarely allows himself to consider that his poverty and his neighbor's riches are inextricably linked, for this would require action, and it is easier for him to think of all the reasons he is superior to his other neighbors, who are just poorer than he is.

As the crowd pressed around the fallen derrick, the lake of oil growing larger, the driller, whose back teeth were still well afloat, could not decide whether or not to ignite the well. Gas can travel hundreds of yards aboveground, flashing at the smallest provocation; it is not uncommon for spectators to be immolated in this fashion, hours or even days after a well comes in.

After more whiskey to clear his head, he decided not to flare the well. The oil was flowing, not gushing. There could not be much gas. Or so he reckoned. I reckoned he was drunk. I told everyone to stay clear of the well, though when I saw Niles Gilbert and his two porcine offspring clomping out of the viscous mud, having stood nearly at the mouth of the burbling black spring, I began to wish for a divine spark. It occurred to me, as I watched the oil flow down the hill, that soon there will be nothing left to subdue the pride of men. There is nothing we will not have mastered. Except, of course, ourselves.

The vaqueros are using horses and fresnoes to build a dyke, but they are losing the battle. A jimberjawed Yankee farmer offered to rent us his new Hart-Parr tractor. Had he been born here, he would have simply driven it over, but being from the North he thinks only of what fattens his pocket. After some consideration I agreed to pay him. The oil is flowing strongly into the stream—the fresnoes are not designed for emergency work.

Nonetheless everyone was in a good mood and proceeded to get drunk, including the fallen derrickman and the partially crushed floorhand. People from Carrizo began to show up, though what attraction there was—a black pit, a sulfurous stench, even more money flowing into their wealthiest neighbor's pocket—I did not understand. The Colonel appeared at midnight, having driven all the way from Wichita Falls at sixty miles an hour, blowing out a tire from the speed.

He found me in my office. Through the windows came a faint odor of brimstone, as if Old Nick himself were having a smoke on our gallery. By sheer coincidence, I am sure, this is also the odor of money.

"Son," said the Colonel. He hugged me. He was
already as drunk as the others. "From now on, you can
pay for all the brush-clearing you want."

Not a word about María. In a moment of panic I
went and checked her room: she was asleep in her bed,
sighing about something. I watched for a long time
until she stirred.

July 8, 1917

This morning I find her waiting for me downstairs.

"Very exciting news, no?"

I shrug. I am only thinking about what she's lost; I'm
happy the oil was found on our land, instead of hers.

"Will you have much work today?"

"I don't think so," I say. "I have some errands in
Carrizo, if you want to come."

She agrees, which puts me in a good mood about
everything, even the steady stream of cars going to and
from the drilling site, the gates left open—fifty heifers
found on the road this morning.

When we get to Carrizo there is nothing in particular either of us want to do. On a whim we decide on
Piedras Negras for lunch (Nuevo Laredo is brought up;
María does not want to go there). It will be a three-hour

drive; we will be home late; we do not discuss this. She ties her hair back to keep it out of the wind; I steal glances, her warm mouth, dark eyelashes, the fine hairs at the nape of her neck.

When we finally reach the town, around four in the afternoon, I am nervous, wondering about the Carrancistas, Villistas, Zapatistas, but María does not seem concerned. We ignore the shoeshine boys and lottery vendors and find a cantina where we sit on the patio under an arbor. We order *arrachera* eels, grilled fish, *tortillas sobaqueras*, chopped avocados and tomatoes. She has a tequila sour; I have a Carta Blanca. We cannot fish all the food; she stares at it. We hesitate at ordering more drinks. We hesitate again at the car.

Instead of heading home we drive farther into the country to see the old San Bernardo Mission. It is a small old ruin, a single story, nothing on the scale of the cathedrals of Mexico City, but in its time it was the upper reach of Spanish influence here. All the northern expeditions left from and returned to it; you could sense the relief the riders must have had when the mission, with its dome and archways, appeared on the horizon. And the fear they must have had when they left it. This land was far more dangerous than New Mexico ever was.

It occurs to me that the San Bernardo is not much older, fifty or sixty years, than the Garcias' casa mayor. I become quiet. María either reads my thoughts or thinks my silence is due to something else, because she takes my hand, and puts her head against my shoulder.

"It is nice to be out of your house," she says.

We walk slowly, small steps, waiting for something important to be said. She does not let go of my hand, but she will not look at me either.

"And your wife? When will she return?"

"Never, I hope."

"Will you divorce her?"

"If I can."

"She is the beautiful woman in the pictures."

"She comes from a good family."

"She looks it."

"You know she married me because her family is bankrupt. She thought she was marrying a younger version of my father, but unfortunately that is my brother Phineas."

"Perhaps she preferred you because you are handsome."

"Certainly not."

"Certainly," she says. "Your brother has a weasel face."

"My wife wants me to be a different person." I shrug. "I am happy she is gone."

We continue to walk. I expect her to let go of my hand, but she swings our locked arms back and forth, as if we are children, and holds on firmly.

When we reach the car she says: "We will be very late driving home, no?"

Some part of me, the part that takes over when there is something at stake, says: "I'm expected back."

"Oh," she says, and looks away.

She sits in the car, arms crossed, looking out over the mission and the *brasada* to the south, while I get the engine started.

When I get in with her, I swallow and say: "Perhaps it will not be safe to make the drive after dark."

"Perhaps not," she says.

We find a hotel by the railroad depot.

"How is this?"

Now she won't look at me. We are silent as if we are an old couple having a fight. It's cooler and the ceiling fans are turning but I feel the sweat running down my back. Every noise amplified, my boots scuffing the floor, the counter creaking when I lean to sign the register. I hesitate, then write Mr. and Mrs. Garcia. The clerk winks. Our room is on the second floor. We walk up the stairs, silent, then into the room, silent.

"Well?" I say.

She sits on the bed and looks at everything but me. The furnishings are cheap; someone has carved their initials into the headboard.

"This is wrong," she says. "We should go back."

I blurt out, "*No quiero vivir sin ti.*"

"Say it in English."

"I will not live if you leave me," I say.

She goes back to looking at the floor, but I think she is smiling. "I wondered if your hesitations were because of the way I look."

"No," I say.

"This is when you tell me I'm beautiful," she says. She laughs. She pats the bed next to her. "Come over here."

"I love you," I say.

"I believe you," she says.

JULY 9, 1917

We are on the bed facing each other, her leg is thrown over me, but we are not moving; she is lying sleepily against me. I watch my finger go along her arm, her shoulder, her throat, then back down her arm. The glow from the railroad comes through the window.

"Touch my back," she says.

I spend a long time drawing lazy shapes, then kiss her to let her know my intentions. She pulls me on top of her and sighs. She begins to move her hips.

Afterward we fall asleep like that. When we wake we do it again.

"I would be happy if we never left this bed."

"Me too," I say.

She kisses me and then again and again and again and I close my eyes.

In the morning, when the light comes through the curtains, I wonder if the spell will have passed, but she looks at me with the sun shining brightly on us and puts her head against my neck. I can feel her there, breathing me in.

Chapter Forty
Eli McCullough

It was not long before Judge Wilbarger was making arrangements for a necktie social, because once Whipple blabbered, the slaves were blabbering as well and then the whole town caught the whispering fever; everyone knew I'd been pirooting the judge's wife eight and ten times a day, drinking his wine, stealing his horses, feeding his cigars to the hogs. It was reckoned a miracle he had not shotgunned his untrue companion, though it was equally reckoned that someone would have to meet Old Scratch in her place.

I had hopes I might win on popularity, but that was youthful ignorance, as the whites had no love for horse thieves and hog killers, even good ones. The only thing that saved me was Judge Black in Austin, who got the statehouse involved, and accused Wilbarger of mentally abusing me, a helpless returned Indian captive, son of a martyred Ranger, and so the trial and hanging were put off until Wilbarger found a way to get rid of me, namely mustering me into a Ranger company. Which, in those days, was considered near the same as a neck-lining.

The idea of riding with the Rangers appealed to me the same as riding with the Comanches would have appealed to my father, but the seriousness of my situation was made plain. I was taken to Austin in bracelets and released into Judge Black's custody, though I was only there for a few hours. He had a small bay waiting for me, a good saddle, a second Colt Navy and a Springfield carbine. The children came and saw me but his wife would not, and the judge was down at the mouth, and nothing I could say would make it better.

I mustered into the company at Fredericksburg, near our acreocracy, which my father had deeded to my stepmother. Rangering was not a career so much as a way to die young and get paid nothing for doing it; your chances of surviving a year with a company were about the same as not. The lucky ones ending up in an unmarked hole. The rest lost their topknots.

By then the days of the ace units, under Coffee Hays and Sam Walker, were over. Walker was dead, killed in Mexico. Hays had given up on Texas and gone to California. What was left was an assortment of bankrupt soldiers and adventure seekers, convicts and God's abandons.

At the end of each tour, the ones who survived were given a square mile of unclaimed land somewhere in the state. It was a sharecropping of blood, in which we killed Indians and took a portion of their lands in payment, but like any other share work, you always came out a loser. The safe land was all claimed and the only acres still redeemable would not have value for decades. And so the vouchers were always traded for equipment, mostly to speculators who lived in big houses and offered us horses or new revolvers, picking up the land for ten cents on the dollar. Our only other remuneration was ammunition, which we got in unlimited supply. Everything else—from corn bread to side meat—we were expected to forage or otherwise annex.

We dunned the state for powder and lead and spent a few weeks training before riding out. All we did was shoot. We set up a fence post and the captain told us we were not leaving until everyone could hit the post five out of five times from horseback, at a lope at least, a gallop being better, with no preference for handedness, those appendages being considered disposable.

After those few weeks it was clear that a gun fit my hand better than a bow. Those who afforded it carried two Colt Navys, as reloading in those days took several minutes. A few of the men carried Walker Colts, which were twice as powerful but also twice as heavy, and had to be carried in saddle holsters, rather than a belt holster, which was not safe if you were separated from your horse. Not to mention the loading lever would sometimes drop and jam the cylinder; despite all that has been written about them, there was a reason not many Walkers were made.

My first tour we did not see a single Comanche. We saw their tracks and leavings, but could not catch them. Being better raiders they were better at avoiding raids, being better trackers they were harder to follow, and so my fears that I would one day see Nuukaru or Escuté over the barrel of my Springfield turned out to be laughable.

With the exception of a few tired Lipans and Mescaleros, most of what we caught were Mexicans and vagabond Negroes, or starving Fort Indians whose skills had rusted by close proximity to the whites. Meanwhile, any outlaw group worth its name carried an old bow and arrow and after making their killings they would shoot a few arrows into the victims, so the Indians would get blamed for whatever they'd done. Wherever you looked, the red man was at a discount.

When game was scarce or settlers stingy it was normal for us to go hungry a few days, so whenever we recovered a big lot of property, say horses or cattle, unless we recognized the brands we would take a detour to sell them in Mexico, along with any saddles and guns. To the settlers we sold scalps, lances, bows, and other Indian accoutrements that people wanted to hang as trophies. Ears were especially popular.

Despite this pilferage we usually rode home with empty pockets, our gear was always breaking and our horses dying and it all had to be replaced in the field. The legislators encouraged our thieving ways, *plunder the plunderers*—which of course was the same as stealing from our own people—but so far as the elected ones cared, anything not recorded in the register did not count as a tax increase, which was all that mattered to their owners, the cotton men.

As for the cotton men, they admired and respected the state's public servants, who unlike them worked for glory rather than money. They passed this wisdom to the cattlemen, who passed it to the oilmen. It was a smooth-working system, as any foolish servant who suggested he might be paid in dollars, rather than pats on the back, was tarred as a Jayhawker or Free-Soiler, or, worse, an Abolitionist, and run out of the state.

In the Rangers there were a number of former captives, some of whom were glad to get back at their old captors, though mostly they had joined for the same reasons I had, namely that the habits of whites had stopped making sense. They felt crowded in cities or even settlements, they longed for their old lives on the plains, and the closest they could get to their old lives, and their old friends, was to chase and occasionally kill them.

My second year I rode with Warren Lyons, who had spent ten years among the Comanches. After getting into a fight with some chiefs, he'd defected back to the whites, checking in with his birth family only to discover he had nothing left to say to them. Then he signed up with the Rangers. The men were not sure if he was a genius or mass murderer.

Thirteen of us rode out in May, and in June we lost an Ohioan to fever and in August our captain caught a ball along the lower San Antonio–El Paso road. Lyons was elected the new captain and we continued to range in the area between the Davis Mountains and the border. One day in September we were looking for some Mexicans who had stolen horses from Ed Hall, nooning on a nice ridge a day or so east of Presidio. A spring came out of the rock, as they did in those days before all the water was used up, and the country dropped below us to the green flats of the river, with the Sierra del Carmen showing blue in the distance. It was a peaceful scene. The last time I'd been there, with Toshaway and Pizon and the others, I had not had time to notice it.

We lunched on fresh venison, ate some fruit we'd gotten off the settlers, and were generally enjoy our jobs when Lyons spotted eight riders making their way toward us on the Mexican side, heading for one of the fords on the old Comanche war trail. He passed me the spyglass. I could barely make out their colors, but there was something about them and I was sure they were Comanches. They were driving a small *caballada*, maybe two dozen horses.

"What do you think?" I said to Lyons.

"I'd say they are *Nʉmʉnʉʉ* for damned sure," he told me.

"The numbers aren't exactly on our side." There were only eleven of us. Unless you were fighting two or three to one, someone was going to get shot.

"They're probably tired. They don't have many horses."

"That doesn't mean they're tired."

"It means things went bad."

I went back to tell the others. There was whooping and excitement; Comanches were as rare as elephants and everyone wanted to bag one.

Lyons was collecting himself in an orderly fashion. Meanwhile I was jumpy as I'd ever been, which was odd because we'd been getting in a fight once a week. We dropped from the bench down a cottonwood-lined drainage, sticking to the damp sand so as not to kick up any dust.

The Comanches had only two muskets between them and we decided to sneak just within gunshot of the ford and get as many as we could with rifles before they could close the distance. I wondered if Lyons was as rattled as I was. The others had their sap up, having never fought anything but Fort Indians.

When we got near the river I checked my guns a third time and put a fresh cap on my rifle. The Comanches were still on the other side of the water. We were ghosting through the rocks and willows and they hadn't seen us and I knew if we could catch them in the river it would be a slaughter. I thought about Toshaway again.

When I turned to look for Lyons, he had thrown off his boots and was donning a pair of moccasins he'd pulled out of his saddlebag. He'd been with the

Comanches almost a decade, he still talked to himself in Comanche, he didn't even think of them as Comanches but as Numunuu, and I realized why he wasn't nervous about taking them on when we were nearly evenly matched in numbers: he was heading back to fight alongside his old friends.

I unshucked my pistol; he stood up and walked straight into the muzzle.

"What the fuck are you doing, McCullough?"

"What the fuck are *you* doing?" I kept the gun pointed.

"I like my moccasins to fight in," he said. He pushed the barrel away. "You got real troubles, McCullough. You got 'em all down but the nine."

I could hear them laughing and talking, we were waiting for them to all get clear of the brush so we could lay a clean volley into them, but then Hinse Moody and the other half-wits fired their rifle shots and called out their war whoops and hubbed themselves in, kicking their ponies and charging down the hill. The Comanche was the wall-hanger; no one wanted to miss his chance.

The Indians took to the rocks and when Moody and the others got to pistol range the arrows started coming in.

After ten minutes, two of the Comanches made a break for the river. Moody and the others had gone down in the first volley and most everyone else had gotten a dogwood switch in the meantime. Except Lyons. He fought like a purebred *Numu,* rolled off to one side of his grullo, shooting under the animal's neck. His horse looked like a pincushion when it finally gave up; the Indians must have picked him as a turncoat because they were all shooting for him. When his horse went down I expected him to cover behind it, but he dodged through the arrows and was not even touched; they were clattering off the rocks all around him and he was closing on the Indians by himself.

There was a shadow in the brush I had a feeling about; I put a shot into it, adjusted a half foot, put another shot in, adjusting and putting a ball here and there until the gun was empty. I had barely got the first cylinder charged when Lyons went running up the left.

It was quiet. The arrows had stopped coming and my ears were ringing and there were horses squealing and snorting. Someone was moaning and calling for his wife. Other than Lyons and myself, there were only three on our side still up and they were dug in way behind me. Lyons was way ahead. My horse was down and I was happily covered behind it, but I made a rush and closed six or seven yards. Then Lyons made a rush. I watched the pile of rocks where the Indians were, but I'd lost my hat and the sun was glaring. I made another rush. Nothing happened. I made a longer rush and an arrow came out of the willows and clipped my thigh. I saw Lyons charging in, heard him shoot his gun empty, then made myself get up. I was not sure where I ought to be aiming. Lyons came out of the bushes.

"Well, I think that's all of them."

"How 'bout down there?"

"Well, go look. But I counted five dead ones, plus the two that ran off."

"There's one more by the water," I said.

"Then there's your eight."

I didn't feel so sure. "Do you have any left?"

He shucked the pistol and pulled out his second and checked it. "Two. Should be enough for some dead Indians." Then he turned around: "Hey, you fucking women."

The other three were eighty yards behind us.

"Move up the right." He pointed toward the river.

Though the two of us were standing out there in the open, they all made the shortest possible rush and ducked down again.

"Who the fuck is that in the way back?" said Lyons.

"I think it's Murphy and Dunham. And maybe Washburn behind them."

"What a bunch of cockchafers." He looked over. "You might want to check that leg."

I did. By miracle of a quarter inch, the spike had turned to the outside of the hip instead of going inside where the big artery was. I made a wide circle of the rocks. Lyons went overtop. I could feel the blood running into my boot. But there were no more Indians and their horses were grazing along the water.

"You want us to come in?" shouted one of the laggards.

I looked at Lyons. "Not yet," I shouted back.

We moved carefully among the fallen Comanches, some lying in deep slicks of blood while others looked asleep, a lucky ball to the neck, a clean, dry end, we lifted their faces and checked them carefully and Lyons must have seen someone he recognized, because when we called the other three in, he didn't share in any of the scalping or stripping; he went off by himself and didn't talk to anyone.

Just when we were starting to gather the dead, MacDowell, one of the men we thought was down for good, stood up. He had been hit in the head by a fragment and after he collected his senses he was able to ride. I bandaged my hip—considered again what a miracle it was that the arrow deflected away from my innards—and got our five dead loaded. We took them to Fort Leaton, where they had shovels.

The next morning, three of the four remaining Rangers, Murphy, Dunham, and Washburn, turned their badges in to Lyons. "We don't want none of the aborgoin horses," said Washburn. "We just want to keep the guns and scalps and such."

"Keep 'em," said Lyons.

"You startin' to miss your turpentine?" I looked at Washburn. He was a cross-eye from East Texas and he had stayed a hundred yards behind us during the fight.

"There ain't pay enough for this," he said. "Even a clay-eater like me can tell that." He indicated the others: "Dunham had ran with Hinse Moody since he was eight years old. You even know that?"

"No," I said. Dunham was already walking off. I didn't know why I was taking the blame.

The three deserters went to attend to their packing, which left only me, Lyons, and the young horse thief MacDowell. He had a good nature and I was happy he had made it. Later we stood on the parapet and watched them ride off toward the mountains, but they felt us looking and put the gaffs to their ponies.

"Well," said Lyons. "Looks like our take just doubled."

We spent the rest of the day scrubbing guns and fixing tack. Two of the horses we'd got off the Comanches had U.S. markings; we traded them to Ed Hall so he could sell them in Old Mexico. I got a beautiful pumpkin-skin gelding, which I later lost in a card game.

Ed Hall said, "How many do you think got away?"

"Two."

"You sure you boys won't stay awhile longer?"

"You'll be fine," I said. "Just invite 'em for dinner in front of your cannon."

He chuckled: "I don't think they'll fall for that one twice."

Of course it was not his cannon; it was Ben Leaton's. Leaton had died a few years earlier and Hall had married his widow but was having trouble filling his shoes. Leaton had been a scalp hunter extraordinaire and I'd always suspected he ran the party that had nearly got Toshaway and me. He was most famous for inviting a group of Indians to dinner, then slipping out halfway through the meal to touch off a cannon he'd charged with canister and hidden behind a curtain. The shot obliterated the unsuspecting Indians along with everything else in his dining room. No one stole his horses after that.

When we got up in the morning we found that Mac-Dowell died during the night.

"I'm cursed," Lyons told me.

"I think MacDowell was cursed worse than you." I was in no mood for his antics. My leg was throbbing and I hadn't slept and I was too tired to dig another grave.

"No," he said. "I mean I've always known it, that everyone around me will die and I will never even get a scratch."

"I'm the same way," I told him.

He looked at me. "Just in the six months I've known you, you've been stuck with two arrows."

"But not seriously," I said.

"Still. There's a big fuckin' difference."

I could not make him understand that there was no difference at all. He quit the Rangers a year before we mustered out to join the Confederacy. Then he moved to New Mexico and died despite his luck and good health.

After selling the horses and captured guns and saddles in Austin, Lyons and I split the money and he rode out again toward the border. I kitted myself out in a new shirt, pants, and hat, dropped my guns off to get the timing fixed, and went to pay the judge for the horse and pistol he'd given me two years earlier. He would not take it, but he was happy to see me, he said, looking and acting like a white man. I had dinner with his wife and three daughters, who were happy to see me also, and I could tell his wife was warming up to me.

"I just knew this would be good for you," she said. "I knew it would help civilize you just a little bit."

I didn't tell her I was doing the same thing I'd been doing with the Indians. The oldest daughters were making eyes at me, and that was not bad, except that it put me in a certain mood and within a few days I'd emptied my pockets.

The city was above my bend. It was nothing but guttersnipes and gaycats, whoremongers and Sunday men. I sold my derringer pistol for a dozen doses of calomel, poured in both ends, as I thought I'd caught the French pox. Then I pawned one of my Colts and got the cheapest room I could find, waiting for another patrol to be funded by the Chosen Ones.

A man found me at the rooming house. He handed me a rawhide wallet like he was making a delivery I was expecting. I took the bag but didn't open it, and I reached toward my back pocket until I remembered I'd sold my derringer. The man had a weak chin and four days of stubble and a rotting hat pulled to his eyebrows. He looked like a mortuarian's assistant.

"I saw Sher Washburn the other day," he said. "He mentioned he had rode with you and I thought I knew your name. Then I found I had wrote it down."

I looked at him.

"Your daddy talked about you a fair bit. We all knew."

"Who are you?" I said.

"I rode in from Nacadoch. I'm trying my hand at granging up there but I have kept this a long time to give to you."

Inside the wallet was a scalp vest. Dozens of scalps, some with the hair on, others with the hair off, sewn together in a careful pattern. They all looked dark.

"Oh, they're all Injun," he said. "You can be god-damn sure of that; I probably helped your daddy with about half of 'em." I handled the vest; it was soft and finely made and I thought of Toshaway, who had his own shirt made of scalps. I had buried him in it.

"Can I give you something for it?"

"Nope." He shook his head and went to spit and then stopped himself.

"Let's get into the air," I said.

We walked toward the edge of town.

"You know he went after you, don't you? He was always worrying if you knew that. They got as far as the Llano before they lost the trail."

"Huh," I said.

"Oh, he went after you all right."

We reached the water and stood there and there was not much to say. A few boatmen were poling supplies for the settlers upriver. I took out my piece of thick and offered it and he cut off a chunk and put it in his lip.

"Your daddy was somethin' else," he said. "He could smell the Indians better than a wolf."

"What happened to him?"

He was looking over the water. "I remember you could stand on Congress and hear billiards in one ear and whoopin' aborgoins out the other. There was thirty, forty houses, maybe. And now look at it." He looked behind us at the town, where there were now thousands of people. Down on the riverbank, the ferryman was doing a brisk business.

"What happened to him?" I said again. He was quiet and I thought of my father coming back to his house and wife and daughter and then I thought of him riding out after us. I watched the water. I could feel my fear drifting away from me.

The man just stood there. He never answered.

Chapter Forty-one
J.A. McCullough

She knew she was not alone, there was someone in the room, the person responsible for her condition. *I'm living through my own death,* she thought, and let herself drift. *A cold place. An old pond. But the mind,* she thought, *the mind will survive,* that was the great discovery, it was all connected, it was roots beneath the earth. You had only to reach it. The great hive.

She was not sure of herself; she felt like a child. The mind was just . . . it was the soul, they had always said it. The body shrank, it shrank and shrank while the soul grew and grew until the body could no longer hold it. You could build a pyramid or vault but it did not matter, the body shrank and stooped, they were right, she thought, they had been right all along, it was an error, the worst of her life. *You have to wake up.*

She opened her eyes but she was not in the room, there were colors, a landscape, a green plain going on as far as she could see and in front of her, an immense canyon drifting among clouds in a bright sky. *This is not my memory,* she thought, *this belongs to someone else.* She could see a coyote padding in a bar ditch, scents sounds it was taking in everything; she thought of a lock, a gate, a man shooting a gun.

She opened her eyes, latched on to the room, counting the chairs tables drawings, embers on the hearth, she was back in the house in River Oaks. Hank was by the window. He was angry about the children. Or something else: the television. The president had been shot and his wife was climbing over the seat.

"H.L. fucking Hunt," Hank was saying, "we just killed the president."

There was a voice, hers: "They say Oswald was working for the Russians."

This is not real either, she thought. Hank had died before JFK. She was mixing things up.

But Hank did not appear to notice. "Hunt has a thousand people waiting for him at the airport with signs saying TRAITOR and YANKEE GO HOME. A few hours later, they shoot him."

"It's a little obvious," she said.

There was the fireplace burning. Hank was looking out the window, but what he saw she couldn't say. "When God dumps a lot of money in your lap, you start thinking you are closer to him than other people."

Then he was kissing her. It went on, he didn't notice that she was old, that she had lost her teeth. Then they were making love. She winked out, then came back again.

They were standing by the bar.

"Are we in on anything with Hunt?"

"No," she said.

"That is a relief." He sipped his whiskey. "If he weren't such a hick, he'd be dangerous."

"You're a hick, darling."

"I'm a hick with an art collection. A hundred years from now, we'll be the Rockefellers."

Of course it was not the Rockefellers he meant. It was the Astors. Or the Whitneys. As for their collection, half of what they'd first bought was fake and it had taken her the rest of her life to replace them with the originals.

As for JFK, it had not surprised her. The year he died, there were still living Texans who had seen their parents scalped by Indians. The land was thirsty. Something primitive still in it. On the ranch they had found points from both the Clovis and the Folsom, and while Jesus was walking to Calvary the Mogollon people were bashing each other with stone axes. When the Spanish came there were the Suma, Jumano, Manso, La Junta, Concho and Chisos and Toboso, Ocana and Cacaxtle, the Coahuiltecans, Comecrudos . . . but whether they had wiped out the Mogollons or were descended from them, no one knew. They were all wiped out by the Apaches. Who were in turn wiped out, in Texas anyway, by the Comanches. Who were finally wiped out by the Americans.

A man, a life—it was barely worth mentioning. The Visigoths had destroyed the Romans, and had themselves been destroyed by the Muslims. Who were destroyed by the Spanish and Portuguese. You did not need Hitler to see that it was not a pleasant story. And yet here she was. Breathing, having these thoughts. The blood that ran through history would fill every river and ocean, but despite all the butchery, here you were.

Chapter Forty-two
Diaries of Peter McCullough

JULY 13, 1917

Four days since we returned from Piedras Negras. Of course they noticed our absence—my Chandler was gone overnight—but nothing was said. María believes we were missed in the bustle.

Landmen have flooded the town; strangers appear at our door at all times of the day and lights burn at my father's house all night. Both the Midkiffs and Reynoldses have been selling leases, but my father has turned down every offer that has come our way. I went over to his house to talk to him and found him sitting naked in the pool by his spring. His eyes were closed. In the water he looked like a small pale imp.

"I dunno why this heat never got to me before," he said.

"You are getting old," I told him.

"So are you."

"We ought to sell some leases and forget about this."

"That girl still in the house?"

I didn't answer.

"You know, if I hadn't kept your mother locked up I would swear you got made by an Indian."

"You wouldn't have been home to notice if I had," I said.

He considered that, then changed the subject.

"Let them find some more oil and then we'll consider selling leases."

I sat down on the rocks.

"It's all right, son. You're a good cattleman. But you don't know a goddamn thing about making money. And that's why you got me."

"Thanks for the reminder."

"Do some figuring on what our minerals are worth at a hundred an acre, which is where Reynolds and Midkiffs are selling."

"Tens of millions," I said.

"Then figure what they'll be worth at a thousand an acre. Or five thousand."

"Why do you even care?" I said.

"This is what is going to happen. A couple dozen drillers and oilmen are going to spend the next year or two proving our leases. That is when we will sell."

I want to believe he is wrong. Unfortunately, I know better.

"What's happening with that girl?" he said, but I was already walking away.

What is happening with María is that we have both been sore for days. The first night after Piedras Negras I slipped quietly from her room, but within an hour I'd returned and since then we have not spent more than a few minutes apart.

This morning I woke just after sunrise. I lay there, listening to her breath, taking in the odor of her hair and skin, dozing, then waking up to look at her again, washed over in the light and the pleasant feeling of being near her.

It occurs to me that I have not seen the shadow in several days; I have not thought about Pedro's ruined face or Aná's scream. In a moment of sheer perversity, I try to call the images back to mind, but I cannot.

I have always known I am not the sort of person other people are inclined to love. They are blind to what I see in myself; with a glance they decide that my judgment ought not to be trusted. My singular luck, so far as they are concerned, was to be born into this great family; elsewise I would be some scrivener, renting a dim room in a filthy city.

It occurs to me that María may wake up one morning and see me as the others do, that her love may prove deciduous, though so far it is nearly the opposite; I see my own childish gaze reflected in hers, I catch her looking at me when my back is turned, I wake up and she is leaning on an elbow, watching me. We are drunk on each other. As for my so-called ailment—which I had presumed was a symptom of age, and Sally had presumed was yet another symptom of my unmanfulness—there has been not a single sign. If anything, the opposite: my body is possessed by an unending desire to be connected with her (just the thought . . .); we never separate after making love and she will often roll on top of me and fall asleep while we are still attached.

This morning she read to me from the Song of Solomon; I read the second of the Heloise and Abelard letters to her; when we are together it seems our mere existence is a transcendence of all that is wrong with the world, but as I sit now I wonder if there is some darker element, a man having relations with someone who is not his equal, though of course she is, in every way except in power, which means she is not. She is free to go and yet not free, as, aside from our room here, she has no place to call her own.

"Where did you go?" she says, when I return.

"To my office."

"You were gone so long."

"I'll never do it again."

"Do you ever write about me?"

"You are most of what I write about," I say. "What else would I write about?"

"Since when?"

"Since the first day."

"But then you were unhappy. Perhaps you should destroy those pages."

"I was confused," I say.

"I've been thinking about the story of your father and the dead men . . ."

I hesitate for a moment; this could be nearly any story of my father. Then I realize what she is talking about.

" . . . and there is one I'd like to tell you. Perhaps you wouldn't mind getting your journal?"

"I have a strong memory."

"But a lazy body."

"No, it's true. My memory is my curse."

She runs her fingers through my hair. I get up and get my journal, just for her sake. On the way to my office I pass Consuela straightening up my bedroom, where I have not slept in five days. She doesn't look up.

He was a Coahuiltecan, the last living one on earth. His people were older than the Greeks and Romans; they'd been living here five thousand years by the time the pyramids were built, and to them, all the other races of the earth were like scurrying ants, who appear in the first warm days but die off in the first frost.

But finally their own winter arrived. The Spanish appeared and then the Apaches, who continued the work of the Spanish, and then the Comanches, who continued the work of the Apaches, until, by this day in the spring of 1836, this man was the only survivor.

On that day my great-uncle Arturo Garcia saw the Coahuiltecan kneeling in his pasture, looking for something, and as the Indian was nearly blind, Arturo went to help him. After several hours in the buffalo grass and nopales he found the missing item, a marble of black obsidian, which Arturo presumed had mystical properties. Arturo had been born on this land, as had his father, and he knew that no rocks of that nature are found in the area.

Arturo was a wealthy young man, with a remuda of blooded horses, a beautiful wife, and a sixty-league grant from the king of Spain himself. His house was full of silver, pieces of art, and the weapons of his family, who had been knights in the olden times. Every morning he woke before the sunrise and watched the light come in, illuminating his land and his works and all he would leave for his sons.

Arturo had blood, and was known to cut out the hearts of his enemies, but he was also the sort of man who—despite having one hundred men working for him, a small town to look after, a beautiful wife and four children—would help an old Indian look for a marble.

Of course he didn't believe in seers or oracles; he was not a stupid peasant. He and his brother had both attended the Pontifical University, his ancestors had founded the University of Sevilla, he had grown up fluent in French and English and Spanish. But that day he was not feeling so intelligent. The Anglos had, against all odds, won the battle against his people at San Jacinto, and he was worried for his family.

The victory made no sense. On one side was a professional army, a powerful and ancient empire on which the sun never set, and the other a pack of ignorant barbarians, condemned criminals and land speculators. Though Texas had briefly been open to the Anglos, the borders had been closed since 1830, and yet they continued to illegally sneak into the state to take advantage of the free land, free services, loose laws. It was not unlike what happened on the fringes of the Roman Empire, when the Visigoths overran the imperial army. Perhaps God curses the proud.

Arturo asked the seer if he could put a question to him, and the seer said of course, but there was no guarantee of any answer.

Arturo said: "Will I lose my land?"

The seer said: "Go away, do not disturb me with questions of a material character; this is a place of the spirit, of philosophy, of the nature of the universe itself."

(This is not really what the Indian said, I interrupt.)

(The fact that he was an Indian has no bearing on his intelligence. She puts her finger to my lips.)

That night he couldn't sleep, thinking about all he had to lose. He returned to the seer the following morning.

"Seer, will I lose my land?"

And the seer said: "You have the best horses for five hundred miles, the biggest house, the most beautiful wife, an ancient lineage, and four healthy sons. I am a blind, penniless Indian. You should be the one giving me the answers."

"But you are wise."

"I am old. So old that I remember playing at your house before it was there."

"I suspect you are mistaken," said Arturo. "That house has stood nearly a hundred years."

"Nevertheless, I remember. There was an enormous rock I used to sleep on with my wife and all my children, for it was very warm, even in winter, as if it went down to the center of the earth. It must have been removed, as it was a growing rock, and became a little taller each year."

Arturo knew there had been such a rock. The top had been blasted off and the house was built over what was left. But as the years passed, the rock had begun to grow, cracking the plaster and bowing all the floors, so that a marble placed in the center of the room would roll toward any of the walls. Finally the floor was removed and the rock hammered and chiseled away. But there was no way for the Indian to have known this. Arturo said: "Old Man, I have done you a favor, and now you will kindly do me this favor as well. Will I keep my land or not?"

The old Coahuiltecan did not take a single breath for ten minutes. Then he said: "You will not like my answer."

"It is as I suspected."

The man nodded.

"I must hear it."

"I am sorry but you will not keep your land. You and your wife and all your sons will be killed by the Anglos."

That evening Arturo stood on his portico, watching his sons play in the grass, his beautiful wife standing near, his vast pastures where his vaqueros and their families tended his herds.

He could not understand why a man like him, a good man, should suffer such a terrible fate and that night he took the most ancient weapon of his family, an *alabarda* that had seen combat against the French, the Dutch, and the Moors, and honed the edge so fine that it would split a hair. The next morning he returned to the camp of the old Coahuiltecan, where he cut off the man's head with a single stroke. But even as the head lay there, detached from the body, it looked at him and uttered a curse.

(But the lungs, I say. Without the lungs there can be no air . . .)

(The finger goes again to my lips.)

A few months later, deciding on the course of maximum caution, Arturo sent his family to Mexico City for their safety. But before they could even cross the river, they were waylaid by white militiamen, who committed enormous outrages upon his wife as she lay dying and murdered Arturo's four sons as well.

Arturo resolved to never marry again, and did not. In 1850, after the second war, he went to Austin and paid all his property taxes, and it was only because of his mastery of both written and spoken English, which exceeded that of every Anglo lawyer in the capital, that he was allowed to retain any property at all. Half his lands were immediately confiscated because the Anglos claimed the title was flawed, though they could not point out how, or where.

Twenty years later he disappeared, murdered with all his vaqueros. My father, who was his nephew, inherited the property. My mother wanted no part of it. She wanted him to sell the land to the Americans.

"But they are murderers," my father said.

"Better to sell to them than live among them," said my mother.

But my father began to go crazy thinking about the vast pastures he might own and six months after Arturo's murder, he and my mother moved here, along with a dozen vaqueros he hired in Chihuahua.

The house was untouched, the family treasure still intact. After reading my uncle's journals, he went and dug up a skeleton at the place they described. He reburied the man, whose head was indeed detached, at the most peaceful place he could find, under a persimmon tree next to a spring, with a good knife and a sack of beans to carry the man through his journeys in the next world. He was certain this would lift the curse and keep our family safe.

(She looks at me. "As you can see, it did not do any good.")

Chapter Forty-three
Eli McCullough

1854–1855

That winter, instead of being sent down to the border, we were sent north to range the breaks from the Washita to the Concho. Winter was usually when the Indians holed up, but the previous year, the government had settled five hundred reluctant Comanches on the Clear Fork of the Brazos and another two thousand Caddos and Wacos on a larger reservation farther east.

As was normal, the reservations were short of food and the attempts to teach the Indians our superior white ways only convinced them of the opposite. The crops they grew were killed by drought or eaten by grasshoppers; there were more of them squeezed into a smaller space than they'd imagined humans could live. Locals complained about the reservation Indians stealing livestock; Indians complained the settlers were stealing horses and grazing their stock on Indian pastures. But we never caught any Indians, and the whites we caught we couldn't do anything about.

Meanwhile, there were houses going up within gunshot of the caprock. The settlers had pushed far beyond Belknap, Chadbourne, and Phantom Hill, a hundred miles past where the army could protect them. They did not care that there was only one Ranger company patrolling the entire eastern Llano. As for the legislature, lice-ridden clodhoppers did not vote or donate to political campaigns, so their problems, quietly viewed to be of their own causation—though necessary for the betterment of the state—were ignored. No new taxes. Rangers cost money.

One night in April we'd made camp on a mesa. Unlike the other ranging companies we were careful with our fires, building them like the Indians did, in arroyos or depressions away from any trees that would reflect their light. We could see thirty or forty miles, an expanse of badlands going on in every direction, the river snaking between mesas, buttes, and hoodoos, uncountable side canyons and rolling hills, motts of juniper and shinnery oak. The land was greening up, the hackberries and cottonwoods along all the streams, the grama and little bluestem on the river flats, and it was pleasant with the red rock buttes and green valleys and the darkening sky overhead. The Dipper was riding high and though we had not caught a single Indian in six months, the weather was warming and we were not going to lose any more toes. We were all ready to turn in when we saw a glow off in the east, in a small valley, that grew brighter the longer we watched it. Five minutes later the horses were saddled and we were making our way off the mesa, toward the fire.

The house was still burning when we reached it. There was a charred scalped body in the doorway; we could see it had been a woman. Off in the brush we found a man stuck with arrows. The arrows had two grooves and the moccasin prints narrowed at the front and I knew it was Comanches. The homestead had not been there long—the corral posts were still leaking sap—and there were the framed beginnings of a smokehouse and stable. Yoakum Nash found a silver locket and Rufus Choate found a barlow knife and after drinking our fill at their spring and making a quick scout for other valuables, we cut stick and rode after the Indians.

Their trail was clear enough, and a mile or so along it we came on a young boy with his head caved in, barely starting to stiffen. When we hit the river the tracks crossed and recrossed in every conceivable direction and the captain put me out front. All the trails were too obvious. I took us up the middle of the water until there was a long patch of rocky ground. I knew they'd taken it and sure enough, where the rocks ended, the pony tracks began.

The grass was high and the tracks were clear but there were not enough of them. They aimed toward a bluff, which the others presumed the Indians had climbed to watch their backtrail, but it was too early for that so I led us back to the river, losing another half hour. Then we found a pale blue dress in the rocks. It was something a teenager would wear, too small to have fit the burned woman, who was tall and chunky.

"Well, it appears we have a live one," said the captain.

"Maybe," said McClellan. He was the lieutenant. "Or maybe they just threw her off in the brush like the other one."

I knew she was alive. They had taken her and her brother, but her brother was too young, or he had cried or been noisy and she was smart enough to take a lesson from that, despite what they had done to her before tying her to the horse.

We stood on the banks another minute, collecting our thoughts, looking around at the hoodoos and canyons and tall grass and cedar; the Indians might be anywhere. It would not take Napoleon to make an ambush in country like this and we all wanted to stay in the flat open plain along the water.

After a few more miles we came to a bend thickly overgrown with cottonwoods and there was something about the light. The sun was coming up behind us. The captain and I eased forward and he looked through his glass while I looked through mine; there were some specks along the red rock, maybe five miles out.

"You seeing horses?"

"Yup."

"Do they know we're following?"

"I don't think so."

The sun was rising into their eyes but we turned around and cut through the brush anyway, keeping the trees and buttes between us and the Indians, gaffing hell out of our ponies. But when we got another look at them again, this time from the top of a small mesa, they'd put even more distance on us.

Midway through the day our horses were blown. The Comanches would have changed mounts twice and the captain was reckless, leading us through funnels and thickets at top speed. "They don't want a fight," he said. "They just want to get away."

Meanwhile we were getting close to the Llano and the badlands had narrowed to a single canyon a few miles wide. Blocks of stone the size of courthouses had tumbled from the upper walls; there were forests of petrified stumps and logs, herds of pronghorn watching from the ledges. The Indians would have to climb out.

We were getting close to the canyon mouth and as we emerged from some cottonwoods, there they were, only a half mile ahead but six hundred feet above us. One of them turned to look and waved his arm. I was squinting through my field glass. It was Escuté.

I couldn't make out his face, but I could tell by his straight back and crooked arm and the way he'd done his hair, which was unlike most Comanches. I wondered if Nuukaru was with him. It occurred to me that Nuukaru might not even be alive.

Then a flat crack rolled across the valley.

One of our men had a Sharps rifle with a tang sight, but he must have missed the Indians by a comfortable margin because they continued to wave as they disappeared over the ledge.

After three hours of riding into box canyons and other dead ends, we found the trail the Indians had taken. There was bear grass and juniper hanging above us, water splashing over shelves of rock nearly too high for our horses to climb. A few men with bows, firing down into the chasm, could have easily gotten all of us, so we moved slow. Our arms were shaking from keeping the pistols up. The ravine ended in a cul-de-sac. There was a wall covered with drawings and carvings, snakes and men dancing and horses and buffalo, a shaman in a headdress, the swirling figures you see when you fall asleep.

It had the feeling of a sacred place and we expected the Indians to appear above us and rain arrows from every direction. Then there was a rustling or whirring all around us and Elmer Pease began shooting. The rest of us jumped behind the closest rock.

There were no arrows. Instead there was a kind of dervish hanging in the air, a small tornado, though there was no wind, it was some kind of Indian spirit, and it floated about for a long time before moving back down the canyon, where it vanished.

The captain came out from behind his rock. "McCullough and Pease, get up behind that face and see if the path goes anywhere."

An hour later we were on the Llano. The Comanches' trail was faint but clear. In the tracks I saw three riders split west from the group, driving a dozen unsaddled ponies, leaving a large, clearly beaten trail, a diversion. The main body had continued north in single file, their tracks nearly indistinguishable among all the buffalo sign and rocks. I thought about the girl they had taken. Then I thought about Escuté.

"Here they go," I said. I pointed toward the diversion.

After five or six miles it petered out. I guessed they had been dragging brush and dropped it. Or they began to ride single file. Or they knew tricks I had never learned. We turned and followed our backtrack; we were six hours behind them and they all had fresh mounts. I got off my horse and stood looking around in the dirt, ignoring the trail they had left across the rocks, invisible to everyone else, but clear enough to me, a faint disturbance, scuffs here and there in the dust.

"I'm about stumped," I said.

The captain looked at me.

"We could split up and see what we find."

"We aren't splitting up," the captain said.

"We know they didn't go west and they probably didn't go south, either."

"You don't see anything?" he said. "Anything at all?"

"There's no tracks," I told him.

He didn't believe me but there was nothing he could do. We went north along the caprock, putting the spurs in and hoping to get a glimpse of them against the horizon before the sun faded. I watched as we rode, our track slowly diverging from Escuté's until finally we were on a different course entirely.

The captain didn't trust me after that, but it didn't matter. Two months later, we made an unplanned resupply trip to Austin and he found his wife entertaining a sutler. The captain's pistol misfired and the sutler stabbed him to death.

After the burial we went to the jail and took the sutler into custody. The sheriff handed us the keys.

"You ain't gonna do nothin'?" the man said, as we marched him past the sheriff. "Just let them hang me, is that it?"

As we led him out into the sunlight, he protested that he'd been one of the filibusters to survive Mier, but we pointed out that was a long time ago, and in another country, and it was time to acknowledge the corn.

A few blocks from the capitol we stripped him, cut off everything hanging between his legs, then fixed him with a riata and dragged him up and down Congress. By the time we strung him up he had stopped kicking.

I thought we ought to scalp him, but everyone else thought he made a fine blossom just as he was and there was no sense cuttin' it too fat. We went to the tavern and I was elected captain over McClellan. I waited till they were good and damaged and then went back to scalp the sutler. I had always been fond of the captain.

With the exception of Nʉʉkaru and Escuté, I had no doubts about my loyalties. Which were in the following order: to any other Ranger, and then to myself. Toshaway had been right: you had to love others more than you loved your own body, otherwise you would be destroyed, whether from the inside or out, it didn't matter. You could butcher and pillage but as long as you did it for people you loved, it never mattered. You did not see any Comanches with the long stare—there was nothing they did that was not to protect their friends, their families, or their band. The war sickness was a disease of the white man, who fought in armies far from his home, for men he didn't know, and there is a myth about the West, that it was founded and ruled by loners, while the truth is just the opposite; the loner is a mental weakling, and was seen as such, and treated with suspicion. You did not live long without someone watching your back and there were very few people, white or Indian, who did not see a stranger in the night and invite him to join the campfire.

People came and went in the Rangers. I was not always elected captain, but I always had a slot to ride. I looked after the new arrivals, whether they were younger or older, and I was beginning to see my life laid out in front of me, one year no different from the next; the faces around me would change, I would put them into the ground or give them a clap on the back as they mustered out, then I would go and see to my equipment, drop my revolvers off at the gunsmith, my tack at the saddlemaker, buy a new shirt and pants, then trade my land vouchers for a horse or whiskey or something useful.

Then I shaved off my six-month beard, figured out what company was riding out next, and put my name back on the list.

Chapter Forty-four
J.A. McCullough

It was dark, it was loud, she could not make out where she was, there was the sound of water, a rushing like standing in the tides. Two people arguing: *it is a girl,* said one, *this one will be a girl,* then another voice, which she recognized as her father's, saying, *okay, honey.* The drumming of a heart, the swell of breathing. She couldn't move. There were children's voices. *My brothers,* she thought.

Then she wasn't sure. There were voices in Spanish and in another language she didn't recognize, though it made a kind of sense. A burning feeling. The grass was tall and the sun was in her eyes and there was a man with a dark beard and shining helmet looking as if he wasn't sure what to do. He stepped forward and stuck something into her again. It caught; he pulled it out and tried again and this time it went all the way through and then the man and the sun were nothing but black spots.

She opened her eyes. She was back in the enormous room. *There have been times before this one,* she thought. She felt a relief come over her; it was the beginning of something, not the end, she had been wrong all along, wrong her entire life.

Then it was gone. She'd made it all up. It was nothing but the mind inventing stories. Anything that did not involve its own end. The house vanished, dust blowing, she could see into the stars . . . she willed herself back into her thoughts.

The truck was going too fast, fishtailing through corners, as if the driver thought he was on tarmac instead of dirt. Something was wrong, she knew immediately, though the vehicle was just a speck still, a mile or more away, an immense cloud rising behind it. Someone had been hurt; that was plain. *Do not let it be Hank.* It was more a feeling than a thought. She stood in the great room and watched the dust come closer. *If it is not Hank, I will never miss a day of church.* Then this seemed overdramatic, a ridiculous promise, they had run out of beer for all she knew. Still, she had a feeling.

She picked up the phone and called the doctor before the truck arrived, before she even knew for certain. "This is Jeannie McCullough," she said. "I think someone's been hurt at our place here, I think they were bird hunting."

She went out onto the gallery. One of the hands saw what was happening; he was riding toward the gate to intercept the truck. He rolled off his horse and pushed the gate open just as the truck shot through and then she had a different feeling, that a mistake had been made, that the man should not have let the truck through at all; she was suddenly very cold and wanted to go upstairs.

When the pickup came to a stop near the gallery, she ran down to meet it. There was Hank in the cab with one of the insurance men. All the worry went out of her, she felt foolish, she felt *thank God thank God,* she was smiling, she was a ridiculous person, but then the two men jumped out without looking at her and she saw she'd been wrong.

Then she was behind the truck. There was Hank, his face white, his shirt heavy and dark, bright handprints over the paint, all over the windows, the third man was holding Hank in his arms and crying. *That is okay,* she thought. *There is more blood in him than that.* She climbed into the bed, it was littered with quail, the man did not want to let go, he was holding on to Hank so tightly; *honey,* she was saying, *honey can you hear me*; his eyes were closed but then he opened them. She put her face to his; someone was saying they were sorry they were sorry. *Hank it's me. Open your eyes.* He did; he saw her. He was trying to smile and then nothing happened. His eyes changed.

A few moments later Hank's dog arrived; it had run the entire way from the quail fields, it leaped into the truck and began licking Hank's face and barking, trying to wake him up, tugging at his shirt and barking; it would not be pushed away. "Get this fucking dog out of here"—that was her—"someone get this fucking dog." The pointer bit someone's hand, then went back to licking Hank's face, the barking was never going to stop and finally the insurance men got hold of it and lifted it off the truck. "Shhhhhh," someone was saying, "shhh shhhh shhh," but she didn't know if they were talking to her or Hank's dog.

No, she thought now, *no no no.* She did not want to think about this. She wished she had been struck down before she had even looked out the window. The pointer would not leave her side. She flew with it everywhere and eight years later, when it finally died, she had been incapacitated with grief, she had not been able to go to work, it was like losing her husband a second time.

He was a great man. There were men who were born like that, the hand of God all over them, Hank had been one. Losing him . . . she was choking. When people spoke she was underwater. She heard them and didn't. She would think about something else. She could still feel pain, she knew she was still alive. Was it true what they said, you were like a butterfly stretching its wings, one day you were trapped here, the next you weren't? She didn't know. She did not want to forget. *I want to remember,* she thought. *I will remember I will remember I will remember.*

Chapter Forty-five
Diaries of Peter McCullough

JULY 22, 1917

Drilling begun in the Reynolds and Midkiff pastures. Not a single room available in town. The streets are packed with men, trucks, carts, stacks of equipment; there are people sleeping in tents and ditches. Niles Gilbert is letting his pig stall for eighty dollars a week. As usual I expect anger at our skyrocketing fortune; of course it is the opposite. They see our prosperity nearly as their own, as if rent for a hog sty is no different from a few million dollars in oil.

And—for the time being—everyone *is* making money. Selling clothes, old tools, food, water, rooms, renting use of their cars, trucks, mules and carts, horse teams, and backyards. Grover Deshields has stopped tending his crops and is instead driving around on his tractor, charging ten dollars (a week's wages) to pull stuck trucks out of bogholes in the drilling fields. It is rumored he waters the bogholes at night. Someday this boom will end. Though not for us.

There are now four derricks, in various states of assembly, visible from our back ridge. My father's driller is not impressed. He thinks there will soon be a hundred or so. This despite the fact that the only other oil around here was found at Piedras Pintas. There are the Rieser and Jennings fields, but they are only gas.

As for María, I have stopped even pretending to go out to the pastures. Sullivan finds me in the evening and gives me a report of the day's activities. He has nearly caught us several times. . . . I expect the novelty of her to wear off but it has only gotten more intense. If I spend even an hour apart from her I can't think of anything else, I forget the names of people, what I am supposed to be doing, any reason I have for being.

I want to know everything. The way a child learns the world by tasting it . . . I want to take every part of her into my mouth; I find myself wondering about her former lovers, how she was with her sisters, her father, her mother, who she was at university, where the separate parts of her come from.

I am up before the light and she is still sleeping, relaxed, her hands thrown behind her head, face to one arm, her knees leaning in as if she has fallen asleep on a beach . . . I watch the sun brighten as it touches her, the smooth skin along her neck (a red mark I clumsily left), an ear, the hollow behind her cheek, her chin (slightly pointed), her lips (slightly chapped), while her eyes, which are nearly black except for a few flecks of gold, flicker in a dream. Without waking, she realizes I am not lying next to her and she reaches for me and pulls me over.

Still the shadow has not appeared. Have begun to look in all the dark places, out of the corner of my eye, but . . . nothing. Pedro—I can only recall his face as a younger man, and Lourdes, too, as a younger, more beautiful woman, as if, in my mind, they are aging in reverse.

July 23, 1917

A rush of air from the north, high of eighty degrees. We wake up alert and clearheaded—we must be outside. As there is an unspoken agreement about spending any time near the Garcia land, we pack a basket into the Chandler and head for Nuevo Laredo. As I drive, she encourages my hands to wander; we make a brief stop along the way. I consider the fact that I have never done this before—never made love to a woman outside the confines of a bedroom. I wonder if she has, feel briefly jealous despite my former sentiment about her old lovers, but the feeling passes and I am content again.

When we reach Nuevo Laredo the ugliness of the city is somehow overwhelming.

"This will not do," I say.

"We will make it beautiful for everyone else," she says. She leans her head against my shoulder.

We are looking for a cantina (or hotel, she reminds me) but as we approach the *plaza de toros* there are several drunk Americans, well dressed, calling loudly after the Mexican girls; one of them stares into the car, says something to his friends about María. I nearly stop to have a word, but she tells me to keep driving. We make another slow circle through the town, past the Alma Latina, where a trio of mariachis sit with no one to play for, and then somehow our eyes seem to catch on all the *congales,* and we decide instead to drive along the river.

After we have put a good distance between us and the city we stop where a small hill affords a good view over the savannah. There is an old long-armed oak with soft grass underneath.

We are lying on a blanket, looking out over the endless land and sky, when María says: "I like to imagine this at the beginning of time, when the grass was very tall and there were wild horses."

"Horses have only been here a few hundred years," I say.

"I prefer to forget that."

"It's buffalo you would see."

"Except there is little to like about a buffalo," she says. "What is the point of a buffalo?"

I shrug.

"But you prefer them. Okay, I will imagine buffalo instead, though they are hairy, smelly, inelegant, and have horns."

"They belong here," I say.

"In my mind, the horses do as well. And if the horses do not, I do not. And if I do not, you do not. In your world there is nothing but buffalo and sad Indians."

"And then a gallant Spaniard appears on horseback. And shoots them."

"It's true. I'm a hypocrite."

I kiss her neck.

"My father thought there were still mustangs here. He said he often saw their footprints, without shoes."

"It's possible," I say.

"I used to dream about them."

I think of all the mustangs we shot. But Pedro had done it too. Everyone had done it.

I look around. At the bottom of the hill is a stream that feeds the Rio Bravo. Along the water are persimmons and hackberries and pecans, cedar elms. I can hear green jays calling.

We lie and make love in the sun, despite the fact that we can see, in the distance, the workers moving in the onion fields along the river. María finds them picturesque; I can't help feeling sorry for them.

"Are you sure you want to be with me?" she says. "I think you would prefer a revolutionary."

I kiss her again.

"I am just old and sentimental," she says.

"Younger than me."

"Women age in dog years."

I look at her.

"Even me," she says. She shrugs again. "But for now I think our wine has gotten hot."

She stands and walks down the hill to put the bottles in the stream. I worry she'll catch a goathead, but her soles are tougher than mine. I watch her disappear over the hill, her small hips swaying, the scars on her back, her hair curled on top of her head.

When she is gone a few minutes I guess she might be relieving herself, but when she still doesn't return

I decide to find her, consider putting on my boots, don't, then make my way through the tall brown grass, worrying about snakes and burrs and thorns. I find her lying in the creek. Her hair is loose and streaming around her, the stones white beneath her. I take three or four bounding steps and then she looks up.

"I have always liked being outside," she says.

She pats the water as if it is our bed. I lie down in it. I notice how white and freckled I am, tan only at the arms, scraggly hairs everywhere . . . but then that feeling passes.

We lie as if we are the first people on earth, or the last, the sun coming down on us, the water cold, our every action of the utmost importance, as if, like children, we know that no one else really exists.

Finally we climb the hill to the blanket. The sun dries us and she curls against me and falls asleep. There is nothing missing. I wonder if I have ever been this happy and then I wonder again about my father, if he has ever felt anything like this. Even as a young man, I cannot see it. He is like my brother, a gun aimed squarely at the world.

Chapter Forty-six
Eli McCullough

Our commission ran out in 1860. The state was split over secession, with the cotton men and everyone who read their newspapers in favor, and everyone else against. But the Rebels needed Texas; without our cotton, beef, and ports the Confederacy could not stand.

That summer, Dallas burned. As in any conspiracy of prophets, a series of miracles surrounded the fires. The first was that all the buildings had been empty—not a single soul hurt—though an entire block had been torched. The second miracle was there were no eyewitnesses. The third and final miracle was that even though there was nothing an Abolitionist liked better than the sound of his own voice—every time an oxcart or soapbox caught fire in Kansas, a dozen Free-Soilers would turn themselves in, hoping to be hanged for their crimes—no soft sister came forward to claim the Dallas fires. The cotton men had burned their own buildings to bring us into the war and before the sun came up the next day, their newspapers were blaming escaped slaves and Yankees, whose next step would be to burn all of Texas, right after they got done raping all the white women.

By the end of summer, most Texans were certain that if slavery was abolished, the whole of the South would Africanize, no proper woman would be safe, amalgamation would be the order of the day. Though in the next breath they would tell you that the war had nothing to do with slavery. It was about human dignity, self-governance, freedom itself, the rights of the states; it was a war to keep us free from the meddling hand of Washington. Never mind that Washington had kept us from becoming part of Mexico again. Never mind they were keeping the Indians at bay.

It is worth noting that even then, no one thought slavery would last forever. The tide was strongly against it, not just in America, but all the world over. But the plantation owners figured if they could get another twenty years out of the institution, it was worth convincing everyone to fight. That was when the acquisitive spirit began to wake inside me. There was no point being a small man.

_____

After the secession vote, the state began to empty out. Half the Rangers I knew lit for California—they were not going to die so a rich man could keep his niggers. Close on their heels was any Texan who had ever said a word against the slaveocracy, or the cotton men, or was suspected of voting for Lincoln. And plenty of secessionists left as well. Over many of the wagon trains headed west, away from the war, the Confederate flag could be seen flying proudly. They were in favor of the war as long as they did not have to fight it themselves, and I have always thought that is why California turned out the way it did.

While not exactly sound on the goose, slavery struck me as the natural state: we had slaves, the Indians had slaves, you shall enjoy the spoils of your enemies, which the Lord your God has given you. The faces of Christ and his mother have adorned many a sword; all the heroes of Texas had made their names in the fight against Mexico. For them the war had been a golden arrangement and I could not see why this one ought to be any different.

If you weren't lined into a Texas cavalry unit, you'd be drafted and sent east to fight afoot, and so any right-thinking man who didn't have a horse quickly begged, borrowed, or stole one. I signed with the Mounted Rifles under McCullough (no relation) and we were put under Sibley and sent to take New Mexico from the Federals.

Things went agee from the start. Our leader, Colonel Sibley, found the march considerable boring, and a few weeks into it, he retired to the bed of his wagon, accompanied by two prostitutes and a barrel of who-hit-John. There was an uproar from the fire-eaters, who imagined they were fighting for human dignity and freedom from the northern elite, but more cat wagons were requisitioned and the complaining stopped. The rest of us were already calling ourselves the RMN men—Rich Man's Niggers—in honor of those brave souls who'd inspired our fight for freedom. As for Sibley, as long as he shared his whiskey, we did not mind him.

The newspapers said we'd have an easy fight against the Yankee farmers but it was not long before we detected a miscalculation. There were not many grangers to be found among the New Mexicans. In fact they appeared to have grown up the same as we had, hunting and fighting Indians, and after a few months they got behind us and burned our whole supply train. Sibley became down in the mouth and retired again to his whore-equipped ambulance; the rest of us took a vote and decided to return to Texas. The newspapers said that since New Mexico was teeming with aborigines, we didn't want it anyway, and thus our retreat was more properly considered a great victory.

Richmond was fifteen hundred miles away; they mostly forgot we existed. Belts were tight—the new governor was inaugurated in homespun—but everyone had enough to eat. Except for the shortage of young men on the streets, and occasional news of Yankee ships sunk in our harbors, you would not have known a war was going on at all. Being now a lieutenant I could come and go as I pleased, but there were not many places to go. The Comanches had taken back a smart sprinkle of their old territory; the frontier had collapsed several hundred miles. On every stretch of lonely backroad where the Indians didn't lurk, you'd find the Home Guard. There was a fifty-dollar bounty on Confederate deserters, and if they didn't know you personally, they were likely to tear up your leave papers, put a noose around your neck, and take your carcass to trade for their pieces of silver.

Judge Black had plenty of pull, so I stayed at his house when I got bored with the barracks, drinking his claret, sleeping in his office, calling for sandwiches on the dumbwaiter. I read a few books but mostly I drank whiskey and smoked cigars and planned my future. It had become clear to me that the lives of the rich and famous were not so different from the lives of the Comanches: you did what you pleased and answered to no one. I saw myself finishing out the war as a captain or major, at which point I'd go into cattle or shipping. One thing I knew: I was done working for other men.

As for the judge's three daughters, one had died of a fever and the other two were still unmarried. The elder was twenty-two, a cremello like the judge, fair of skin and temperament, with my brother's tendency toward books and deep thoughts. There had been some scandal associated with her, but no one would discuss it. The younger was more proper, in the exact form of her mother, a dusky beauty with a taste for the finer things and impeccable public behavior.

I abused myself thinking about them, but the judge had expectations that his daughters would marry Harvard men, or sons of Sam Houston, or at least sons of bankers. I was an unreliable lieutenant, whose time on earth would likely be short, and it would not do to make any investment in me. So when the door to my room opened and closed quietly one night, I wagered it was Millie, the quadroon who'd just been added to the judge's household.

She came and sat on the bed. I looked at her in the light from the window. It was Madeline, the older daughter.

"I didn't think you'd mind," she said.

I didn't. She had pale skin and red hair; her face was covered in freckles but she had big green eyes and a soft mouth. Everything about her was finely done, and though in the past I'd found kissing girls that pretty to be like biting into a green persimmon, I patted the mattress and she lay down next to me.

Her breath was sweet, which I guessed to be from her mother's sherry. When she saw I would take no initiative, she straddled me. It was not long before I determined that she had waylaid her maidenhead sometime in the distant past.

Unfortunately I felt cowardly as a Dutchman. The judge would never forgive me; at best he'd expect me to marry her. Not to mention she was drunk, and, I thought, slightly crazy; there was no telling how the story might play when the sun rose. She detected my cowardice and lay on top of me. Unlike most of the women who consented to my company in those days, she was sweet and clean. I ran my fingers through her hair—finer than corn silk—but I did not think she'd appreciate the comparison so I kept it to myself.

"Am I not pretty enough?"

"You're too pretty," I said.

"But . . ." She touched me and reminded me of my failure.

"There is a lot on my mind," I told her.

"Because you're going back to fight this awful war for the slavers."

"It's for Texas," I said.

"Texas is not Jefferson Davis," she said.

"This is not good talk."

"Who will hear me?"

"I can hear you."

"Don't be silly. Texas is worth fighting for, but not the slavers. And I am not sure there is a difference right now."

"This is some house to be a Free-Soiler in," I said.

"I told my father he was a coward and the reason slavery hadn't ended was that men like him didn't speak up. And men like you, who are going to fight for it. Though of course unlike him, you have no choice." Then she said, "Do you have syphilis?"

"No," I said.

"He has been warning me against you since I was twelve."

"Did he say I had the pox?"

"He said if I looked the word up in Johnson's there would be a picture of your face."

I was quiet.

"I am joking you," she said. "I was just wondering. Given your history."

"Well, I don't have it," I said.

"I'll lay with you despite your pox. I love you and now you're going off to die."

I did not know what to make of her.

"Well," she said. "Do you love me?"

"Jesus," I said.

"I'm kidding." She sighed. "All right, I'll go."

"I'm going to die of old age," I said.

"Don't be hurt."

"I'm not."

"You shouldn't be afraid of him."

"I'm not afraid of him. I'm afraid of what will happen if you spend too much time with me."

"Well, I'm sure you would like that honor, but you're about five years too late. As I'm sure you've heard." She began to move her hips. I allowed my hands under her shift. I knew even then I was not doing right. I will not lay it on anyone else. But I told myself she was a young girl and whatever affection she possessed would be gone by the time the dew burned off the morning grass.

For most of the night we were enthusiastic and in the morning she snuck back to her room. I expected a speech about us being married in the eyes of God, as that was the price of milk in those days, but all she said was: "My mother and father are going to San Antonio."

That night we did it several more times and each time I took precautions.

"You're afraid you'll have to marry me," she said.

"I don't mind marrying you." I hadn't thought about it until that moment, but I knew it was true and I didn't regret saying it.

"Well, that is a very sweet way to put it."

I ignored her. "Nothing's going to happen to me," I said. "You don't have to worry."

"You really shouldn't talk like that."

I nearly told her that there were things God and I had buried the hatchet on, though it was just as likely Old Scratch. But I decided to keep quiet.

A few weeks later we got orders to ride on Kansas. The judge summoned me to his office. He was unbarbered and his hair was askew and I could see he'd slept in his clothes. He was a big man in every way and except for his ginger color I had never noticed anything to link him to his daughter. But now I saw that Madeline had his eyes and his large mouth, and something about this made me happy.

"You are nearly a dead man," he told me. He took a pistol from a drawer and thumped it on the table. "I tried to get her to admit that you'd abused her honor, but she insists you have not. Is this true?"

"Yes," I lied.

"I told her you had syphilis and her face would be marked by pox."

"That is not true, so far as I know."

"I told her you laid with whores."

"I'm leaving," I said. "You shouldn't worry about it."

"I'm not," he said, "but I am very worried for my daughter. I am terrified for my daughter, in fact. I don't approve of this. I approve of you but not with Madeline. Unfortunately she gets what she wants. You will marry her."

"I intend to."

"Good man," he said. "Good man."

The whole time he hadn't looked at me. He was staring out the window. I knew what he was trying to find: the exact moment in time he'd made his first mistake. Was it taking me in when I came back from the Indians, or was it saving me from the hanging in Bastrop, or was it allowing me to come around all those years since, the whole time against everyone's best judgment? His eyes were wet.

"Say something terrible, Eli." He began to straighten the papers on his desk, pushing them into neat stacks, and then he stood up and picked up an armful of books that had been sitting on the floor as long as I could remember. He carried them to the shelves.

"Don't make my daughter a widow." He looked at a title and shelved it and looked at the next one and walked a few steps and made a space.

I was nearly to the door when he called after me: "You have to understand I wanted something different for her, Eli. You're a good man, and I love you like my own son, but I know the life she will have with you."

He continued to shelve his books.

"I wanted her to marry someone with a house in a city, some banker or clerk or Yankee. I didn't want her living in a cabin and dying in childbirth or from drinking bad water or being kicked by a horse or scalped or shot." He shook his head. "My daughter . . ."

"I promise."

"You can't," he said. "You can't make a promise about what other people will do to her."

Chapter Forty-seven
J.A. McCullough

She was back in the office in Houston. Milton Bryce in his thick lawyer's glasses, already combing his hair over, telling her to make an offer on Brown and Root. But there was very little oil flowing anywhere; she couldn't see the point in a pipeline company.

"They also do dams, military bases, things like that," Bryce was saying. "A lot of work for the Corps of Engineers. You know Herman Brown died . . ."

"I heard that."

"And now George is trying to get out of the business. I mean now. This week."

Something about his insistence put her off; she stopped listening.

"It's clean and you could probably get the whole thing for forty. If I had the money myself . . ."

She made a note to look into it, but a few days later, Ed Halliburton scraped together an offer, despite the fact that, along with the rest of the industry, his well-cementing company was hitting bottom. George Brown sold out for thirty-six million dollars; within a decade the company was grossing seven hundred million a year, building bases for the army in Vietnam.

It was hardly her only mistake. For years after Hank's death, she'd felt the need to calculate and recalculate every risk, as if everything she did was being recorded for others to judge, as if her most private thoughts would become public. She became deliberate to a fault, building cases for every decision, she was never not reading, she was never not thinking; it was unusual for her to have a conversation that she had not already rehearsed in her mind, and there were times she convinced herself that not even Hank could have kept pace. Though in more sober moments, she knew there was something missing. The men around her were always sure they were right, even when there was no good reason. That was what mattered. Being sure of things. If you were wrong, you just defended your position even more loudly.

Meanwhile, everyone was stealing from her. T.J. Block, their partner on several drilling projects, had for "purposes of convenience" moved into Hank's office. In her haze she had signed off on new leases, not having the energy to look into them herself, though the problem was also Hank: he had made so many verbal agreements, had his fingers in so many projects, so many promises . . . she could not keep track. She could not tell when someone was lying to her. She was being charged twice for the same orders of casing pipe and drilling mud, she couldn't tell if it was her drillers ripping her off or the suppliers or both, everyone saw an opportunity, there were offers to buy her out. Hank's sisters sued her for half the company and her own employees thought she was stupid; they were slow to follow orders, seemed to think she could not tell the difference between a good job and a bad job, they were reluctant to start big projects that they were certain she would abandon. There were casing problems, cementing problems, flow problems, the equipment broke constantly . . . to Hank they had given their best, to her they gave nothing.

Of course, they all assured her this wasn't so. She was not sure if she was being paranoid or going crazy or was just in over her head and ought to sell the company to T.J. Block, who acted like it was already his. Everyone seemed to know things she didn't; she wondered if her phone had been bugged.

So far as everyone was concerned it was Hank they had worked for. She was nothing more than an appendage, a pretty blond housewife who—instead of opening a clothing boutique or horse stable or something sensible—had decided to amuse herself at her husband's office.

She began to suspect she might really crack up, that she would have to take the kids and leave Houston and move back to the ranch, and then she and Milton Bryce were going to lunch and instead of stopping to park she kept going. Down the street and out toward the countryside.

"I was not hungry anyway," he said.

She continued to drive out of the city until there was nothing but tall straight pines and oaks, the light coming green over the road. She said, "Who is definitely *not* stealing from me?"

He was quiet and then he stayed quiet . She wondered if he had turned against her like the others.

"Bud Lanning is not bad," he finally said.

"Bud Lanning ordered four thousand feet of casing pipe to finish a two-thousand-foot hole."

"Gordon Lytle?"

She had made a mistake.

He mashed his hair over.

"What do you think of Mr. T.J. Block?"

"He is fine," said Bryce. "Except for being a liar and a thief."

She felt herself smile and the relief came over her and then faded and then she was furious. They continued down the road in silence.

"You didn't ask," he said. "And it's not really my place to offer these opinions."

"What if I just fired everyone right now?"

"You'll want to change the locks first. And you'll need to hang on to at least one of the secretaries. Maybe two."

She turned the car around at a logging road and headed back to town.

They spent the rest of the afternoon walking around the Museum of Fine Arts. Finally she decided she could hold down a sandwich. Even that turned out to be too ambitious but nonetheless, that night she had the locks changed and in the morning, as people began to show up at the office, she fired them all except Edna Hinnant, the secretary.

The new employees were better and yet . . . in order to be respected she had to know their jobs as well as hers; if she did not understand fracture flow and jet perforation versus gun perforation and different methods of sand consolidation and acidizing and propping agents . . . she wanted only to sleep but there was so much to review, more than would ever have been expected of Hank. She felt herself wavering again; there was no point in working so hard at something that no one wanted her to be doing.

Later she would realize that it was simply that she'd had nothing else. Her children were not enough and she had always known she was nothing like her grandmother, nothing like the other women in the neighborhood, whose lives were sunk into their outfits and fund-raisers, who might spend a week trying to get the seating at a party just right. She had always seen herself a certain way; the fact that others felt entitled to an opinion on the matter—on who she ought to be—should not have come as a shock, though it did. While other women got prescriptions for Valium, she got one for Benzedrine, and every time she felt herself fading or she wanted to stay in bed or take a long lunch she reminded herself of the Colonel, who had kept working until he was ninety years old.

Endless reports, mental exercises to keep her mind fresh. Any numbers she saw—a license plate, house number, street sign—she would multiply, divide, manipulate in some way, 7916 Oak Drive, seventy-nine times sixteen, which was eighty times sixteen minus sixteen. Twelve hundred eighty. Minus sixteen. Twelve sixty-four.

As for the men around her, they remained polite while resisting everything she did. She convinced Aubrey Stokes to sell her a lease instead of passing it up to the majors, but just as she was about to hang up the phone, he said:

"I'll get some papers over there this afternoon. Just to make sure we're on the right page."

She was too surprised to reply.

"Nothing personal, Jeannie."

But it was personal. There wasn't a single oil operator in the state who didn't consider his word as good as his bond, who didn't look down on the easterners and their endless need for lawyers and documents. But men who'd taken Hank's word would not take hers. They acted as if she'd landed from outer space or they sweetly ignored her attempts to talk business and turned the conversation toward her family and her health (she was under a lot of pressure); they did not trust that she could be relentless or focused when nature demanded she stay home with her babies.

She took all the pictures of the kids out of her office. She could not have people suspecting she was thinking about her family when she ought to be thinking about work, and equally—though it took much longer to admit this to herself—she could not disturb the fantasy that these men had about sleeping with her. She wouldn't, and didn't, but you did not want them thinking that door was closed. You did not want pictures of your kids.

After she fired everyone she spent seven days a week in the office and, knowing she would need the same of Milton Bryce, tripled his salary and gave his wife a credit line at Neiman Marcus. As for her children, Tom and Ben sensed they would have to bear up. Susan was lost for good. The boys had always been well-behaved and self-sufficient; Susan had been a colicky baby and as a toddler she was always sneaking into bed with Hank and Jeannie, claiming she'd had a bad dream. By the age of four or five, if she were not getting enough attention she would reach for something convenient, perhaps a vase, perhaps her water glass, and, while pretending to inspect it, drop it to the floor.

Hank had known how to deal with her. He had patience and an ability to compartmentalize that Jeannie could not muster. His mind was a neatly ordered place and if Susan threw a fit he could give her his complete attention and then forget her the moment he walked out the door. *The nanny is taking care of her—there is no more need to worry*—that was how his mind worked, it was switches inside a computer. But Jeannie, even after getting to the office, would stay angry with her daughter for half the days. She took the fits personally, she took her daughter's softness personally, there were strains of weak blood in all families, there were those who sat and soaked in their own problems and those who got up and helped themselves. Jeannie, at her daughter's age, had taught herself how to ride and rope, she had taught herself to compete with men on their own terms. Her daughter competed by being loud and disruptive, an impossible princess; even before her father died she saw him as a saint and her mother as something else; whatever Jeannie did it was never enough.

Of course her daughter was only being what a girl in Texas was supposed to be. It was Jeannie who was the odd one.

Chapter Forty-eight
Diaries of Peter McCullough

August 1, 1917

Most of the drillers are progressing twice as fast as the Colonel and his alcoholic henchmen. At least forty rigs visible from the road. Quiet nights are a thing of the past.

The town is overwhelmed not just with drillers and landmen and speculators, but now with the men who build storage tanks and dig trenches, who haul pipe and wood and fuel, who repair tools and other equipment. Everyone is working at twice last year's wages.

In news of the dead: a man's body was found behind the Cabot Inn (what Wallace Cabot is now calling his house). A moonshiner's still exploded in the tent city. A roustabout sleeping under a truck was crushed.

Our driller claims this is nothing. Wait till all the rest of those rigs get running, he said. It will be a river of blood and bodies.

I ask María what she thinks of all this. She says she is trying not to.

AUGUST 3, 1917

My father sold twenty-eight hundred acres of leases under the old Garcia pastures to Magnolia Oil. Nearly a thousand an acre. Drillers on the Midkiff and Reynolds pastures are getting shows a few hundred feet beneath the surface, and the Colonel's rig (now staffed professionally) hit a good show of oil at eight hundred feet. That or my father spiked the well corings. Regardless, it appears that our money worries are over for the next ten or so generations. This depresses me enormously.

Naturally Magnolia wants to drill near the house, where my father's discovery well was (the only one actually flowing), but I said I would not allow it.

That area is now a half-mile pit of stinking black sludge. Sullivan and I rode past it today. He is bitter about the oil, and worried about his job.

"You know I am glad about this oil," he said. "But I can't even get a glass of water in town without someone trying to charge me for it."

"Well, now we can afford to get all this brush cleared off, get these other pastures cross-fenced . . ."

"What's the point of getting the brush off if we have to look at this shit all day and listen to those drillers all night. Not to mention they leave every goddamn gate open."

We continued to look at the oil spill.

"Think he'll sell the cattle?" he asked.

"I won't let him."

"That's what I've been telling the boys. He's always had his mind on other things but you . . . you are not the type to let that happen."

It is quiet and I consider that Sullivan has not said a word against my father in the thirty years I've known him.

"We've got twice as many head as we did two years ago," I said. "We've got twice the work." The reason for this occurred to me and I winced. I began to wonder where María was.

"But the cattle won't make money like this stuff. That's what everyone is worrying over."

"Well, they shouldn't."

Then I added: "Have you heard about this Garcia girl?"

He didn't answer. I wasn't sure if he was chewing his thoughts or if he hadn't heard me. We continued to ride and then he said: "I believe everyone has heard of her, boss. In these three counties, anyway."

"It's a difficult situation."

"That is putting it lightly."

"What do you reckon about my wife?"

"Maybe she'll get kicked by a horse. Or fall into a river."

"My luck has never been that good."

"That is true," said Sullivan. "If anyone will fall into a river, it will be you."

AUGUST 4, 1917

Today, for the first time, we go to McCullough Springs together. At first she keeps a comfortable distance, as if she is an employee, but I take her hand. We have lunch at Almacitas, drink Carta Blancas, linger in the street holding each other. I am not sure I have ever felt better. Though part of me wonders if we are doing this as a bulwark against the tide that is rising around us. As if we might stop it with love. Which, of course, is ridiculous.

Tonight we are sitting in the library, my head in her lap, when I say: "Why didn't you ever get married?"

She shrugs.

"But really."

"I had lovers, if that's what you're asking."

It isn't, and it gives me a bad feeling to think about, but I persist.

"I won't give myself to anyone who doesn't respect me," she says. "I would rather be dead."

"They couldn't have all been so bad."

"I should have been born a man," she says.

I pinch her thigh.

"They expect you to look at them adoringly, regardless of what they have done, and if they don't expect you to wash their clothes, they expect you to keep after the woman who does." She shrugs. "And the Mexicans are the worst. A Mexican man will take you to a place, say a nice hotel, or a nice view in the mountains, and show it off as if he made it. And part of him really believes it."

"It's bravado," I say.

"Regardless," she says. "He believes it. And that is why I never married. And never expect to."

I give her a hurt look.

She leans over and kisses me. "Except to you, of course."

I nuzzle into her lap and wrap my arms around her waist. But when I look up at her again, she is staring out the dark window, and doesn't appear to notice me. "There is another story," she says.

Long ago, here in the Wild Horse Desert, there was a young vaquero, very handsome, though very poor, who was in love with the daughter of a Tejano rancher.

This girl, who was almost too beautiful to look at, was desired and courted by every rancher's son on both sides of the river, though being of pure heart, she was more interested in horses than men, and dreamed only of a certain stallion that ran with the wild mustangs. This horse was unusual in both his pure white color and his size, sixteen hands. In addition to his perfect form, he had the toughness of a paint, the speed of a Thoroughbred, and, like the girl, he was coveted by every man who had ever seen or heard of him. But none could ever catch him.

When the young vaquero learned how much the girl loved this horse, he decided to make her a present. For months he studied its tracks and discovered its secrets. Then he waited all night at a hidden watering hole, and when the stallion came in, he roped it. He fed it plums and persimmons and chunks of *piloncillo*. He repeated this process for many weeks until the horse allowed himself to be stroked and touched, and then led with a halter, and then saddled. But even then he would stand only in one stirrup, never trying to mount the horse, until he knew the horse would not mind. And in this manner he broke the horse to the saddle without breaking his spirit.

After more gentling, the vaquero brushed and groomed the white stallion and rode him to the house of the Tejano rancher, where he called softly to the rancher's daughter. When she opened her window she recognized the vaquero instantly, and the horse as well, and knew that this was the man she would marry. They shared one chaste kiss, but agreed to find a priest before they did anything else.

Unfortunately they were not alone. The fat son of an Anglo rancher had seen the entire thing, because when he was not forcing himself upon servant girls he was hiding in the bushes outside the window of this beautiful Tejana, watching her disrobe and doing unspeakable things to himself.

(Was this in your mother's version of the story, I ask.)

(She ignores me.)

He returned to his father with news that the most beautiful girl anyone had ever seen was about to marry a common vaquero. And then he and his father laid an ambush.

With their specially made rifles they waited until the vaquero's back was turned and then murdered him, and, for the rest of their days, told all their friends of the beautiful shot they made, at a very great distance, on a Mexican.

But when they reached the body of the young vaquero, the white stallion had returned to protect him. He bit and kicked at the rancher and his son and so they murdered him as well. Then they cut off the vaquero's head.

The ranchero's daughter, when her vaquero did not return, took her father's pistol and murdered herself. But God does not allow noble beings to be separated, and thus the vaquero can be seen on his horse at every full moon, with his head in his lap, riding his ghostly white stallion with the other mustangs, looking for the spirit of his intended.

(I believe you have the story wrong, I tell her.)

(How so?)

(That is an old folktale of ours as well, I say.)

For many years there was a black stallion, not white, that ran with the mustangs and carried a ghostly rider on its back. The sight of the rider made the mustangs stampede, and thus people always knew when the black stallion appeared, because it sounded like a tornado had touched down in the desert, thousands of mustangs galloping across the caliche.

Very few men ever got close to the horse and its rider, but the few who did said he was sitting normally, except that his head was not attached. His head, along with a sombrero, was strapped to his lap. And so for many years, the cowboys shot at the ghostly rider, but the bullets went through his body like a paper target, and he continued to ride.

Finally, a few cowboys decided to solve the mystery. They waited all night at a watering hole, and when the black stallion and the headless rider appeared, they shot the horse.

On the back of this beautiful mustang there was an old dry corpse tied upright with rawhide, the head tightly bound to his lap. After many months of inquiry, it was discovered that a young Mexican by the name of Vidal, who was a notorious womanizer and horse thief, had met his end.

The men who caught him were Creed Taylor and Bigfoot Wallace, legendary Texans about whom many books have been written. They were great practical jokers, and so to make an example out of Vidal, they cut off his head and tied both his head and body to an unbroken black stallion that had been caught in a trap with other mustangs. They released the stallion and his headless rider, who confused and terrorized the populace for over a decade.

———

"Yours is the true one," she says.

"It's an old story," I say. "It's well known."

"Of course," she says. "There are many convincing details. First, there is a dead Mexican who was a horse thief, as all dead Mexicans are. Second, there are two famous Texans, who decided, after killing a man, that they would decapitate him for fun. Third, they decide that merely decapitating this man is not funny enough. It will be hilarious if, instead of burying him, they tie his body to a wild horse."

"Hmmm," I say.

"And the final convincing detail is that a group of Anglo cowboys, when faced with the task of capturing a legendary black stallion, instead of roping him, or building a simple trap, decided to shoot him, because it required the least effort."

"That is why I don't tell stories."

"No, it was educational."

"Yours is the one our children should hear."

"No," she says. "Our children should know the truth." Then she kisses my forehead and strokes my hair, as if I am a child myself.

Chapter Forty-nine
Eli McCullough

1864

A t the beginning of the year there was a shakeup and most of the RMN men were sent east. They tried shipping me to the Frontier Regiment, but I didn't feel like riding against the Comanches and I didn't like McCord, either, and so as punishment I was sent to the Indian Territories. Most whites didn't want to work with Indians—they were considered only a step above Negroes—but I suspected it would be high living and I was right.

Of the five civilized tribes, two—the Creeks and Seminoles—had sided with the Union. The other three—the Cherokee, Chickasaw, and Choctaw—were fighting for the Confederacy. There was a brigade of Cherokee under their own general, Stand Watie, and a Choctaw brigade under Tandy Walker. I was given the temporary rank of colonel and put in charge of a battalion of ragged Cherokees. They'd signed enlistment papers the same as whites, but they didn't believe in boots or uniforms, or remembering their orders, or fighting when they were outnumbered. They believed in eating well and staying in one piece, which made them just about useless, as far as the army was concerned.

By then, we were getting most of our equipment from Union supply trains. We wanted Union-made pistols, which had steel frames instead of brass, and we wanted their repeating rifles, Henrys and Spencers, though we were happy with their Enfields as well. We wanted their wool pants and blankets, their field glasses, their saddles and tack, their horses and ammunition, tinned beef, coffee and salt, quinine, factory-made shirts, their writing paper and sewing needles.

Our only orders were to disrupt the enemy's rear, which meant riding into Kansas or Missouri, burning barns or bridges or just stealing chickens. Eventually, when our bellies were as empty as bankers' hearts and there was nothing left to plunder from the locals, we would go south to resupply.

It was a familiar way of living and I did not mind it one bit, sleeping outside and roaming where I wanted, and I did not mind being with the Indians, either, who, civilized or not, lived closer to the natural ways than most whites. But in summer I got a few days' leave and decided to head back to Austin.

I was heating the axles the whole way but when I came across the hill and saw the judge's house, I reined up short. I wasn't sure why I'd come home. I could remember sitting on a horse in my Comanche gear, shooting arrows for the reporters; in the backyard there were hackberries thirty feet tall that I remembered as seedlings. I suddenly felt old, and I nearly turned around and rode north again, but Madeline was standing in the doorway of the guesthouse, so I got off and fixed my horse to the snubbing post and went to her.

She was holding Everett. He was nine months old, or it might have been eight, or eleven.

"Daddy's back," she said.

He looked like he might cry and she looked like another person—she'd aged ten years since the war started. She'd had no trouble getting back her old figure, and looking at the dark circles under her eyes and her skin that bruised at the lightest touch, I knew I'd made a mistake for the ages.

We went inside and she put my hands on her chest and then I was in a fierce rutting mood. But once we made it to the bed, I could tell she wasn't.

Still she wanted me to do it anyway but right before we started she said, "Put it there instead," and raised her legs a little higher. "I don't want my milk to get thick.

"Does that feel good?"

I nodded.

"As good as . . ."

"Sure," I mumbled.

"It feels good to me, too. It also hurts, though."

I took it out. She rolled over and examined me.

"I thought it would be filthy." She looked closer. "It does smell."

"I better wash I guess."

"I thought you would like it," she said. "Did you?"

"Sure," I said.

The Negroes had kept some water hot so I walked over to the main house and took a bath. When I came back she was dressed again.

"Is it the baby?" I said.

"Probably."

I looked around the cottage. It was small and dark. I told myself that I loved them.

"I feel a little far away from you, maybe."

"I'm right here," I said.

"You're gone and then every few months you're back for a few days and we do it and then you're gone again. I feel like a cow."

"You're beautiful."

"Not the way I look. I mean you come home and leave and that's all there is to it."

I started to say something but she interrupted. "My father could get you something here. I know he told you that. I see officers around town all the time and there must be men on the coast who see their families all the time as well."

"That wouldn't be fair."

"To the army or to me? To a bunch of men you've known a year, or to me? You like to pretend it's not a choice but it is, Eli."

"Why are you mad?" I said. "I just got here."

"I'm trying not to be."

Everett was glaring at me. "I made you," I said.

"That's just his normal face," she told me.

That afternoon, after we'd been to see the judge and his wife, we were back in bed. Madeline had stolen a bottle of sunflower oil from the kitchen.

"You don't want another Everett," I said. "Or a little sister for him?"

"I do," she said. "One day I really do, just not by myself."

She looked at me and took my hand in both of hers and kissed it. She was a beautiful woman. I reminded myself she was plenty strong.

"Do you ever think about what my life is like here?"

"I imagine it's hard," I said, though I didn't.

"It is hard. I'm stuck in this house with a little animal who can't even talk to me. Sometimes I wake up and think today will be the day that I forget how to speak."

"Isn't it nice to have the baby, though?"

"Of course it is," she said. "But not any nicer for me than it is for you. When he's crying I sometimes want to leave him in his crib and run as far away as possible."

I didn't say anything.

"Sorry. I'm tired of playing the long-suffering wife. I thought it suited me and now it doesn't. I will do all the work of raising your son but if you think I am going to be silent about it you have another think coming."

"Can't the niggers look after him?"

"My mother keeps them busy enough," she said.

"You know when I'm not here I'm either sleeping in the rain or living off wormy biscuits. Or people are shooting at me."

"I feel like your mistress," she said. "So don't pretend it is nothing but misery, because I know you, Eli, and I know you wouldn't be doing it if it were."

Then we were both quiet. She looked like she was going to cry. "I don't want this to be your last memory of me."

"Nothing's gonna happen."

"And please stop saying that."

"All right," I said.

"At first I thought there was another woman up there. Now I wish that's all it was."

Chapter Fifty
J.A. McCullough

Things had gone wrong from the start. She'd walked onto her plane and her pilot was missing and his replacement—a woman—had a certain look. For the first time in her eighty-six years, decades of flying ten or twenty times a week, she wanted to get off the plane. Of course everything was fine. The woman was an excellent pilot, she'd flared so perfectly that Jeannie had barely been able to tell they'd touched down. But still there was that feeling.

Later she was sitting on the gallery, the sun was going down and it was quiet and she had begun to weep, the entire sky from front to back was red and purple and fiery orange, one day soon would be her last, perhaps this one, everything was so beautiful she could not bear the thought of leaving it. Then Frank

Mabry had made his presence known. He took off his hat and waited for her to acknowledge him. She wondered if he were blind, or deaf, but he was just stupid. She ignored him, but still he would not leave, he stood there like a scolded dog and waited.

"Ma'am," he said, after a minute.

She nodded. Dabbed at her eyes.

"I was wondering if you'd thought about what we talked about last time."

"No," she told him. She had no idea. He flew the small helicopter they used on roundups. She dabbed her eyes again and hoped he would drop dead but he didn't retreat, he seemed to have a sense that he might yet be able to weasel his way into her good graces.

"How long have you known me, Frank?"

"Thirty-four years. And in fact that is just it. I have been wondering if something . . . were to happen, if any arrangements had been made, any considerations, for the people who had been in your employ so long."

She wondered what he was talking about. Then she understood. "Please leave," she said.

He clomped away. She hoped he might be kicked by a horse or that his truck would flip or that the rotor might fall off his little helicopter. She watched him drive away, had the sense everything was ruined, and went up to bed without dinner.

The next morning she woke up earlier than she wanted. Normally she turned on the computer, checked the oil and S&P futures, where Asia had closed and Europe was trading, but this morning she had no interest. She dressed and padded down the long hallway, the light just coming in on the dark wood and busts of old Romans, but instead of going downstairs she stood at the top and watched the sun come up through the stained glass. There was something about it. She'd seen it thousands of times but now there was something different. *You're being sentimental,* she decided. She began to make her way down the stairs.

In the kitchen she made breakfast but when she went to put her plate away, she found the dishwasher full of clean dishes and glasses. Not hers; she'd only been here a night. Someone—some employee—must have thrown a party, she didn't remember being asked, *no,* she thought, *I was not asked,* of course it was Dolores, who ran the house, no one else would have dared.

Dolores had worked for her thirty years and they'd always maintained a tactful sort of friendship, hugs and air kisses, J.A. making the occasional showing at Dolores's family gatherings, birthdays or graduations, a benevolent presence. Certainly she had helped them live far above what was normal in Dimmit County. And, unlike Mabry, Dolores *was* being taken care of, though she did not know it yet.

She felt a heat rising in her; she should not be having these feelings. They were no longer healthy. She pulled back into her mind. The anger went out of her, the sun came brightly through the windows, she could see hummingbirds just outside and the scent of vanilla—the agaritos were blooming—but it didn't matter, everyone was against her, they all saw the end was near. She wondered if she should have remarried. Which was ridiculous—Ted had died years ago, another husband to bury—but still, she had not led a natural life.

Your pills, she thought, *and your drink.* But even the small container seemed like too much effort. She wondered when Dolores would come, she would mention the incident but make it clear all was forgiven, she could have parties but only with permission. The light was spreading through the house, across the old rugs and dark floors, the portraits of her father and grandfather and great-grandfather along the main stairway; of course there ought to be one more, the person who had run the ranch longer than her father and grandfather combined, but one did not hang a portrait of oneself. And there was no one behind her to do it. Her grandson: perhaps he would be happy. That was all she could hope for.

The front door opened and closed and Dolores appeared at the end of the dining room, a tiny figure, out of proportion to all her surroundings. There was a long minute as she walked closer; she was carrying a new white handbag and when she reached the near end of the dining room, she smiled and said, "Good morning, Mrs. McCullough."

"Good morning," she said. "How was your little party?"

The woman looked away. Jeannie could see her mind working. "Party?" she said. "It was not a party, it was just a gathering, it was not planned."

This was clearly rehearsed and she became angry again: "Well, let me know next time. It is still my house."

Dolores continued to look away and then Jeannie felt bad; what would it be like to be nearing the end of your life, still being scolded? She came around the counter, intending to hug her, to show this was nothing serious, they were old friends, but if Dolores noticed her intention she didn't let on. She said, "I'll go see about your room," and turned back toward the stairs, giving Jeannie the feeling that she, not Dolores, was the one who ought to be apologizing.

And there was that feeling—that Dolores no longer thought it worth hiding what they both knew, which was that in most important ways she no longer needed J.A. McCullough. Within her own community, Dolores was considered wealthy, a matriarch, people calling on her for favors, at every holiday there were cars parked on both sides of the road to her house.

In the old days it would have been the opposite. Jeannie would have been the one with the house full of lively children, weddings and birthdays and graduations to plan, while Dolores would have lost most of hers—perhaps all of them—to dysentery and malnutrition, to overwork and bad doctoring and the *coraje* and jealous husbands (they used to butcher each other, she thought, it was always in the paper that some *peón* had woken up and found he'd cut his wife's throat). But now . . . now . . .

The sun was bright. Soon it would be summer and the light would extinguish everything, all the colors. But for now it was green and cool. She had a feeling, which became a clear thought, that she would not live to see it. She looked at her hands. Something was moving in the corner. She felt cold.

After Hank died, there were times when the face that stared back at her in the mirror meant exactly nothing; given the right circumstance she would have obliterated it like a fly on a window. But they had not let her alone. If there was anything you could say about oilmen, they knew about suffering and loss; most were only a generation or two out of some tarpaper shack and for weeks after Hank died they had not let her alone. No matter how much she wanted silence there were people in the kitchen, living room, guest rooms, there was food out, servants she didn't recognize, strangers coming and going, the kids going to school, coming back, how she didn't know.

The Texans had been relentless; they might hate the blacks and Mexicans, they might hate the president enough to kill him, but they had not let her alone, they had cared for her like a mother or daughter, men she barely knew, men whose absence from their offices cost them thousands of dollars an hour, and yet she would come downstairs and find them asleep on her couch, and call their drivers to pick them up.

Though of course it was these same men who had nearly refused to do business with her in the years that followed. It was better not to think about. It was all forgiven, they had all gone back to the earth, they had lived only to die.

———

Ted had come into her life a few years after Hank left it. He was older and he came from an even older family, he spent most of his time playing polo—when he was not running or swimming—though he gave off the aura of someone who had done a lot of drugs, a man going to seed.

Not physically; at fifty he was over six feet, with a thirty-two-inch waist and the rugged looks of his ancestors, though his calluses were particular to polo mallets and dumbbells and he had never broken a bone in his life, most of which he had spent chasing women. But as if a switch had turned, he'd decided to settle down. He was smart, though it took her a long time to realize it, he paid attention to her in many ways that Hank had not and she had slowly come to see that Hank, as good as he was, had lived mostly for himself, though neither one of them had known it at the time.

And Ted, just in this difference, had given her hope, that she had not totally figured out life or people, that things might be different; it was a pleasant feeling. It mattered to Ted how she looked, he noticed all her haircuts and new clothes, he knew the difference between a mood he could talk her out of and one he couldn't. He didn't fawn, but he noticed. And yet he was not a serious person. He was an aging playboy who wanted company; who had grown tired, she guessed, of putting on an act for every waitress or stewardess who caught his eye. He'd decided he was old, and he wanted to be around his own people.

The boys liked him well enough. They did not quite take him seriously, though he was good to them, and filled a role she could not, taking them shooting and riding; he was too lazy to hunt deer but enjoyed hunting quail. The boys never seemed to learn anything from him; neither their riding nor their shooting improved in his presence, but he did not demand anything of them, either, and nights she would come home and find them sitting together on the sofa watching television, Ted with a bottle of wine, the boys with their pop, *The Avengers* or *Bonanza,* none of them with anything to say, but as happy as a pile of dogs in winter.

As for Susan, she had begun to summer in Maine with Jonas's children, three months of blessed silence and privacy and after the second summer she came back asking to leave Kincaid and go away to Garrison Forest, like Jonas's daughters. The idea that her daughter might disappear from her life for eight months was not entirely appealing, though it seemed better— barely—than having to put up with her. By then Susan was not just needy; she was a saboteur. She would go through her mother's things, she would walk into their bedroom when she knew Ted was there, she would pretend to sneak to the kitchen for a snack, wearing only her T-shirt and underpants.

"That girl is a handful," Ted told her.

"She will be lucky if she isn't pregnant by her next birthday," Jeannie said.

"I think you will be the lucky one."

Of course he was right. But somehow, even then, it had not felt that way.

Ted didn't have children of his own; she might have given him one while it was still possible, but neither one of them had been willing to commit to that. Mostly what Ted wanted was a family, without having to raise it himself; a woman who had her own money, a woman who accepted him as part of her pack, but otherwise asked nothing. She would never have guessed it, but she'd been more happy with him, more settled than she'd ever felt. Of course she could not help but be drawn to people like Hank, people with their own fire, but no matter how much they thought they loved you or their family or their country, no matter how they pledged their allegiance, that fire always burned for them alone.

Chapter Fifty-one
Diaries of Peter McCullough

AUGUST 6, 1917

Sally called to say she will be coming to visit. "Don't worry about your little *pelado,*" she told me. "I won't interfere."

For a moment I saw everything falling in around me. I didn't say anything. Finally I told her, "There is no reason for you to be here."

"Except that it is my home. I would like to visit my own home. All sorts of excitement going on, I hear."

"You are not welcome," I said, though I knew it was pointless.

"Well, get that idea out of your head. Because I am coming back."

My father was sitting on the porch with the driller and a few other men.

"I just spoke to Sally," I said.

He gave me a look.

"And if anything happens, I will make certain things known."

"I'll see you boys this evening," he told the men. They got up as one and left.

"Whatever you are about to say, do not say it. In fact do not even think it."

"Stop her from coming."

"I have nothing to do with that," he said.

I shook my head.

"Anyone but that girl, Pete. In fact I would like it if you got every wetback in town pregnant, because unless I am given a proper Goodnighting, my days of prodding are over, and I could use a few more heirs."

"We have nothing to worry about from María," I said.

"I know that."

"Then tell Sally to stay away."

"You know, if you were a Comanche you could just cut Sally's nose off, and throw her out, and get married to the new one."

"Her name is María."

"Unfortunately you are not a Comanche. You are subject to the laws of America. Which means you should have gotten rid of Sally before signing this other one on."

"I'm embarrassed for you."

"The feeling is mutual," he told me.

"So your wife is returning?"

I look at her; there is no point denying it. "Don't worry about her," I say.

She shrugs. I can see she has been crying. "I knew it had to end sometime."

"It doesn't," I say.

She turns from me.

I try to hug her but she shakes me off. "It's fine," she says.

"It's not fine."

"I will be fine."

I realize she is not even talking to me.

After she fell asleep I took a bottle of whiskey and walked out into the chaparral until I reached Dog Mountain, which is nothing more than a large hill, though it is the tallest around. At the top is a large rock with a backrest cut or hacked into the stone and I climbed up and lay against it. The house was a mile or so behind me; I could see a few lights, but otherwise, it was dark.

When I had sat long enough I began to get a strange feeling. This has always been a warm place and men had likely sat on this exact rock for ten thousand years at least, as it provides the best view of the surrounding country. How many families had come and gone? Before there were men there was a vast ocean, and I knew that far beneath me there were living creatures turning to stone.

I thought of my brother, who has always pitied me for my temperament, who spends his life inside, obsessed with his papers and bank accounts. When the agarito ripens he can't smell it, when the first windflowers bloom he will not see them. As for my father, he sees everything. But only so he can destroy it.

AUGUST 7, 1917

Sally arrived this morning. She kissed me politely on the cheek, then greeted María. "Nice to see you again, neighbor." Then she laughed and said: "This heat can make for strange living arrangements."

She said she would take a bedroom on the other side of the house and had her things brought up there.

Meanwhile, I was supposed to spend the day with Sullivan, as we have hired a crew to do more cross-fencing.

I intended to tell him he would have to do it without me, but María assured me it would be fine.

"Your wife and I are going to have to be alone at some point. Better sooner than later."

We met the crew at the gate and drove to the middle of the ranch, explaining what we wanted done. Gates here and here and there . . . after a few hours I was so antsy my hands were shaking. I told Sullivan I had to go.

Back at the house, Phineas's Pierce Arrow was parked in the driveway. I got a terrible feeling. Phineas, Sally, and my father were all sitting in the parlor, waiting.

I went from room to room, calling for her, the kitchen, the great room, the library, then searched every closet. Consuela was in my bedroom, stripping the sheets off the bed. She would not speak. I went back downstairs and found the three of them still sitting there.

Sally said: "María has decided to go back to her own people."

"I am her people."

"Apparently she felt differently."

"If you hurt her," I said, "either one of you," looking at Sally and my father, "I will kill you."

They looked at each other and something crossed their faces, some expression of humor. If I'd had a pistol, they both would have died an instant later. There was a red mist and I took my jackknife out of its sheath, opened it, and stepped toward my wife.

"I will cut your fucking throat," I told her. She smiled and I stepped closer and she lost all her color.

"And you," I said, pointing the knife at my brother. "Did you know about this?"

"Pete," he said, "we offered her ten thousand dollars to move back with her cousin in Torreón. She decided to take it."

"Her cousin is dead."

"She knows other people down there."

"Where is she now?"

"She's in a car."

"Son," said my father, "it's for the best."

I went upstairs to my office. I loaded my pistol and was making my way down the hall when I saw the dark figure, leaning on the banister, waiting for me. The sunlight was on him and I stood for a long time watching: first he had a face like my father's, then it was my own, then it was something else.

I went back to my desk.

Waiting for them to make the car ready. Leave for Torreón in an hour.

Chapter Fifty-two
Eli McCullough

June 1865

The Federals stuck to our tracks all winter and by
Christmas we'd lost half our number. It was plain
that if we didn't leave Kansas we would all end up
either shot or hanged; Flying Jacket and the remaining
Cherokees decided to absquatulate west to the Rockies.
The five RMN men—Busque, Showalter, Fisk, Shaw,
and me—decided to go with them. The last we'd
heard was Sherman had taken Georgia. If there were
other bands of Confederates, we'd stopped running into
them.

The Cherokees collected a few Ute scalps but we
avoided the Federals entirely, camping at tree line
and generally sticking to the owl-hoot trail until
one afternoon in the Bayou Salado we chassed into

a small regiment. Normally this would have sent us scurrying over the next ridge, but there were two dozen wagons for only a few hundred men, and they all had eight-mule hitches, and this was not lost on Flying Jacket, either. We hunkered in the rocks and watched them.

"They are pulling something heavy," he said.

I stayed quiet. I knew exactly what they were carrying but unless Flying Jacket agreed with me, it was pointless. He was near fifty and he'd insisted on being called a colonel and that's why they made me one as well. He wore his jacket with the oak leaves even when it was a hundred degrees out.

"They're going to the assay office in Denver," I said. The war had been nothing like I thought—even the judge was nearly bankrupt—but the longer I watched the wagons, the more I wondered if something might yet be saved from the wreckage. I thought about Toshaway and the raid we'd made into Mexico and I could not see why this was any different.

"If they're not carrying hides," Flying Jacket was saying. "Or timber. Or, who knows, perhaps they're simply that strong now. Perhaps they ride this way for fun."

"Well, they won't make the pass at that pace. They'll have to camp on that bench."

We continued to watch. The men riding the wagons got off to walk as the road got steeper. It was gold country and they were pulling something heavy. Of course, it could have been anything. But Flying Jacket was coming around.

"I hope we don't go in and find it's just a pile of rocks."

"If we do," said Flying Jacket, "it will just be a continuation of my entire life."

He called a few Cherokees over and they talked. Then he turned back to me.

"This cannon they are pulling?"

"Probably a mountain howitzer."

"With canister shot, if they are worried about being robbed."

"Yes, but they only have one shot, and they will be firing into their own men."

"And yet it is strange," he said.

They made their camp where we thought they would. There were butterflies in the grass, a hundred-mile view of the mountains, a cold stream running past them. We were at the tree line. It was rocks and dust. The Union men were relaxed, taking their time to set up their tents, making bets on the bighorn sheep, which were white dots on cliffs high above them. A few had Sharps rifles. Once in a while one of the white dots would come tumbling off the mountain, looking like a falling snowman.

All the boys were against it. Except for Showalter, who was down with the Indians, we were on our bellies in the rocks, passing the field glasses back and forth.

"This might be a persimmon above our huckleberry," said Fisk.

"Well," I said, "it's what the Indians want, and it's what Jeff Davis wants, and it's what we're going to do."

"Listen to the fire-eater. The living legend."

Shaw said: "May I humbly suggest to the boss that his attitude is outdated. By about four years."

I passed the glasses to Fisk. He was the oldest of us; he had a big family back in Refugio.

"This is a dumb idea." He began to wiggle back down through the rocks.

"Where are you going?"

"I gotta write a letter," he said.

"Same here," said Shaw. "Let me know if y'all change your mind. Otherwise you'll find me and my horse heading down that draw we came up."

I looked at him.

"I'll be back at the camp," he said. But he wasn't smiling.

Then it was only Busque and me.

"What do *you* think," I said.

"I think it's stupid."

"It'll be high livin' if it goes off."

"You know they'll find some way to take it off us."

"That is a sorry attitude."

"It's time to piss on the fire and call the dogs, Eli. For all we know, Jeff Davis is already a cottonwood blossom."

I didn't say anything.

We continued to watch the bluecoats, who had stripped down to their underwear and were lying in the grass, enjoying the sun, gambling on saddle blankets or writing in their journals. Others were skinning the sheep, getting a fire going.

"I feel sorry for those Indians," said Busque.

We watched as the Federals ate their supper, we watched them watch the sunset, we could still see them even as the first stars came out, passing around a bottle, enjoying their jobs, acting like there wasn't any war.

Most of the tents were in a small depression, their wagons and horses on the outskirts. Around midnight we shot arrows into their pickets. Then we stampeded the horse herd through the tents and it became a proper massacre; the Federals were easy to pick out as they were all wriggling under collapsed sailcloth or looking about confusedly wearing bright white union suits. We came into the bowl from all sides, shooting with our repeaters while the Cherokees raced around, ululating and smashing heads with their flint axes. Most of the Yankees died before they even knew who was tormenting them and I began to feel sorry for them, it was not even an honest fight, and then Flying Jacket was trying to get my attention.

A dozen of the Union men, all in their underwear, had escaped to the rise where the cannon was parked. They were fetching things from a wagon, making no attempt to stiver off, and I thought they had lost their heads. Then their gun started up and I knew why they hadn't run.

One aimed it while others worked to feed it or watched the flanks and the gun was popping so fast it was like twenty men shooting at once.

Some Cherokees made a charge on horseback and then there was a second charge. The gun had not stopped firing since it started and Shaw and Fisk and I hunkered in some scraggly brush on the other side of the meadow. The Federals were on a rise directly across from us and in the grass below were dozens of trampled tents and dead and dying men and horses and the sound of moaning like a cattle auction.

They ran out of targets. They began to work over the wounded. The moon was bright and Fisk shot a man standing near the gun and then the branches overtop of us were swaying and crackling and Shaw said, "Leon's hit," and went quiet.

There would be a shot from our side and the Federals would see the flash and put twenty or thirty rounds in and get their credit. Shaw's face was dark and I reached for Fisk. He was wet. One of the Cherokees broke cover but the gun caught him, then came back to me. I pushed up against a rock no bigger than a saddletree and the bullets were slapping against it, something punched my arm, my face was stinging, and then they were working the bushes over my head. The ground all around me was flat and open and I knew my medicine had run out. I tried to remember the death song. I'd forgotten it.

The gun stopped again. Flying Jacket was yelling something. I looked for a ditch or rock or dead horse. There was a flipped wagon but it was too far, and there was an Indian behind the wagon shooting his bow nearly straight up, and then more Indians were doing the same and the air above the gun began to shilly and waver, as if there were heat from a great fire. The loaders were shrieking and calling out and then all the Indians were shooting and the gunner was alone firing blindly into the dark.

The Cherokees were moving among the tents, finishing off the wounded with clubs. There was an occasional shot farther down the valley.

I bandaged my arm, then I found Busque and Showalter. We went to the gun. The ground around it was stuck with hundreds of arrows—the Indians had shot them almost straight up so that they would fall on the Federals from above and there were scattered bodies with the switches sticking into them at strange angles, into the tops of their shoulders and heads.

One of the bodies began to move. A man slid out from under it. He appeared to be unhurt.

"I surrender," he said. He held up his hands. "Are you bandits?"

"We're with the Confederate States of America," I told him.

He looked at us strangely. Then he said: "I'm a civilian. I'm a sales representative."

Busque said: "What does that even mean?"

"I represent the Gatling company. We're not under contract with the army, but we offered a few production samples for their use, as I . . . as I believe we had difficulty contacting your government."

The remaining Cherokees were beginning to gather.

"How does that gun work?" said Busque.

"It's actually very simple. You take a standard paper cartridge, insert it into this carrier . . ." He picked up a small metal cylinder from the ground, where hundreds or thousands were littered. "The cartridge and carrier unit then fit into this hopper at the top of the gun, like so."

Flying Jacket had come up.

"Who is he," he asked. "A deserter?"

"He works for the company that made the gun. He says he is a salesman."

Flying Jacket cocked his head as if thinking. He said something to his men. Six or eight of them rushed forward and stabbed the sales representative to death.

The Indians attempted to take the gun apart so that it couldn't be used again. But they couldn't make sense of it in the dark and instead began to bash it with rocks.

Flying Jacket took me aside and led me to the other wagons, where a crate had been pried open.

"This is heavy but it does not look like gold. It looks like wheat."

"That's gold dust," I said. "That is gold for sure."

"There is a lot of it."

"How much?"

"Hundreds of sacks like that one. Hundreds at least."

The sack looked to be about two pounds.

"We'll have to bury some of it and come back later."

"Why?" he said.

"It'll be tough to move it all."

He looked at me.

"What?"

"Eli, did the sight of that gun not convince you of anything?"

"No."

"I believe that you are not telling the truth. Did you know of the existence of this type of gun?"

"Not exactly."

"So you did."

"I didn't know they were in production."

"But you knew the other side would eventually have them. A gun with which one man can kill forty."

I looked off into the dark valley below us and the mountains beyond it. I wondered if we would make it home.

"Ah, Eli. Our band is nearly a thousand women, children, and old men. When we began this trip there were nearly two hundred warriors to support them. It was not enough. Now there are perhaps forty."

"It's a tragedy," I said. "I am extremely sorry."

"It is an even greater tragedy that we are on the losing side of this war. The land we have been given by the federal government, which was not very good, and which we hoped to improve by fighting, we may lose entirely. Just to see that gun fired it is clear."

I shrugged.

"And these men! Look at how fat they are, and how good their horses, when we are starving and our horses starving as well. And the ammunition they carry . . ."

"It's always been like this," I said. "We were always the underdog."

"We are done fighting," he said. "I'm sorry."

"That is a poor decision."

"Your government will not even exist a year from now, Eli. You are five white men . . ."

"Now three."

"Three. I am sorry for your loss of two men, but when this war is over, you three will be able to do whatever you like. But I will be stuck on the reservation, along with my family, paying the price for supporting the wrong side. As will all my men. Who, when they are finished burying their brothers, will likely come to the conclusion that the best action is to kill the three of you. Both because you led us to this gun, which you did not bother to tell us about, and also because when whites steal something, it is no problem—whites can steal from each other—but if Indians steal something it is another matter. Do you understand? Indians who steal gold will not be forgiven." He shrugged. "And yet we need this gold."

I didn't say anything.

"This was a great battle, Eli. The last we will ever win. After this there will be only losing. And I think that if I were you, I would get off this mountain as soon as possible."

"You're their chief," I said.

"Unlike your people, we are democratic. Each man is free. My word is simply advice, not law." He patted my shoulder. "I am telling you this because you are the best white man I have ever known. The thought of you living gives me great pleasure."

"Me too," I said, but he ignored me.

"It will be best if you ride all day and all night, at least for the first few days."

I turned to go. He had loaded sacks of the gold into a rawhide parfleche. "Magic will not touch you, Eli. I saw it from the first time I met you. But of course that is also a curse." He handed me the bag.

What do you think," said Busque. Rummaging in the moonlight, he and Showalter had each found a clean Union uniform, which was not hard to do as most of the bluecoats had died in their underwear. They packed the uniforms into their saddlebags.

"We're going to California," said Showalter.

"I'll report you as killed in action."

"Asshole," said Busque, "the action is over. Those bluecoat motherfuckers all had Henrys and Spencers and that fucking automatic gun. Not to mention those Yankee boots they were all wearing. I would have killed any one of them just for those boots."

"And this fucking gold," said Showalter. "Our guys are getting paid in scrip that'll be worthless by the time the peaches come in."

"I'm a colonel," I said.

"Eli, very shortly we will have lost the greatest war in history; in fact it is possible we have lost it already, and that the news has not reached us yet. I don't plan on being put in a Union prison camp, or shot by the Home Guard between now and then, or, even worse, dying in the final battle for a house of bullshit."

I didn't say anything.

"If you go back to Austin you'll be shot for desertion. And the war will end anyway, whether you're alive or dead. Come out west and send for your family."

"I can't."

"You think we lived this long because of what great soldiers we are? Is that what you think?"

I didn't say anything.

"You're a real sonofabitch," he said. "I always wondered about you."

"Girls," said Showalter, "you think these prairie niggers are gonna let us into any of that gold?"

There were over two hundred Union dead, mostly in their underwear. Usually the time after a fight felt like after a deer hunt, but now I began to get a terrible feeling.

Twenty-eight Cherokees had been killed outright and at sunrise, fourteen of the wounded would be shot by their friends. We buried Shaw and Fisk, whose faces were staved in. I thought of Fisk's children, and the children of all the other men, they were all somebody's darling.

From the supply wagons I loaded up on salt pork and cartridges for my Henry rifle. Flying Jacket allowed Busque and Showalter a bag of yellow dust apiece. They were happy and I decided not to tell them what I'd been given earlier.

His men wouldn't look at us. They all thought we'd known about the gun and the three of us trotted off down the mountain, leaving the Cherokees with the gold and all the Federals' weapons, ammunition, and horses. Just off the road was a dead man in his long underwear, and farther off the road, at the edge of the stream, was a second one.

I could not shake the feeling I'd stepped over some line over which I would never return, but maybe I'd crossed it years earlier, or maybe it had never existed. There was nothing you could take that did not belong to some other person. Whatever strings that held me had been cut.

"Stop fretting," Showalter said. "As soon as the sun comes up and they see all their loot, they'll want to take it and run. They'll forget we exist!" He grinned at me.

"You're probably right," I said.

Busque stayed far ahead. He hadn't looked at me since the burial.

At the base of the mountain, when we reached a long stretch of rock, I split off on my own, promising to see them in California when the war ended. It was the end of the RMN. I said a few words to distract from what was showing on my face.

We heard the shots as the Cherokees finished their wounded. I watched Busque and Showalter disappear to the west and then I pried the shoes off my horse and looped around the base of the mountain, staying under cover, changing direction every time I crossed a stream or patch of rock. I guessed Busque and Showalter wouldn't be careful about their tracks. I hoped the Indians wouldn't find them, but I knew better, the people around me did not live long, the Cherokees would catch the others, but not me, I was as sure of that as anything.

A month later I got to Austin. The war had been over since spring.

Chapter Fifty-three
J.A. McCullough

She was a slut or a dyke or a whore. A man trapped in a woman's body; look up her skirt and you'll see a cock. A liar, a schemer, a cold heart with a cunt to match, ridden hard and put up wet, Though she shouldn't take it personally. No one meant anything by it.

To be a man meant not living by any rules at all. You could say one thing in church and another at the bar and somehow both were true. You could be a good husband and father and Christian and bed every secretary, waitress, and prostitute that caught your eye. They all had their winks and nods, code for *I fucked that cheerleader or nanny or Pan Am stewardess, that maid or riding instructor.* Meanwhile, the slightest hint she was anything but a virgin (excepting the

three children), would get her banned for life, a scar-
let letter.

Not that she was complaining, but it had never
stopped being strange that what was praised in men—
the need to be good at everything, to be someone
important—would be considered a character flaw in
her. This had not been the case when Hank was alive.
Perhaps they thought her ambition came from him,
perhaps they did not mind a woman if she was under
the control of a man.

But why did she care? Most men bored her, people
bored her; she'd spent fifteen years watching Hank's
mind grow and change and constantly being surprised.
She was not going to give up her freedom for anything
less. In the first few years after Hank's death, she'd
slept with only a handful of men and of all of them the
only one she'd fallen for was married, and as far as the
others, her feelings had faded, or turned off abruptly;
they were not Hank, could not be Hank. Most nights,
if she had the energy, she reached for her massager and
fell asleep.

Yes, she was jealous, there were two sets of rules, a
man could have mistresses and abortions, sleep with
every cheerleader on the Dallas Cowboys . . . to be
free that way, to do whatever you wanted, though
it was not just about being free, it was about being

desired. No matter how old, fat, or ugly you were— you were desired nonetheless. She could not think about it without feeling like a failure, as if she had to live her life in a sort of cage, a narrow and particular path, watching the others sprint about like a pack of children, or dogs, breaking the rules, going in circles, this way and that.

She was not a prude. She'd used a few men for sex, or tried to, but each time it was less than she wanted, it was something half-complete, and even men did not not enjoy being treated that way, no matter what they told their friends, *you acted like I was some kind of vibrator,* one had told her, they were sensitive creatures, monsters and sensitive creatures, they were whatever they wanted to be.

And yet they had begun to accept her. They were all getting old, they were all getting rich, she didn't know, but they had begun to treat her like the lady who'd been on the cover of *Time,* the woman you should have known way back, when she was a looker, a man-eater. Of course, she had never been a man-eater; of course, even at fifty, she was still striking. But that was not part of the agreement. The agreement was she was old and fat, just like them, though being old and fat did not matter for them.

Lucho Haynes invited her to his hunting camp, and she'd immediately turned him down. It was Lucho, not Clayton Williams, who'd come up with the idea of the Honey Hunt: prostitutes hired by the dozen and set out in the woods with a blanket and cooler—as a bird handler would place pheasants before a hunt—at which point Lucho and his friends would go out and find them.

She mentioned the invitation to Ted.

"Well, I doubt they'd rape you or anything," he said. "They probably have younger girls for that."

"Sex could be an interesting novelty," she said.

He faked a hurt look, then went back to his magazine. "I would not mind trying it later."

"Fat chance."

"Well, if you are seriously interested in my opinion, I think it's a terrible idea. They'll figure out some way to humiliate you or it'll happen naturally without them even planning it, because they aren't so stupid that they can't see what you really want."

"Which is what?"

"To be like them," he said. "To be accepted into their little club."

"There is no club," she said. "And if there is, I am in it."

"I suppose that is true."

"That is ridiculous."

"No, you're right. I don't know what I was talking about."

The next day she called Lucho and told him she was coming.

The camp was three hours northeast of Houston, deep into the Pineywoods. There were families living in shacks, fields of wrecked farm equipment, it was as poor as Mexico, poor as the last century. In her trunk were three days' worth of clothes and a pair of shotguns: a 28 gauge for quail, a 20 gauge if she needed something heavier, and her normal revolver under the driver's seat.

She made her way down the sandy road, the car fishtailing the entire time. The vegetation was thick, vines hanging, smells of flowers she didn't recognize, she thought of white sheets, her father, old longleaf pines and white oaks and magnolias a hundred feet tall. It was like going back in time, mosquitoes and dragonflies and the air so wet and heavy—it did not seem possible this was Texas.

By the time Lucho showed her to her cabin, the sun was going down and most of the men had returned from fishing or shooting. She was wearing heels and a skirt and blouse and cursing herself for forgetting the bug spray. None of the men appeared to have showered or shaved in several days. The average oilman's ranch had a main house of limestone with heavy wood floors and leather furniture; the lodge here was a crude plank structure with stapled screen windows and unfinished walls. It might have been the hunting camp of some backwoods mayor, jury-rigged electrical cables, old refrigerators and televisions. She knew all of the men present, Rich Estes, Calvin McCall, Aubrey Stokes, T.J. Garnet, a half-dozen others, all dressed in their oldest clothes, pale legs under Bermuda shorts, bellies hanging. She had brought jeans but decided not to change—the worst thing would have been to give off the impression that she cared to fit in, to let them know how flattered she was. They were all good men, but they were the type who demanded submission.

Dinner was beans and tortillas, beef or cabrito, piles of fried catfish caught that morning, a platter of fried squirrel riddled with number-six pellets; if you counted what these men might have been earning had they not been hunting and fishing, it was probably the most expensive meal ever eaten. Travis Giddings was picking out the squirrel heads and methodically sucking them, his shirt covered in gravy. Drinks were Big Red or sweet tea or Pearl beer, but mostly whiskey in a paper cup. Then there were trays of peach cobbler and buckets of ice cream. But there was no loud talk, no cursing; it was like a locker room when the teacher walks in. She let slip that she would only be staying a night or two at most, saw the relief. Lucho began passing a handle of whiskey; she put the bottle to her mouth, lifted it high and held it for a long time as if she intended to drink the whole thing. Of course she kept her tongue pressed to the rim, letting barely any into her mouth, but there were cheers and laughter and within a few minutes a stream of *fucks* and *shits* like a dam had broken, *everyone likes the drunk girl,* she thought. Maybe that was not fair.

She pretended disgust at the mess, laughed at the dirty jokes, and when four women showed up (strippers? prostitutes?) she didn't react. Lucho gave her a look and she knew it had not been his idea; she winked to show he shouldn't worry. She was safe—any one of these men would have jumped in front of a train for her—but they were not above making her feel uncomfortable. She wondered who had ordered the girls, maybe Marvin Sanders, who had never really liked her, or maybe Pat Cullen, or maybe it was Lucho himself, whatever he was pretending now. Maybe they had invited her to test her. Or maybe they had presumed she could handle it, or maybe they had not thought of her at all.

Sitting in the dirty armchair, watching the girls circulate, the lights dim, the windows open, a record player going with Merle Haggard, she sipped from her 7 and 7, drunk despite her best efforts. Everyone looked terrible; everyone said what they meant. It was a pleasant feeling of companionship; she had known these men for decades. Many of them had sat with her when Hank died, and despite their behavior since, here she was, safe and protected. She began to relax and then Marvin Sanders looked at her and said something and then the girls looked at her, too. There were three bottles of whiskey circulating. She wondered if any of the men were doing harder stuff, though this was not that kind of place, and these were not, for the most part, those kinds of men. Drinking until your car went into the bar ditch or you blacked out at the controls of your Cessna: yes. Smoking reefer: no. One of the girls was standing next to her, a brunette with theatrical black eye makeup, wearing nothing but a bra and panties. Then she was sitting in Jeannie's lap. Jeannie could feel the girl's crotch rubbing somewhere above hers, it was soft and entirely wrong, she wished she had put on pants or something thicker. She started to push the girl off, then stopped, everyone was watching, the girl was watching, did she care what Jeannie wanted? No, the man who was paying her had told her to do this; the girl would see it through. It went on a half minute, then a minute; there was cheap vanilla perfume, there was a strange intensity in the girl's eyes. *She is enjoying this,* Jeannie thought, and then the girl kissed her, openmouthed, hard and fake, all for show. Jeannie turned her head. She wondered how much the girl made in a year. What she would do if she knew how much Jeannie made. Then the song ended and the girl climbed off. Jeannie winked at her in solidarity, but the girl ignored her; she was already looking around the room. *I was prettier than you even ten years ago,* she thought, but she knocked that from her mind, the girl was not the problem, it was Marvin Sanders, red-faced and fat; his comb-over flopped to the wrong side, his pants covered in cherry soda, a ridiculous figure, though it did not matter, he was rich and could buy whatever he wanted.

Not much later she got up and yawned and said it was getting late for an old lady. Everyone stopped what they were doing and shouted good night, raised their drinks. It was very early but no one protested. As for the girls, they ignored her.

She walked in the dark toward her cabin, the pines enormous above her, everything closed in. She wondered if Hank had done things like this; of course he must have, it was likely he had touched plenty of strippers, he'd spent weeks with other operators at their hunting camps and private islands, for all she knew he became an entirely different person. He certainly would not have gone to bed early—it would have been a mark against him—and she was suddenly sure that he had slept with another woman, absolutely sure, he could have done so, at no risk and no consequence, hundreds or perhaps thousands of times, the code of silence would never be broken. She wondered why she had never realized this. A loneliness came over her.

Why it might disturb her so much, he had been dead twenty years, it made no sense, she listened to the cicadas whirring, laughter and music from the main house, who was she to say who her husband had been? She sat in her underwear on the strange, hard cot. She wondered if she ought to get dressed and drive home, home to Ted, who had asked her to marry him twice now, she would see if he was still up for it. She was tired of being alone.

She lay back down. Too drunk, too far to drive. She fell asleep and the next morning washed her face in the stream, put on makeup in the dull cracked mirror, dismissed the thought of marrying Ted, and spent the morning shooting grouse with Chuck McCabe. After which she got in her Cadillac and headed back to Houston. No one asked why. They pretended they were happy she had come.

She was driving. It was hot and she had a sudden memory of the branding fire, defying her father and all the rest, and now here she was, forty years later, desperate to belong. They had broken her. She had given up. She should have given Ted a child, she had been selfish, her entire life for her father and for Hank, but you could not measure yourself against the dead, they retained their perfection while your flesh got weaker and weaker.

And her father had been weak himself, and even Hank, she could see that now. He had been an idea longer than a real person, but he was only an idea, he was no longer real, she had not done badly, there was no one like her. That ought to count for something. She was not like other women. A dozen lifetimes of tennis or polo could not have made her happy, and, as for a child, if Ted had asked she would have given him one. But he had wanted children like he wanted everything else, it was an old song somewhere in his mind, dim and faint. Though he had been right about this. She should not have come. It was a mistake, an enormous mistake, she would learn from it.

Chapter Fifty-four
Diaries of Peter McCullough

August 8, 1917

Hot. Blew two tires driving fast on the rocks. Half a day lost; believe we will reach Torreón tomorrow. Sullivan and Jorge Ramirez are with me. Jorge knows the area somewhat. He is very nervous—if we get stopped by the Carrancistas it will be a dice roll on whether we live or die.

I do not particularly care. It feels as if someone might push a finger through me. There is nothing inside.

August 9, 1917

From some workers along the road Jorge acquired sombreros and proper clothing, which we change into, giving the men our own. Anger at Americans high here especially given Pershing's recent expedition (*la invasión,* they call it). We pass donkeys dragging lumber and mules laden with pottery and thick-footed men padding slowly in the heat, all in white except for the blankets across their shoulders. There are children wearing nothing but hats and ragged blankets that barely reach their waists and we stop often for herds of sheep and goats and bare-ribbed cattle that see no reason to move out of our way.

I asked Sullivan and Jorge if they thought it possible that Phineas had María hurt or worse. Sullivan vigorously denied. Jorge silent. I pressed him and he said no, he did not think so.

Sullivan pointed out that Phineas is preparing to run for governor, and Sally's father is an important judge. Suggested it was probably because of those reasons they wanted María gone. I pointed out there were other reasons as well.

In Torreón, which is bigger than I thought, we drove until we found a cantina Jorge judged to be safe (what logic he used is beyond me) and spent a few hours sitting in the back corner (after $150 bribe to owner) while Jorge went out to scout. We were both wearing the soiled white shirts and pants of workers, reeking of the sweat of other men. Sullivan kept his .45 on one empty chair and the carbine on the other. I had my pistol under my shirt but doubted I would have the energy to use it. Sullivan sensed this and it angered him.

When Jorge had not come back for several hours, Sullivan pointed out, though he said he had promised himself he would keep quiet, that ten thousand dollars is a lot of money. Enough to start an entirely new life. *I am nervous here, boss, to tell you the truth. The longer we stay here, the lower our odds of staying above the snakes.*

Am not sure what I am supposed to feel. Jorge finally returned and we ordered food. He had found us a good hotel.

Did María know this would happen? Was she waiting for it? I find it unlikely—she just as well expected to be led into the *brasada* and shot.

But it is the unstated question for the rest of the day. There are no signs of her that Jorge was able to detect—she might have come through last night, or might not.

I watched as Sullivan and Jorge silently pondered what they might do with ten thousand dollars. Five years' wages. They would leave me, certainly. I see it on their faces about María. I cannot explain the situation. No longer certain I know it myself.

That she was desperate remains unsaid; that she had everything to gain and nothing to lose also remains unsaid. That she is ten years my junior and beautiful; no one mentions that, either.

AUGUST 10, 1917

Car stolen. Barricaded in hotel room. Waiting for Phineas to wire money for a new vehicle. They now know Jorge's face and it is dangerous even for him to go outside. Strangely we see a European photographer walking around in the streets; no one seems to harass him in the slightest.

AUGUST 11, 1917

Phineas and my father apparently making calls: chief of police this morning brought a suitcase full of pesos and a 1911 Ford he is willing to sell. I point out that his price is the same as for a new Ford on a dealer lot. Sullivan and Jorge give me a look to shut the hell up.

Jorge's arm nearly torn off by the starter handle, but we get police escort out of town. They encourage us to make the most of our journey today, it being Sunday, as the people will be taking their leisure. No one seems to know anything about María.

AUGUST 13, 1917

Drove to San Antonio to talk to Pinkertons.

"You want us looking in every city in Mexico."

"Yes," I told him.

"That is impossible. It is financially impossible and it is logistically impossible. There is a war going on there."

"Give me a figure."

He put up his hands. "One hundred thousand dollars."

I didn't say anything.

"I am taking you at your word when you say you want us looking everywhere. There are ways to do it for a tenth as much."

"Will that get me the same result?"

"Either way, the result will likely be the same."

"Let's do it," I told him.

He looked at the desk. "Everyone knows your family, but . . ."

"My family is not to know a word about this."

"What I was getting at is that we will need the money up front, Mr. McCullough."

I took out the checkbook, the money I have been socking away for myself, all I have ever put aside. I thought: I will never be free if I write this.

"I can give you eighty thousand today. The rest I can bring you next week."

"Just so you know, you are wasting your money. Villa is still running around in the north, Carranza and

Óbregon have the middle, and Zapata has the south. Even if she is still . . . in good health, finding her will be extremely difficult."

"I am well aware of that."

I wrote the check. A drop of sweat smeared the numbers.

"Are you sure you want me to take this?" he said.

AUGUST 18, 1917

Sally asked when I was going to accept the reality of our situation. I told her I said prayers every day that she would roll her Packard into a ditch. She laughed and I pointed out I was not joking.

After she collected herself she said she was willing to spend only half the time here, and half in San Antonio, just for appearance's sake. I didn't answer.

This afternoon she returned to my office with a bottle of cold wine and two glasses. Admitted she had not been perfect, though I had not been either. She wants to start over. A second marriage, of sorts.

I told her I did not want her around, now or ever, that I would sooner lie with a rotting corpse.

"You were with the girl a month," she told me. "It is time to grow up."

"That is the only month I have ever been happy."

"Well what about the boys?" she said.

"The boys do not respect me. You have taught them that. You and my father."

She smashed the glasses and stood leaning in the doorway, as María used to do. After she left I looked at the jagged wineglass and wondered what it would be like to push it into her neck. Then I was nearly sick. Follow your footprints long enough and they will turn into those of a beast.

I think about María. I tell myself she was a luxury, like fruit out of season, lucky to have but temporary.

AUGUST 19, 1917

They have buried me alive.

Chapter Fifty-five
Eli McCullough

1865–1867

The best of the Texans were dead or had left the state and the ones who'd run things before the war came back. The cotton men wept about paying their slaves, but they kept their land and their Thoroughbreds and their big houses. There is more romance roping beefs than chopping cotton, but our state's reputation as a cattle kingdom is overboiled. Beef was always a poor cousin to the woolly plant and it was not until thirty years after Spindletop that even oil knocked King Cotton from his throne.

I moved back in with the judge but I could barely stand to be in town, with the better classes strutting around in carriages and the errant freedman or Unionist to be cut down from the trees every morning. It was more and more like the Old States, some neighbor's nose in all your business, who did you vote for and which was your church, and I considered buying a parcel along the caprock, where the frontier was still open, though the judge was dead set against it. I pointed out the Comanches were on their heels; it was just a matter of time. And we did not have to move there; I could simply buy it. But the judge reckoned the temptation would be too much, and he was likely correct, as I often sat on his smoking porch wondering about Nuukaru and Escuté and if I ought to ride out and find them. Likely they were already in the Misty Beyond, but had it not been for Everett I would have left Madeline all my money and lit off to find out.

It was an idle period. I put on a bloom and my pants got small and I developed a taste for nose paint I never shook. The judge encouraged me to find a regular job but I had money in the bank and I was determined to make it work for me—as it did for the better classes. I tried to buy back my father's headright, which was now well settled, but it had already been split into four parcels and the new owners wouldn't sell and all my other plans fizzled. My best days were behind me, that was plain.

Meanwhile, the judge thought the opposite. He had moved to Texas to watch it settle up, and now that he'd gotten his wish, he was planning a run for Senate. It was touchy business as Custer's troops were occupying the capital and no one knew what would happen when they left. The judge rolled the dice and announced on the Republican ticket, which his friends had counseled him against, though he would not hear them. He thought times were changing. A few weeks later he was found shot by the river.

Whatever had been left in me after Toshaway was buried along with the old ram. I refuted my kinship with other men. If anyone knew who did it, they were not saying, and I began to plot a campaign of murder among the Roberts, Runnels, and Wauls, felt the old holy fire begin to spark, but Madeline detected my plan and her words got the better of my judgment. The big house was sold and we moved to the farm at Georgetown. The slaves were now called servants and they worked on shares.

Madeline's mother and sister felt content to lie around crying about the judge, but so far as they were concerned my job was to sit on a pot-gutted horse watching the freedmen as they trudged up and down the rows of cotton. The days of high living were over; we survived on venison, side meat, and the holy trinity. But I was not content to see the great house fall. And I was not cut out to be an overseer. And the Comanche in me held grubbing in the dirt to be lower than hauling slops. And I wanted to make my money work.

For twenty-eight cents an acre I picked up sections in LaSalle and Dimmit Counties. I considered parcels on the coast but the Kings and Kenedys had already driven up the prices, and the Nueces Strip was rich, well watered, and so cheap I could acquire a proper acreocracy. There were bandits and renegades but I had never minded packing my gun loose, and in that part of the state a man with a rope could still catch as many wild cattle as he wanted, which sold for forty dollars a head if you could get them north. It was not panning for gold, but it was close, and I rode out to save the family's good name.

There were forty-eight souls in the entire county, the nearest being an old Mexican named Arturo Garcia. He had once owned most of the surrounding country but was down to two hundred sections, and the same day I met him he tried to outbid me on a four-section parcel that linked all my other pastures. My ranch was useless without it. I went to the commissioners' office and offered forty cents an acre, a gross overpayment, which they accepted.

"Happy to have you in the area," said the commissioner.

"Happy to be here."

"We are trying to move folks like Garcia out, if you know what I mean."

I looked at him. I was thinking I could have bid less for the land but he mistook my meaning.

"Not just because he's Mexican. My wife is Mexican, in fact. I mean because he associates with known thieves."

"That is interesting knowledge."

"I'm guessin' you got a gun?"

" 'Course I do."

"Well, I wouldn't stray too far from it."

I would like to say otherwise, but this only convinced me I had come to the right place.

Chapter Fifty-six
J.A. McCullough

Once again she was a fool, they all knew it, even Milton Bryce. Domestic oil was a dead end, you lost money on every barrel you pumped. But she had a feeling. That was what she told them. Then she put it out of her mind. It was the biggest bet of her life and she was at peace.

She was happy with Ted, she was happy with her children, they were all doing well, even Susan and Thomas. Ben had finished at the top of his class and gone off to A&M. He did not care much for sports but he was conspicuously bright, interested in others, a good listener, the opposite of his siblings, who seemed to believe they had some special arrangement with fate (Susan) or were barely aware of anything outside themselves at all (Thomas). Susan had survived a single semester at Oberlin before moving to California; she would be unreachable for months and then the phone would ring at three A.M. and there she was, asking for some outrageous sum of money. Though she seemed happy. Jeannie would agree to the sum and Susan would tell of her adventures. As for Thomas, the oldest, he continued to live in her house. She was happier about this than she liked to admit, she knew she ought to push him out, but—his eccentricity—it seemed better for him to be close to home. There was the example of Phineas, but Thomas was not him.

Thomas was content to live with his mother and she was content to have him, he had a car, a large allowance, trips with his friends. He'd been a gorgeous child and it had ruined him; even now he expected to be the center of things. A man in love with his own face, that was how Ted put it, and she supposed she couldn't blame him, he really did look like a young Peter O'Toole, the fact of which he was enormously proud, so much so that she was often tempted to point out that Peter O'Toole did not live with his mother.

As for his eccentricity, he hid it so well that she sometimes wondered if she were mistaken, though other times she was certain, and scared, and waiting for him to be caught in public. In truth, there was not much to be worried about. Everyone knew Tom McCullough, and Texans were good at ignoring things they didn't want to see, it was a leftover from the frontier days when you couldn't choose your neighbors.

Yes, her children were happy. It was a real pack, even Susan. These were good years. And perhaps because of this she continued to unwind her properties, to undiversify, she sold the steel company and the insurance company she had bought with Hank, most of the real estate, she plowed it all into oil, domestic acreage, which everyone was happy to sell her. It happened so easily she sometimes wondered if she was walking into her own suicide—financial suicide, at least—which would leave her family greatly diminished.

She wondered if it was the same liberated feeling that allowed her father to blow his inheritance on the ranch. Though her father was an actual fool. This was something else. She had gone touring around the Middle East with Cass Rutherford and while he found nothing amiss, in fact he thought things were getting better— the infrastructure, the competence of their drillers and geologists—she found the whole thing disturbing. Twenty years earlier, it had been men on camels. Now it was housing blocks, trash everywhere, people staring you down on every street corner. That was the problem with television—everyone saw what you were taking— what these Arabs saw was rich foreigners buying up their oil at ten cents on the dollar. By the end of the trip, she felt so corrupt and depressed that she'd considered getting out of the business altogether.

After a few weeks at home she came to her senses, but the uneasy feeling remained. Something was going to happen and the overthrow of Mosaddegh was a miracle unlikely to ever be repeated. And so she had begun to look at domestic acreage. She was a fool, though later they would call it women's intuition, though it was not, it was just a question of seeing what was actually in front of you, instead of what you wanted to see.

Oil went nowhere. Then Bunker Hunt bet big in Libya and got massacred and the Egyptians went into Israel and the embargo hit. The boom had lasted ten years. And still this dissatisfaction. She had won her bet but they would not recognize her. *They* being . . . she was not sure. The world? Her dead father and brothers and husband? *You expect a medal,* she thought. And she did. It was not entirely unreasonable, some notice from the other operators, a bit of recognition, a mention of her alongside the Richardsons and Basses and Murchisons, the Hunts. She was certain— ragingly certain—that if Hank had pulled off what she had, his name would have been included. Maybe she had a victim complex. That's what they wanted her to think.

She focused on her home life, maybe for the first time ever. Here was her medal: a happy house, happy children. Ben and Thomas and all their friends, who, like them, had gotten exceptions from the draft. They made her house their own, drinking and swimming at all hours, it was like being an older sister, young people drunk in the kitchen, drunk in the yard, they would tell her their problems.

Then, quick as that, as if a single twig had been holding it all up, it was over. Ben was down at the ranch; his truck went into a bar ditch. Milton Bryce had gone with her to see him—he did not look himself, she was not sure how, he had only a single black eye—they had parted his hair wrong—she walked out of the room and they had handed her something sweet—a Coke?—and then she was thinking of her brothers and then she remembered nothing.

They had buried him and then nothing more was expected, she had sat down in the old familiar house and everything became gauzy and unreachable. She had allowed, in some far corner of her mind, that something might happen to Thomas or Susan—their judgment was terrible, the risks—but Ben had been the linchpin, the steady soul. And if he . . . she had a feeling she would lose them all. She had failed in some fundamental way. They had been right about her all along.

Thomas also seemed to sense this, to sense that his brother's death was her fault, that there was some power she had failed to exert, over the driving habits of young men, or the sharp curve in the road, or the bar ditch that flipped the truck. One day he went out and never came back. Susan called to say that he'd arrived in California; he'd driven all night. Gone forever, as it turned out. She sold the house in River Oaks and moved in with Ted.

She could admit it was different from losing her husband. She knew she would survive, she knew she would recover, *do not take this as a lesson,* Jonas told her, but she did, she had expected too much, and if it was not a lesson, then what was the point?

Even if God existed, to say he loved the human race was preposterous. It was just as likely the opposite; it was just as likely he was systematically deceiving us. To think that an all-powerful being would make a world for anyone but himself, that he might spend all his time looking out for the interests of lesser creatures, it went against all common sense. The strong took from the weak, only the weak believed otherwise, and if God was out there, he was just as the

Greeks and Romans had suspected; a trickster, an older brother who spent all his time inventing ways to punish you.

She was bitter, Ben had changed her, first for the better and then for the worse, she was furious and defeated, when she was not too low she assembled a vast dissertation, praise from various figures, approval from the Colonel, success in business, the covers of magazines, her marriage and worthy lovers and her saving of the McCullough name, it buoyed her for a time, it held her above the darkness, but always, always, she plunged. None of it mattered.

The boom continued. *Time* magazine came around again: now she was the woman who'd predicted the embargo. Incidentally, was she a feminist? No? Back on the cover she went, not entirely defeated, though it was not the same, not the same. A publisher approached her about a memoir, something inspirational for other people, women, they meant, your life story, the way you think and solve problems, something for the young to take inspiration from, though likely they meant housewives.

But what would she say? That the Colonel had been right? That you could only depend on yourself? It would not exactly fill a book. She tried anyway, and for a time a dream came back to her from youth, sitting behind a desk, answering letters from all her subjects, the cameras lingering on her every word, she wrote about her father and two brothers and the mother she had never known, her husband and son, where should she stop, children in the graveyard, the dead pouring forth until she set the papers aside. She knew why the Colonel had hated talking about the old days. Because the moment you looked back, and began to make your tally, you were done for.

By '83 there were wildcatters going bankrupt left and right, but for Ted and most of their friends, the boom had been nothing more than a period of unusual wealth, in which the royalty checks they all lived on had been preposterous instead of merely large.

Jonas was fine, frugal as always; no belt tightening necessary. He still commuted down to Boston a few days a week in his old Volvo, maybe from Martha's Vineyard, maybe from Newport, maybe from his lake house in Maine, though if he really did anything at his legal practice, she didn't know. Mostly he seemed to wake up at the same time every morning, spending hours writing lists of what needed to be done: *winterize boat, paint railings on porch* (he considered himself handy), *call about Volvo noise, Bill squash (racquet), porch screens, tuition, Bohemian Club, reservations at . . .* He got great satisfaction crossing things off his list; sometimes he would write things he had already done (*breakfast with Jeannie*) just to cross them off again.

She considered selling the ranch, keeping the house but selling the land, she had no family left in Texas; in Midland you could buy a Rolls-Royce or office building or even a Boeing for pennies on the dollar, there wouldn't be work in the oil business for a long time, that was clear. It was time to sell. There was no point being so far from her only living brother and her children.

She and Ted were at the ranch, fighting about this very thing (one did not sell land, he thought), when Consuela came to tell her there was someone at the door.

It was a Mexican woman around her own age, wearing a dress and jewelry as if expected for a party. Jeannie hadn't yet showered that day; she brushed back her hair and smoothed her blouse and felt short.

"I am Adelina Garcia."

This meant nothing.

"I am Peter McCullough's daughter."

This meant nothing as well. Then it did. She reached for the doorknob.

"Peter McCullough did not have any daughters," she said. "I'm afraid you are mistaken."

"He is my father," the woman repeated.

When Jeannie didn't react, the woman got an imperious look. "You are my niece," she said. "Regardless of our ages."

Maybe it was the language barrier, but she could not have picked a worse thing to say. "Well you have met me. And I am busy." Jeannie closed the door. The woman stood on the porch a long time then walked slowly back to her car. Jeannie wondered how she'd gotten through the gate.

It was an old trick. Though usually you heard about it through a lawyer. Still, she felt unsettled, and back in the library, she lost all her strength and collapsed against Ted. He leaned around her to see the television.

"Anyone important?"

She felt sick; something told her to follow the woman but she could not make herself get up.

"What do you want to eat?" he said.

"That was a Mexican person claiming to be my relative."

"Your very first?"

She nodded.

"Welcome to the club."

She sat there.

"Call Milton Bryce," he said, not looking up from the television. It was *Dallas.* People were obsessed with it. "Call him right now if you're really worried about it."

But she was not sure that was she was worried in that way. She decided to think about it. She waited until dinner and decided it was nothing.

What else might she have been? She had plenty of friends from old families who were always carrying on about how helpless they were, no driver's licenses or social security cards, the worst sort of bragging, they were helpless, absolutely helpless, and proud of it.

The things that made them happy meant nothing to her. She was a leftover from another time, maybe, like her great-grandfather. But even that was not true. She was not like him at all. She'd had no imagination, she'd chased only what she could see, she could have done more.

She had a feeling she ought to apologize, but to whom, and for what, she didn't know. She looked around the room. It was still dark. When it finally happens, she thought, I won't even know it, and then she wasn't afraid.

Chapter Fifty-seven
Ulises Garcia

There had always been a rumor that they were descended from wealthy Americans, it was a story his mother liked to tell about his father's side of the family. His father had died when he was two. The Dirty War was going on, and the last anyone heard of his father, he was being taken into a police station.

After that, they had moved around a lot, finally settling in Tamaupilas with his grandparents. His grandfather worked on a ranch, tending the fences, repairing the windmills and outbuildings, more time on a truck than on a horse, but this is what vaqueros did now. In America, the cowboys now flew helicopters. Or so it was said.

His grandfather had worked for the Arroyos his entire life and was no richer now than when he started;

the Arroyos had owned the land since the 1600s and paid as if no time had passed since. Sitting at the fire with the old-timers, he could see his entire life from birth to death, it was good work, he was lucky to be born into it; his friends would end up in the refineries, or selling trinkets to tourists, or with the narcos.

Still, there were nights he woke up thinking he was as old as his grandfather, he would turn on the light and go to the mirror and look at his face. He was dark, people thought he was mulatto, he had a soft nose and a heavy brow.

In winter the men would trickle back from the north with thousands of dollars in their pockets and some would blow it all—a season's work—in a night or two of gambling. His grandfather just shrugged. Mercedes Arroyo would spend three thousand dollars on a scarf, what was the difference?

As for Ulises, he watched the Arroyos' pretty grand-daughters come and go, their drivers and BMWs; when they passed he smelled perfume from inside the cars. The house was full of stuffed jaguars and elephants, exotic rugs, bathrooms done in gold, but he'd only heard this; he'd never been allowed inside.

His mother went to work in Matamoros and he stayed with his grandparents. One day he was going through a suitcase she had left, which was full of her junk, old pictures and keys, birthday cards from people he didn't know, letters, faded receipts, his father's university ID, and then, in its own paper bag . . . his grandmother's birth certificate. The document was in Spanish but the name of the father was not: Peter McCullough. And there were letters written in English.

He knew that his grandmother had tried to get in touch with the American side of her family, but they had spurned her, and then his father had tried as well, and also been sent away, and he could not imagine how the McCulloughs (he now knew their name) had done this. He tried to imagine their point of view, a person showing up on your doorstep and asking for money. The details mattered; it would have to be handled a certain way.

He began to daydream about visiting them, and being received, and given land, and made wealthy. Of course they would not simply do this for no reason; he would show them that he knew cattle, he knew their business, he was not simply some freeloader, he was a hard worker, and then, once he had proven himself beyond question, he would make a formal presentation.

Those daydreams had gone on for several years; they were straight out of a telenovela and he was not clear when they had materialized into a firm plan. But in September of 2011, he crossed the river and rode onto the McCulloughs' ranch. His grandfather knew someone on an olive plantation on the Mexican side, just a few miles upriver from the ranch, and he and this old man had waited for a dark night and crossed. After that it was easy. He was not some pollo, he was a vaquero, and he belonged.

He found the white foreman and offered to give up his hand-tooled saddle if any bronco in their remuda could throw him. The foreman burst into laughter, then explained they did not have any broncs in the remuda, it had probably been half a century since they had broncs. They did their big roundups with helicopters and bought most of their horses as three-year-olds from other ranches.

But he could see the foreman was impressed with his appearance, he had not thrown Ulises off the ranch immediately, he'd carefully inspected his tack, his chaps. Ulises threw a few loops for him, caught a calf by the neck and then the foreleg. *I roped an eagle in flight once*, he said. It was not exactly true—it had been a turkey. But he could see the man liked his face. *I can also use a welder.*

He spent the rest of the day in the man's truck, helping with chores, repairing a fence, running a tractor with a bale spike. At the end of it, the man said:

"Two fifty a week. *La Migra* mostly stays off the property, but if you stick your nose out and get caught you'll spend a few months in the pokey. Normally we'd never do this but we are shorthanded and getting shorter."

He noted this, but decided not to ask why.

"If you're still here after a few months, we can talk about applying for a permit. Though none of us are sure if this place will even be around that long. I lost two guys this week alone. So if you've got other prospects, I suggest you follow them."

His salary was not much by *norteamericano* standards but he had nothing to spend it on. On smaller ranches the ICE agents came and went daily but the McCulloughs kept their own security and *La Migra* was rarely around. It was dangerous to leave the property, though: the white-and-green trucks were everywhere; it was a bit like being under house arrest.

He had a bunk and a few nails to hang his shirts. When he wasn't working he sat around watching TV with the other vaqueros. When they wouldn't let him watch the American programs—they did not care about their English—he borrowed a rifle and went out into the *brasada* and shot an occasional javelina or rabbit, or trailed the big-racked deer that were everywhere.

They were too valuable to kill; the Americans would pay thousands to shoot them.

He snuck to town once a month and sent his grandparents half his salary and bought a new shirt, though he had to ask for the hanger it came on. At Christmas he spent a long time looking at some Lucchese handmade boots but decided on Ariats, as they were a quarter the price. He also picked out a Leatherman tool. He felt rich. Then a white man with a gun walked into the store and everyone got quiet. Some kind of deputy. Ulises stood by the cash register, waited for his items to be bagged, watching the man's reflection in the window. He felt disgusted as he walked out. He paused near the trash bin, considered throwing away everything he'd just bought. It could not be worth this.

It will be better when you get your permit, said Romero, when they were back in the truck. *No estoy recibiendo mi permiso,* said Ulises, but Romero pretended not to hear. He had worked for the McCulloughs five years but still got stopped by the ICE, who pretended not to recognize him. Ulises could see the pride he took in the new white truck, though it was not his any more than the ranch was, and it struck him that Romero was a fool and he was a fool as well.

————

The old lady was dying and had no one to take over the business. Her daughter was a drug addict and her son, it was said, was not fully a man. There had been a grandson everyone liked, but he had drowned in three feet of water. The other grandson visited the ranch with his friends: they wore sandals and never shaved and were constantly smoking *mota*. One look and you knew why the vaqueros were leaving. This place would die with the old lady.

His plan was ridiculous. The old lady rarely visited the ranch and the foreman, who was likely looking for another job himself, forgot his promise to apply for a permit. But still it was better than the Arroyos. So he stayed.

Chapter Fifty-eight
Diaries of Peter McCullough

SEPTEMBER 1, 1917

The shadow follows me everywhere; I see him in the corner at supper, biding his time; he stands behind me as I sit at my desk. As if a great fire were burning in front of me. I imagine reaching for it . . . letting the flames carry me off.

I ride to the casa mayor and put my ear to the rock. I hear the bell of the church, children calling, women's shoes.

A memory from the day after the killings:

My father postulating, absentmindedly, that María's survival was a kind of tragedy. Had she died, all the Garcias' anger and sadness would have disappeared from the earth. His words have become a moving picture, playing over and over in my mind. I imagine putting a revolver to his head while he sleeps. I imagine the well shooter parking his truck next to the house, setting a match to the nitro bottles.

Of course this has always been inside me. It was only waiting for a moment to escape. There is nothing wrong with my father: he is the natural. The problem is those like myself, who hoped we might rise from our instinctive state. Who hoped to go beyond our nature.

SEPTEMBER 4, 1917

It came to me this morning: she is dead. I paced my room but then I was sure of it, she is dead, I have never been so sure of anything in my life.

My father came to find me in my office.

"You know I am sorry," he said. "You know it hurts me to see you like this."

I didn't respond. I have not spoken a word to him since that day.

"There are responsibilities," he told me. "We don't just get to act like normal people."

Still I ignored him. He walked around my office, looking at my shelves.

"All right, partner. I'll leave you alone."

He came forward, raised his hand to put it on my shoulder, but something in my face . . .

"It will get better," he told me.

He stood there another minute like that. Then I heard him shuffle down the hall.

Of course in person . . . the idea of hurting him is repulsive. Because, unlike him, I am weak. He did not mind trading a wife and a few sons to get what he wanted . . . each of us walks in his own fire for his own sins, lies down in his own torment. Mine the sin of fear, timidity . . . I might have carried María away from this place . . . it did not even occur to me. Held by the chains of my own mind.

My sun has set, the journeying ways have darkened. The rest of my life hangs above me like a weight; I remind myself that my heart for a brief time ran feral . . . my most preposterous thoughts came true.

Perhaps another great ice will come and grind all this into dust. Leaving no trace of our existence, as even fire does.

SEPTEMBER 6, 1917

Sally continues to make overtures. As if I will simply forget what she has done. It is only because I no longer defer to her that she is interested in my company. Today she asked if I would continue looking for María. Then she asked, *Would you look for me if I disappeared?* She is baffled. She did not see María as entirely human; she does not see herself as having done anything wrong. Like stays with like—that is her only principle.

I content myself to think that one day we will all be nothing but marks in stone. Iron stains of blood, black of our carbon, a hardening clay.

SEPTEMBER 7, 1917

This family must not be allowed to continue.

Chapter Fifty-nine
Eli McCullough

In 1521 a dozen Spanish cattle were landed in the New World; by 1865 there were four million living wild in Texas alone. They did not take to domestication; they would happily stick a horn through you and go back to chewing grass. Your average hayseed avoided them as he might a grizzly bear.

But they could not help being herd animals. Once you had a big enough bunch even the mossy horns would fall in. Starting from nothing it might take a year to build your brand, roping and cutting and marking seven days a week, and if you weren't gored or trampled there was always a neighbor who found it more enjoyable to spend that same year grinning up at the sun; all he had to do was come into your pastures one night with ten of his boon companions, where, in a few hours, he could take your entire year's work and make it his.

For room, board, and a sliver of the future profits, I hired two former confederates, John Sullivan and Milton Emory, along with Todd Myrick and Eben Hunter, who had spent the war dodging the Home Guard in Maverick and Kinney Counties. They knew the land better than I and were not allergic to sweat or blood. All knew Arturo Garcia and hated him, but as it was common to dislike Mexicans in those days, I did not think anything of it.

You began a cattle drive owing your hands a year's back wages and after borrowing money from everyone you knew. The brutes were gently walked and allowed to graze and drink at will, so they would not drop even an ounce of weight. They were treated as precious eggs. Meanwhile, a storm might cost you half the herd.

The life of the cowboy has been written about as if it were the pinnacle of freedom in the West but in fact it was a sleepless drudgery almost beyond imagination— five months of slavery to a pack of dumb brutes—and had I not been riding for my own brand I would not have lasted a day. The fact the country was tame enough to drive valuable property across tells you all you need to know; the days of Bridger and Carson and Smith were long gone, the land was already going domestic.

We lost two of the thirty-dollar men when their horses went off a cliff in the dark. The others we released in Kansas. They were happy to see the big city and look for other work; they had more money in their pockets than they'd ever seen. On 1,437 head I cleared $30,000 and two hundred Indian ponies no one wanted. We drove the ponies back down the Chisholm and I stopped in Georgetown to see the family while Sullivan, Myrick, Emory, and Hunter took the ponies back to the Nueces.

Madeline was still living on the farm with Everett, Phineas, and Pete. Her mother, still a known beauty, had remarried and there were dining room servants again.

We were in the kitchen in the sun. The money was in the bank and I was happy to be home, happy to be looking at my pretty wife. She had a white hair among the red ones on her head. I leaned and kissed it.

She smacked her hand there. "Is it one of the gray ones?"

"More white," I said.

She sighed. "Now you're going to miss me even less."

I kissed her again.

"Do you miss me?"

"Of course."

"Sometimes I'm not sure if you even like me."

"That is crazy," I said, though I knew what she meant.

"I mean, I know you like the idea of me. But I am not sure you like the thing itself."

"I love you."

"Of course you do. But that is different than liking me."

It was quiet.

"The year before last, when we were all together here, I still think about that. I don't want another bite of venison in my life but when I think about it, it was the happiest time I've ever had."

"We were broke," I said. "There was no future in it."

"Well, one day I'll be dead. There is no future in that, either."

I looked at her with the sun coming in and her elbows on the whitewashed table. Her hair went softly over her shoulders and I looked at that and her red lips and high cheeks and pale chest still heavy under her dress. I thought any man would be happy to have her in any way he could.

"Let's go to the bedroom," I said.

She gave me a tired smile. "Okay," she said.

Then I was looking at her in the white sheets. Her eyes were closed.

"I needed that."

"Me too," I told her.

She shook her head. "You don't need anything." She pushed the sheets off herself and lay there in the sun. I ran my fingers up and down.

"If you keep doing that I am going to want you again."

I kept on but I wondered what was wrong with me. She saw and crawled over and took me into her mouth. I wondered how or where she had learned it. Then I was ready again. As we were doing it I almost told her that if she had to do it with someone else I wouldn't care but then I changed my mind again. I tried to slip off but she held me where I was.

"Ten years from now we'll have the biggest house in Austin."

"And then you'll come back from the middle of nowhere?"

"Yes." I kissed her on the neck.

"I think you like the middle of nowhere."

"I like people, I just don't know how to make money where they live."

"Well, soon you won't have to."

"Soon I won't."

"That's right," she said.

When I got back to the ranch Todd Myrick was dead in the yard and Eben Hunter was on the porch. They had been there for days. I went looking for Sullivan and Emory. In the lower pasture were more buzzards and by his lathyness I realized the man I was looking at was Emory.

Sullivan was at the Brackett army post. He had been shot through the lung but he had lived this long, and they were optimistic. He was a big man with a strange high voice he would pass along to his son. I asked him how he was feeling but he did not want to talk about that.

"It's a real piece of pudding how we were gone five months, then happened to get visited right when we got back," he said.

"And expecting us to have a wallet of money from a cattle sale."

The thieves had pried up the floorboards and tore the cupboard off the wall but there had not been any money. I had put it in the bank.

"A thinking man would allot upon your Mexican neighbor." He had to breathe awhile. "The buckras here paid him a visit, but it did as much good as a dog smelling his own piss."

"We get any of them?"

He looked out the window and I knew I shouldn't have asked.

"All I care about is you keep breathin'."

"Emory got a couple shots off. That boy was always quick."

I offered my handkerchief but instead he took my hand and held it. My throat got thick. I was thinking about the others. Then it was quiet.

Sullivan let go of my hand and took my bandanna. "I'm not leavin' this county without naturalizing at least a few of them. I wondered if you might stake me until then."

I spent the day burying Emory, Myrick, and Hunter. Then I went to see Arturo Garcia.

He lived in a big white house that looked like a fortress of old. There was a long covered porch around the front and he came out to greet me. Through the open door I could see the house was filled with gold-framed paintings and weapons, furniture of the sort kings owned.

He was sorry for my loss. By some miracle his stock and horses had not been touched. I wanted to ride his fences and look for my two hundred Indian ponies, but I knew they had already gone to Old Mexico.

"What bamboozles me," I said, "is to get to my pastures, they must have passed pretty close to your house. Unless they wanted to ride twenty miles around. And to get my stock out, they had to lead them through your pastures again. Which is obvious because the tracks are all still there."

"It is big country, Eli. I am sorry."

"They also knew within a day that we'd got back."

"Eli, I will say this once, because I know you are upset, but the fact that I live on the border, and am Mexican, does not mean I had anything to do with stealing your horses, or killing your men."

"I didn't say it did."

A young white man came out of the house wearing bright yellow trousers and a blue silk shirt. His boots were spit shined and he had a pistol on each hip. He looked like a stage actor, an easterner's impression of a badman. "Jim Fisher," he said. "Very sorry for your loss, sir."

Then other men were coming from the pastures. I took my leave and spent a few nights sleeping in the brush, far from my house, thinking it over.

There were no other neighbors, no roads going in or out.

Let me say that Garcia being Mexican had nothing to do with it. White or Mexican, the bigger a rancher was, the more liable he was to run his neighbors out. Your slice of pie is one less I can eat myself, that was his attitude, and for every orphan he helped in public there were ten he made in private.

Garcia had lost half his estate. That the state had stole his land I do not deny. But I had nothing to do with it and furthermore he was not the first to have lost it. He figured there was nothing I could do. I would dig out sooner or later.

Except I was not playing a lone hand. There was a twisting *barranca* to climb from his back pasture, where the walls were steep and you could only ride single file, a place where two men with ten-shot Winchesters, if they were patient, might stop any number of others. When Garcia died he was speaking in a language that was not English or Spanish or even Comanche, it was like nothing I had ever heard. Still, I understood him. He thought he was cursing me but it was nothing I didn't know already.

When Sullivan healed to ride the distance we hired a half-dozen sympathetics and drove Garcia's horses and cattle to New Mexico. Every unmarked calf and colt we drove into my pastures. I should have burned that house then, and salted the earth, because a year later, his nephew came and picked up where his uncle had left off.

Chapter Sixty
J.A. McCullough

To lie around and do nothing but think—if you'd asked her yesterday she might have wanted a year of it; now all she wanted was to get up. It was bright again in the room, the sun was coming in, but something was wrong: tables and chairs had been flung, pictures were off the walls, busts and pedestals scattered about. Aphrodite was facedown in the corner. The roof would fall in and animals would build their nests.

I am not really seeing this, she thought. She decided to ignore it. She decided to be glad to be in this room, the one place her father hadn't had the gumption to redecorate, he had filled the rest of the house with Remingtons and Russells and Bierstadts. But the Colonel would not have abided that. For him, this was what success looked like: dark wood, old sculpture,

Eastern money. Which was trying to look like European money. Of course that had changed. The Italians now made movies about cowboys.

Even before the boom ended she had begun to diversify again, oil was overheated, every housewife in Midland was driving a Bentley. Along with most everyone she knew, she got into the savings-and-loan business. The S&Ls had been deregulated, allowed to loan money in commercial real estate, oil, and gas, the ceiling had been removed on the interest that could be paid to depositors. She bought a small one, offered high rates to attract depositors, then used the money for real estate projects in Houston and Dallas, taking a ludicrous up-front fee. But then real estate crashed along with oil, and Southsun was bailed out, which she felt guilty about, though not so guilty she wanted to lose the hundred million dollars herself. She thought she might have to testify in Washington, but she didn't.

Meanwhile Thomas was making plans to come out to all his old friends, to everyone he'd known in Houston, she had discouraged him, she had relentlessly discouraged him, there was not a single bit of upside to his plan. He would only be making things harder on himself. He never saw those people anyway.

"Why should I have to hide who I am?" he said.

She was so surprised she couldn't think of anything to say. He was finally standing up for himself, she ought to support him. And yet, she was not sure, it was a cry for attention—to identify yourself in public by what you did in your most private moments—it was wrong, entirely wrong, he ought to look to Phineas, who had taken the world in his fist and crushed it.

She had made some error. Neither of her children had any confidence, they were both muddle-headed, Susan in her addiction to gurus and therapists, Thomas in his liberal politics, his insistence on coming out. They could not seem to grasp that what mattered was what you did. Not what you said or thought about.

The coming-out had been a nonevent. She had sensed his confusion, she had felt terrible for him, he had thought it would be important, a pivotal moment, but nothing had changed, he was the same person.

It was not fair of her. She did not know what he'd been through. She had begun to wonder again if it was her fault, both her children had become unhappy, she guessed because neither one had ever engaged in any meaningful endeavor. She had flown to see them, a formal proposal, a few million each, or twenty, whatever they needed, whatever they wanted to do—a gallery for Thomas, a vineyard for Susan—there was no reason to start small. They were confused. She had always left them alone. And then they saw. They understood. She considered them failures, she considered them trivial, she was trying to save them from themselves.

By then Susan had two young boys, Jeannie barely saw them, it was as if her daughter, without ever hinting at it, knew this was the only war she might ever win with her mother. But then Susan's boyfriend, father to neither of the two children, ran off somewhere and Susan was calling to ask if she might move to Texas, though she didn't actually mean that, what she meant was could her mother look after the children while she went off to hunt another man.

Jeannie was delighted, though she tried not to show it. The boys were six and eight, but had little recollection of ever meeting her. Ash was pale and blond, Dell a pure Spaniard; they looked like exactly what they were, boys with different fathers. She loved them. They had not seen the ranch since they were very small and she took them over it in a helicopter, the vast kingdom, they were its princes.

"One day this will belong to the two of you," she said.

"Mother," said Susan.

"One day this will all be yours."

She loved the boys. They sat there in front of the television, she bought a few tame ponies they enjoyed riding, but in general both were possessed by a clumsiness, a wariness, as if the physical world were conspiring against them. She could not help comparing them to her brothers, even to Ben and Thomas. It was likely an illusion. It was likely her failing memory. She loved them anyway; sitting there on the couch watching jangling cartoons, she forgave Susan everything she had ever done.

But the slackening. By five she and her brothers were throwing loops. By ten she was at the branding fire. Her grandchildren were not good at anything and did not have much interest in anything either. She wondered if the Colonel would even recognize them as his descendants, felt briefly defensive for them, but of course it was true. Something was happening to the entire human race.

That is what all old people think, she decided.

She took them on walks for as long as they would put up with her, *this is a javelina track, this is a deer track, that is a green jay. That is a kettle of buzzards and there is where a rabbit has been making his run and here is where a hawk ate a woodpecker.*

When the first men arrived, she told them, there were mammoths, giant buffalo, giant horses, saber-toothed tigers, and giant bears. The American cheetah—the only animal on earth that could outrun a pronghorn antelope.

Her grandsons listened politely. Maybe they sensed where the story was going; where all her stories went. The American cheetah had disappeared and antelopes had gotten slower—the laggards got to keep breeding. People had become slower as well.

They went inside to watch television. She sat on the gallery alone. McCullough land, as far as the eye could see. There was no reference. There was the Colonel of course, but what kind of man had it taken to thrust a spear into a twenty-thousand-pound animal? The bears were twice the size of a modern grizzly, they must have died horrible deaths, as many words for courage as an Eskimo had for snow. For suffering as well. *That is who we came from,* she thought.

They'd left nothing but tracks and bones. In Australia, frozen into rock, there were the footprints of three people crossing a mudflat. At twenty-seven miles per hour—all three moving as fast as the fastest man on earth today. They were speeding up when the tracks ended.

———

What should she tell her grandchildren? There were too many facts and you could arrange them in any order you wanted. Eli McCullough had killed Indians. Eli McCullough had killed whites. He had killed, period. It depended on whether you saw things through his eyes or the eyes of his victim as he pulled the trigger. Dead people did not have voices and this made them irrelevant.

She didn't know. Perhaps he had sown the seeds of his own ruination. He'd provided for all of them, and they'd become soft, they'd become people he never would have respected.

Of course you wanted your children to have it better than you had. But at what point was it not better at all? People needed something to worry about or they would destroy themselves, and she thought of her grandchildren and all the grandchildren yet to come.

Chapter Sixty-one
Ulises Garcia

The ranch made all its money from oil and gas, and the men from those companies were always driving around checking the wells and tanks and pumps. They were mostly white and their soda cans were always found along the roads. The vaqueros did not care for them and every time they saw a piece of surveyor tape marking some turn, they would stop to cut it down.

But the work was not bad; there was something to be said for air-conditioning when you wanted it, and the money, compared to Mexico, was unbelievable. In late January he'd gone to a rodeo with the other vaqueros, all of whom had work permits. They had been reluctant to take him—a truck full of Mexicans was a prime target and if they were caught they would lose their permits—but he pretended not to notice their hesitation. He quickly realized that three-quarters of the men in the competitions did not live or work on ranches—they competed at rodeos for fun.

He and Fernando got third in the team roping; he was going to collect his ten dollars when he saw a pair of ICE men talking to the promoter. He walked the other way. He waited in the brush outside the parking lot and watched for Fernando and the others to come out.

No one spoke on the ride home. It was no small thing to have a work permit; even being around them, he was putting them in jeopardy.

He was going stir-crazy. He could not even leave the ranch. One Sunday he rode up to the old Garcia place; it was just crumbling walls now, but it had once been a big house, a fortress even. There was still a spring running nearby, and trees and shade, and a view. He entered the ruins of the house and knew instantly, felt in his gut, that his people had lived here. Though Garcia was not exactly an uncommon name.

A truck came up the road, and he slipped out of the ruins and considered hiding; he felt as if he were doing something wrong. Though of course he was not. He might be trailing a lost cow.

The man who got out of the truck was short and baggy, old pants and an old shirt and thick glasses, the look of a person who spent all his time alone. The other hands had mentioned that Mrs. McCullough was paying someone to write a history of the ranch. He had never met a writer, but he thought this man looked like one, like he had not washed his hair or his glasses in a long time. Ulises introduced himself.

"I like to come up here and eat lunch," said the man. He seemed embarrassed to be breathing. "It's about the best view on the property, plus"—he indicated the spring—"it's nice to be near water."

After they had been sitting and talking, Ulises asked: "So what happened to the people who used to live here?"

"They were killed."

"Who killed them?"

"The McCulloughs. Who else?"

Chapter Sixty-two
Diaries of Peter McCullough

SEPTEMBER 15, 1917

Feel my heart growing moderate. An even worse punishment. The might-have-beens filling in my years.

I think of my son's wounding, his near-death, as an excuse for other deaths. Both my children in some barracks, waiting to be sent overseas. This house nothing more than a mausoleum. Just in recorded history the polestar has changed four times. . . . yet men insist we will endure on this earth.

SEPTEMBER 18, 1917

Went out to help the vaqueros check the fences after last night's rain. In an arroyo, sticking out of the bank, I found a bone so ancient it had completely turned to stone; it rang like steel when I struck it.

SEPTEMBER 20, 1917

Ab Jefferson at Pinkerton came by today in person. Pretended it was a social call. We went for a drive and he informed me that in Guadalajara there are three possible María Garcias, all recent arrivals. Gave three addresses.

I had to pull the car over. He patted me on the back.

"It's one of the most common names in Mexico, Pete. They are probably farm girls."

"It's a start," I said.

"Do you want me to send someone?"

"No," I said.

Wrote letters to each of them, begging them to take me back. Lay on the sofa all day. The shadow is no longer standing over me. He has retreated to one of the corners.

Chapter Sixty-three
Eli McCullough

Early 1870s

Beef was up four straight years but in '73, with the economy falling over, most went back to killing steers for hides.

I would not allow it. By then I owned 118 sections in fee simple with another 70 on lease. I held my stock. Our losses we kept to a minimum as we shot any mounted rider inside our fences. It was all according to Gunter.

Those afoot we let pass: it can never be said I denied an honest man his day's work. It was known in Carrizo that any man who found his family short rations could entitle himself to one of my calves, so long as he left me the hide. Only bullets and walls make for honest neighbors and a single night in my pastures would net any rustler a year's wages, a year of my own life. If they had built a cow-proof fence between us and the river . . .

There are plenty of old pistols still to be found in the brush country. Bone rots faster than iron. It was all according to Gunter.

Madeline and the children had moved to a big house in Austin. The children had schools and tutors and I would have sooner burned the ranch than had them out to it, though Madeline had been asking for a proper house on the Nueces, so that we could all live together. I put it off. There were no schools. And she would not have cottoned to our treatment of fence crossers.

One day a black mood came over me for no reason, I was ornery as a snake and could not stand for anyone to look at me. I went off by myself. I guessed it was the heat.

The next morning they were shouting it in the streets: Quanah Parker and the last of the Comanches had surrendered. There were barely a thousand left on earth—the same number that had lived in Toshaway's village—and now the whole of Texas was open to the white man. I told Madeline I needed time alone, saddled my horse and went up the Colorado. I was riding and riding, but no matter how far I got there were hog callers and boatmen. I rode well into the night until finally it was quiet. I climbed a ledge and built a fire and howled out to the wolves. But nothing howled back.

That I had done wrong was plain. I was not thick enough to believe I might have saved the ponies from Ranald Mackenzie's troopers, but you could never say for certain. A single man can make a difference.

I thought how I might have gone back to the *Numunuu* when the war started. It hit me that fifteen years had passed since. I could not believe it; I could barely name a thing I'd done. I sat there looking out over the cliff, running it through my mind. It was not that I did not love my family. But there are things no person can give you.

Then I could not stand looking at my fire; I kicked the logs into the river and watched their spark quench. Then I rode home. I arrived well into the black morning, filled a lamp, and went into my office.

I took out my ledgers and securities and laid them on my desk. Deposits, shares in the Pacific Express, a steel concern in Pittsburgh, a sawmill in Beaumont. I considered how good the rains had been and the pastures I had just leased and all the new cowbrutes the green grass would nurture. I sat in my chair and thought about these things. I began to feel at ease.

Chapter Sixty-four
J.A. McCullough

Ted had not left her so much as asked to be released. There had been some final revolution of the blood and he'd gotten tangled with a woman half his age. She was angry, she was worried about him, about the convenience this woman—a schoolteacher—might see in him. Which only made him furious. You could have kept me, he said, you could have kept me a hundred or a thousand different times. But of course she could not have. It was not in her.

It was true that she was lonely, that she was occasionally struck by a physical need that she had not felt for him in decades, but mostly there was a lightness. She wondered what was wrong with her. She had always been a person who did not need much affection, she did not need much from other people, but of course there was the downside; she did not have much to give, either.

Her worry that Ted might be her last lover turned out to be ridiculous. There were other companions, men who could have, and still did have, younger women, but they were companions nonetheless; there were things they could not share with young people, and she suspected, though not a single one had admitted this to her, that decades of being the less attractive partner might take a toll. She wondered what it would be like to look into the mirror and see yourself, white haired, slough skinned, your wilting everything and uncountable skin tags, right next to some perfect young specimen of the human race.

She was not sure. She had not compromised. She had not compromised and in that way, she'd escaped. *I am the last of my kind*, she thought, *the last the last the last* . . . but even that was a kind of vanity, there could be no last of anything, there were uncountable billions to come.

Milton Bryce became a widower, there had been another chance, she had known him nearly fifty years, and they had talked about it, how the two of them might form a sort of partnership, they had kissed but not otherwise touched, they were both into their seventies, he was a good man, but there was not a drop of fire in him. It was better to be alone. She was not some spinster. There were things she had not done, perhaps she had missed out, but the Colonel had not remarried, either. There was a reason for that.

Maybe if she'd gotten sick she would have felt differently. But even then she would not have wanted a lover taking care of her, even after two decades she had not liked using the toilet in front of Ted, had not liked brushing her teeth in front of him and when she got out of bed she always put on a nightgown, it was not modesty. It was just that without keeping something to yourself, the only thing left was comfort.

She had always suspected (*known*, she thought) that she might outlive Thomas. There were people with a will to survive, people who might drag themselves across a desert, but Thomas was not one of them.

At a certain point, she had begun to think he would dodge it, he had been with the same partner (*lover*, she thought, *husband*) for over a decade, then quick as that, his partner was dying and they all knew what that meant for Thomas. It did not make her special. All stories ended that way. And yet it seemed to her that she had willed her son's fate, that by somehow suspecting it, considering it, she had witched it up out of the future, where a child's death was supposed to remain.

As for the man Thomas lived with—Richard—she had never cared for him. He was not sure of himself and he compensated. Thomas and Susan both found him hilarious, but he was not and she hated the sight of him at the hospice, *you have killed my son,* that was all she could think. She had to fly back to Midland in the morning. "When will you be here again?" Thomas asked her. *For the funeral,* she thought. Richard hated her even as he was dying; she hated him right back. But there was something in her son's face.

"All right," she said. "I'll be here tomorrow."

She'd been trying to unload some acreage in the Spraberry to Walt and Amos Benson. They wanted to take her out at $16.26; she was looking for $19.00. It was high but things were happening.

"Come out to the ranch," they said. "We'll get the quail opener."

There was nothing she would have liked better; the Bensons were old friends, Walt's wife had died a year earlier and there had always been some spark . . . but she couldn't. She had to go back to San Francisco. She did not want to tell them why.

So she had flown back and spent the night in the hospice, staring at the gaunt-faced man in the bed, knowing she would be looking at her own son there soon enough. The man's parents had not been told. She wondered if she ought to find out who they were and call them. She decided she should, they had a right to know, but then she wasn't sure, and then she had never been more afraid of anything, she made one bargain after another, her own life, all her money, speaking to God the entire night. None of it meant anything. She would lose her son. In the morning she slept two hours on her Gulfstream and woke up in Midland to meet with the Bensons again. She told them that Saddam Hussein was going to invade Kuwait.

"Is that what your price is based on?"

She was too tired to explain.

"Honey," they said, "what's wrong?"

She wanted to go to their ranch, she wanted to sit on their patio and drink wine with Walt, she wanted to stop thinking about her son. Instead the driver took her back to the airport.

All of this for money. Money she did not need, money her daughter did not need, money her son did not need. No one she knew needed money. And yet, apparently, she would do anything for it. She would spend her days in Midland and her nights in San Francisco. She was crazy. She agreed to the Bensons' price.

Walt invited her to the ranch again. They looked at each other a long time, here was her chance, she'd rejected him years earlier, he would not try again. Instead she went back to San Francisco, got a room at the Fairmont, and stayed two months helping Thomas clean out his condo, agonizing over Richard's awful paintings. And Thomas had lived. He had gone on the drugs and they had saved him. He went back to calling her Mother; he called her Jeannie only when he was mad.

She knew that other people felt sorry for her. She knew that her life looked empty, but it was the opposite. You could not live for yourself while also living for others. Even lying here she was free. She was not in some hospital where they kept you alive when they shouldn't, where you had no say over your own end.

She was back in the enormous room. The light was blinding now, the sun was shining directly through the roof, the furniture askew, everything in shambles, but she did not mind it.

There was a scent in the air, soothing and oversweet and she recognized it: balm of Gilead. Cottonwood buds. Were they blooming? She couldn't remember. She could not remember the day or year. She and Hank had planted a row of saplings around the stock tank, they were now enormous, a grove of cottonwoods. She

had left things better than she found them. She remembered the Colonel rubbing the sap into her fingers, she
remembered how the smell lingered all day, every time
you lifted your hands to your face, every sip of water,
you drank in that smell. The Colonel had showed her
and she had showed it to Hank. Now they were waiting
for her. She could feel it.

Chapter Sixty-five
Ulises Garcia

He had heard and then seen her jet land yesterday; it was quite a sight, a plane that looked as if it might carry thirty or more people, landing to discharge a single person. It was a Gulfstream. The same one the *narcotraficantes* preferred. A car picked her up from the runway.

Even watching her from a distance gave him a nervous feeling. He had worked all day, but had not been able to eat lunch.

Later he saw her being driven around the ranch, sitting in the back of her Cadillac. Her chin held high, surveying all she owned. Near dinnertime he had made a point of passing by the house, just to get a glimpse of her, when he noticed an old person sitting by herself on the vast porch, looking at some papers.

He rode up and tipped his hat. "Good evening. I am Ulises Garcia."

She looked at him. She was annoyed at being interrupted. But he smiled at her and finally she couldn't help herself. She smiled back and said: "Hello, Mr. Garcia."

He couldn't think of anything more to say, so he wished her a good night and rode off cursing himself.

The next day the plane was still there. The sun was going down and he was heading back to the bunkhouse. He supposed it was now or never. Of course if she rejected him, he would have to leave. It was a good job, Bryan Colms liked him, the other hands liked him, even if they thought he was a showoff.

Of course he was a coward if he didn't try. After dinner, he changed into his good shirt and packed his papers into a small leather bag his grandfather had given him.

Chapter Sixty-six
Diaries of Peter McCullough

OCTOBER 13, 1917

Received two telegrams from Guadalajara asking me to come down, but neither is the real María. Today a letter arrived. Very short.

"Received your note. Good memories but see no way of continuing."

I wait until I am certain Sally is out of the house, then call Ab Jefferson and tell him what happened.

"We could bring her up here easy," he says.

"How would you do that?"

"It has been done, Mr. McCullough."

Then I understand. "No," I tell him. "Absolutely not."

It is not much of a plan. Composed a letter to Charlie and Glenn explaining as best I could. Do not expect they will forgive me—especially Charlie. He is the Colonel's son as much as mine. Tomorrow is a Sunday so I will have to wait.

OCTOBER 14, 1917

Woke up this morning with a happiness I have not felt since she left, replaced slowly by the old feeling. Did not know I had so much fear in me.

If she consents to see me it will not be the same, she was a refugee then—we will be like old friends who no longer have anything in common. Our bonds revealed as illusion. Better not to see it. Better to hold on to something I know is good.

OCTOBER 15, 1917

Did not sleep last night. Packed three changes of clothes and my revolver. In a few minutes I will pass through the gates of the McCullough ranch for the last time. One way or the other.

The bank in Carrizo will not have what I need so I am going to San Antonio. Ronald Derry has known me twenty years—he will not question me. Unless he does. Two hundred fifty thousand dollars for oil leases. *Oil leases*, I will say, *you know these farmers, they all want to see cash.*

Then I will cross the border. Of course the money is not mine. If they decide to call my father . . .

I have no illusion about my chance of reaching Guadalajara alive. I am of sound mind and body. This is my testament.

Chapter Sixty-seven
Eli McCullough

With the surrender of the Comanches, an area as big as the Old States opened to settlement and every easterner who owned a whaling ship or hotel began to fancy himself a cattle baron. There were Frenchmen and Scots, counts and dukes in scissortail coats, peacocked Yankees with their faces shining like new mirrors. They overpaid for range, overpaid for stock, overpaid for horses, they were trying to catch up to the rest of us. Meanwhile the southern grasslands were already run-down; the smart stockmen drove their herds to Montana to get fat on what grass remained.

Half the cowhands were Harvard men in lisle thread socks, with mail-order pistols and silver-decked tack bought straight from a leathershop drummer. They'd come west to grow up with the country. Meaning see the end of it.

I said I would sell out by '80. The part of me that was still alive hated the sight of cowbrutes, hated chewing every waking minute on how I would profit or lose by them. The rest of me couldn't think of anything else. How to protect them, how to get the best price for them, and, when the money had gone out of them, how I might make it another way. I was caught in the thorns of my own undertaking, unmaking, I considered the beasts more than my own wife and children, I was no different from Ellen Wilbarger with her laudanum. She had not needed it until she tried it, but soon saw no other way.

Madeline thought I was interfering with some senorita. She gave me too much credit. The problem was much bigger than any girl.

By then I had moved them to San Antonio, but I still spent my time in the *brasada* or along some dusty waterhole and Madeline was not any happier. She told me to get a proper house built on the Nueces or else. I told her I had only a few years left—I could feel it doing something to me.

"Like what?" she said.

I started to tell her, but couldn't. Old Nicky himself had pinched my jaw shut.

She paced the living room. She'd fallen in with some other grass widows and had taken to wearing paint; just a touch but I noticed it. The servants were off being servants and the boys were in the yard.

"I hate this house," she said.

"It's a hell of a nice house," I said. It was a big white one in the Spanish style, big as the one she'd grown up in, with a good view of the river. It was two years' wages and a sizable note to match.

"I would rather be living in a hut."

"We'll be out soon enough," I said.

"Why not now?"

"Because."

"We do not have to live in the biggest house. Now or ever. I believe you have confused me with my sister."

She smiled but I wanted to keep it serious. "Three years," I told her. "Come hell or high water I swear I will not touch a cow after that."

"That is the same as never."

"There is no school."

"We will build one. Or hire a teacher. Or we keep this place and go back and forth and hire a teacher half the time." She threw up her hands. "There are any number of ways," she said. "We are not exactly building a railroad."

"Well, it's a waste of money to build a place and leave it."

"The fool who buys the land will also buy the house. Meanwhile I am here with your children, who spend all their time pretending they *are* you when they don't really know you."

"It's not the right place," I said. "I am sure of it."

But she was already not listening. I could see her thinking. "The representative is going back to Washington," she said. The representative was her mother's new husband. "There is a nice house for sale next door to theirs. Which is where I am taking the children unless you convince me otherwise."

I walked away from her and stood by the window. The best part of me knew I ought to let her go but I could not get the words to my mouth. Outside, Everett was wearing my old buckskin shirt. He had a feather in his hair and he was stalking the other boys. I had been promising to show him how to make a bow for so long that I realized he had stopped asking me. Pete and Phineas were digging at something in the yard— they didn't have the fire of a firstborn. I had also promised Everett I would let him ride with me a few days during roundup. In truth I liked that the boys were in school. I had not wanted to start them on the outdoor life; soon it would be fit only for hobbyists and outcasts.

Madeline was still talking. "Or," she was saying, "you can move us to the Nueces."

I didn't say anything.

"Wonderful. September, then."

"That is barely enough time to build a dugout."

"Then hire twice as many men. Or ten times as many. I don't care. But three months from now the children and I will not be living in this house."

In Abilene a new tailor opened shop every week, and, after making a drive, most of the hands would sell their horses, buy suits, and take the train home. The ones who'd seen a Ned Buntline or Bill Cody show would brag on the incident for months, as if the shows were more real than their own lives. The others passed the winter reading Bret Harte.

The drives got shorter. The International and Great Northern surveyed a line through our pastures. The grass was disappearing but it didn't matter—the railroads brought the farmers and nesters, people who wanted to live in towns—the land I had bought for a quarter was worth forty dollars an acre when they built.

Had it not been for the children I would have moved to the Klondike. The country was ruined, as a woman would have been after riding the cat wagon. I had never known it could fill up. I had never known there were so many people on earth.

Chapter Sixty-eight
J.A. McCullough

She'd come into the great room to see her father sitting next to the fireplace. He didn't notice her—she remained in the shadows—he was sitting in a chair he had pulled onto the stone hearth, reading from a leather-bound notebook. When he finished a page, he would tear it out, lean forward, and drop it into the flames. There were three other notebooks— they appeared to be some sort of journal—on the floor next to him. She watched for several minutes. Finally she walked over. "What are you doing?" she said.

He was sweating and his face was pale as if he had a fever. For a time he didn't speak.

"Your grandfather was a liar," he finally said. He looked as if he would tear up and then sat there like that and she was reminded of the father of her school friend, who had also sat weeping in front of the fire, and she wondered if it was something that fathers did.

He collected himself. "I should get some work done." He stood and picked up all four of the notebooks and tossed them among the burning logs. Then he kissed her on the head. "Good night, sweetie."

When she was sure he was gone, she took the poker and pulled the journals out. The flames had barely touched them.

She had not shown her brothers, or anyone else. She had known better. She had known she was the only one who could be trusted with them.

Jonas had been acting strangely all day; after school, instead of going out to the pastures to meet their father, he had gone up to his room. She had watched him at dinner, there was something wrong with him, probably the flu. He barely touched his food.

The dishes had been cleared away and Paul and Clint had gone to the library to play cards. She went out to her sleeping porch to read and looked out into the dark and saw a figure walking down the hill toward the stables. His shoulders were hunched and his head was down as if he was embarrassed and she knew immediately it was Jonas.

Even later, she was not sure why she followed him. She walked to the stables and sat in the dark, watching. A light went on. She wondered if her brother was meeting a girl; she wondered who the girl was. But then he was leading all the horses out to the pasture, slapping to get them moving.

She went closer and watched through the cracks in the boards, standing in the dark night, as he dragged hay bales down and stacked them under the loft. When he was satisfied with the pile he'd made, he took a jug of coal oil and poured it over the hay.

"What are you doing?" she said. She opened the door.

He was looking at her and she stepped into the light.

"Jeannie," he said. He looked stricken.

"What are you doing?" she said again.

"This is the only way he'll let me leave."

She had not understood.

"Daddy," he said. He shrugged. "I thought I would see what happened when I start costing him real money. That's always been the way to his heart. You can tell on me if you want, I don't care."

"I won't tell," she said.

"Then go through the stalls and make sure I didn't leave any of the horses. I'm not thinking straight right now."

She had walked through the stable, checking each stall.

He had made a torch out of a stick and an old shirt and she watched through the door as he doused it in kerosene and lit it. Then he threw the torch onto the pile. There was a noise and it was bright. He came out and shut the door behind him. They sat on the hill and watched as light began to come through all the cracks in the building, as if a small sun were rising inside it. Smoke began to pour out into the night and her brother stood up and held her to him and then he took her hand and they walked quietly together back up the hill toward their father's house.

Chapter Sixty-nine
Ulises Garcia

He had shaved and his hair was wet and neatly combed. He was wearing a fresh shirt and pants. The shirt was brand-new, as were the trousers; his boots were polished. He brought his leather bag with all the birth certificates, and his great-grandfather's old Colt revolver, which no longer worked but was clearly engraved *P. McCullough.*

He walked around the porch, looking for her, and saw a pair of open glass doors.

He walked up to them and there she was, sitting in a chair, reading.

She recognized him.

"You must be looking for Dolores."

"No," he said.

"I like to have a fire when I come here," she said. "Even if I have to leave the door open so it doesn't get hot."

"It seems nice."

She waited for him to say something else.

"I work for you."

"I remember."

A long time seemed to pass before he could say anything. His head felt light.

"I'm the great-grandson of Peter McCullough," he said. "I wanted to work for you because . . ." He couldn't say the rest; it would make him sound like a crazy person.

Her face showed nothing.

From his leather bag, which he had also cleaned and oiled before coming over, he removed all the letters and papers. He took a few steps into the room and handed her everything, then stepped back. He looked around as she read. The room was enormous, thirty meters by forty, he guessed. The ceilings were ten meters tall, a beam construction like an old church. The room itself might have contained three of the houses in which he'd grown up, and he began to think about the Arroyos' house.

She read the first few pages, but then she was going through the papers faster than she could read them.

"We are family," he repeated.

Her eyes showed nothing, but he could see that her hands had begun to shake.

"I'm afraid I'll have to ask you to leave," she said.

He pointed again to the papers.

"You will leave this house right now," she said. "Mr. Colms will have your check."

He was about to say more but she was not paying attention. As if he were not there, she casually pushed herself up from her chair and walked to a low marble table and picked up the phone there.

She dialed and their eyes locked.

"This is Mrs. McCullough. There is a man in my house who refuses to leave. Yes, he is here right now in the room with me."

She nodded at him and waved him out. He could feel his body begin to move, toward the door.

"His name? Martinez, or something."

It felt like he'd been splashed with hot water. He marched forward to take back the papers, but she misinterpreted him, she backed away too quickly and tripped over her own feet, he reached to catch her but she twisted away and fell in front of the fireplace. Her head made a noise on the stone hearth. The phone went out of her hand. He could hear someone talking on the other end.

"Mrs. McCullough?" He was whispering.

She did not respond. Her eyelids were trembling, they were not quite closed and not quite open.

"I did not touch you," he said to her.

She said nothing. She made no move, her eyes were open now but they did not fix on anything and he knew that she was going to die.

He collected his papers and put them into his case, looked around to see if he'd forgotten anything else, then walked toward the door. He had killed her. Not by touching her, just by existing.

He went outside but in the distance he saw one of the ranch trucks cresting the hill and came back in. Of course they would find him, they would figure it out, they had ways of doing that. He had not touched her. *You are a Mexican in the house of a rich lady,* he thought. *They will not care if you touched her or not.*

He waited for the truck to pass outside and wandered through her house, looking for another exit; what a house it was, the rugs so soft his feet made no noise at all, art and statues everywhere, dim light, it was like something from the movies. He shook himself out of this, reached the kitchen; beyond it was a door that led outside.

His mouth was dry. He went to the sink and drank from the tap, he had not touched her. *They will kill you,* he thought. *They will not care.* This was obvious.

The water was helping. His heart began to slow. He smoothed a few drops from his shirt, thought of all the ways he might explain himself, but no one would believe him, he would not have believed himself.

Later he was not sure how he came to this solution, but it occurred to him this quickly: there was an immense gas stove and he dragged it away from the wall. The gas came right from the property, that was what all the hands said, directly from the ground beneath. He took his Leatherman from his belt, reached behind the stove, and unscrewed the copper line.

Out on the porch, he closed the door quietly behind him. All around the land spread out in the dusk, there was nothing in sight that did not belong to the McCulloughs.

He considered stealing a truck but that would leave him afoot once he reached the border. He could see the lights in the housekeeper's cottage, in Bryan Colms's house, in the bunkhouse; he began to walk toward the McCulloughs' private stable, praying there was no one there, but there were no vehicles, and when he reached the stable he left the lights off.

He had been inside before to muck the stalls and he knew which horse he wanted. He put on a bridle, threw a blanket over her, and saddled her quickly. Bryan Colms insisted on calling her a gray, but she was white, of course.

Then he led her out of the stable, downhill, away from the house, and put his heels to her. The stirrups were short.

He had not made it far when there came the loudest noise he had ever heard. The horse took the bit in its teeth, but he didn't care, as long as he was heading toward the river. He hazarded a look behind him; there was a dust cloud all around the house, though it was still standing. Then there were flickers and he saw the flames. A few miles later he looked back and the light had spread from one side of the horizon to the other.

When he got to the river he reined up to look around. The sky was enormous. The lights of America, which had blotted out the stars, had faded. His legs were beginning to seize and his abdomen and back were cramping as well. "You're a strong horse," he said. He kissed it on the neck.

Then they eased down the bank. It was easy to cross, the river was shallow; it was no longer even a river.

What had the historian said? Nineteen or twenty people. He had stopped by the man's house and the man had shown him the picture they had taken of the Rangers and townspeople posing with the bodies of his family.

"Who are they?" he had asked. "Who is who in the picture?"

The historian had shrugged. "No one knows. No one knows what any of the Garcias looked like."

The white men were standing in the sun, their faces clear, while the faces of the men on the ground might have been molded from clay. The historian had shrugged again and shown him some other pictures, Colonel McCullough's dugout, long-dead cowboys, horses and old cars. To him, the picture of the dead Garcias meant no more than these other things.

Ulises had not been able to stop thinking about it, it was like discovering a cancer in your own body, the thought of the uncles and aunts, great-aunts and -uncles, an enormous family, wiped out. He continued to ride. But of course he had equal blood from both sides. He was not some victim. One half of his family had killed the other. Both of those things were inside him.

The Americans . . . he allowed his mind to roam. They thought that simply because they had stolen something, no one should be allowed to steal it from them. But of course that was what all people thought: that whatever they had taken, they should be allowed to keep it forever.

He was no better. His people had stolen the land from the Indians, and yet he did not think of that even for an instant—he thought only of the Texans who had stolen it from his people. And the Indians from whom his people had stolen the land had themselves stolen it from other Indians.

His father had come to this woman asking for help and the woman had denied him. His grandmother had come and had been denied. And now he had been denied as well. Yet this same woman had given twenty million dollars to a museum. Millions for the dead, nothing for the living, it was people like her who ended up in charge. He had to remember those things. He was still young. He would remember.

In the meantime he would go back to his grandfather, and then, he thought, to Mexico City, where there were no problems with the cartels. Business, politics, he didn't know, but it was as he'd suspected, the days in which you held your head up because you were a man, because you had roped an eagle, those days were gone. The Americans, it seemed, had known this.

He would go a few more miles and rest for the night. After that . . . he didn't know. But he would be someone. No one would forget his name.

Chapter Seventy
J.A. McCullough

She had seen the Garcia boy come in; she had known him from across the room. She had known from the moment he spoke that he was telling the truth.

She no longer fit inside herself. All her life she had known she would ride off into the dark, but now the land was as green as it had ever been, the sun was running, she had been wrong, she could see her brothers far ahead of her. They were young, and she made up her mind to catch them.

Chapter Seventy-one
Peter McCullough

After four days of driving he reached Guadalajara. He stopped in front of her house, a small adobe structure with peeling yellow paint and a tended garden.

That night, after she had fallen asleep, he put on his pants and shirt and went out to make sure the car was still there. It was dark and quiet; most of the lights in the neighborhood were out. He had been surprised that so many had electricity at all.

He wondered if he had stolen the money because he was a coward, because he was worried about changing his mind. He decided it didn't matter. He went back inside to wake her up. They loaded the car and drove off into the darkness.

For a time they moved every few weeks, staying in hotels under different names. It was quieter in the south and they had one child in Mérida and a second near Oaxaca, but when the war ended he began to worry they would be found, and in 1920, after Carranza was deposed, they moved to Mexico City.

There was a new government and the city was overflowing. There were bankers and industrialists, exiles and artists, musicians and anarchists; there were cathedrals and sprawling markets and gaudy *pulquerías*, murals going up everywhere, streetcars running through the night. Motorcars jostled with donkeys and horsemen and barefoot peasants. He guessed it would drive him insane. It didn't. He would lean over the edge of their apartment building and watch the street; he had never seen so many people in his life.

"You don't like cities," she said.

"It's better for the children."

It was not just that. He was losing his memory; Pedro and Lourdes Garcia seemed impossibly young, likewise his mother and father; he could barely remember his own childhood; he could barely remember last year. If there was anyone watching from the dark corners, he never knew it. Each night after the sun set he would go and stand over the street and put his hands to the warm stone, a million lives passing just beneath him, millions more yet to come, they were all just like him, they were all free, they would all be forgotten.

Chapter Seventy-two
Eli McCullough

1881

I had told myself I would sell out by '80. The rains were good and my two-year-olds had brought $14.50 and then a German baron, looking to stock a range in Kansas, promised ten dollars for spring yearlings. The hands sold their horses and took the train home, but I wired Madeline that I would be delayed. I had built her the house on the Nueces but by then she had stopped expecting I would come home at all.

I rode the long way down, past our old hunting grounds. I shooed cows from our camp on the Canadian, where the dogwoods had grown up straight and tall, higher than a man could reach. I looked for days, but I could not find the graves of Toshaway or Prairie Flower or Single Bird. The ground had gone to rocks and the trees had all been cut for firewood.

As for my brother's grave, at times I have been certain the Indians led us up the Yellow House, and other times I have been equally certain it was the Blanco, or Tule, or the Palo Duro. I rode the length of the Llano, following the edge of the caprock, hoping I would be sparked, that I would feel the spot when I came to it. There was nothing.

I arrived home to find my men all waiting for me on the gallery.

"Nothin' better to do?" I said.

Then I saw the house.

"What was all the shooting?" I said.

No one answered.

"Who did the shooting?"

They had buried them under a cottonwood on a hill overlooking the house. It had a good view of things. Madeline, Everett, and a hand named Fairbanks.

Madeline had been shot in the yard and Everett had been shot trying to pull her into the house and the three surviving hands, two of whom were shot as well, had driven the bandits back. All anyone knew was it was renegade Indians. No one knew which ones.

"Were they scalped?"

Sullivan followed me up the hill. He had a sense for things. I took a shovel and set to digging and when we could smell the grave gas and Sullivan saw I wasn't going to stop, he held me to the dirt. A penny for three measures of barley, hurt not the oil and the wine. My wife and son had not been scalped and neither Peter nor Phineas had been scratched.

The army thought the perpetrators to be a renegade group of Comanches. They had trailed them to Mexico but had not gone over the water. Sullivan led me to where the Indians had stood in the corral. It was Lipans. The toe of an Apache moccasin is much wider than a Comanche's, which comes to a point, and the fringes are shorter and drag less. The Apache has a bigger foot. And the arrows had four grooves.

There were three and twenty hands and they all stood up to ride. The oldermost was twenty-eight, the youngest sixteen, and to ride on a group of Indians— they had thought those days were gone forever. If you were free to go back in history, to fight the great battles of your ancestors . . . you should have seen their shining faces.

The party of Lipans split seven times on rocky ground and the trail was weeks old but if I ever believed in a Creator it was for this reason: it had rained before the Lipan attack and then gone dry, leaving their tracks as frozen into the earth as the marks of the ancient beasts. Twelve riders, tracks of the unshod ponies leading right to the water's edge.

We did not slow down when we reached the river. In Coahuila the tracks stopped; it was hard dry ground. I did not get off my horse. I looked into the book of the earth: I was Toshaway, I was Pizon, I was the Lipans themselves, afraid to stop looking behind me, knowing I'd killed where I should not and yet the ponies I'd taken would save my tribe another year.

The others saw nothing. A grieving man on a pale horse. They followed on faith alone.

By dusk we stood on a hill overlooking the last of the Lipan band. They had lived in the country five hundred years. We waited until their fires had gone dark.

We dynamited the tipis and shot the Indians down as they ran. A magnificent brave, his only weapon a patch knife, charged singing his death chant. A blind man fired a musket and his daughter ran forward, knowing the gun was empty; she swung it toward us and we shot her down as well. It was the last of a nation, squaws and cripples and old men, our guns so hot they fired of their own will, our squarecloths wrapped the foregrips and still every hand was branded.

When the people were finished we killed every living dog and horse. I took the chief's bladder for a tobacco pouch; it was tanned and embroidered with beads. In his shield, stuffed between the layers, was Gibbon's *Decline and Fall of the Roman Empire*.

When the sun came up, we discovered a boy of nine years. We left him as a witness. At noon we reached the river and saw the boy had followed us with his bow—for twenty miles he had kept up with men on horseback—for twenty miles he had been running to his death.

A child like that would be worth a thousand men today. We left him standing on the riverbank. As far as I know he is looking for me yet.

HARPER LUXE

THE NEW LUXURY IN READING

We hope you enjoyed reading
our new, comfortable print size and found it
an experience you would like to repeat.

Well – you're in luck!

HarperLuxe offers the finest in fiction and
nonfiction books in this same larger print size and
paperback format. Light and easy to read, HarperLuxe
paperbacks are for book lovers who want to see
what they are reading without the strain.

For a full listing of titles and
new releases to come, please visit our website:

www.HarperLuxe.com